Crazy In Love 2

Crazy In Love 2

Yoshe

www.urbanbooks.net

Urban Books, LLC
97 N 18th Street
Wyandanch, NY 11798

ISBN 13: 978-1-62286-904-6
ISBN 10: 1-62286-904-4

First Trade Paperback Printing May 2015
Printed in the United States of America

10 9 8 7 6 5 4 3 2 1

This is a work of fiction. Any references or similarities to actual events, real people, living, or dead, or to real locales are intended to give the novel a sense of reality. Any similarity in other names, characters, places, and incidents is entirely coincidental.

Distributed by Kensington Publishing Corp.
Submit Orders to:
Customer Service
400 Hahn Road
Westminster, MD 21157-4627
Phone: 1-800-733-3000
Fax: 1-800-659-2436

Crazy In Love 2

Yoshe

Prologue

November, 2009

It was approximately 6:30 p.m. in East New York, Brooklyn, and the late November wind could be heard whipping around the tall apartment buildings of the Spring Creek Towers apartment complex. Thirty-six-year-old Brandi Wallace had just gathered up her grocery bags and hurriedly exited her parked car to escape the chilly air. She wrapped her oversized cashmere sweater coat around her shapely frame and quickly walked across the one-way street toward her building.

Brandi was pretty excited about her life these days. For one, she couldn't wait to get upstairs to call her new boyfriend. The man in question was the handsome Sean Daniels, who was three years her junior. There was nothing better than listening to him whisper sweet nothings in her ear, as she dipped a spoonful of her favorite Ben & Jerry's ice cream into her mouth.

Little did Brandi know, her peaceful night was about to turn into a drama-filled nightmare.

Before Brandi could enter the foyer of her building, she felt someone grab her hair from the back. Alarmed by the intrusion, she immediately began to struggle with the mystery person.

Suddenly, Brandi felt cold steel being pressed into the nape of her neck. *It's a gun!* Her body froze instantly. A gun could only mean that someone meant business.

Brandi couldn't believe what was happening to her. She winced in pain from the pressure of the gun being applied to the back of her neck and she could feel warm pee rolling down the legs of her dark denim skinny jeans. Fearing for her life, Brandi complied. She dropped her grocery bags to the ground, ready to give the person whatever they wanted. She just wasn't ready to die.

Brandi closed her eyes, waiting for the perpetrator to say something. Not wanting to make any sudden moves, she slowly raised her hands in the air.

"I told you to stay away from my man, didn't I, bitch?"

Brandi recognized that voice right away. That voice belonged to a woman named Yadira Cruz.

Yadira was a coworker of Sean's, whom he had a brief fling with a month or so before Brandi came into the picture. Since then, the woman had been stalking her and Sean for the past two months. Now it seemed like Yadira had taken the stalking thing to a whole new level. She was definitely out for blood.

"What do you want from me, Yadira?" the nervous Brandi asked.

"Ever since you came into our lives, Brandi, it's been nothing but fucking drama! Turn around and look at me!" she ordered.

Brandi slowly turned around, only to come face to face with the emotionally disturbed Yadira. She was holding a huge gun in her hands and the woman's eyes were bloody red, swollen, and bulging out her head. She looked like she had been crying all night. But what scared Brandi the most about Yadira's eyes was that vacant stare. She knew that murderous gaze all too well.

"Why are you doing this, Yadira?" Brandi asked, in a pleading voice. "You and Sean were never in a relationship with each other!"

But Yadira wasn't trying to hear that. She waved the loaded gun in Brandi's face.

"Oh, is that what he told you?" she asked. She began laughing hysterically. "Sean has always been my man, Brandi, and you're the side chick! Me and Sean were all good until you came into the picture and spoiled everything for us! You're the fucking reason why he's been disrespecting me and acting like he doesn't want to be with me anymore! It's all because of you, bitch!"

Brandi scoped her surroundings. Spring Creek Towers was usually busy around that time of the evening. But strangely enough, there was no one around at the moment. She silently prayed that someone would walk or drive by her building and see Yadira pointing the silver semiautomatic at her.

"Yadira, can we please, please just talk about all of this?" Brandi asked, again pleading with the maniacal woman. "Maybe we can come to some type of happy medium—"

Yadira cut Brandi off. "Shut . . . up . . . you . . . bitch," she whispered, as if she was getting irritated with the sound of Brandi's voice. "What we're going to do now is go pay my man a visit! And once we get there? I'm going to need for you to tell my man, face to face, that you are not going to see him any fucking more. Do you understand me?"

Brandi nodded her head.

Yadira raised the gun so that it was pointed toward her forehead. "And you're going to drive us over there," Yadira exclaimed, pushing Brandi in the direction of her parked vehicle. "Let's go!"

The bewildered Brandi painstakingly followed Yadira's orders. An eerie chill ran through Brandi's body, as she pressed the keyless alarm to open the passenger door to her vehicle.

Everything was happening so fast and Brandi didn't understand why it was even happening at all. For one fleeting moment, she thought about running away from

Yadira. But with the state of mind that the deranged woman was in, she decided to not take that chance.

And how lucky was she! Brandi was glad that she didn't have her young grandson when Yadira rolled up with that gun. If that were the case, things would have definitely gotten ugly. Brandi slowly slid into the driver's side of her car.

As soon as Yadira got in on the other side, she poked the gun into Brandi's side. Yadira slammed the passenger door closed. "Now hurry up and get to Sean's house, bitch. And you better not try shit or else, I promise you, you will regret the very day that you were born," she yelled.

Brandi reluctantly started her vehicle up, making her way to Sean's Bedford-Stuyvesant home. As she whipped her Audi through the light traffic on Pennsylvania Avenue, she was almost too afraid to even breathe the wrong way.

"I cannot freaking believe that Sean had the nerve to choose your tired, five-dollar ass over me," Yadira said. She pushed the gun deeper into Brandi's right side. "You just don't know how much I hate you, Brandi. You just don't know, girl," she added, drifting off into a zone.

Brandi kept her eyes on the road and didn't say one word to Yadira. Getting killed by a female stalker was not the way that she pictured herself leaving the earth.

By the time Brandi and Yadira arrived in front of Sean's house it was 7:15 p.m. and she was a ball of nerves. The drive from her East New York residence to Sean's house was such a harrowing experience for her. What was normally a twenty-minute drive seemed like hours and she desperately tried to figure out what her next move was going to be.

The sound of Yadira's voice startled Brandi. She was ordered to take the key out of the ignition and get out of the car.

"No funny business, bitch, or else I will blow your motherfucking brains out!" Yadira warned, as if she was reading her mind. She kept the gun pointed at Brandi while she walked around the vehicle. "I am so sick of you basic chicks acting like y'all are better than somebody!" Yadira said, out of the blue. "What makes you think that you could compete with me, huh, Brandi?" she asked.

Brandi glared at Yadira and just shook her head. She could feel herself losing patience with Yadira and all of her dramatics. The old Brandi would have never tolerated this behavior from any woman or man, for that matter. She instantly regretted not handling the erratic, lovesick lunatic after their first run-in.

All of sudden, Yadira grabbed Brandi and shoved the gun into the small of her back, while pushing her toward Sean's house. They approached the steps located at the lower level of the brownstone.

Meanwhile, Brandi tried her hardest to hold her composure. She had a few guns pulled out on her back in the day but never had she felt more defenseless then she did at that moment. It was clear that the mentally unstable Yadira had finally gone off on the deep end.

Brandi rang Sean's doorbell while Yadira lurked in the dark corner with the gun pointed directly at her head.

The clueless Sean was downstairs relaxing in his family room. He was stretched out on the couch, while sipping on some Hennessy and Coke and watching the ESPN channel on TV. The sound of the downstairs doorbell startled Sean. *Who the fuck could that be?* He hadn't been expecting any visitors but he wasn't stupid. The security-conscious Sean quickly walked over to his bar and grabbed his Ruger. Then he slowly walked over to the door with the gun in his right hand.

"Who is it?" he asked, in a stern voice.

"It's me, babe," Brandi softly replied from other side of the locked door.

Sean smiled at the sound of Brandi's sweet voice. "Oh, it's my baby," he said to himself. The Rikers Island correction officer tucked his off-duty firearm into the waistband of his jeans and opened the door. Just as he was about to hug Brandi, the smile on his face instantly disappeared. The wild-eyed Yadira had emerged from the dark corner with the gun still aimed at Brandi's head.

"What the fuck is this?" Sean asked, with a shocked expression on his face. "What the hell is going on here?"

Yadira pushed Brandi through the threshold of the doorway, causing her to fall face first at Sean's feet. When he went to help her up, Yadira pointed the gun at the both of them. Sean reached for his gun but instantly decided against it. Yadira had the upper hand and he didn't want her to shoot him or, even worse, Brandi.

"I really should kill the both of y'all motherfuckers!" the jealous Yadira screamed at them, with saliva spewing from her mouth. "And you, Sean! You haven't done nothing but use me and made me look like a got damn fool!"

Yadira held the gun in her hand so tightly that her knuckles were protruding from her small hands. She began pointing the gun back and forth between Sean and Brandi.

"Sit down!" she ordered them.

Both of them did as they were told. Brandi was quivering with fright while the stoic Sean closely watched Yadira's every move.

"See how you got me acting, Sean?" Yadira asked, in a sarcastic tone, with her trusty off-duty weapon pointing at him and Brandi, whose eyes were tightly closed. "See what happens when you choose another bitch over me, Sean?" She began pounding on her chest. "I'm a good fucking woman and you chose to skip over me to be with this lame-ass trick!" Yadira looked at Brandi. "A low-budget bitch with her fucking jailbird son! This ho can't even hold down her child!"

When she said that, Brandi went from being terrified to angry in a matter of seconds. She was unable to compose herself after Yadira mentioned her son and the time that he had to do on Rikers Island.

"You stinking bitch," she began, in the nastiest tone of voice that she could muster up. "My got damn son has absolutely nothing to do with you, Sean, or nobody else!" Brandi yelled at her. "Keep anything that you got to say about my son out of your despicable, motherfucking mouth before I make you swallow that got damn gun! You really do not know who you're fucking with, Yadira!"

Sean intervened and put his forearm in front of Brandi's chest to keep her from going at Yadira. The two women continued to have a screaming match with each other before Sean interrupted them.

"Yo! Yo!" Sean yelled. "Leave Brandi and her son out of this, Yadi! You don't have no beef with her! It's me you have the beef with! Ain't I the one you claimed rejected you? Huh?" he asked, trying to take Yadira's attention off the visibly irate Brandi.

Yadira waved the gun over her head, not taking her eyes off Brandi. "Fuck her! Fuck you, Brandi! This bitch thinks that she's better than some got damn body!" She stared at Brandi. "You ain't nobody, bitch! I'm the got damn law!" Yadi screamed, pointing the gun in Brandi's face. "That's right! You couldn't walk a block in my shoes!"

That was the last straw for Sean. "You're the law?" Sean asked. "Now you wanna talk about being the law? Who are you fooling, Yadi? You don't give a fuck about your career!" he added. "Look at you. Yeah, you're a correction officer and everything but you know motherfucking well that you shouldn't be doing none of this shit right here! If you kill me and Brandi, just know that you're going to do a shitload of time; our families are going to see to that! Do you understand that you will go to jail? And you wanna talk about being a good mother? Why would you wanna subject your daughter to that?"

Yadira started pacing around the room, as if she was thinking about what Sean said to her. "If anything happens to me, my daughter has her father and her grandparents to take care of her! She's better off without me anyway. I know that I'm messed up and I know that you don't love me, Sean. My daughter's father never loved me; my family and friends think that I'm fucking crazy. I just don't give a shit anymore!"

Sean began thinking about what Yadira was saying to him. It sounded like she wanted to end her own life. But he wasn't about to let her go out like that. He didn't want that to be on his conscience. Suddenly, his anger turned into concern.

"Yadi, just put the gun down, please!" he pleaded with her. "You don't need any more drama and neither do I! Maybe we could work something out," he said.

"Sean, baby, you just don't seem to understand me, do you?" Yadira asked, with a pitiful look her face. "I just love you so much. It's you I want; you're what I'm holding on to." Yadira slowly began breaking down right before Sean's and Brandi's eyes. "I don't have anyone to love me except my baby girl and she is much too young to understand her mama's pain! That's why I need you, Sean! You know, what it takes to make me happy!" she cried out, still holding the gun in her shaky hands.

Sean took a deep breath. Unfortunately, he couldn't find the words to console the distraught Yadira and he didn't want to say anything that would set her off. But Sean knew that he had to come up with something that would make her put that gun down.

Sean got up from the couch and attempted to soothe the tense Yadira from a distance. "Look, Yadi, you need to calm down, babe! You're going to get into a whole lot of trouble if you do anything stupid, sweetheart! Just put the gun down, please!"

Suddenly, the frustrated Yadira regrouped and let off a warning shot in the air. Sean jumped back and looked up at the dust falling from a gaping hole in his ceiling. He plopped back down on the couch and shook his head, in annoyance.

"Why are you doing this to us, Yadi?" Sean asked her again, too livid to be afraid of the gun-toting woman.

Yadira laughed. "Doing this to *us?* I do not believe this Negro!" she said. She looked at Sean with a scowl on her face. "You're still taking up for this pathetic little heifer, huh, Sean?" she asked.

Yadira raised the gun and aimed it in Brandi's direction again. The reflection from the light in Sean's family room made the gun shine like platinum.

"Would you still love the bitch if I just blow her head off right in front of you, Sean? Would you take up for the bitch then?"

All of a sudden, Yadira walked over to Brandi and grabbed her by the hair. She dragged her from the couch and onto the floor. Once Brandi was on the floor, she gave her a swift, hard kick to the ribs. "Now get the fuck out of this house so that I can be alone with my man, bitch!"

Brandi tried to stand up but her sore ribs felt as if they were cracked in half from the impact of Yadira's foot. If a younger, hot-tempered Brandi had anything to do with it, Yadira would have definitely been six feet under. It was that moment that she realized how much she had evolved as a woman.

Brandi wasn't moving fast enough for Yadira. She grabbed her by the shirt collar and physically helped her get to the door.

"I'm going to need for you to hurry up and get the hell out of here! And if I see your ass around here again, I'm gonna blow your got damn head off your shoulders!"

Yadira shoved Brandi outside and locked the door behind her.

Seeing how things were being played out with the two women, Sean felt bad for Brandi. She didn't deserve to be caught up with his messiness. Everything that was happening was because he couldn't keep his penis in his pants. In the meantime, Sean hoped that Brandi could put any bad feelings to the side and get the police over there before Yadira killed him.

Outside of Sean's house, a battered and bruised Brandi slowly got up from the stained concrete. She brushed the dirt off her bloody, scraped-up knees. Then she went through her jeans and sweater pockets to retrieve her car keys. Thankfully, she still had those.

As Brandi limped to the car, she began crying. How and why she became a target in all of the craziness that was going on between Sean and Yadira was beyond her. The only thing that she ever strived for was a relationship with a decent man and all she got in return was some deranged, obsessive bitch wanting to kill her.

Ironically enough, Yadira Cruz was nothing but a replica of Brandi's former self. She too had been crazy in love with Maleek, the father of her son. Brandi snapped out of her daydream. She could have easily gone home and let whatever was happening with Sean and Yadira play itself out. But she couldn't bring herself to do that. Sean was in serious trouble and it was up to her to get him some help.

Brandi pulled off and grabbed her cell phone. As soon as she went to dial emergency, her phone went completely dead. "Noooooo!" she wailed out in despair, throwing the phone in the back seat of her truck.

She turned left onto Stuyvesant Avenue, unsure of where the neighborhood precinct was. Just as luck would have it, she spotted two cops walking around the corner from Sean's block. Brandi beeped the horn to get the police officers' attention. When they walked over to her truck, she told them what was going on at Sean's house. They immediately radioed for a patrol car to go directly to Sean's address and they began running in that direction. Brandi pulled off, in an effort to meet the police there. She just hoped that it wasn't too late.

Inside of Sean's house, Yadira was pacing back and forth with the loaded gun still in her hand. She listened intently as Sean talked about how much he really cared about her and even suggested that he was just stringing Brandi along. For a brief moment, it looked as if Yadira wanted to believe everything he said.

"So, come on, Yadi, put the gun down, baby girl, please," he said, in an attempt to coax her with his soothing words. He even managed to smile at her. "You don't need the gun anymore! We're good now! Brandi is outta here!"

Now it was the infatuated Yadira's turn to smile. Instead of putting the gun down, she walked over to Sean and tried to kiss him on the mouth. But he wasn't interested in kissing Yadira. He was just trying to smooth talk her into putting down the weapon. The idea of actually kissing her made Sean's skin crawl and he quickly turned away from Yadira's puckered lips. She was taken aback by the gesture and Sean just sat there, unable to hide the disgusted look on his face.

"Oh, Sean, Sean!" she said, shaking her head, after realizing that he was playing her. "You are such a stupid man! Do you think that I'm gonna let you get away with playing with my feelings . . . again?" Yadira went from being angry to pleading with him. "Sean, we should be together, baby! We both can live in this house together and eventually I can become your wife! Don't you want me to have your baby, Sean? We can make such beautiful babies together!"

Sean was getting more and more upset by the minute. He slowly put his right hand behind his back and gripped the handle of his own gun. Yadira was a very lucky woman; she was supposed to have been dead. But Sean didn't really want to kill Yadira. He couldn't see himself sitting in a courtroom full of jurors trying to claim self-defense on a woman who was only five feet five inches in height and almost a hundred pounds lighter than him. And he thought about Jada, Yadira's five-year-old daughter. Not only would the prosecution hang him by his testicles but he could never live with himself knowing that he killed that little girl's mother. Yadira didn't need to die; she needed help.

Sean frowned. "What in the hell are you talking about, Yadira? How do you even have the nerve to talk about being my wife and starting a family with me when you got a motherfucking gun pointed in my face?"

"Because . . ." Yadira began, after she became aware of her contradictions. She started waving the gun over her head again. "You know what? I'm tired, Sean! I'm just tired of everything! I'm tired of y'all trifling-ass men taking advantage of me! I'm tired of people talking about me. I just wanna be happy, you know what I'm saying? And is that a crime to wanna be happy? I wanna be able to love somebody and they love me back! Is that so hard?"

"You want someone to love you back, huh? What about trying to love your damn self, Yadi? Look at what you're doing now! You're trying to force me to be with you. Is that supposed make me love you?"

Sean paused. He knew that he was coming off too harshly. "At one time, I thought that you were a complete package," Sean calmly said. "You're a gorgeous woman and you was a good friend to me; what more could I ask for? And you had me thinking that this baby daddy of yours was some fool for messing things up with you. So when you decided to leave him, I opened up my door to you and your daughter with no problem. I wanted to help you. But after one moment of weakness, one lovemaking session, you turned into this weak-ass, whining basket case, always wanting a nigga's undivided attention and shit. It's like . . . It's like you can't function unless you got a nigga up under you twenty-four hours a day!"

Yadira's bottom lip began to quiver, as if she was about to cry. She pointed the gun at Sean. Unable to take any more of her intimidation, Sean finally got up from the couch and pointed his Ruger in her face. Now it was Yadira's turn to be petrified.

"I guess we're both gonna die tonight," Sean said through clenched teeth.

Yadira stood her ground. She didn't say a word but did not take her eyes off Sean, either. After a few more seconds of their showdown, her hands began shaking. Sean watched as she started to crack under the pressure.

When Yadira finally broke down, Sean was able to carefully remove the loaded gun from her hands. She collapsed to the floor and began moaning in despair. In the meantime, Sean gripped the handle of his Ruger for dear life, afraid that it might slip from his sweaty grip. He was unsure what Yadi had up her sleeve or if she had another gun on her. Instead of patting her down, he let her sit on the floor and continue to cry. Sean hid Yadira's personal firearm behind the bar.

"I am so sorry, Sean," Yadira whispered, finally expressing some remorse for her actions. "I know that I fucked up with you. It's just that I love you so much.

You have always been good to me and I'm the one who took our friendship for granted. After I broke up with Devin, I needed somebody. You were that somebody! I thought that there was a possibility that you and I could be together."

Yadira's wild hair framed her face, as she shook her head in anguish. Even at her worst moment, she was still strikingly beautiful. "I just needed to be with somebody, Sean. Don't you understand? I didn't want to be alone," she whispered, while breaking down in more tears.

Sean knelt down and began rubbing her back. For a fleeting moment, he felt sorry for Yadira.

"First of all, Yadi, you don't need me or any man to make you feel complete. You have a family and a daughter who worships the ground that you walk on. Forcing me to be with you is not going to make me want to build this imaginary life with you. Sometimes you just have to accept things as they are and move on."

Yadira buried her head in hands again. Sean sat on the nearby barstool and just watched as she cried her eyes out. From the moment he welcomed Yadira into his home wreaking havoc was the only way that she had repaid him for his good deeds.

It was a clear fall night in 2009 and Brown Sugar, a local Brooklyn bar, located on Marcus Garvey Boulevard, was buzzing with patrons. Inside of Brown Sugar, Sean and one of his childhood friends, Unique, had just finished playing a few games of pool. The two friends were having a few beers and catching up on each other's lives, as they waited for the weekly comedy routine to appear on the small stage.

But Sean didn't need the comedy show to laugh. Unique, who was visiting from Atlanta, had all the jokes that he needed. He was a temporary escape from the situation with Yadira. And Sean needed his friend's advice. He figured that Unique would know what to do in circumstances like that.

"What's up with that psycho chick? Is she still bothering you, man?" Unique asked.

Sean took a gulp of his Corona beer. "Man, that broad is a certified lunatic! Straight Fatal Attraction, *man," he said, shaking his head.*

"And I'm the black version of Michael Douglas, man!" Unique laughed. "I'm just waiting to walk in my kitchen and see a fucking rabbit boiling on my stove!"

Unique choked on his beer from the laughter. "Yo, you are stupid!" he replied. Sean laughed, too. "That Fatal Attraction *movie was the shit, though and Glenn Close was one sexy bitch! She was giving up that pussy any- and everywhere! On the kitchen sink, the elevator . . . Old-ass Mike couldn't resist that ass, neither!" Unique said.*

They slapped each other five then Sean got serious. "Maybe that shit was sexy for the movies, but in real life it's not. And don't get me wrong, Yadi is a gorgeous woman, man, but the things that she does and the way that she's been carrying herself is not sexy or cool! What makes it even worse is she could have any man she wants! I'm just trying to understand why the fuck does she keep bothering me?"

Unique put his beer on the bar and looked at Sean. "Look, man, I hate to tell you this but homegirl don't want any other dude! She wants you, homie! She don't care nothing about looking like a fool because she's doing exactly what she wants to do! In her mind, you and her are already in a relationship with each other!"

Sean stared into space. "Damn, I didn't look at it that way, man." He shrugged it off. "But anyway, fuck her feelings! She's not my woman and I wish that she would just leave me the hell alone! I have a woman already and her name is Brandi. Yadira has no other choice but to get me out of her system so that me and Brandi can move on with our lives!"

Unique shook his head. "Don't you and this Yadira chick work together, man?"

Sean sighed. "Yeah, we do. Shit's got so bad at work that she started messing with Brandi's son."

Unique looked confused. "Brandi's son?"

"Brandi's son ended up getting jumped by some general population inmates because he was in the wrong area. Yadira had some new jack officer bring him to the unauthorized area and now that poor officer is about to be brought up on charges. He might even lose his job behind that shit! And it was all because Yadira was trying get back at me and Brandi!"

"Damn, man! She's doing all of that? You need to write the bitch up!"

"And say what? It's her word against mine! I'm really ready to choke the life out of this bitch but I have to chill. I have too much invested for me to lose everything because of this ho." Sean looked Unique up and down. "Maybe I should hook her up with your black ass!"

"Hell no!" Unique exclaimed, almost choking on his drink. "I don't want no stalker chick following me all the way back to ATL! You can save that bullshit, man!" They both laughed at the thought.

"Man, I just gotta get this woman off me! Judging from the way that things are going down between me and her, I wouldn't be surprised if all the things that she used to tell me about her daughter's father are a lie."

Suddenly, Unique turned his attention away from Sean. His eyes went to the entrance door of Brown Sugar.

"Damn! Who in the hell is that?" Unique said.

Sean turned around and his jaw dropped. It was none other than Yadira. Before he could say anything to

Unique, she was bouncing her way over to the bar. Sean turned around and leaned on the bar. He put his head in his hands.

"That's her, Unique, that's Yadira! I don't believe this shit!" he said with an attitude. "What the fuck is she doing here?"

But Unique wasn't paying Sean any attention. He was too focused on the sexy Yadira. "That bitch is bad as hell, nigga, damn!" he said, still staring at the woman.

Yadira walked up to the two friends and looked at Sean with a smile on her face. "What's up, Sean? I went by your house to see if you wanted company but you weren't there. I figured that you would be here." She peeked over their shoulders and saw their beers on the bar. "Care to treat me to a drink or two?" she asked, fluttering her long eyelashes.

Unique couldn't take his eyes off Yadira. A few other male patrons at the bar began checking her out too.

"How you doing, miss?" Unique said, reaching for her hand. He put the back of her hand up to his lips and kissed it. "I'm Unique, sweetheart, and your name is?"

Yadira blushed, relishing the attention. "The name's Yadira but you can just call me Yadi. Nice to meet you, Unique. How you doing, honey?"

Unique let her hand go and slowly walked around her. "Girl, I'm fine but damn, I ain't as fine as you! You are gorgeous, baby!"

Yadira rolled her eyes up in her head, as if he was telling her something that she heard a million times a day. "Thank you, Unique. You seem like you're a really sweet guy, unlike your boy here," she said, looking back at Sean and rolling her eyes. "He don't appreciate none of this!"

Sean began to walk away from them. "Look, Unique, I'm going back over here by the pool tables."

Yadira clapped her hands. "Oooh, I love playing pool!" she said. "Do you wanna play me in a game of pool, Unique?"

Unique walked toward an empty pool table. "Sure, baby doll! I'll play with you!" he said, with a sly look on his face. He couldn't wait for her to bend over the pool table in her short skirt.

As Yadira and Unique walked to the table next to where Sean was standing, he grabbed her by the arm. "What in the fuck are you doing here, Yadi? I thought I told you to stay away from me!"

Yadira snatched her arm from Sean's grasp and pointed her manicured finger in his face. "No, baby, you told me to stay off your property! And right now, we are in a public fucking place and you don't have the right to tell me to leave, okay? I have a right to be here so get the fuck over it!" As Yadira started to walk toward the pool tables, she turned around and blew a kiss at Sean. "Oh, yeah, and just because we had this little tiff, it doesn't mean that it's over between us!"

Sean was on fire but he realized that Yadira was right. There was nothing that he could do about her showing up at Brown Sugar. It was a public place. But for her to appear at one of his local haunts wasn't just some coincidence. She was definitely following his every move. Sean knew that if the shoe were on the other foot, he surely would have been arrested by now.

Sean stood there and watched as Unique shared laughs and had a ball with Yadira, the same woman who was giving him a hard time. Unique was like so many other men who thought that because Yadira was such a beautiful woman, there was no way that she could be as crazy as what Sean described. But she was and no amount of beauty could overshadow that.

After calming down, Sean walked over to Unique and gave him a pound. "Look, U, I'm outta here, man. I'm a little tired," Sean said.

Unique looked disappointed but then he looked at Yadira, who was bending over the pool table. She was wearing a red lace thong under the short mini-skirt she had on.

"All right, my dude, you do that. You go on home. I think I'll be okay with Miss Yadira over here," he said, unable to take his eyes off her plump rear. "You're gonna hang out with me tonight, right, Miss Yadira?"

Yadira struck a yellow ball with her pool stick. "Yes, sir! We're going to be just fine!" she replied, flashing a million dollar smile.

Unique grinned from ear to ear. "Yeah, baby girl, that's right!" He looked at the annoyed Sean and winked. "Okay, see ya, boy. Call you later!"

Sean shot Unique a strange look and shook his head. He couldn't wait to give him a serious tongue-lashing.

As Sean was driving home, he couldn't keep his mind off Yadira's antics. A part of him didn't care about her dealing with any man, as long as it wasn't him, but not one of his best friends. He didn't want Unique to be subjected to any of her craziness.

Ten minutes later, Sean pulled into a parking space near his home. He opened the front door, walked into the foyer, and pressed the code on the burglar alarm. Then he went upstairs to his bedroom. He stripped down to his birthday suit and ran the shower inside of his master bathroom. Before stepping into the tub, he turned on the CD player. He was in the mood to hear some slow jams. The soft, sultry sounds always calmed his nerves.

While Sean lathered up and sang along with the singer Joe, he never heard his downstairs door being opened. The intruder pressed the code on the burglar alarm, just like Sean had done a few minutes before. They slowly crept up the steps and walked toward the bathroom. By the time Sean hit a high note, the intruder was standing directly outside of his bathroom door.

The intruder tiptoed inside of the bathroom and peeked into the slightly open shower curtain. Sean had his back facing the door and was temporarily blinded because of the soap all over his face. And the music was so loud, he hadn't heard a thing. That was when the unthinkable happened.

The intruder took the blunt object that they were holding in their hand and came crashing down on the back of Sean's skull. Sean fell forward and banged his forehead against the tiled wall before slipping in the tub. The intruder swung the object again. This time, they hit the fallen Sean on the other side of his head.

As the fatal blow was about to be administered, police cars passing through the block with their sirens blaring startled the intruder, who hurriedly ran back downstairs and out of the front door. The unconscious Sean lay slumped in the bathtub, stained with his own blood.

The following morning, Miss Miller, Sean's mother walked into the quiet house with her spare key. She and Sean, her youngest, were supposed to meet for an early breakfast but he didn't call her or answer his phones. When Miss Miller walked up the stairs, she heard the shower running in the master bathroom.

"Sean?" she said, calling out his name. Miss Miller walked into the bathroom and pulled back the shower curtain. She screamed loudly when she saw her son, slumped over in the tub with blood all over his face. "Oh, my God!" she exclaimed. "My baby!"

Suddenly, the upstairs bell rang. Sean prayed that it was Brandi with the cops. He walked over to the staircase and looked back at Yadira. She was still on the floor, balled up in a fetal position and crying in front of his fireplace. Sean hesitated to leave the emotionally unstable Yadira unattended but it wasn't the time to babysit. He ran up the stairs to open that door.

When Sean opened the door, two police officers walked in his house with Brandi following closely behind them. Thankfully, she had already filled them in on what was happening. The officers came more than ready to remove Yadira from Sean's residence, in handcuffs. One of the officers looked down and spotted the Ruger in Sean's hand. Instinctively, the officer's hand went to the Glock in his holster.

"No, Officer, I'm a CO and this is my personal firearm!" Sean laid the gun on the top of the staircase banister. "If you want to see my badge, I can run upstairs and get that for you but the person you want is downstairs," Sean said. "I removed the gun from her possession so she's unarmed right now."

The two officers and Brandi followed Sean down a flight of stairs, leading to the family room. But before they could reach the bottom of the steps, they heard a single gunshot. Both of the police officers immediately drew their guns and told Sean and Brandi to stay back. The cops walked down the last couple of steps, leading to the family room. There, they saw Yadira's limp body sprawled on the floor. One of the cops walked over to Yadira and checked her pulse, while the other one held his firearm over her. A grim look came over the face of the pulse checking officer. He motioned for his partner to holster his gun.

The cop stood up and looked back down at Yadira, who was still holding the weapon in her bloody hand. He pointed to the lone gunshot wound on the right side of Yadira's temple.

Brandi and Sean were standing a few feet away from the horrific scene. Brandi began crying and buried her head in Sean's chest. Yadira's thick hair was matted with blood and there was brain matter all over Sean's hardwood floors and wall. The pellets from the bullet looked like they were lodged in the wall nearest her body.

"I think that this young lady is dead," the officer said, as he radioed for more backup and an ambulance. "Two patrol cars are outside and the paramedics are on their way," he told Sean.

Sean just stood there in shock, staring at Yadira's lifeless body and embracing the crying Brandi. Then he remembered one horrifying detail. The gun that Yadira had used to kill herself was her own firearm! He had carelessly left it behind the bar and she was able to get a hold of it.

Throughout the entire ordeal, Sean was able to maintain some self-control. But after thinking about everything that led up to Yadira's suicide, his guilty thoughts and the image of her dead body became too much for him to bear. Sean felt himself slowly losing his composure.

He let go of Brandi and tried to walk over to Yadira. "Why, Yadi, why? Why did you do this to yourself?" he yelled at the dead corpse, forcing the cops to restrain him.

As the police officers tried to calm the inconsolable Sean down, Brandi couldn't stop crying. She had her own thoughts about Yadira's death. The vast similarities between her and the woman were entirely too much for her to bear. And for some strange reason, the memories of what her son's father, Maleek last moments may have been like before he was murdered, came flooding back into her memory with a vengeance.

"Oh, my God! What did I do to you, Maleek?" she whispered under her breath. "Why did I do that to you?"

***

It wasn't until five months after Yadira's suicide that Sean was able to sleep peacefully. The cool April breeze that was blowing through his open bedroom window put him to ease. But just as Sean was about to close his eyes, his ringing cell phone interrupted his restful slumber. Sean reluctantly answered the call, slightly annoyed that his sleep was being interrupted.

"Hello?" he answered, groggily.

"Hey, Sean."

Sean knew that voice all too well but needed to make sure that he was hearing right. "Hello?" he repeated, sitting upright in his bed.

"Hey, Sean. It's me. Brandi."

Sean got real quiet. He didn't know what to say. He hadn't spoken to Brandi since the suicide. Shortly after the incident, she changed her numbers and hadn't bothered to reach out to him. So there was no use in Sean beating around the bush. He wanted to tell Brandi exactly how he felt.

"What the hell do you want, Brandi?" he said, in a voice that was callous as ever. "It's been five months since I heard from you and now you fucking decide to call me? What's up with that?"

Brandi let out a long sigh. "Look, Sean, I don't have any excuse for not attempting to contact you. It's just that I needed some time to get myself together."

"Get yourself together?" Sean replied. Deep down in his heart, he knew that Brandi was right. She was the one who suffered physical violence at the hands of the mentally disturbed Yadira. But Sean could only feel sorry for himself and how much he had been through. "Brandi, Yadi killed herself in my got damn house, remember? What about how I was feeling at the time?"

Sean's selfish attitude made Brandi lash out in anger. "I don't believe that after all of this got damn time, you're only thinking about yourself, Sean!" she yelled. "After everything that happened that night, you never called to see if I was all right or ask me how I was doing! So you know what I did? I changed my got damn number! That's right! And do I need to remind your ass that you were the reason why I was in that fucking predicament in the first place? Huh? Do I?"

Sean took a deep breath and tried to calm himself down. Having never taken the time to think about how Brandi must have felt, he felt bad about the way he reacted to her. She must have been just as traumatized as he was. The fact that Yadira could easily have killed her, too, must have crossed Brandi's mind hundreds of times.

"Got damn it, Brandi!" Sean exclaimed, getting up from the bed. He began pacing the room. "Look, you're right, babe. I apologize for lashing out on you. And I apologize for not calling you after everything went down. It's just that I wasn't up for accepting any phone calls from nobody other than my family members. It was about a month later when I tried to call you. But it was too late. You had already changed your numbers and from that alone, I knew that you weren't messing with me," Sean admitted.

Brandi sighed. "Maybe I need to apologize too. We both had our reasons for not calling each other. But I didn't change my number because I was upset with you, Sean. It's just that people were calling my phone like crazy—news reporters, detectives; and then there were my problems with Shamari. Anyway, what we went through on that crazy night was devastating for the both of us but we survived it. Now let's get off that. How are you, Sean? How have you been holding up these past few months?" Brandi asked.

Sean shook his head. "I've been doing all right, sweetheart. I just wish that things wouldn't have turned out the way that they did."

"Yeah, I know. It was definitely tragic. So sad. Did you attend Yadi's funeral?"

Sean wiped the beads of sweat from his forehead. Yadira's suicide was always going to be the big elephant in the room. There was no way around it.

"No, I didn't go to the funeral but I was able to speak to her mother and her daughter's father not too long after the funeral. They both told me about Yadira's deteriorating mental condition. She was suffering from bipolar disorder and something else that I can't remember. Her daughter's father told me that she was on medication, too, but she refused to take it."

Brandi gasped. "For real? Yadira was on psych medication? Wow! That's crazy! She was such a beautiful woman! Who would have ever known that she was dealing with that?"

Sean shrugged. "As the old saying goes, 'Don't judge a book by its cover,'" he said.

"Ain't that the truth!" Brandi paused. "Look, Sean, I just called to let you know that I still care about you and that I miss you so much."

"I still care about you too, Brandi." There was a brief silence between them. "Would you like to come over? I would really like to see you."

"Sounds like a great idea."

An hour later, Brandi arrived at Sean's house. When he opened the door, he was taken aback by how good she looked. She had lost a few pounds but she still had some weight in all of the right places.

Sean invited Brandi into the living room where he had some chilled Moscato and wine glasses waiting for them. Sean poured them some glasses of wine and they made a toast. Afterward, they stared at each other for a couple of moments but didn't say a word.

Brandi was the one to speak first. “You look damn good, Sean,” she said, rubbing his toned bicep. “You look really good.”

Sean rubbed his washboard abs. “Yeah, I’ve been working out. I had to alleviate some of that stress. Plus, I started training again, you know, with the boxing and all that. And you look good too, babe.”

“Thanks.” Brandi cleared her throat. “I wanted to clear the air with you. I know we had some drama in our lives. I also know that you and I are still trying to put the pieces together. But what I came here to say is—” she began before Sean cut her off.

Sean looked down at his glass. “Brandi, I don’t think that it’s a good idea for us to be together,” he said, out of the blue.

Brandi had a look of surprise on her face. “Excuse me?”

Sean was too caught up with what he was saying to see the hurt in Brandi’s eyes. “That’s what I wanted to talk to you about. I think that being with each other will just be a constant reminder of what happened with Yadira. And honestly, babe, I don’t want to ever remember that shit.”

Brandi stood up and walked away from Sean. He got up to comfort her but she pulled away from him. “I’m so sorry, baby,” Sean continued. “I care about you, Brandi, you know I do but after everything that happened, I’m too afraid to take a chance and be in a relationship with any woman right now.”

Brandi grabbed her pocketbook and headed to the door. “Where are you going?” Sean asked, with a confused look on his face. “I didn’t say that you had to leave!”

“Couldn’t you have told me this bullshit over the fucking phone?” Brandi screamed at him.

Sean tried to convince Brandi to sit back down but she pulled away from him again.

"I didn't want to tell you this over the phone, Brandi." When she didn't reply, Sean started to explain. "Brandi, I just want the best for you, babe; that's why I'm keeping it real with you! This shit with Yadira has scarred me and you don't deserve to be with someone who's not going to give you all of him."

Once again, Sean tried to comfort Brandi. But she pushed him off her and walked out of the front door. He followed her outside and stood on the stoop, watching helplessly, as Brandi walked down his front steps. It was that moment that Sean wished he could take Brandi into his arms, make love to her, and tell her that everything was going to be all right. But the truth was everything wasn't all right. Sean was still dealing with Yadira's suicide and he didn't trust himself or anyone else for that matter. And because of that, all he could do was stand there and watch the woman he had fallen in love with disappear from his life for good.

Chapter 1

October, 2012

It was a hectic Friday for Brandi Wallace. She was so looking forward to her weekend off from her demanding job.

A career-driven woman and a stickler when it came to her job, Brandi loved her position as a director for the Administration of Children's Services. She had a great rapport with her subordinates and, more importantly, they all got the job done. But even though Brandi was quite successful in that area, there was something missing from her life: a meaningful relationship. She sighed loudly, as she thought about her lackluster love life.

Brandi hummed along with Beyoncé, as she drove her Audi Q5 truck across the Brooklyn Bridge. She was a little exhausted from putting in some hours at work but for some strange reason, she was not in the mood to go straight home. So instead of heading straight to her East New York residence and letting a Calgon bubble bath take her away; Brandi made an unexpected detour.

As soon as Brandi arrived in the borough of Brooklyn, her hometown, she headed straight for Halsey Street in Bedford-Stuyvesant. She wasn't going to visit anyone in particular, or even had a real destination. She just wanted to recapture the memories of what could have been.

Brandi pulled up on Halsey Street and parked her car. She got out of the vehicle, standing a few feet away from a lovely brownstone. She took a few seconds to admire the oak double doors and natural stone steps. But the beautiful home wasn't what brought her to the Halsey Street address. The home belonged to her former flame, Sean Daniels.

Brandi smiled to herself as she thought about the fun times she had with Sean. They met each other in September of 2009, in a place that she would have never expected to meet any man. He was a strapping thirty-three-year-old man, three years younger than the thirty-six-year-old Brandi. But the small age gap didn't bother the sexy cougar one bit; she just loved Sean's laidback demeanor. And what she really liked most about Sean was that he wasn't intimidated by her at all. He had a silent confidence that even men her own age lacked.

It was obvious that Sean left quite an impression on Brandi. It was refreshing for her to have met a man who had his act together. Brandi wouldn't have it any other way.

Brandi laughed to herself. She couldn't believe that she was actually standing in front of Sean's house! But she couldn't help herself; it was hard to stop thinking about him. It was also part of her that made her curious to find out how his life turned out after they went their separate ways. Brandi sighed. The end of their budding relationship started with a woman by the name of Yadira Cruz. Yadira's deadly obsession with Sean was what really ruined their chances of ever having a normal union.

Now it was almost four years since the death of Yadira. The emotionally disturbed woman had taken her life, right in Sean's house. But even after so many years had passed, Brandi just couldn't bring herself to sympathize or even empathize with Yadira. It was hard for her to feel sorry for a woman who committed suicide because she couldn't have a man.

Brandi hated Yadira for killing herself. Her tragic death was always a reminder of why Brandi never got with Sean, a man who could have potentially been her husband.

Brandi took one last look at the brownstone and sighed. She was probably the only one out of the two of them who was still obsessing over the what-ifs. And Sean hadn't tried to contact her in three years. It was painfully evident that he had moved on. It was definitely time for Brandi to let go of the past and move on too.

As Brandi walked back to her parked vehicle, the thoughts of Sean didn't end there. She began reminiscing about the very first time that she met the charming bachelor. In the late summer of 2009, Brandi's nineteen-year-old son, Shamari, who was facing robbery charges, had to be detained on Rikers Island. Before the incident, no one could have ever told her that her only child would be in jail at all, let alone for some robbery offense. Brandi was heartbroken, for she had given him everything that a child could ask for and more; in other words, Shamari wanted for nothing. But although the idea of her son being locked up had her upset, she stood by his side. After all, she was all that he had.

Brandi remembered how it used to take everything for her to walk through the doors of the jail to visit Shamari. She was so stressed out about the entire ordeal. Jail was no place for anyone, especially her baby, and she found it hard to believe that the intelligent Shamari put himself in that position. Brandi knew her son was much smarter than that.

Walking through the doors of that same facility was where Correction Officer Sean Daniels entered her life. He was very helpful to them and assured Brandi that he would keep an eye on Shamari for her. Being a mother, she was more than grateful for that. But while she was looking at the attractive thirty-three-year-old, she couldn't deny the strong physical attraction that she had to him. Aside from everything that Sean said that he was going to do for Shamari, Brandi found herself wanting to get to know him better.

On the day that Brandi met Sean, she had left work early. She had to do that in order to make the miserable trek from her job in Manhattan to Rikers Island in Queens to see Shamari, her incarcerated son.

Usually, on the days that Brandi visited Shamari everything would go smoothly. But on this day, things weren't getting off to a good start. For one, Brandi had forgotten her change of clothes at home. She hated wearing her professional clothing to that jail. When she did, she got the stares and dirty looks from the other visitors. Even a few correction officers looked at her funny. It was as if they were wondering who she was coming to Rikers Island to visit.

After arriving at Rikers and going though the grueling registration process, search, and waiting procedures that day, Brandi was finally seated at a table on the crowded visit area floor. As she anxiously waited for Shamari to walk through the sliding metal doors, she could feel the butterflies fluttering in her stomach. Brandi was looking forward to seeing her son, even though every time she saw him in that Godforsaken correction-issued jumpsuit, she just wanted to break down and cry. But she did her best not to do that in front of Shamari. He hated when she cried and she wanted to be strong for the both of them.

When the sliding door opened, Shamari walked out onto the visit floor. He appeared to have adjusted to his environment well; it even looked as if he had grown an inch or two in height. Brandi didn't think that it was possible for Shamari to gain any weight but he had managed to put some pounds on his lean frame. And peach fuzz on his chin had gotten a little thicker since the last time she visited him.

When Shamari approached the table, Brandi stood up and greeted him with a smile and hug. Shamari hugged her back and kissed her on the cheek.

"Hey, Ma," he said, while attempting to smile back at her. "Thanks for coming to see me."

Brandi felt a lump building in her throat. "Now you know that I was gonna come and see my baby, Shaki," she said, calling him by his childhood nickname. "Even though I despise this got damn place, I can't let you sit in this jail without coming to visit you."

Shamari managed to smile at his mother. He held her hands in his own and kissed them. "Love you, Ma," he said, looking as if he was about to tear up. "You know that I appreciate you, right?"

"I know you do, baby. I know you do," Brandi gushed.

A visit officer approached their table, interrupting their mother-and-son moment. Brandi wanted to protest but when she looked up at him, she was staring in the face of an exceptionally handsome man. Damn! Who the hell is this? *Brandi tried to take in all of the officer's manly attributes in one glance. She saw that his uniform was fitting him to a tee. When she felt her eyes wandering to his crotch area, she caught herself. Brandi almost forgot that Shamari was sitting there, watching her reaction to the officer's presence. She could tell from Shamari's facial expression that he caught an instant attitude.*

"Hey, what's up, young blood?" the officer said to Shamari. "How's everything going over here?"

"Everything is fine, CO," Shamari replied, giving the officer a suspicious look. "We're good, man."

The handsome officer looked at Brandi. "And how are you, miss?" he asked.

Brandi smiled at him. "I'm okay, Officer. I'm just here visiting my son," she said, looking at his nametag. "Officer Daniels."

When Brandi said that she was visiting her son, CO Daniels quickly extended his hand to her. Shamari sighed loudly and crossed his arms.

"Oh, wow!" Daniels exclaimed, ignoring Shamari's nonverbal gestures. "This grown man right here is your son?" he asked, pointing at Shamari.

Brandi sighed too. "Yep, this is my baby," she replied, with a faint smile on her face.

Daniels rubbed his chin and stared at Shamari. "Oh, okay, say no more! Your baby boy is in good hands." He looked at Shamari. "By the way, what housing area are you in?" he asked.

Brandi rolled her eyes. She prayed that Shamari didn't embarrass her on that visit floor. But her prayers weren't answered. He gave Daniels a nasty look. "I'm in Five North, man. Why?" Shamari replied.

Once again, Daniels acted as if he didn't notice Shamari's callous attitude toward him. "Oh, yeah? That's my old steady housing area right there. I'll put the word out and tell the officers up there to look out for you, man."

Shamari impatiently shifted his behind in the hard seat. "Look, man, you ain't gotta do nothing for me! I don't fu . . ." he began, looking at his mother before he cussed. "I mean, I don't fool with too many of these cats in here anyway! And I damn sure don't fu . . . I mean, fool with no po-lice!"

Now Brandi was getting pissed with her son's ungratefulness. "Will you just shut the hell up, Shamari?" she said, scolding him and talking through clenched teeth. "Your attitude and your hard head is exactly why your ass is in the trouble that you're in now!" Brandi looked at CO Daniels apologetically. "I want to apologize for my son's ignorance. He's always had this problem with authority," she added, rolling her eyes at Shamari in the process. "My son really doesn't belong here. I didn't raise him like this," she continued, feeling the need to explain herself to the officer. "Being in this . . . this shithole is nothing but a pit stop before death. And I don't know what it's going to take for him . . ." Brandi's eyes began to get watery and she drifted off.

CO Daniels cleared his throat. "Oh, man. Okay, listen, I'm so sorry for interrupting you and your son, miss. It looks like you two need to have a serious talk. I'm gonna go back to do what I'm paid to do. Enjoy the rest of the visit," he said, before quickly walking off.

As soon as Daniels left their table, Brandi went off on Shamari. "What the hell is wrong with you, Shamari?" she asked, while looking around the visit floor to see who was listening to her. "That officer was being nice to you and you acted like a complete jackass to him! You need somebody to look out for you while you're in this place!"

Shamari looked his mother straight in the eye. "Like I said, Ma, I don't need nothing from nobody, especially from no got damn po-lice!"

Brandi felt like slapping the taste out of Shamari's mouth. In his display of defiance and stubbornness, he reminded her so much of his father, Maleek. Maleek had been dead since Shamari was five years old but it was amazing how their personalities were so similar.

"And what about you, Ma?" he whispered, holding out both hands. "You sitting here flirting with some po-lice nigga right in front of your own son! The only reason that that nigga came over here to do was to holler at you and here you go acting like you ain't see what he was doing. Damn! You fell the fuck off!"

Brandi's right eyebrow shot up. "Boy, what in the hell are you talking about and who are you talking to?" she whispered back. "First of all, I'm a grown-ass motherfucking woman and damn, the got damn man was just trying to be nice!"

Shamari huffed. "I done already told you and that lame-ass cop that I don't need anybody looking out for me, especially some police nigga! I'm not going to tell you or him that shit again!"

Brandi let out a sarcastic chuckle. "Oh! Is that right?" she replied, looking at Shamari like he had flipped his wig. "So you got this, huh? Well, if you got this, Shamari Wallace, then give me back my five thousand dollar retainer that I had to put out for that got damn lawyer of yours! And how about the commissary money that you're always begging me for? Huh? And please, let's not forget about the packages that I send you in the mail every other week!"

A dumb look came over Shamari's face but he didn't say one word.

"That's what the hell I thought!" Brandi said, tightening her jaw. She shook her head and took a few seconds to compose herself. "As a matter of fact, I cannot be aggravated with you right now. I'm going home!"

Brandi stood up to walk off the visit floor but as she was about to do that, Daniels rushed back over to the table to ask her to sit back down. He then explained to her that the inmate was always the first to leave the visit area.

Brandi plopped back down in the chair. "I'm sorry about that but we have a serious problem here," she replied angrily. "My son obviously doesn't appreciate his mother coming to this filthy place to visit his unappreciative ass!"

Shamari sucked his teeth and waved his mother off. "Ma, c'mon, cut it out! You are bugging out right now!" he said. "A few minutes ago, I just told you that I appreciated you coming to see me and now you're saying that I'm ungrateful? Wow!"

Brandi pointed a French manicured finger in Shamari's peach fuzz face. "I was sixteen going on seventeen years old when I got pregnant with you, Shamari. I made all kinds of sacrifices trying to provide you with everything that you needed so that you wouldn't be out in these streets trying to steal, cheat, or rob! I gave you the best so that you wouldn't have to go through shit like this!"

Shamari had a smug expression on his face while some nearby visitors and fellow inmates stared at him. He sat there with his arms folded, acting like the child he was. And he did not bother to respond or even apologize to his mother. Instead, Shamari got up and stomped out of the visiting area without even saying good-bye to her.

Brandi took a deep breath, trying to hold back tears of frustration. She immediately left the visit floor, wondering where she had gone wrong while raising her child.

Daniels followed the upset Brandi back to the registration area and watched as she retrieved her personal items from the visitors' lockers. After gathering her things, Brandi sat in one of the empty seats to wait for the visit bus to take her and other visitors back to the parking lot. When she looked up, Daniels was right there with a look of concern on his face.

Brandi shook her head. "I have to apologize again for his bratty behavior," she said, forcing a smile. "Thank you, Mr. Daniels, for wanting to help my son."

Daniels sat beside her. "Oh, it was no problem," he replied. "And don't worry, I'm still gonna look out for him so don't get yourself too upset. He was just trying to prove to his mother and to me that he's a fucking tough guy." Brandi laughed a little. "But seriously, I've been doing this for a while so that attitude of his is nothing new to me." He paused. "Oh, by the way, I'm Sean."

Brandi giggled. "Oh, shoot, please forgive me. I forgot to introduce myself. I'm Brandi. Brandi Wallace."

"Well, Brandi, I hope I'm not being too forward but I think that you're a very beautiful woman. I hope you don't mind me saying so."

Brandi blushed. "Thanks, Sean. I appreciate the compliment. You're a handsome guy."

Sean smiled at her. "Thank you, sweetheart."

Brandi rumbled through her bag to retrieve one of her business cards. When she found one, she placed it in his hand. Before she could say another word, she lined up at the door with the other visitors to board the bus.

Brandi looked back at Sean and waved good-bye. Then she mouthed the words "call me." He smiled back at her and gave her a head nod. When she looked back one more time, Sean was still standing there, watching her. He stood there until she was completely out of his sight.

Since she and Sean went their separate ways, Brandi dated men who didn't quite measure up to what she really wanted. But in 2010, Brandi met someone she thought was special. She even endured an eleven-month relationship with the man and everything. She just couldn't get into him. Out of fairness to the guy, she had to let him go.

Brandi turned up the radio in her truck. "Ascension" by Maxwell came blaring through her speakers. It was her and Sean's favorite song.

Chapter 2

An hour after Brandi pulled off from Halsey Street, newlyweds Sean and Milan Daniels exited the door of their brownstone. They were walking down the stairs together when suddenly the affectionate Milan turned around and placed a soft kiss on her husband's lips.

"Damn, baby," she said, wiping her Bobbi Brown lip gloss from his mouth. "I'm gonna miss you this weekend! It's messed up that they're sending me on this last-minute business trip on your days off! We could have spent this entire weekend in bed together."

Sean smiled at his wife of one year. "Yeah, me too, sweetheart," he replied, as he made his way down the stairs with her luggage in tow. "By the way, what the hell do you have in this suitcase? You're only going to Atlanta for the weekend, babe!"

Milan pressed the alarm to her Mercedes-Benz coupe and the trunk popped open. "I know, I know! But I couldn't make up my mind about what I wanted to wear," she said, pouting her full lips.

Sean shook his head at her and smiled. He threw the heavy suitcase into the back of the trunk.

Milan held out her arms. "Hey, hey, hey! Be careful with the bag, brother man!" she joked. "I gots all my good shit in there, man!"

Sean laughed and closed the trunk. "That's my bad, beautiful," he replied, giving her another kiss on the lips. "I know you have your own money and everything but do you mind if a brother adds to your riches, my queen?" Sean asked, pulling out his wallet.

Milan held out her hand. "Why, of course, you can, my king!"

Sean counted out five hundred-dollar bills for Milan and put them in her hand. She dug in her bag to retrieve her wallet. She put the money away and wrapped her arms around Sean's broad shoulders.

"I love you so much, Mr. Daniels," she whispered. "Now you better be a good boy until mama gets home. Once I come back from my trip and walk through that front door, you can be bad all over again."

They shared yet another intimate kiss. Sean grabbed Milan's plump derriere and squeezed tightly. She giggled and playfully slapped his hands away.

"Stop playing, nasty!" said Milan. "You must want me to miss my flight."

Sean stepped back. "Nah, babe, I don't want you to do that. As much as I wouldn't mind having some more of that good stuff, you have to go and take care of business."

Milan sighed. "Yeah, I do." She kissed Sean again, got into the driver's seat of her car, and started it up. "I will call you as soon as I'm about to board the plane. I love you, babe."

"I love you too, sweetheart. See you Monday."

Sean stood by the curb and watched Milan pull off. When she made a left turn at the corner of their block, he walked back into his house.

Minutes after Milan's departure, Sean put on some tunes and began tidying up the sprawling brownstone. As he dusted, swept, mopped, and polished furniture, he sang along with the song, while grinding his torso to the beat.

Sean laughed at his horrible attempt at singing. He could recall a time when something as simple as laughter was something that he wasn't able to do. But thanks to Milan, his entire life had changed.

He recalled the first time that they met.

Sean first laid eyes on the stunning Milan Garrett at a cocktail mixer in the summer of 2010. A close friend of his was having the event in the spacious backyard of his Dix Hills home. Sean spotted Milan sashaying across the yard in a white flowing maxi dress that clung to every curve. He couldn't take his eyes off her. He thought that Milan was a knockout, with her small waist and wide hips; not to mention she had one of the most inviting smiles that he had ever seen. Sean knew that he had to meet her. He quickly made his way through the crowd of people and over to Milan, who was chatting it up with a small group of women.

"Um, excuse me, ladies," Sean said to the other women. "I hate to interrupt y'all but I couldn't help but notice this beautiful woman right here," he said, taking Milan's hand into his. "I just had to come over here and introduce myself."

The women applauded and laughed at Sean's chivalrous gesture. They walked away to tend to some other activities at the mixer while Milan just stood there, looking at the charismatic Sean with an apprehensive look on her face.

"How you doing, sweetheart?" he greeted her. "I'm sorry to be so forward but you are irresistible. What's your name?"

Milan still seemed a little skeptical but she smiled at him anyway. "The name's Milan Garrett. And yours?"

Sean placed a kiss on her baby soft hand. "My name is Sean Daniels. It is a pleasure to meet you. You have to excuse a brother but I have to get straight to the point. Do you have a man here or is that problem at home? Are you married? Any children?"

Milan shook her head and laughed. "Boy, slow down!" she said. "First off, I don't have a child! And I don't have much time for a relationship because I'm focusing on my career right now."

"Ah, damn," Sean said, letting go of her hand.

Milan looked confused. "What does that 'damn' mean?"

"That damn means what do I say to you now? You just said that you don't have time for a relationship and I was looking forward to you being my lady one day. You're definitely the one."

The flattered Milan wrapped her arm around Sean's muscled bicep. When she did that, she paused. "Wow," she said, while feeling him up in the process. "You have some really nice arms on you, buddy! Maybe I need to reconsider that relationship thing, huh?"

Sean laughed. "So you're just going to stand here and molest me, huh? Right here? In front of everybody?" he asked.

Milan gave him a flirtatious look. "I can molest you in private, if you'd like."

Sean licked his lips. "Now I wouldn't mind that at all!"

From that day on, Sean was head over heels in love. Not only was Milan young and gorgeous; she was an ambitious, college-educated woman. Her marketing assistant position for Universal Music Group definitely added to her go-getter appeal. And just like him, Milan was extremely close to her family. These great attributes made Sean fall deeper in love with her.

So after dating each other for a year, Sean made a life-changing decision. He realized that he didn't want to just date Milan anymore. He asked her father for his daughter's hand in marriage and even consulted with her mother as to what kind of engagement ring he should purchase for her. He finally proposed to Milan during an intimate family dinner in September of 2011.

Instead of having a grandiose wedding with hundreds of guests and a massive bridal party, Sean and Milan got married in a private ceremony on the beaches of St. Lucia. The two of them shared a very touching moment with each other, with Sean pushing all of the tragic events that occurred in the previous years out of his mind. With Milan came a breath of fresh air and Sean embraced the much-needed change. And for the last year, he was happier with her than what he had ever imagined he could be with any other woman.

After Sean finished cleaning the upstairs of the house, he walked downstairs to the large family room. When he stepped into the dark room, he hesitantly clicked the light switch to the on position. It was funny but every time Sean stepped into that room, there was a creepy, haunting feeling. Something in that room reminded him of what a complete mess his life had been a few years earlier.

It seemed like it was only yesterday when Sean, a thirty-three-year-old bachelor at the time, found himself caught up in a deadly love triangle with Yadira Cruz, a coworker/friend, and his lovely paramour, a woman named Brandi Wallace.

At the time, Brandi was a sexy thirty-six-year-old single mother. Sean met her when she came to the Rikers Island facility to visit her inmate son. And his coworker, Yadira, was an exotic-looking, curvaceous, half-black, half-Latina *mami,* who oozed pure sexiness.

When Sean first started his career with the Department of Corrections, he found himself being extremely attracted to Yadira. He initially wanted to have sex with her. But after he tried to come on to her, she straight out told him that she was in a committed relationship with her daughter's father. The disappointed Sean had no other choice but to respect that. So instead of hopping in the sack with each other, they became platonic friends.

As for Brandi, when Sean saw her walk through the door of the facility visiting room, he was immediately taken aback by her attractiveness and classy demeanor. Just from looking at Brandi, Sean knew that she was a different type of visitor from any of the females who visited inmates at Rikers Island. She had the look of a professional career woman; the business suit that she wore to the visit said it all. And judging from the serious look on her face, he knew that she was nothing to be played with.

While it wasn't proper protocol for a correction officer to talk to anyone coming to visit an inmate, Sean found the urge to holler at Brandi overpowering. He was ready to break all of the rules for the caramel-skinned beauty. Fortunately for Sean, it wasn't as hard as he thought it would be to get with her. Brandi definitely entertained the attention. She caught a little flack from her jailed offspring because of it but that didn't stop her.

Not too long after their first meeting, Sean began dating Brandi. He found out that she was even cooler and down to earth than what he initially thought she would be. To say that Brandi was enjoyable and a pleasure to be with was an understatement. A former bad girl, she had a vibrant personality and most of all, she was a tigress in the bedroom. But unfortunately, their union was short-lived, thanks to Yadira Cruz's jealous antics.

Sean's troubles began when Yadira called him one night, looking for a place to stay.

It was not too long after getting into a physical altercation with Devin, her live-in boyfriend, and she was extremely upset about what happened. Sean hated to hear his friend cry. Yadira claimed that she had nowhere to go. So being a supportive friend, Sean insisted that Yadira and Jada, her five-year-old daughter, come to stay with him while she sorted some things out. What Sean didn't realize is that he opened a huge can of worms.

The first week of Yadira staying in his home was pretty much drama-free and uneventful. That is, until one moment of weakness between him and her changed the dynamics of their friendship forever.

After returning from a delightful first date with his newfound love interest, Brandi, Sean was unaware that he was in for a big surprise when he got home. Not bothering to walk upstairs to his bedroom, Sean chose to stay downstairs in his family room. He stripped down to his underwear, turned on the big-screen television, and made himself comfortable on the couch. Just as he was about to doze off, Yadira appeared downstairs. He hadn't expected her to still be awake because it was pretty late. But there she was, standing in front of him with a T-shirt and no panties on.

With the help the dim light coming from the television, Sean caught a glimpse of Yadira's D-cup breasts. Her hardened nipples protruded through the thin material of the T-shirt that she was wearing and her freshly scrubbed thick mane of hair hung down her back. Yadira's bronze-colored sun-kissed skin was practically glistening from the coconut oil that she rubbed on all over her body.

Out of the blue, Yadira began thanking him profusely for welcoming her and her daughter, Jada, into his home. Then she went to embrace him. If her mission was to seduce Sean, it was definitely working. He had always been physically attracted to Yadira and she knew that so Sean was immediately turned on by the gesture. He felt his manhood rising and immediately after that, their friendly hug turned into an intimate kiss.

Yadira cut the kiss short to take Sean's erect penis into her juicy mouth. He felt like he was in heaven as she sucked and licked on his rod like a porn star. For several minutes, Sean massaged the insides of Yadira's mouth, as the saliva dripped down the shaft of his long dick. She sucked on his testicles and ran her tongue around the "taint," a highly sensitive area under his testicles. Sean grabbed onto the arm of the couch and began moaning. He couldn't take any more of the delicious foreplay. He wanted all of Yadira.

Sean quickly pulled her up from her knees. "Bring your sexy ass up here and sit on this dick," he whispered.

Yadira smiled and climbed on top of his stiff erection. Sean entered her, slowly grinding inside of her tight walls. He closed his eyes, taking in the sounds of Yadira's wet pussy making gushy noises.

As their session got more intense, she grabbed Sean's waist, pulling him deeper into her. In the meantime, Yadira whispered nasty nothings into his ear.

"Fuck me harder, baby," she said softly. "You know that you wanted this pussy for a while now, baby."

That much was true. Their sexual escapade had been a long time coming for the both of them.

After a long night of unadulterated sex, the next day, Sean mistakenly thought that things were going to be back to normal. But like most women, Yadira's whole attitude changed after they had sex. She became extremely jealous and her control issues began rearing its ugly head.

Judging from her actions, Sean knew that they had crossed the line and their sexual interlude may have possibly cost him a ten-year friendship with Yadira. Unable to deal with Sean's bachelor lifestyle, Yadira moved out of his house. And his casual reaction to her leaving angered the highly sensitive Yadira even more. That was when she started making Sean's life a living hell.

The first incident with Yadira occurred one evening while Brandi was visiting his house. On this day, Brandi and Sean had spent hours making passionate love to each other in his plush king-sized bed. Sean wanted Brandi to spend the night but that was a no-go; she had to work the next morning. Disappointed, he got dressed and walked her downstairs to the front door.

After watching Brandi pull off in her vehicle, an exhausted Sean turned off the lights downstairs. As he was headed back upstairs, he put his hand on the banister, and a key fell to the floor. Sean paused for a moment, trying to remember if he had put the key there. Then it hit him. That mystery key was indeed the spare that he'd given to Yadira while she was staying with him.

Yadira must have let herself in the house, hoping to find him at home alone. It was a pretty good chance she heard all of the sex noises coming from his bedroom. So she left the key on the banister and walked back out of the house.

Sean's paranoia set in. He checked all of the rooms in the house. When he discovered that the coast was clear, he felt a little better. But it didn't stop him from worrying.

Now, Sean felt himself getting upset all over again. To that day, he was still unable to believe that Yadira took her life, leaving him to live with the guilt of it all. And he never once mentioned Yadira to his wife. He preferred to act like the suicide never happened. It was so much easier to do that.

After Sean finished cleaning the family room, he ran upstairs to the kitchen and grabbed an ice-cold Corona from the refrigerator. It was a Friday night, Milan was out of town on business, and he didn't have to work that weekend. With a little free time on his hands, Sean didn't want to spend a restless night at home, watching Netflix movies; he wanted out of that house.

Sean picked up his cell phone to call Rasheed, his partner in crime. Rasheed Gordon was one of Sean's oldest and closest friends. They had known each other since they were babies and their now-deceased grandmothers were extremely close to each other. Even their mothers were best friends.

Both of the men were raised in the same Bedford-Stuyvesant neighborhood that they presently lived in. It was a place that they never strayed too far away from. And in that same neighborhood was where the two rambunctious boys would constantly get into some mischief. Sean laughed as he recalled the numerous butt whippings that he and Rasheed received from their grandmothers and other extended family members. Those whippings and the village that they grew up in were what shaped Sean and Rasheed into the men they were.

But unlike Rasheed, who continued down the path to become a criminal, Sean put the brakes on his roguish behavior. He chose a career as a NYC correction officer while his boy ended up on the other side of the cell. But their loyalty to each other was incomparable to most friendships. Their different lifestyles never affected their close bond with each other.

"What's up, my brother?" Rasheed said, as soon as he answered the phone.

"Yo, Big Rah!" Sean said with a hint of enthusiasm in his voice. "What are you getting into tonight, man?" he asked. "A nigga's bored to death, it's Friday night, and Milan is out of town for the weekend. What's up?"

"Man, listen, if you're ready to go, I got dough to blow! What time do you want me to pick you up?" Rasheed said excitedly.

Sean laughed. "I know you got the dough to blow! Why do you think I'm calling you to hang out? Drinks on you, man!" he said.

Rasheed laughed. "Fuck you, slime!" he replied, calling Sean by their nickname for each other. "Maybe you should be the one treating me tonight. Last time I heard you were making six figures and your wife works in the music industry, motherfucker! I smell money, nigga!"

Sean nodded his head in agreement. "Yeah, yeah, yeah, I'm not gonna lie, shit is pretty good on my end. Me and wifey are doing our thing."

"Damn! I can't believe that my boy, Sean Diggedy Dog, is really married!" Rasheed said. "Who woulda thunk it?"

Sean took a swig of his Corona. "Yeah, man. A brother's married. And as much as I tried to avoid this bullshit in my younger years, I'm not gonna front, I kind of dig it now. Milan is my soul mate, man. Word!"

Rasheed brushed off Sean's last statement. "Man, please! You said the same thing about Brandi, nigga!" he teased.

A confused look came over Sean's face. "I don't remember saying nothing about Brandi being my soul mate," he lied. "As a matter of fact, why you even had to bring her name up? Damn! Gonna have me thinking about her ass!"

Rasheed laughed. "Well, I clearly remember you telling me that that broad was your soul mate, nigga," he said. "Don't make me into a liar!"

Sean groaned. "I really don't remember saying that," he said in a low voice. He felt a pounding headache coming on.

"By the way, man, what's up with the broad anyway?" Rasheed asked.

"Man, how we even start talking about Brandi? I don't know where Brandi is nor do I give a fuck about what's up with her."

Rasheed laughed. "Ah, man! Don't take shit so serious. I'm just fucking with you."

Sean didn't know whether to be frustrated with Rasheed for reminding him of Brandi or aggravated with himself for thinking about her. He was definitely into Brandi back then. But after Yadira's suicide left him emotionally drained, Sean didn't have the willpower to be the man she needed him to be. He ended having to let her go and had been secretly regretting it ever since.

"Yo, Sean!" Rasheed screamed into the phone. "What's up with you, man? Are you daydreaming or something?"

Sean's mind was always drifting, which was another one of his problems. He was constantly thinking about how he could have done things differently with Yadira and Brandi. If only he would have known better back then . . .

Then again, there was no need for him to cry over spilled milk. After all, he was happily married to Milan.

"Like I told you, man, Brandi and I haven't spoken to each other in years," Sean said, brushing off the notion of ever seeing or speaking to the woman again. "And besides, I wasn't nothing but drama for that chick. She ain't trying to see me no more."

"You don't know what homegirl is thinking," Rasheed said, who was suddenly advocating for Brandi. "You let that suicide shit fuck you up, man! I don't understand why you never gave Brandi another chance after that."

"Yo, Rah," Sean began. "What's up with you, dude? Are you a spokesperson for Brandi now? You don't fucking like my wife or something, man?"

Rasheed chuckled. "Man, I'm not no spokesperson for anybody! And Milan is cool; I ain't got nothing against her. It's just that when you said that Milan was your soul mate, I remember you saying the same damn thing about Brandi! Just thought a nigga would remind you of what you said, that's all."

Sean sighed. "Okay, so if I did say that, maybe I thought that Brandi was my soul mate back then. But it ain't no need to bring her name up anymore, man. Brandi probably got herself a man or husband by now."

Rasheed wasn't trying to leave the topic alone. "I will bet you money that Brandi don't have a man! She's probably still hanging around and waiting for some knight in shining armor nigga to rescue her ass. Or maybe she's waiting on you, homie!"

"Nah, she ain't waiting on me, man! I have my wife. I'm good!"

"Yeah, a'ight. But if you were to run into Brandi right now, tell me you wouldn't try to fuck her?"

Sean was beginning to get impatient with Rasheed. "Please, man! I ain't thinking about no Brandi, Yadira, or any other fucking broad right now," he said, in a defensive tone. "I'm married now and that's it!"

"Okay, okay, calm down, young man!" Rasheed said.

Sean quickly moved from the Brandi topic on to something else. "Anyway, man, what's up for tonight, yo?" he asked. "Are we hanging out or what? Milan is about to board a plane to Atlanta and I'm a free agent for the next forty-eight hours. I wanna have me some fun."

"Word, man, I wanna hang out too. Shit, I'm in search of a new side chick. I had to drop the last one."

"Damn! She had a fat old ass! What happened with her?" Sean asked.

"The usual bullshit! The broad lied. She told me that she could handle being the side chick. Then after about six, seven months of us fucking around, this bitch started calling and texting my phone all times of night so I had to let that go! Told the broad that this shit ain't gonna work!"

Sean began cracking up. "Yo, take it from me, man, it was good to dead that situation before it got out of control! Them side pieces always wanna get mad at a nigga and spill the beans. That's why I'm faithful to my woman. So what time should I be ready?"

"Look, man, I'll be in front of your crib at twelve-thirty a.m. on the dot. Don't have me waiting outside all night for your bitch ass, neither! Be ready or else be ready to get left, slime ball!" Rasheed said.

Sean sucked his teeth. "Whatever, man! You gotta wait for me; I'm your boy!"

"I ain't gotta do shit but stay black and die, slime!"

They both laughed at the joke and disconnected the call.

After hanging up with Rasheed, the bored Sean looked at the clock on his living room wall. It was still early. Then his phone rang again. This time, it was his wife.

"Hey, babe," Milan said. "Just wanted to let you that I'm about to board this flight."

Sean began walking upstairs to his bedroom. "That's good, babe! You have a safe flight and call me after you get settled in tonight."

"Okay, my love," she replied. "Love you."

"Love you too."

Sean smiled and put the phone on the nightstand next to his bed. Now that he'd heard from his wife, he could relax before hanging out with Rasheed for the night. Within minutes, he was sound asleep.

Chapter 3

Almost an hour after her excursion to Halsey Street, Brandi finally arrived home from work. She walked into her large two-bedroom apartment, half expecting for her three-year-old grandson, Little Shamari, to greet her at the door with a hug. He always made her feel so much better. But he didn't live there anymore.

And she missed her son, too. Brandi's son and the father of her grandson, twenty-three-year-old Shamari, had recently moved into another two-bedroom apartment. After he moved out, Brandi had a hard time dealing with the empty nest syndrome. But she was proud of the way her son had stepped up his duties as a single father and a man, since the mother of his son, Amber Johnson, passed away during childbirth. Amber was only eighteen years old then and Shamari was still an inmate on Rikers Island at the time of her death.

Amber's untimely death shed new light on the wayward Shamari's life, forcing him to rethink some things. So after doing eighteen months in jail for armed robbery, he was released in September of 2010. That following year, in March of 2011, Shamari was called for a job with the Department of Sanitation. Because of Shamari's demanding schedule with the job, Brandi, along with Amber's mother, was more than happy to step up to the plate and help him out with the baby. Everything definitely worked out for the best.

Brandi walked into her bedroom. She quickly stripped down to her bra and panties, catching a quick glimpse of herself in the mirror.

"Not looking too bad for a forty-year-old grandmother," she said aloud, admiring her shapely frame from front to back.

Brandi wasn't only happy about her appearance. With all of the things that had occurred during her life, she was lucky to still be alive.

Brandi, along with her three older brothers, was raised in a single-parent home with a mother who never volunteered much information about their biological father. Nevertheless, Mama Wallace was a hardworking woman, who worked two jobs in order to support her brood. Because of this, Brandi, the youngest and the only girl, spent lots of time with no parental supervision. Between her mother's demanding work schedule and her fascination with the fast life, the teenage Brandi was well on her way to becoming a handful of trouble.

Like most children who lacked discipline and structure in the home, all four of the Wallace siblings took to the streets. As anyone would expect, serious trouble found the inquisitive Brandi and her brothers.

The boys formed alliances with some of the neighborhood's shadiest characters and embraced a lifestyle that exposed them to lots of street beef and lengthy jail sentences, as well. As for their little sister, her problems began when she turned twelve years old. Because she was so advanced for her age, Brandi ran with a pack of girls who were much older than her. They taught her how to roll and smoke weed-filled blunts. Then they showed her how to boost high-end designer clothing from stores like Bloomingdale's and Nordstrom.

Driven by her newfound popularity, Brandi spent the rest of her teenage years wreaking havoc on unsuspecting females, and guys, too, just for the heck of it. It was no secret that everyone considered her to be a tough cookie and she was, especially after having to look out for herself for so long.

Then one day, not too long before her sixteenth birthday, Brandi met a man who would rewrite the story of her life. His name was Maleek Mitchell.

Maleek was a local drug dealer, who had discovered early on that crack-cocaine was a lucrative way to make him some serious dollars. Brandi used to see Maleek around the hood from time to time and when she did, he always seemed to be driving some hot car and flashing money, too. The pubescent Brandi knew that she was not in Maleek's league; she was nothing but a kid to him. But she didn't care about that. She promised herself that if she ever got the opportunity, she was going to approach him. She was determined to convince Maleek that she could hold her own.

It was 1988 when the fifteen-year-old Brandi and Maleek finally got together and she was ready do anything for him. Even when she was pregnant with Shamari, it was nothing for Brandi to accompany Maleek in transporting kilos of crack along Interstate 95 South. They stood by each other, through good and bad times, with Brandi sometimes bringing that heat to some sucker for her man, if she had to.

But by 1994, the path of self-destruction, the abuse and criminal activities, finally ended for Brandi. Maleek was found dead in his Land Rover SUV on the side of Interstate 64 in Norfolk, Virginia.

After getting off the crazy emotional rollercoaster that she had been on with Maleek during her younger years, Brandi made a promise to herself that she would never lose her mind over a man again. That was, until she met Sean Daniels.

The ringing house phone startled Brandi. When she answered the call, it was Sheba, her best friend of almost thirty years, on the other end.

"Hey, Miss Thing," Sheba said excitedly. "Just getting home from work?"

Brandi held the phone to her ear while hanging up her work clothing in the closet. "Yes, girlfriend," she said with a smile. "I was just thinking about calling you, too. By the way, I have to tell you about what I did today, girl. I did something really freaking stupid."

Sheba laughed. "Oh, Lord, what in the hell did you do now, Brandi Lynn Wallace?" she said, calling her friend by her full birth name.

Brandi began pacing back and forth. "Well, I was driving home from work, minding my own business, right, when . . . when I got this strong urge to drive through Halsey Street."

"Okay," Sheba said. "What's so stupid about that?"

"Halsey Street is where Sean lives."

"So you drove through Sean's block? What's wrong with that?"

"I didn't exactly drive 'through' Sean's block, Sheba. I parked a few doors away from his house and waited around to see if he was going to step outside his front door."

Sheba groaned. "Oh, my God, Brandi! You were getting your stalk on? Girl, please, don't tell nobody else that shit! And why are you even entertaining the thought of seeing that man? Didn't old boy cut your ass off like a light switch?"

"Yes, he cut me off but let's be real, can you blame him, Sheba? After Yadi killed herself, he didn't know who to trust!"

Sheba sucked her teeth. "Do you hear yourself, girl? You are making excuses for that cowardly son of a bitch!

First of all, wasn't Sean the reason that the crazy, suicidal bitch put a gun to your head in the first place?" She stopped her ranting for a brief second to see if Brandi was going to reply. When she didn't get any response, Sheba continued.

"You know, Bran, you're my girl and everything but seriously, you need to stop taking the blame for the stupid shit that these motherfucking men do! You used to do the same damn thing with that sorry-ass Maleek!"

As usual, Sheba was right. Sean was the one who suggested they go their separate ways. And yes, Brandi could admit that she was guilty of making excuses for the men she loved. But there was no way that she was going to admit that Sean was partly responsible for what happened with Yadira. She just wasn't ready to do that.

"I hear what you're saying, Sheba, but I really don't think that Sean was being a jerk when he let me go. Actually, he did me a favor! I mean, let's face it. He and I were in the beginning of a brand new relationship. With all the drama that went down within those few months, I didn't know what kind of person Sean had become."

Sheba wasn't trying to hear any of that. "Okay, I'm confused," she said sarcastically. "What exactly did Yadira do to him, Brandi? The only thing that that pathetic woman did was fall in love with a man who obviously didn't feel the same way about her. And at the end of the day, Sean had control over that! Didn't he tell you that he was always attracted to her?" Before Brandi could answer Sheba, she asked her another question. "And who was she living with when she left her boyfriend? Mmm hmm! For all you know, Yadira could have been his real girlfriend and you were the side piece! At that time, you didn't know Sean well enough to actually know if he was telling the truth about that woman and their situation." Sheba sucked her teeth. "Anyway, girl, when you came into the picture, Sean tried to push homegirl to the side and Miss Psycho Bitch was having none of that!"

Brandi shook her head at Sheba's delivery. Ever since they were little girls, Sheba had always given it straight with no chaser, not caring about who she offended. But Brandi loved her outspoken friend to pieces.

"Do you really have to call that dead woman a bitch, Sheba? No kind of respect, I swear!"

"Ah, fuck that ho!" Sheba replied, in a dismissive tone. "Why should I respect that bitch when she tried to kill you, my best friend, my sister? How am I supposed to feel sorry for a woman who stuck a gun to her own head and killed herself over some lying-ass man? And how do I care about her when she didn't care nothing about her daughter, her family, or herself?"

There was nothing that Brandi could say to dispute what Sheba was saying. But that still didn't change the fact that she missed having a man like Sean in her life.

Sheba stopped ranting and moved on to something else. "Look, girlfriend, I didn't call to talk about that damn Sean or the dead nutcase. I just wanted to know if you were down to paint the town with me tonight. Let's get spiffy then let's go get drunk! We need to have us some fun!"

Brandi agreed. "That sounds like a really good idea, girl. I'm tired of coming straight home and looking at these walls. What time?" she asked.

Sheba let out a chuckle. "Be at my house around eleven o'clock."

"Oh, okay! I'll see you then."

"And, Brandi?"

"Yes?"

"Please don't make no excuses, okay, sweetie? It's been awhile since you broke up with that last guy and I think it's time for you to find somebody to beat the cobwebs off that coochie of yours!" Sheba said, referring to Brandi's involuntary celibacy. "I know that you gotta be good and horny by now!"

They both began laughing uncontrollably. "Sheba! I'm not no—" she began.

Sheba stopped her from saying anything else. "Yeah, yeah, yeah, I know, I know, you're not a ho, not anymore! You know I know how your ass gets down!" They both laughed again. "Anyway, be at my house at eleven o'clock, boo. I'll talk to you later."

"Okay, girl, see you then," Brandi said.

After hanging up from Sheba, Brandi felt a lot better. She realized that in the last few years, she had been taking herself a little too seriously. It was time that she stopped worrying about everything and anything that happened before 2012. The night out with Sheba was going to mark the beginning of Brandi's new life—and a new Brandi.

Chapter 4

It was the wee hours of Saturday morning; 12:05 a.m. to be exact. The R&B music coming from inside the Hive Lounge on Atlantic Avenue had the crowd of partygoers two-stepping to the beat. Men and women from all walks of life were at the popular Brooklyn haunt, sipping on alcohol and sharing a laugh or two with each other. The patrons were a jovial crowd of people, for this wasn't the type of lounge bar that catered to a younger, more rah-rah mob. The Hive Lounge was definitely for the grown and sexy.

People were lined up against the brick wall adjacent to the bar, chatting it up with each other over the sounds of DJ Chase. And the bar was filled with customers, waiting to get their hands on their drinks that were being prepared by sexy bartenders dressed in all-black body-hugging outfits. Also standing at the bar were various ballers and self-proclaimed shot callers, who were more than willing to spend top dollar on a bottle of tequila or some pricey champagne. Their ideas of having a good time were to pop bottles and surround themselves with attractive women.

The Hive Lounge crowd was definitely turned up.

When Sheba and Brandi walked in, all eyes were on them. The two very attractive friends shimmied through the crowd of people, making their way to the crowded bar. While Sheba ordered their drinks, Brandi looked around. She was scoping the place to see if she saw any familiar faces in the crowd of people. She recalled a time when places like the Hive Lounge were somewhere that she assumed the lonely and desperate lingered. Now she was part of the same scene.

Sheba interrupted Brandi's idle thoughts by handing her a fishbowl-shaped glass filled with a bluish concoction inside of it. Brandi frowned at the massive-sized drink then looked at Sheba.

"What in the hell is this?" Brandi asked, yelling over the loud music. "How in the hell am I supposed to drink all of this shit, Sheba?" she yelled.

Sheba laughed. "Ah, bottoms up, bitch!" she joked, waving the uptight Brandi off. "It's a fishbowl! After this, I promise, you won't need nothing else to drink! And don't worry about driving home. If we get too tipsy, we can always leave your truck on this end and catch a cab back to my house. Now drink up!"

Brandi took a sip of the drink and surprisingly enough, she liked the taste of it. "Okay, okay, this is really cute. I likey!"

Sheba smiled at her friend. "See, I told you, boo!"

They took their drinks and walked to the rear of the lounge bar. In the back of the Hive, there were couches, a dance floor, and the VIP area. Brandi and Sheba made sure they found themselves a place to sit on one of the white leather sofas before it became too crowded back there.

Once they were seated, Brandi bopped her head to the music while Sheba sang along to the songs and danced in her seat. Brandi was glad that she had agreed to hang out with her girl. When Brandi looked around she noticed a few of the male revelers. Much to her delight, most of them were certified eye candy. She was glad that she was looking good and feeling even better. She couldn't wait to see who was going to be the lucky catch of the night.

***

Meanwhile, back on Halsey Street, Rasheed sat in his Range Rover, waiting for Sean to come out of the house. In the passenger seat of the truck was another one of his good friends, a man named Kane Porter.

Almost fifteen minutes had passed since they pulled up to Sean's house and he still hadn't appeared in the doorway. The impatient Kane reached over to the driver's side and pressed down on the horn. Rasheed shook his head at the gesture.

"Yo, Rah, what's up with this dude Sean, man?" Kane asked, with a frown on his face. "Every time we hang out with this nigga, we're always the ones who end up waiting for him! What the hell is wrong with that motherfucker?"

Rasheed laughed. "Come on, man! You know how my boy is! He's very meticulous about his looks."

Kane shook his head. "Meticulous? Did you just say meticulous, man?" he asked Rasheed, who was laughing at his friend's reaction. "We both know got damn well that it don't take a man hours to get ready to go anywhere! What the fuck?"

Rasheed was still laughing when Sean finally stepped outside of his door. As he walked toward the Range Rover, his entire facial expression changed when he saw Kane sitting in the passenger seat. Sean was never really fond of Rasheed's "other" longtime friend.

"What's up, Rah? What's up, Kane?" Sean said, sliding in the back seat of the truck.

Kane turned around in the passenger seat to face Sean. "Hey, man," he began. "Why in the hell do we have to wait a hundred and one hours for you to bring your black ass out of the house? I mean, damn, what the hell were you doing in there? Playing with yourself, homie?"

"Nah, man, the real question is what is your Geritol-popping ass doing hanging out without us young thirty-somethings anyway? You shoulda stayed your 'black ass' home, motherfucker!"

Rasheed couldn't stop laughing at Sean's joke. Kane had a smug look on his face.

"Okay, okay, boy," Kane said, calling it a truce. "I see you got some snaps tonight! I'ma let you have that one, boy." He gave Sean a pound.

"Yeah, a'ight, homie," Sean said, with a look of self-satisfaction on his face.

Rasheed turned up his music while they cruised through the backstreets of their neighborhood. When they got to Atlantic Avenue, Sean asked where they were going.

"We're going to the Hive Lounge tonight," Rasheed said.

Sean frowned. "The Hive Lounge? Never heard of it."

Kane sucked his teeth at Sean. "Man, you don't know about the Hive? Sounds like you need to pull your head out of your wife's ass, man! Or maybe you just haven't really been nowhere since the shit that happened with the dead broad," Kane blurted out. Tactfulness was not one of his better characteristics.

Rasheed shot Kane a dirty look. "Whoa, man, watch your fucking mouth!" he scolded. "I think that you done had one too many Patrón shots. You're doing a little too much right now, my man!"

Sean waved Kane off. "Good looking out, Rah, but I ain't paying this dude no mind! Let me find out you're jealous of me, son."

Kane blew him off. "Jealous? Now you sound like a got damn fool!"

Sean smiled. "Yeah, okay, motherfucker! I don't believe that shit for one minute!"

"Get your boy, Rah! This dude is an idiot!" Kane replied, pointing at Sean.

"Both of y'all dudes need to shut the hell up!" Rasheed yelled at them. "I didn't sign up for this shit. I wanna go out and enjoy my night! So y'all dudes need to press that chill button and relax. Save all that energy for these hoes we're about to bag tonight!"

When Rasheed, Sean, and Kane walked through the doors of the Hive Lounge, females began flocking to them almost immediately. And why wouldn't they? They were three handsome, well-dressed men with a bad boy swag. This only made women want to get to know them better.

Kane, who was the bachelor of the trio, was what some would call a 'hood celebrity.' What helped fuel this reputation was his father, a man named Jasper Porter, better known as J.P. J.P. was an illegal numbers runner and a self-made millionaire. Of course, there was never much evidence to support that claim because the Porters lived a modest yet financially comfortable life. But the truth was J.P. never wanted to rub shoulders with the rich and elite, considering that he was nothing but a hustler. He'd much rather live among the working-class people, who consisted of his old friends and family, and that he did until the day he died.

But when J.P. passed away in 2010, Kane and his older sister, Tabitha, reaped the benefits of their father's estate. They rented out their home in Bedford-Stuyvesant, Tabitha and Mama Porter purchased homes in Long Island, and Kane bought himself a one-family home in Canarsie. The two siblings proceeded to invest their monies into other lucrative business ventures. Their beloved father J.P. would have definitely been proud of how wisely they managed the money.

Being the son of the well-known Jasper Porter definitely paid off for Kane. Unlike J.P., who was a humble, low-key man, the spoiled Kane was the complete opposite. And being extremely good-looking only added to his arrogance.

Even though Kane was what most would consider the model type, he was no one's pretty boy. Standing at six feet three inches with his well-toned frame, Kane's rugged outer appearance screamed all man. That tough guy persona, matched with his looks, had the women clamoring for his attention.

But aside from being a hot commodity with the ladies, there was one thing missing from Kane's life and that was someone to settle down with. He was secretly bothered by the fact that most of his closest friends were in committed relationships with the love of their lives. Kane had plenty of women groveling at his feet but none could really keep his interest. He yearned to be with someone who was independent and who had a mind of her own; he wanted a challenge. But unfortunately, that hadn't happened yet. And Kane was beginning to think that maybe it was he who was incapable of loving a woman.

Kane walked over to the bar and pulled out a knot of hundred dollar bills. He purchased two bottles of coconut-flavored Tequila 1800, his favorite liquor. One of the bartenders grabbed two buckets filled with ice and followed him the rear of the Hive Lounge where his boys were already seated. They were in the VIP area, sitting near the DJ booth and, as usual, they were surrounded by a small bevy of sexy women. They waited patiently, as the bartender set up their table with ice buckets, pineapple juice to mix with their tequila, and some plastic cups. After that was done, Kane cracked opened the first bottle and poured out some liquor. Everyone held up their cups and prepared to take a shot of straight tequila at the same time.

A few shots later, Sean was smiling like the Cheshire cat and hugging all over one of the female guests. Both Rasheed and Kane looked at their boy and shook their heads.

"Please don't tell me that you're twisted already, man," Kane asked, staring at Sean in disbelief.

"Nah, man, I'm not. I'm just nice," Sean replied, as he stood up to two-step to the music. "What I need to do is get out there on the dance floor with this cutie pie right here!" he said, grabbing the female's hand.

Rasheed nudged Kane and poured Sean another shot. Sean took the shot to the head.

"Ah! That's good!" Sean looked around at the throng of partygoers. "I'll be back, man. I'm going to the bathroom," he said, leaving the female behind.

Rasheed and Kane laughed at Sean, as they watched him stagger his way through the crowd toward the restroom. While he was gone, they continued to savor the effects of the liquor, loud music, and women.

As they partied in VIP, an attractive woman caught Kane's eagle eye. He nudged Rasheed on the arm. "Yo, homie, I think I see my future wife over there!"

Rasheed raised his cup. "Well, what you waiting for, man? Go find out what's up with her, man! And see if she have a friend for me, too!" he added, while enjoying a lap dance from one of their female guests.

Kane made his way over to the woman he had his eye on.

"Damn, I have to pee," the tipsy Sheba announced, putting her drink on the table in front of them. "Watch my drink, girl. I'll be right back."

Brandi nodded her head and watched as her friend walked toward the restroom. When she turned back around, an extremely attractive gentleman was sitting on the right side of her.

"How you doing, miss?" the man said, extending his hand.

Brandi shook his hand. "I'm fine and yourself?" she asked, surprised that she hadn't tried to run the man away.

The man smiled. His perfect white teeth gleamed in the dimly lit lounge bar. "I'm fine now," he replied, licking his lips. "I'm sorry to intrude but I couldn't help but notice how gorgeous you were from where I was sitting. I just had to come over here and tell you that."

Brandi didn't know where the guy came from but he definitely had her attention. "Aww! That's sweet! What your name?" she politely asked.

"Kane Porter."

"Oh, okay, Kane Porter! I'm Brandi Wallace."

Kane's eyes narrowed. "Brandi. Mmm. That name definitely fits you."

She smiled. "Thank you."

Suddenly, Kane stood up. "Look, babe, I would love to sit here and talk to you all night but I know that you came out to have a good time. If I give you one of my business cards, can you give me a call tomorrow? Maybe we can do brunch and get to know each other a little better with less noise and lot less company, of course."

Brandi nodded her head. "Sure, Kane. I don't have a problem with that."

Kane went into his pocket, pulled out his wallet, and handed her one of his business cards. He waved at her and walked away as quickly as he came over to her.

Just as Kane disappeared into the crowd, Sheba came back from the restroom.

"Brandi!" the excited Sheba said. "Girl, guess who I ran into near the bathroom?"

When Sheba stepped to the side, Sean was standing there. Brandi almost spit out her drink.

"I told him that we were just talking about him today," Sheba added.

Sean stood there, starting at Brandi and smiling from ear to ear. "What's up, Brandi? How you doing, babe?" he asked.

Brandi instantly hopped up from her seat to give Sean a big hug. "Hi, Sean! How are you? Long time, no see, man!" She couldn't believe that she was actually happy to see the man who had broken her heart. *It has to be the alcohol.*

Sean kissed her on the cheek. "How have you been, sweetheart? Funny I see you here," he said, yelling over the loud music.

"I know, right? Sheba convinced me to come out." When she looked in Sheba's direction, she was dirty dancing with a gentleman a few feet away from where they were standing. "What are you doing out tonight?"

Sean pointed to the VIP area. "Just hanging out with a few of my boys!"

Brandi nodded her head. "Oh, okay! That's cool. I'm just here, having some drinks with my girl and you know, enjoying the scenery."

Things began to get awkward between the two and for a few seconds, they were at a loss for words. Sean was the first to break the brief silence by pulling out his cell phone.

"If you don't mind, can we exchange phone numbers?" he asked. "I would really like to keep in touch with you."

Brandi was a little skeptical about that but couldn't resist the pleading look on Sean's face. That was the same face that used to always win her over.

"I don't see why we can't do that," she said, as they put their numbers into each other's phones.

After their transaction, Sean kissed Brandi on the cheek again. "It was really good seeing you, sweetheart. I'm gonna definitely give you a call."

Brandi sighed as Sean walked through the crowd. "Yes, please do that," she said to herself.

After leaving Brandi, Sean walked back to the VIP area. While he should have been happy to see her, he was having some mixed emotions. The love that he thought was nonexistent had definitely resurfaced once he saw Brandi in person.

Sean grabbed the bottle of tequila from the table and poured himself a full cup. He quickly guzzled it then plopped down on the couch and held his head in his hands. He knew that he couldn't let temptation get the best of him; he was a married man. But Brandi looked so damn good.

Meanwhile, Rasheed took a moment from the women to check on his friend. He patted Sean on the back. "What's up, man?" Rasheed asked. "You a'ight?"

"Yo, Rah, I just saw you-know-who, man," he said, slightly slurring from the effects of the liquor.

"Saw who?" Rasheed asked, with a hint of confusion in his voice.

"I just saw Brandi, man. And damn, she looked so good!"

Rasheed frowned. "What do you mean, you just saw Brandi? Where is she at?" he asked.

"She's out there in the crowd somewhere," Sean said, pointing to the packed dance floor.

Rasheed smiled. "Okay, so you saw Brandi, here at the Hive. What happened?"

"Well, I ran into her friend, Sheba, as I was coming out of the bathroom. She was the one who recognized me and walked me right over to Brandi."

"So how did you feel about seeing her?"

"I'm pissed, man!" Sean said, through clenched teeth. "Here I am, married to Milan and then I run into this bitch!"

"So when are y'all fucking?" asked the curious Rasheed.

Instead of being annoyed by Rasheed's off-color questioning, Sean rolled his eyes. "I didn't say anything about fucking her, man!" He took another swig of the tequila. "Now that I've seen her, I really don't think that I'm over that chick, man."

"I knew that you weren't over her, man! I knew it!" Rasheed said, pounding his fist into his hands.

At that moment, Kane came over and slid in the seat next to the tipsy Sean. "Just met me a new honey to add to my stable!"

Rasheed snickered. "I bet you did, player!"

Kane sucked his teeth. "Now why a dude gotta be a player, Rah?" he asked, in a slurred voice. "You never know, this broad just might be the one for me!"

Sean snapped out of his daze. "You mean to tell me that a player like you wants a real woman now?" he asked with a look of amazement on his face. "Damn! I'll have to make a toast to that shit!" he said, slightly raising his cup in the air.

Kane threw his head back and laughed loudly. "Man, fuck you, you fake motherfucker!"

Sean was too deep in his thoughts to reply to Kane's potshot. All he kept asking himself was one question: *is it possible to be in love with two women?*

Chapter 5

It was seven o'clock Saturday morning when Dollar pulled up in front of a bodega on Livonia and Georgia Avenues in East New York. Fresh off a road trip from Raleigh, North Carolina, Dollar was in serious need of some relaxation and a cigarette. In the passenger seat of his Infiniti truck was none other than his right-hand man, Peeto. Peeto was fast asleep and snoring like he was at home in his own bed.

After driving all the way back to New York, the worn-out Dollar attempted to wake his sleeping friend. "Yo, man, wake the hell up!" Dollar said, nudging the husky Peeto with his elbow. "You've been sleeping ever since we left the Maryland House, man! Why don't you go in the store and get a brother some smokes?"

The startled Peeto opened his eyes. He spent a few seconds trying to get a clear visual of his surroundings. "Come on, man, I'm sleeping! Go get it yourself," he said, wiping the drool from the side of his mouth and lying back in the seat.

Dollar gave Peeto another shove and reluctantly got out of his truck. As he headed toward the entrance of the bodega, the drowsy Peeto rolled down the window to try to make a request. Dollar ignored him and walked directly into the store.

Inside of the bodega, Middle Eastern music was blasting. Dollar put his hands over his ears and walked to the back of the store, grabbing an Arizona Sweet Tea out of the freezer. He walked up to the register to pay for the drink and get a pack of cigarettes.

"Hey, Money Man," said the young Pakistani co-owner from behind the counter.

"What up, Habib?" Dollar said, his voice smoother than honey. He put the cash on the counter and Habib immediately reached for a pack of Newport 100s to give to him. "What kind of music is that, Beeb? That shit louder than a motherfucker!"

Habib laughed. "This 'shit' is on the top ten music list in my country!" Dollar began cracking up. "Anyway, what you been up to, man? Haven't seen you around in a while," he asked.

Dollar sighed. He opened the pack and immediately lit up a cigarette on the spot. After the first puff, he felt a whole lot better. "Ain't shit, man, I've been down South with Peeto for a few weeks," he replied. "What's been good with you? How's the biz for you and your fam?"

Habib shrugged. "Shit real slow on this end," he replied. "One-time keep fucking with us, you know," he added, referring to the NYPD.

Habib took money from another customer for a purchase. Dollar didn't speak again until after the person walked out of the store. Habib's father, Adnan, and two older brothers were into all kinds of illegal ventures. One of them was smuggling guns, which had become a family business. Getting weapons and ammunition was not a problem for Habib and his family of crooks and they were well off because of it.

After the coast was clear, Habib reached behind the counter and pulled out a silencer. He put it in Dollar's hand.

Dollar inspected the silencer and smiled. "This is what I'm talking about, man! Nice!"

Habib smiled too. "I'm glad you're pleased, man. Do you wanna buy it?"

Dollar sucked his teeth. "Of course, I'm pleased, Habib. Everybody knows that you Akbars got the best ammo in the hood." He handed him the silencer back. "But I don't need nothing right now, man. I'm done with the gun shit."

Habib shrugged his shoulders and tucked it in a secret compartment behind the counter. "If you ever need something, you know that I got you, Dollar, man. You're the peoples."

Dollar gave Habib a pound. "No doubt, Beeb. Listen, I'm out, man. Tell Pop Dukes that I said good looking out but I'm a retired gangster."

Habib smiled and gave Dollar a head nod. "I feel you, man. That's a good look. You know how to reach me though."

"No doubt."

Dollar walked out of the store and back to his truck. When he got back into the driver's seat, Peeto was snoring again.

"Damn, you fat motherfucker!" Dollar yelled at his big-bellied friend. "You're still sleeping, man?"

Peeto lifted his head and eyes instantly popped opened again. He let out a loud yawn while giving Dollar an evil look. "Hell yeah, man! I'm tired as fuck!" he said.

Dollar chuckled and pulled off. He was worn out too and in desperate need of a hot shower. He couldn't wait to drop Peeto off and head back to his condo in Queens.

As Dollar rode through the potholed streets of East New York, he began to reminisce about the old days. He had robbed more people than he could count on the street corners of Schenck Avenue, Jerome Street, and Hegeman Avenue, to name a few.

Dollar thought about how many people were the victims of his wrath back then. He could practically see the images of their distressed faces and still hear their voices, as they begged for their lives. Some of these people were lucky; they were spared from his murderous rage. Then there was the competition. They were the ones who hated Dollar and his crew. Most of them didn't get away unscathed.

Dollar's guns had always been his most loyal allies, his comrades. He couldn't recall any gun that he ever owned—from .25-caliber Saturday Night Specials to a 9 mm Sigma—ever failing him.

Then one day, after some serious consideration, Dollar decided that it was time for him to hang it up. He thought about all of the felonies that he committed. He picked a certain lifestyle and he had to commit certain crimes in order to survive the rough streets.

Now that he was a forty-two-year-old man, Dollar deemed himself too old to participate in the criminal exploits of his younger years. But due to the exploits of his past, Dollar was a lonely man. He didn't know who or even how to trust anyone, which was why none of his relationships with women ever materialized. Even his parental skills were questionable. Because he was an orphan growing up and never had a real family, he was unsure of how to relate to his one and only child. Now his fifteen-year-old son was calling another man Daddy.

The only thing that Dollar had to show for all of the mental, physical, and emotional duress over the years was a safe filled with lump sums of money, a condominium in Forest Hills, Queens, and a successful trucking business. To some, those material things may have been enough, but to Dollar, he still felt unfulfilled. He would trade it all just to have someone special to share it with.

Dollar stopped at a red light. While he waited for the light to change, he began thinking about his deceased friends. He smiled to himself as he relived some of the good times that they all had together growing up; life was just one big party for them back in those days. But that was a long time ago and life was not about fun and games anymore.

And then there was that secret. It was a secret that had been eating him up for the past seventeen years.

In the late eighties and early nineties, the streets of East New York, Brooklyn, was popping. Even the 75th Precinct patrol officers were corrupt back then, leaving the residents of the community with no real protection. They lived in fear for their safety every day. During this violent era, one of Dollar's most loyal friends, twenty-one-year-old Gator, was gunned down and murdered in 1993. It was then that he, Maleek, and Peeto decided that they had to leave Brooklyn and move out of town; things were getting too hot in New York.

By the early part of 1994, Dollar and Peeto were more than ready to desert the concrete jungle. A move to the South sounded perfect for the trio of friends. After all, they felt there wasn't any reason for them to remain in New York City anyway; they had no real family there. On the other hand, Maleek had plenty of family. For one, he had two children. He had a seven-year-old daughter and a young son by the name of Shamari. But for some reason or another, Maleek still seemed very anxious to leave his children and family behind. And he did just that without one iota of guilt.

His children weren't the only ones who were left behind. Brandi, who was his girlfriend at the time and the mother of his son, didn't go along for the journey.

Back then, the twenty-year-old Brandi was a pretty girl from Bedford-Stuyvesant who was tough as nails. At least, Dollar thought she was. She was definitely a sight for sore eyes and the fact that she could roll with the best of them made her even more appealing to Dollar. But upon seeing how she was head over heels for Maleek, Dollar began yearning for that kind of love too.

Dollar saw how Maleek disrespected Brandi on a regular basis and he didn't like it one bit. But because Maleek was his friend, he quietly remained on the sidelines, watching how everything went down between the couple. During some their physical altercations, Dollar would come to Brandi's defense. His urge to protect Brandi made Dollar realize that he was slowly but surely falling in love with her. And if Brandi was with it back then, he wouldn't have had one problem with crossing Maleek just to be with her. But to his disappointment, Brandi only looked at him as a big brother.

The three friends decided that they would take off to the state of Virginia. Once they were there, they made a home for themselves in Virginia Beach. In the meantime, they took the Portsmouth, Norfolk, and Hampton drug trade by storm, eventually making a name for themselves.

It was late 1994, during the Norfolk State University homecoming, when Dollar finally was introduced to Smokey Wilson, a Virginia native who was also heavy hitter in the drug game. He had the Peninsula on lockdown; anything coming in and out of those parts had to be done with Smokey's consent or pay a heavy price. Dollar and Peeto formed a great rapport with Smokey, who was more about making money than beefing with the Northerners. But the jealous-hearted Maleek did not click with man. And Maleek's city-boy arrogance and exaggerated confidence did not sit well with a laidback country bumpkin like Smokey.

That was when Dollar's feelings about Maleek began taking a turn for the worse. Everything about Maleek started to annoy the serious-minded Dollar. Maleek's flashy personality and bad habits became a serious issue, as well; even the sound of his voice became bothersome.

As the months and days went on, it became harder for the ornery Dollar to hide his contempt for the person who at one time he considered a brother. He realized that Maleek's attitude wasn't new; the man had been feeling himself ever since the influx of money started flowing. And Dollar felt that it was only a matter of time before the younger Maleek turned his grandiose attitude against him.

One day, during the spring of 1995, Dollar and Maleek were cruising on Interstate 64 in Norfolk. Brandi called Maleek on his cellular car phone while Dollar remained silent and listening to the pathetic telephone conversation. He shook his head as he overheard Brandi's desperate pleas for Maleek to be a part of their son's life. But unfortunately, the self-absorbed Maleek wasn't having any of the guilt trips that she tried to lay on him.

"Maleek, I need for you to come home! Shamari has a slight touch of pneumonia and I don't know what to do!" Brandi yelled into the speaker phone. "Please, your son needs you! I don't know why you're acting like this!"

Maleek turned on the signal to pull over on the side of the highway. He looked at Dollar and made a pointing gesture at the phone.

"This sorry bitch is getting on my nerve," he whispered to Dollar. Then he got back to his phone call. "Yo, bitch, fuck you and that fucking baby!" he yelled at her. "If you were any kind of mother, that little motherfucker wouldn't be sick, now would he? And fuck is you calling me for? I'm out of town getting money and I ain't coming back to Brooklyn no time soon! So deal with it, bitch!"

"Why are you talking about our son like that, Maleek? He's your got damn son, too!"

"How do I know that?" Maleek asked, with a scowl on his face. "How the fuck do I know that that little bastard is my child? Knowing your trifling ass like I do, you probably was sleeping with one of my homies, you nasty bitch! You need to call his real father and tell him to go to the hospital with you!"

"You're a lowdown dirty piece of shit, Maleek! I hope you fucking burn in hell!" Brandi screamed back.

Suddenly, Maleek got real serious when she said that. "Me? Burn in hell? No, bitch, you burn in hell! Fuck you and that fucking baby! I'm outty!"

He disconnected the call and looked over at Dollar in the passenger seat. He was staring out of the passenger side window and stewing with anger.

Maleek laughed. "Yo, Dollar, did you hear how this disrespectful bitch was talking to me, man?" he asked. "She's gonna tell me that I gotta come back to New York because Shamari is in the fucking hospital! I ain't got time for no fatherly duties, man; there's a whole lotta money to be made down here! The fuck I look like leaving Virginia for some sick kid? She must be fucking crazy!"

Dollar couldn't take it anymore. He looked at Maleek in disbelief. "Man, what are you talking about?" he asked. "Shamari is your son, your offspring, homie! And don't you know that pneumonia is a very serious condition?"

Maleek waved him off. "Ah, come on, Dollar, man! And? What the hell am I supposed to do for that little nigga if I'm hundreds of miles away, huh?" Dollar had a disappointed look on his face. "Look, man, I'm down here for self! I ain't got the time to be worrying about nothing going on up in New York!"

As Maleek continued talking trash, he didn't notice Dollar turning around to see if anyone was behind them. When Maleek put his hands on the steering wheel to turn back into traffic, Dollar grabbed his right wrist. He was surprised the gesture and looked at Dollar like he was crazy.

"Yo, Dollar man, what the fuck are you doing?" Maleek asked, attempting to pull his hand away from Dollar's vice grip.

All of a sudden, Dollar pulled the concealed gun from his right side and held it to Maleek's head. "This is what's going on, you fuck boy!" the angry Dollar said, through clenched teeth.

Maleek never had a chance to reply. Dollar pulled the trigger on the nine millimeter and fired three shots into his dome, killing him instantly. After the shooting, Dollar sat there with the warm gun still in his hand. Some of Maleek's blood and brain matter were splattered on his face and all-black clothing. Dollar pulled a handkerchief from his back pocket and wiped the guck off him. Then he wiped down the door handle and whatever else he had touched inside of Maleek's Land Rover SUV.

Dollar got out of the vehicle and walked a few yards to an idling Infiniti Q45 that had pulled up behind Maleek's vehicle. Sitting inside of that car was none other than Smokey. When Dollar slid into the passenger seat of Smokey's car, he had a huge smile on his face. Smokey handed Dollar a thick envelope filled with money. Then he quickly pulled back onto the highway, leaving the dead Maleek on the side of the interstate.

"Hey, mane," Smokey said, in his thick Southern accent. "You ain't no motherfucking joke for a city boy! You pushed that dude got damn wig back, for real!"

Dollar chuckled and counted the money in the envelope. It was the $10,000 Smokey had offered him to kill Maleek.

Dollar put the money in his inside pocket. "Listen, man, it took everything in me to kill this dude! Maleek was getting out of control but he was my man! But like I mentioned to you before, I knew that it was only a matter of time before the motherfucker went turncoat on me!"

Smokey agreed. "You ain't never the lie, mane! You had your reasons for wanting that crab dead and I had my reasons for wanting him dead, too."

Dollar frowned. "Your reasons? I thought that you wanted the homie dead for the same reason I wanted him dead," he said, with a puzzled look on his face. "You said that you never liked Maleek."

Smokey laughed. "Well, let's put it like this, mane. I agree that ya boy Maleek was getting out of control and no, I didn't like the motherfucker, that much is true. But the real deal is that his baby mama, Brandi, came down here a few months ago and set that ass all the way up! She asked me if I could put a bullet in that ass for her."

Dollar shifted in his seat at the mere mention of Brandi's name. "What are you saying, Smoke? Are you saying that Brandi is the real person who orchestrated this hit?"

"Listen, mane, Brandi called me one day, out of the blue, and told me that she had just landed in Virginia. She asked if we could meet up with each other to talk about something very important. I met up with her, know what I'm saying, picked her up from the airport and all that. As soon as she got in the car, she began telling me about this cat Maleek and how he ain't shit as a man or a father. Then she asked me if I could take care of him for her. She said that she was sorry that she couldn't put up the money for it 'cause her funds were low. And instead of giving me money, she paid me another way, if you know what I mean, mane," Smokey said, with a smirk on his face. "She paid me with some of that good old pussy of hers!"

Dollar narrowed his eyes. "Oh, so you was fucking Maleek's baby mama, huh?"

Smokey took his eyes off the road and looked at Dollar for a few seconds. "Come on, man, ain't you been listening? She volunteered to give it to me! I didn't ask her for shit but it ain't like I ain't want to fuck the sexy bitch from the first time I laid eyes on her pretty ass. She got some tight-ass pussy, too. Mmm hmm! Just how I like it!"

Dollar patted the envelope of money. "If Brandi didn't have the money to pay you, where did you get the money to pay me?"

"Now that right there is some of my own got damn money," Smokey said, while switching lanes on the highway. "Me and my boys got this thang what we call the Fuck Boy Fund!" Smokey laughed. "I was supposed to have killed that dude Maleek a few months ago my got damn self but couldn't get close enough to him. Being that you was the closest somebody to that fuck boy, I decided to come to you with the job. You get the money and I get the bitch! It's a win-win for everybody, you know what I'm saying, mane?"

All of a sudden, Smokey's cell phone rang. "Hey, Brandi, baby," he said. He paused. "Yeah, I called you. I was calling you to tell you that deed is done. It's over. Okay?" Smokey smiled. "Okay, now, baby girl. I can't kick it with ya right now, li'l mama. I'ma call you back in a few so you can tell old Smoke when you bringing your fine ass back down here to see me."

Dollar was getting more and more heated with their conversation.

Smokey laughed again. "Hug my stepson for me. Bye-bye, baby."

Dollar couldn't believe that Smokey had used him to take his friend out, while he schemed on having Brandi for himself. But what Smokey didn't know was that Dollar had waited a long time to get Maleek out of the picture. He wanted Brandi more than he had wanted Maleek dead. And there was only one thing to ensure that Smokey never got with her again: he was going to have to die too.

A few miles down the highway, Smokey pulled over to the side of the road again. "Damn, I gotta take me a piss, mane! I'm pulling over yonder."

Dollar shrugged his shoulders. "Do what you gotta do, homie," he said. Smokey never saw the sinister look in his eyes.

Smokey pulled over on a grassy knoll, put the idling car in park, and got out. He walked a few feet away from the vehicle, found him a tree, and began to urinate.

Meanwhile, Dollar quietly got out on the passenger side of the vehicle. The unsuspecting Smokey was holding on to his exposed penis as the armed Dollar crept up behind him. He aimed the gun to his head and as soon as Smokey went to turn around, Dollar let off a live round, right between the man's eyes.

Smokey fell backward and slid down the embankment. Dollar quickly sprinted downhill toward the dying man and shot him one more time in the face. As he put away the gun, Dollar watched as blood seeped from the large hole where Smokey's left eye used to be. Then he walked back to Smokey's idling vehicle and pulled off, leaving his dead body on the side of the interstate.

Dollar turned onto Ashford Street and pulled up in front of the house that Peeto shared with his girlfriend and their two small children. He shook his head, wondering why his boy still had his family living in the same neighborhood that they used to terrorize.

"Yo, man, you got a nice crib and everything, man, but why don't you move your family out to Queens or Long Island or something? Get them out of the hood."

Peeto opened the passenger door to get out and retrieve his bags. "Man, it's not me," he said. "It's my girl; she's the one who don't wanna move! Most of her family lives around here and, you know, she needs help with the kids when I'm out of town."

Dollar nodded his head. "Oh, okay. I can understand that."

Peeto paused for a minute. "Man, I've been thinking about a lot of shit lately. I'm about to get out the game, man. I'm forty-two years old and I done did all the hustling and illegal money-making that I could do. Fuck it. I'm about to join me a church and get saved, man."

Dollar began cracking up. "Yeah, okay! I'll believe that shit when I actually see it!"

Peeto laughed too. "Now you know ya boy lying, man! I ain't going to nobody's church but I am about to retire from the game." After he got all of his bags out of the car, he gave Dollar a pound. "Good looking out on the ride home, my nigga. It was no way that I could have transported all this money on the bus or train, man. That ten thousand for coming to get me is cool, right?"

Dollar smiled. "Yo, Pee, that's good, man. And you're my brother. Anything for my brother, man."

A solemn look came over Peeto's face. "Damn, I wish that Gator and Maleek was here with us. I miss them dudes, yo. Word."

Dollar didn't respond to Peeto's comment. "Yeah," was all Dollar could say. "Anyway, Pee, I'll call you tomorrow. I'm going home to get me some sleep."

"All right, Gregory Wharton, I'll holla!"

Dollar threw an empty water bottle out of the opened passenger window. Peeto ducked the bottle and laughed. "What I tell you about calling out my government out in the street, Peter Robertson?" he said. They both laughed. Once Peeto was safe and sound inside of his house, Dollar pulled off.

It was funny hearing Maleek's name roll off Peeto's lips. The sound of it made the hairs on Dollar's back stand up; he was trying so hard to forget what he'd done. That murder was fueled by insane jealousy and wanting someone he knew his friend didn't deserve to have. It was crazy but after going through with the heartless task of executing Maleek, Dollar never saw Brandi again. Dollar promised himself that if he ever ran into her, he wasn't going to let her go. After all, he didn't kill her son's father for nothing.

Chapter 6

Across town in the diverse middle-class neighborhood of Canarsie, Kane was awakened by the sounds of a car alarm going off outside of his open bedroom window. Annoyed, he reluctantly got out of his bed to close it. The bright sunlight shining into his bedroom aggravated his hangover headache, forcing him to close the blinds, too.

Kane sucked his teeth and took a look at his unmade bed. Now that he was wide awake, he figured that there was no need for him to go back to sleep on an empty, growling stomach. What he needed for his hangover was a good breakfast and an aspirin for his pounding headache.

Kane slowly traipsed down the stairs and into his kitchen to look for some breakfast food to prepare. When he opened the door to refrigerator, he remembered that he hadn't done any grocery shopping in the past week. He thought about how nice it would have been to wake up to breakfast in bed, prepared by the woman he loved.

"Damn," Kane said to himself. "Now I'm gonna have to go out and get something to eat."

After taking a ten-minute shower and getting dressed for the day, the hung-over Kane reached for his car keys. He walked outside to his parked BMW. Once he was inside of his car, he called up Rasheed.

"Yeah," Rasheed answered, sounding as if he was still asleep.

"Wake up, home slice! Breakfast is on me!"

Rasheed yawned loudly in his ear. "Yo, man, it's nine o'clock in the damn morning, you bastard! I'm trying to sleep this drunk off!" he said.

Kane overheard Rasheed's pregnant girlfriend, Asia, in the background. She asked her man who was on the phone.

"It's nobody but this dude Kane, babe. I'm gonna go downstairs to talk to him," Rasheed said to her. Kane listened as Rasheed walked down the stairs in his house. "Okay, now why you want me go to breakfast with you?"

"Since you won't come with me to the diner, I'm coming over there for breakfast," Kane said, as he backed out of his driveway.

"Why don't you call one of those broads of yours to go to breakfast with you, Big Pimpin'?" Rasheed asked.

Kane laughed. "Yeah, a'ight, man. You got that one. Anyway, I'm coming over there. I got something to tell you or, rather, ask you."

Rasheed reached into his refrigerator and took a few chugs of juice, belching in Kane's ear. "It's a Saturday morning, you're up early, and you're a little too fucking hyped right now, man. What is it that you had to ask me?"

Kane groaned. "Come on, son! I gotta talk to you in person about that! And have me some breakfast ready."

Rasheed groaned. "Are you crazy, slime?" he yelled into the phone. "It's too early in the morning for company!"

"I'll be there in twenty minutes," Kane said, before hanging up on Rasheed.

Not too long after Kane hung up the phone, Rasheed's downstairs bell rang.

"Who is that?" asked Asia, who was now wide awake and getting dressed for the day.

"It's Kane, babe," Rasheed said, turning over in the bed. "Go let him in while I get myself together."

"Okay. I'll make breakfast for y'all before I go out and do some shopping today."

Rasheed smiled. "Thank you, sweetness. Give me a kiss."

Asia gave Rasheed a kiss then went downstairs to open the door for Kane. When Kane walked in, he gave Asia a peck on the cheek.

"Hello, Mommy," he said, greeting her with a smile. "You look beautiful."

Asia blushed and rubbed her protruding belly. "Aw, thank you, Kane! I just made eight months yesterday. Baby is gonna be here real soon. Messiah is going to have a little sister."

Kane's face lit up. "Wow! Okay, okay. Can't wait for the baby shower. I'm gonna have to get my goddaughter something special."

Asia chuckled. "No doubt!" She walked toward the kitchen. "Why don't you go have a seat in the living room and wait for Rah? I'm going to cook you guys a nice breakfast and then I'm gonna head out to the mall with my sister and mother. I have to get an outfit to wear to the shower."

"Tell that sexy-ass India that I said hello," Kane said, with a wink, while he walked to the living room.

Asia waved him off. "I ain't telling my twin nothing," she replied, from the kitchen. "Why don't you just call her yourself?"

Kane laughed to himself. He was thinking about the last time he saw India. Her ass was tooted up in the back seat of his BMW and he was hitting it doggie style. While he was more than willing to have the raunchy India as a booty call partner, he was not interested in committing to her. Of course, the woman had a serious problem with that.

"Yeah, I think I'll do that," Kane said, while rubbing on his manhood.

Shortly after Kane walked in the house, Rasheed came downstairs. He slowly walked into the living room and plopped down on the plush sofa across from Kane. He yawned and stretched then rubbed his eyes. The uninterested look on his face made Kane shake his head.

"Okay, so what's up, slime?" Rasheed said. "This shit had better be good because it's not cool for you to be waking me up out of my sleep. I got to go take care of some business this afternoon and you're interrupting a brother's fucking beauty rest, man. Real talk!"

Kane shrugged. "I had to talk to you, man. I need your honest opinion on something."

Rasheed frowned. "What happened?" he asked, with a look of concern on his face.

Kane leaned back on the couch. "Ok, so I'm ready to hang up this player shit, son. I really think that I'm done with all of these women chasing me. I want to be in a relationship and I wanted to ask how you go about doing that, man."

Rasheed scratched his scalp and looked at Kane in amazement. "Are you serious, man?" he asked. "You? You're really ready to settle down with somebody? Are you for real?"

"Yeah, I'm for real! Why the fuck is that so hard to believe?"

"Because you . . . you always been the type of dude who liked to keep 'the bitches at bay.' Those are your words, not mine. You were never with a female trying to get all close to you and trying to be all up in your business. Now you're sitting here telling me that you want somebody to make an honest man out of you?"

"That's exactly what I'm saying, man!"

Rasheed laughed. “I don’t know what to tell you. I don’t know what type of woman you like. Honestly, I don’t think you know! And if you don’t know what you want, how can you settle down with someone?”

The smell of scrambled eggs and turkey bacon permeated Kane’s nostrils, as he continued to talk with Rasheed about his love life.

Kane shrugged. “I’m gonna start working on that. I mean, look at you. You’re going on kid number two, Sean is married, and y’all cats are younger than me! I have to get on the ball, man!”

Rasheed frowned. “Speaking of Sean, I have to ask you a question. What’s up with you and my boy?” he asked.

“Ain’t nothing up with me and Sean!” Kane replied, waving Rasheed off. “Why you ask that?”

Rasheed gave Kane a suspicious look. “I don’t know, man. It just seems like you have a problem with Sean. Every time we’re all around each other, I noticed that you always try to find some way to get at him. Seems like there’s a little competition thing going on with you and him.”

“Man, listen! I ain’t in competition with nobody! Why should I feel threatened by another dude?” Rasheed gave Kane the side eye. “Plus, I don’t have time to be stressing what the next man is doing. I’m too busy trying to meet wifey. As a matter of fact, that fine-ass feline I met last night at the Hive?” Kane said, changing the subject. “I’m trying to get up with that before the weekend is over, homie.”

“I hear that. But, seriously, if you’re looking for a relationship, man, you can start by staying out of the panties. Let the vagina breathe for once and get to know the woman instead of trying to smash that ass before even knowing her last name.”

"See, that's where all bets are off, man! 'Cause if she's giving up the pussy, I'm taking them panties off!"

"And that's the problem right there! You're just too thirsty for pussy, man. Give yourself a chance to know a chick before you try to lay some dick on her." Rasheed leaned back to see if Asia was within earshot of their discussion. "Damn, baby, that food smells real good!' he called out to her from the living room. He couldn't chance his pregnant girlfriend overhearing any of their conversation. Asia thanked him from the kitchen.

"Well, I like to know what I'm getting myself into before I get serious with a woman! I'm not wifing no broad with some whack pussy and no dick sucking skills! Sex plays a major part in a relationship, don't you think?"

Rasheed sighed and ignored Kane's last question. "Anyway, what's up with this sweet thing you met? What's her name?"

"Brandi. Brandi Wallace," Kane said with a big smile on his face. "Yep, she gave me the entire government, too, man. That's some grown woman shit right there!"

Rasheed stood up. "Wait a minute. Did you just say Brandi? Brandi Wallace?" Kane nodded his head. "Ah, shit! No good!" he exclaimed, holding his hand over his mouth.

"Ah, shit, what?" Kane asked.

"That chick you met last night is Sean's ex-chick! Brandi was the one who was in Sean's house the night that female killed herself!"

Kane, who was unmoved by that news, shrugged his shoulders. "And? What the fuck is that supposed to mean to me, man? Sean is a married fucking man now!"

"It doesn't matter if Sean is married or not! You cannot fuck with that chick Brandi, man! I'm telling you. She's problems!"

"She's problems? What the hell are you talking about, Rah?" Kane asked, catching a slight attitude with his best friend. "Sounds like you have more loyalty to your boy Sean than you do to me, man!"

Rasheed tried to explain his point. "Man, this shit ain't about me or my loyalty to anybody, okay? It's about a woman Sean had some serious feelings for! You have to understand something; Sean confides in me and I know the real deal when it comes to him. So with that being said, you have to leave that one alone, man. There are some chicks who are just off-limits and Brandi is one of them chicks."

Kane sighed. "Yo, Rah, I understand that you're trying to look out for your boy and everything, right, but um, anytime a man let a woman go, unless she was his baby mama or his wife, the bitch is fair game, you feel me? If Sean really wanted to be with the broad, he would have made it his business to marry her, not Milan! And it ain't my fault that Brandi done met herself a real dude!"

Rasheed threw his hands up in the air. "See, man? That's what I'm talking about! You're one hardheaded, stubborn motherfucker! You just got to keep fucking with fire until you get burnt, right?"

Kane rubbed his hands together. "You've known me most of my life, son, and you know that I loves me challenge!"

Rasheed laughed too. "Well, you're about to have one hell of a challenge, slime! And I know that this shit ain't just about Brandi, neither. This is about how much you don't like my dude Sean."

"Why do you keep saying that, man? Sean is cool with me," Kane lied, with a smirk on his face.

Rasheed was visibly irritated with Kane's smug attitude. "Come on, man. Keep it official! You're not a real big fan of Sean's and he only tolerates you. The only common denominator that y'all have is me! And being that Sean's my boy, you're about to put me in the middle of some real bullshit, man! Damn!"

Before Kane could reply, Asia walked into the living room and interrupted their chat. "Breakfast is ready, y'all," she said, putting her coat on. "I made y'all some pancakes, eggs, and turkey bacon. It's all on the island in the kitchen." She walked over and gave Rasheed a kiss on the lips. "I'm out of here, babe. I'll be back later. See you, Kane. And call my sister, man!"

"I'm gonna give her a shout out!" Kane said, telling another lie.

Once the front door slammed, Rasheed and Kane made their way to the kitchen for breakfast. They took their positions on the counter stools and began to chow down on the food.

Rasheed stuffed some bacon into his mouth. "Let me tell you a few things about this chick Brandi, man. She's from around the way. She had a son by this cat named Maleek. He was a get money dude from East New York, Killer Miller Avenue, to be exact. And her brothers? I know you know her brothers."

Rasheed told Kane the names of Brandi's older brothers and he frowned. He knew exactly who they were but he couldn't recall ever knowing Maleek or even Brandi.

"Damn! Those wild-ass dudes are her brothers? I know that two of them are locked up on some serious charges and the younger brother is somewhere out here running around like he's still one of the young'uns!" Kane frowned. "What's up with that baby daddy of hers? Is he still in the picture?" he asked.

"Hell no!" Rasheed replied, while putting syrup on his pancakes. "Rumor had it that dude was murdered in Virginia by some country cats. After that happened, Brandi disappeared for a little while. Shit, when people didn't see her around the way for a while, they thought that she was dead too. Come to find out, she stayed away from the hood and got her shit together. She got a college degree. By the time she started showing her face again, she had that degree and a new attitude, too. The last time I saw her was three years ago when she was still with Sean. She looked damn good, too. No one would have ever guessed that she used to be a wretched ass, wild-ass street chick back in the day!"

Kane shrugged. "Okay and you're telling me all this to say what?" he asked, shoving some pancake into his mouth. "It's not like this info is gonna stop me from making a move on the broad."

Rasheed looked at Kane and sighed. "Forget it, man! Do what you do. But when the shit hits the fan? Don't call me, man! You don't give a hell about it so why should I, right?"

"Listen, man," Kane nonchalantly replied. "Sean moved on from this broad. From what you telling me, they ain't been together in a few years and they weren't together for that long a time anyway! And I just don't see Sean giving that much of a fuck about Brandi, especially since he has a wife, nah mean? Bottom line is that in one minute that pussy of hers is about to be Kane Porter's pussy! That's guaranteed!"

Rasheed continued to eat his breakfast. "Like I said, when the shit hits the fan, don't call me, motherfucker, 'cause I'm gonna act like we ain't never had this conversation."

It was 12:30 in the afternoon when Kane finally pulled off from Rasheed's house. He checked his phone to see if he had received any phone calls. Three different women, including Asia's twin sister, India, had called him and left voice and text messages on his phone. But Kane wasn't concerned with any of those females. His mind was on Brandi and she was the one who hadn't even called him yet.

As Kane made his way back to his house, he kept thinking about what he was going to say if Brandi called him. Telling various untruths and playing with women's feelings were why committed relationships were always a problem for Kane. He was accustomed to dealing with younger women, who were more than honored to be in the company of an older man with money. Brandi was definitely on his level and, judging from what Rasheed told him about the woman, it didn't seem as if he could spit his usual game in her ear.

Just as Kane was about to pull into his driveway, his cell phone rang. He smiled when he saw an unknown number pop up on his caller ID. He prayed that it was a call from Brandi.

"Good afternoon. Is this Kane?" the female politely asked.

"This is me," Kane replied, with a wide smile on his face. "Who wants to know?"

The woman on the other end of the phone giggled. "Hey, Kane, it's me, Brandi. How you doing, babe?"

The Brandi on the phone sounded nothing like the around the way, former hood rat Rasheed had described earlier.

"I'm a'ight now," he said. "I've been hoping that you called me. What are you getting into today, Miss Lady?" he asked.

"As of now, I don't have any plans. I was just going to relax today. I'm still kind of tired from last night. Those drinks, though . . ." she said, drifting off.

Kane quickly agreed. "I understand how you feel! I have a hangover myself."

"You must have had a hell of a night too."

"I sure did." Kane walked into his house, took off his jacket, and lay across the couch. He wanted to know everything there was to know about Brandi. "So tell me about yourself, girl," he said, still feeling elated that she called.

Brandi began telling him about her life, leaving out most of the details that Rasheed told him. Kane raised an eyebrow when she told him that her son's father died of cancer in 1995.

"Yeah?" Kane said, playing along with Brandi's lie. "My father died of prostate cancer two years ago. What kind of cancer did your son's father have?"

Brandi hesitated when Kane asked that question. "I can't really remember what," she replied. "We had broken up and weren't on the best terms when he died so I can't really say."

Kane sat up. "Oh, okay. I understand," he replied, with a smirk on his face. "It's like that sometimes. So where did you say that you were from again?"

"Well, I'm originally from Bed-Stuy. I didn't come outside much though. I was one of those girls who just went to school every day and came straight home, you know."

"I see." *That's not what I heard.* "Do you have any brothers or sisters?"

"I have three brothers and they all live out of state."

Kane frowned at the lie but just like the others, he didn't say a word about it. "And your son? How old is he?" Brandi told him her child's age and volunteered to tell him about her grandson, too. "Oh, so you're a grandmother! You look so young," he added.

"Thanks, babe. I try to keep myself looking and feeling good. I'm not getting any younger."

As they continued with their conversation, Kane discovered that Brandi was very evasive when it came to answering certain questions. He couldn't blame her for not wanting to reveal things to a man she had just met. But there was something about her that made Kane feel as if she was hiding so much more about herself.

When Brandi began inquiring about Kane's life, he gave her just as much information as she had given him. After getting the obvious out of the way, Kane decided to go in for the kill.

"So when am I going to see you, Brandi?" Kane asked.

Surprisingly, Brandi gave him some positive feedback. "I was going to ask you the same thing."

"What about tonight? Do you wanna hang out with a brother tonight?"

She readily agreed to Kane's request. "Sure! Why not?" she happily replied.

They both decided on the time that they were going to meet for their first date. After hanging up the phone, the exhausted Kane began dozing off on his living room sofa. He didn't want to be too tired when he met up with Brandi. He definitely had some serious plans for her.

Chapter 7

It was a Saturday afternoon and Sean was still exhausted. He popped his head up from the pillow and took a glance at the alarm clock on the nightstand beside his bed. He rubbed his eyes, not believing that it was one o'clock p.m. He had slept the entire morning away.

Sean dragged himself out of his bed and prepared to take a shower. He could smell the stench of liquor coming out of his pores.

Before the bathroom got all steamed up, Sean caught a glimpse at his unshaven face in the mirror when a thought came to him, making him stop in his tracks. Brandi's face appeared in his head and he felt the traumatic events from three years ago were starting to resurface again. Sean ran his fingers across the three-inch-long gash on the left side of his head. He stood there and closed his eyes, thinking back to how that gash got there in the first place.

When Sean snapped out of his daydream, he held his hands together and started praying. "God, please, remove these crazy thoughts from my head," he said. "Please!"

Suddenly, Sean felt extra dirty. He climbed into the shower and began scrubbing his skin like crazy. And not too long after drying off his skin, Sean heard his phone ring.

"Hello?" he said, answering the phone without looking at the caller ID.

"What's up, Sean? I'm standing outside of your door. Aren't you going to invite me inside?"

The voice sounded very familiar and it didn't take long for him to catch the voice. It was Brandi. *What the hell is she doing here?*

"Hello?" she said, snapping him out of the daze that he was in.

"Um, I guess so," Sean replied, unsure of what to do.

"Then what are you waiting for? Open the door," she demanded.

Sean wrapped a robe around his naked frame and quickly ran downstairs. "What the fuck?" Sean whispered to himself, as he opened the front door.

Brandi walked into his house, looking good as ever. She had a smug expression on her face, looking as if she was up to no good. Sean knew that he was losing his mind by allowing this woman to step foot into his house.

"Hey, Sean!" Brandi said cheerfully, wrapping her arms around his neck. "How are you, babe?"

Sean didn't know what to say. Brandi had always been a dignified woman, a classy dame. She would have never popped up at his house, even when they were dealing with each other. He had to get to the bottom of what made Brandi appear on his doorstep.

Brandi looked around the house. "I love what you did with your place, Sean," she said, talking as if they had just spoken to each other the day before. "Hmmph. It looks really cozy in here," she added, while rolling her eyes at the ten-by-thirteen pictures of him and Milan on their wedding day. "So you *are* married now," she said, with an attitude. "Your wife is cute."

Sean ignored her comment. "Look, Brandi, I was really happy to see you last night. I'm glad that we agreed to exchange numbers and all that but," he said, "what made you come by my house?"

Brandi sighed. "When I just called you," she began, in an aggressive tone, "you could have easily told me to leave but you didn't do that. So I assumed that it was okay for me to stay put."

Sean rubbed his head. He prayed that this situation wasn't going to be a replay of what happened with Yadira. The nervous Sean looked out of the glass door to see if anyone saw Brandi walk inside.

"What if my wife were here?"

Brandi laughed at that statement. "That's funny; when you were giving me your cell phone number last night you never once mentioned that you were fucking married!" She threw her hands up in frustration. "You know what, Sean? I'll just leave," she said. "Sorry for the intrusion."

Sean grabbed her arm. "Yo, Brandi, look, babe, you don't have to leave. I apologize. It's just that you surprised the hell out of me with this visit."

Brandi nodded her head. "I gotta apologize to you too, Sean. I guess that I was a little too anxious to see you and, honestly, I think our wires got crossed. I mistakenly assumed that you were unattached being that you gave me the number. You must think that I'm crazy."

Sean chuckled. "Um, yeah, just a little."

Brandi smiled.

"And you're right. I should have been honest and told you that I was married. But I was so happy to see you."

Brandi crossed her arms. "So, um, where is your wife now?" she asked, looking around the place.

"Lucky for us, she's out of town on business. She won't be back in New York until Monday morning."

"Hmmph. Monday morning, huh?"

Sean nodded his head.

"So let me ask you another question. Why her and not me?"

Sean sighed. "Brandi, I . . ." He paused. "I don't know, man. I can't even begin to answer that question."

Brandi put her finger to her temple, as if she was thinking about something. "I know what it was," she said. "It was Yadira who fucked everything up for us!" She shook her head. "Look, Sean, I didn't come here to cause any problems. It's just that you've been on my mind for the last couple of months and ever since I saw you last night, a simple phone call wasn't enough for me. I just had to see you in person."

Sean came closer to Brandi and made her look him in the eye. "After all this time, you're still upset with me, aren't you?" he asked, with a look of sincerity on his face.

Brandi threw her arms up in defeat. "Truthfully, I don't know what I am with you." She began walking toward the door then rolled her eyes in frustration. "Okay, enough of this. I have to keep it real. I fucking missed you, okay? I've been missing you all of these years. I can't get you off my mind! And I was fucking pissed when you let me go! I was hurt because none of what happened with Yadira was my fault! It wasn't fair the way you treated me in the end! That wasn't cool at all!"

Brandi began to cry, making Sean feel bad for her. He grabbed her hand. "Come into the living room. Let's talk," he said.

Brandi followed him into the living room and sat on the couch. Sean remained standing and began nervously walking back and forth.

"I still feel guilty about everything that happened between us," he said, as Brandi wiped her tears. "And I know what happened with Yadira wasn't your fault, babe. It's just that I didn't know who to trust after the smoke cleared." Sean gave her an earnest look. "I didn't mean to make you think that we were going to work on a relationship. But I had to be straight up and honest about my true feelings at that time. I was fucked up in the head."

Brandi waved him off. "The reason that I came over here is because I wanted to tell you that I forgive you. I wanted us to let bygones be bygones." She stood up to leave. "Well, it was nice seeing you again, Sean. I'm going to leave now and I truly apologize for the intrusion."

Sean blocked her from leaving. "I still want us to keep in touch with each other, Brandi, if that's all right with you," he said.

She managed to smile. "That's cool. We can do that. Anyway, let me get out of here. I wouldn't want your wife to come home early from her trip and catch me up in her house," she said, gently brushing up against Sean as she walked by.

Sean chuckled. "Oh, so now you care about my wife?"

A mischievous smile appeared on Brandi's face.

"I'm sure that your man wouldn't be too happy about you being here with me!"

Brandi put her hands on her hips. "My man, huh? Now that's funny! I don't have that problem, honey!"

Sean laughed and gave her a tight hug. "I missed you so much, girl," he said. "I missed everything about you, even your smart-ass mouth."

Brandi wrapped her arms around Sean's trim waist and hugged him back. "I missed you too."

Then it happened.

Sean and Brandi looked into each other's eyes and a few seconds later, they were sharing a passionate kiss. While they kissed, Sean began massaging Brandi's round derriere. He pulled her closer to him and he could feel her grinding on his growing manhood, getting him more excited by the minute. Brandi opened his terry cloth robe and let it drop to the floor. Sean unzipped Brandi's leather jacket and practically ripped her button-down shirt off. Then he unbuttoned her tight skinny jeans and yanked them off her. The half-naked Brandi stood there, in her satin Frederick's of Hollywood panty and bra set with a seductive look on her face.

"I want you so bad," she whispered. "But how can we do this right now? Your wife—"

Sean hushed her. "I told you that she's out of town until Monday," the stark-naked Sean replied through clenched teeth.

He picked Brandi up and carried her upstairs to the bedroom that he and Milan shared. Once they were inside of the bedroom, Sean dropped Brandi on his king-sized bed. He took off her panties and immediately buried his bearded face inside of her hot pussy. He licked and sucked on her clitoris, while he finger-fucked her with his thick middle finger. Brandi moaned, as Sean stuck his tongue inside of her box and tickled her ass. She wrapped her mocha-colored thighs around Sean's neck, getting him excited as her juices splashing all over his face.

"Oh, baby, I missed this," Brandi whispered. "You always knew how to fuck me so good!"

Sean didn't reply to her. Instead, he continued to suck on Brandi's wet pussy, all while fingering her into oblivion. His manhood was even harder now. He wanted to fuck Brandi badly but of course, he was going make sure that she was satisfied first. Sean had to make the every minute of their session count so that Brandi would want to come back for more.

"Put the dick in, please, put it in," Brandi whispered between moans. "I want to feel every inch of you in the pussy!"

Sean stood up and pushed Brandi onto the bed. She opened her legs ready to receive him. Not bothering to put on a condom, Sean entered Brandi raw, unprepared for how good her pussy was going to feel as it wrapped around his rod.

Sean closed his eyes, as he slowly began to grind inside of her. As their bodies moved in rhythmical motion, it was apparent that their feelings for each other hadn't changed in the last three years.

Brandi felt the urge to give Sean some of her infamous head. She pushed him off her and made him lay down on his back. She took his soaking wet rod and began sucking her juices off it. She deep-throated his nine inches like a pro, practically sending the mesmerized Sean into convulsions. She spit the white foamy saliva onto the shaft of his penis and slurped it back into her mouth. Then she wrapped her expert tongue around the head of his dick, sticking her tongue in and out the hole, causing him to almost jump out of his skin.

Sean grabbed Brandi's hair and yanked it. She smiled, enjoying making his toes curl and his body jerk; this meant that she was doing her job. Brandi had her own agenda for pleasing him, as well. She didn't want to lose Sean again and she wanted to give his wife some staunch competition. Thinking about Mrs. Daniels roaming Sean's body only made her suck his dick even harder, so hard that he almost shot a load of his semen right into her mouth.

But before he did that, Sean stopped Brandi. He didn't want to cum yet. Instead, he pulled Brandi on top of him. He made her sit down on his dick. Once she was on top of him, she began bouncing and grinding on it like there was no tomorrow. Every inch and diameter of her hot box was filled with Sean's dick and she loved it. This went on for the next hour and when it finally ended, both Sean and Brandi were lying across his bed, spent from breathtaking orgasms.

Brandi exhaled. "Whew! Damn! I guess some things really don't change, do they?" she asked.

Sean chuckled. “Nah, not at all,” he replied. He turned over to face her. “What are we doing, Brandi? Here I am, making love to you in the bed that I share with my wife! This shit ain’t right, man!”

She gazed into Sean’s eyes. “I don’t know what’s going on. This wasn’t supposed to happen.”

Sean lay on his back and looked up at the ceiling of his bedroom. “I don’t want you to get hurt.”

Brandi wiped the sweat from her forehead. “I’m not the one who’s going to be hurt. This shit is cut and dried.” There was a brief pause between them. “Now that you mention it, tell me the truth, Sean, did I just play myself or what?”

“Play yourself? No, not at all!” Sean exclaimed. “You know how I feel about you.”

“Feel about me? I knew how you felt about me but I don’t know now. And if you always felt this strongly about me, please tell me why did you marry someone else, Sean?”

Sean covered his eyes with his forearm. “Are we back on that? Brandi, we both had moved on! And what was I supposed to do? Be by myself forever? Put an APB out on your ass?”

The naked Brandi hopped up from the bed. “You were supposed to have looked for me! Damn! You know where I live! You know where I work! You were so caught up with your own got damn feelings of . . . of guilt and resentment that you didn’t even bother to consider my feelings in all of this. You let Yadira control you when she was alive and she’s still doing it from the grave! She got exactly what she wanted and that was us not being together!”

“Don’t get mad at me, babe,” Sean said, as he walked up to her and rubbed her face.

“I thought that I wouldn’t ever feel a way about you again. But lately, I don’t know, I just keep thinking about what could have been.”

Sean kissed Brandi on the forehead. "Forget all of that. You're back now."

"What do you mean, I'm back? Are you suggesting that we have some torrid extramarital affair with each other?"

"I'm not suggesting anything! All I know is that I want to keep you in my life."

"I'm all for being in your life, Sean," Brandi replied. "But having an ongoing affair with you . . . I just don't want us to lose our friendship again," she said, pointing her finger at him.

"We won't lose this friendship ever again," he said, making a vow to himself to keep Brandi in his life, no matter what. Sean kissed Brandi on the lips. With that kiss, they consummated their rekindled affair, by making love to each other one more time.

Chapter 8

It was a little after four o'clock in the afternoon when Brandi walked out of Sean's house. She was feeling sexually satisfied and liberated, too. He had made love to her for two of the three hours that she spent with him. It was so gratifying. And, of course, Sean gave an excellent performance. But her pleasure didn't only come from the great sex that they had with each other. It came from knowing the control she still had over Sean. All Brandi cared about was when she appeared on his doorstep, Sean was more than willing to allow her right back into his life. Just like that. And all it took was a few of her tears and the guilt trip that she laid on him and, once again, she was all in. Brandi smiled. She knew what powers she had over men and she used that to best of her ability. After all, wasn't she the one who had convinced a man to kill the father of her child?

As soon as Brandi got into her truck, she turned her cell back on. The ringing phone had been such a distraction while she and Sean were handling their business. As soon as she pressed the on button, it was ringing again and that caller was none other than Kane. She'd completely forgotten that they were supposed to be meeting up with each other that evening. Brandi took a deep breath and answered the call.

"Hello?" she answered, slightly exhausted from her sexual romp with Sean.

"Hey, Brandi, what's up, ma?" said Kane. "I was just wondering if we were still on for tonight."

Truthfully, Brandi was really not in the mood to go out with Kane. But she recalled a few months before when no man was checking for her. "Yeah, we're still on for tonight. What time should I be expecting you?" she asked.

"I'll pick you up around seven. Is that cool?" Kane replied, with a hint of anticipation in his voice.

She moved the phone away from her mouth and quietly yawned. "Seven is perfect," Brandi reluctantly agreed.

"Okay, sweetheart. See you then."

After disconnecting the call, Brandi sighed. She had no idea what she was getting herself into. Over time, she had prided herself on finally becoming an upstanding woman with slightly decent morals. The wretched behavior and actions of her youth were replaced with maturity and stability. But within the last few years, she became somewhat disillusioned. It seemed as if the undeserving, bitchy types of women were having all the fun. Now it was her time and she was going to do whatever she wanted to do.

It was seven p.m. on the dot when Kane rang Brandi's phone again. "What's up, babe?" he happily greeted her. "I'm downstairs in front of your building."

"Go 'head, Mr. Porter!" exclaimed Brandi. "I like me a man who's on time," she said, with a smile.

Kane grinned. "I try to be a man of my word, babe," he replied. "Not to mention, I have to make a good first impression on you, don't I?"

"Well, you're doing just that by coming to pick me up on time."

"That's what's up. Anyway, hurry your pretty self downstairs. I can't wait to see you," Kane said, with his baritone voice, oozing with sexiness.

"I will be down in a few."

Brandi ran into the bedroom to put on her pumps. She primped her stylish short hairdo in the mirror, sprayed on some more of her favorite Marc Jacobs perfume. After applying her favorite Sephora brand lipstick, she blew herself a kiss.

"Two men in one day ain't half bad for an old biatch like me," Brandi said aloud. "I hope these motherfuckers are ready for the new me!"

She grabbed her snakeskin clutch purse and her waist-length leather jacket and headed for the door. When Brandi arrived downstairs, she looked around for Kane's car. She heard a horn beep and began smiling as she walked toward the black BMW 5 Series. Kane hopped out of the driver's side and walked around the car to open the passenger door for her.

"Why, thank you, sweetie," she said, flashing her signature smile. "Aren't you a gentleman."

"That's no question, love," Kane replied. "This is what I do."

Brandi was definitely impressed with Kane's chivalrous ways. He slid back into the driver's seat and they pulled off.

"So where are we headed to?" she asked.

"It's this great seafood restaurant on the water in Parsippany, New Jersey. I know that it's a little chilly outside but as long as we have each other to hold on to, I don't think the cold weather would affect us one bit!"

Brandi laughed. "Not at all, hon, not at all!" she agreed, looking at Kane like he was filet mignon.

She hadn't expected to find him so physically attractive. And after they talked, Kane's physical attributes weren't all that Brandi liked about him. On their way to New Jersey, she learned a lot about the man. He told her about how his father, Jasper Porter, an old-time numbers runner from Bedford-Stuyvesant, invested his money wisely and took very good care of his family. He talked about his two college-age children in Virginia and how proud he was of them and their accomplishments.

Brandi loved that Kane was so honest with her. But never once did she mention anything about her convict brothers or her shady affiliates. She wasn't ready to reveal that part of herself to him or any other man for that matter. The past remained the past for a reason.

"So you're forty-one years old?" she asked, after Kane told her his age. "You look great!"

Kane blushed. "Thanks, sweetie! I work out about three times a week and I make sure I eat the right foods, know what I'm saying? I'm not getting any younger and I need for all of my equipment to work, if you know what I mean!"

Brandi couldn't contain her laughter. "You are so right, Kane! I mean, let's face it, guys in their forties begin to, well, you know, kinda lose their vitality, if you know what I mean. And if the dick, excuse my French, ain't working properly? Shoot, he is pretty much finished!"

Kane nodded his head in agreement. "Hell yeah! Shit, I need to use my rod for more than just taking a piss out of it."

Brandi laughed. "You ain't never lie!"

Kane briefly took his eyes off the road. "You are stunning, babe," he replied, with a serious look on his face. "A certified fox."

Brandi got caught up in the moment. "Thank you, Kane," she said, giving him a wink. "You're quite the looker yourself." She looked out the passenger window. "You know, I'm getting some really good vibes from you, Mr. Porter."

Kane took his right hand off the steering wheel and rested it on Brandi's upper thigh. "And I'm going to make sure that it stays like that."

Brandi smiled at him but didn't reply. After having so many crazy experiences with men and love all of her life, that wall was slowly creeping back up. She wanted to believe everything Kane said; it sounded real good. But Kane was a man and, unfortunately, Brandi had learned early on that the male species could not be trusted.

It was almost two in the morning when Kane pulled up in front of Brandi's building to drop her off after their wonderful night out. The Moët Rosé that they were drinking had kicked in and she was feeling good and tipsy. The chivalrous Kane volunteered to walk her upstairs to her apartment.

After parking his car, Kane scooped Brandi into his arms. She giggled loudly, as he followed the cement trail leading to her building. When they got inside, Kane put her down and helped her open the door with the key. Brandi walked in ahead of him, totally unaware of Kane lustfully licking his lips and watching her from behind.

Brandi pressed the elevator button and turned around to face Kane. He was standing there with a naughty smile on his face, as he found her to be irresistible.

"Give me a kiss," Kane whispered in her ear.

Brandi gave in. Her tongue tasted so good that Kane couldn't help but wonder what her pussy tasted like.

"Mmmm," Brandi moaned softly. "Damn, you can kiss, too!" she exclaimed, as she wrapped her arms around his neck and kissed him again.

When they came up for air, Kane smiled at her. He was amazed at Brandi's openness, after she had been reserved for most of the night. He figured that the one shot of tequila and a few glasses of Moët did it for her. The alcohol exposed Brandi's raunchy side and Kane loved it.

"I can eat it, too," he whispered in her ear. "Can I taste you, pretty?" he asked.

Brandi fluttered her eyelashes. "Of course, you can," she whispered back to him. "We're grown, right?" she asked, placing a soft kiss on his lips.

Kane liked that response. "What about showing each other just how grown we are?"

When the elevator doors opened, Kane slowly backed Brandi up against the wall. They began kissing and feeling each other up after she pressed her floor. As they ground in the elevator, things got even more heated. The sexually aggressive Brandi made the first move. She began unbuckling Kane's jeans on the spot and he did the same to her. A few seconds later, the elevator stopped on Brandi's floor and the doors opened up. They walked out and continued to undress each other.

Without saying one word, they stripped down to their underwear, right in the middle of the hallway. There were apartments on either side of the hallway but luckily, no one was able to see what was going on between the two. And Brandi and Kane didn't seem to care about someone catching them in the act. They were all over each other.

With his jeans wrapped around his ankles, Kane got on his knees and moved Brandi's lace panties to the side. He just had to taste her sweet nectar. Brandi tried to suppress her moans of pleasure by covering her mouth with her hand. When Kane's pussy-eating expertise became too much for her to handle, she stopped him. Kane came up for air with her vagina juices dripping off his chin.

"Let's take this inside," she whispered to him. They tiptoed their half-naked butts down the hallway to her apartment door. Once Brandi unlocked it, Kane immediately went back to performing oral sex on her and she was able to moan as loud as she wanted to.

"Oh, please, please, Kane," she said, in a breathy voice. "You're gonna make me cum, baby! Oh, yes, oh yes!"

"That's right, baby, I want you to cum," Kane mumbled, stroking her insides with his middle finger and sucking on her clitoris at the same time. "Cum in my mouth, baby!"

And come Brandi did. It felt so good to release her juices into Kane's eager mouth. Right after she came, he quickly put on a condom and entered her. Brandi's eyes opened wide, as if he was much bigger than she had expected him to be.

Suddenly, their interlude took an odd turn. Kane began to slow things down a bit. While he was in mid-stroke, he stopped and began kissing Brandi on the mouth. He placed soft kisses on her neck and caressed her; being a tender lover wasn't something that Kane was used to doing. Even he was surprised at his own actions.

"You're a beautiful woman, sweetheart," he whispered to Brandi. "And you taste so good, you feel good; you make me want you all to myself."

As Kane was expressing his innermost feelings, Brandi was focused on one thing: the sex. She wrapped her arms around his neck and sucked on his bottom lip. "If you want this pussy all to yourself, you have to show and prove, honey," she replied.

Kane commenced to showing and proving to Brandi how much of a champion he was in the bedroom. She was in her glory, as he threw her legs over his shoulders and dug deep in her insides. Sometime later, the lusty duo lay in a crumpled heap on the couch, spent from the breath-taking orgasms that they had just both experienced.

When Brandi began to doze off in Kane's arms, things began to feel real awkward for him. He was accustomed to having sex with his female paramours and leaving right away; he wasn't into cuddling. But he felt comfortable with Brandi. He didn't want to leave but Kane wasn't sure if she wanted him to stay.

Kane gave the sleeping Brandi a little prod to wake her up. "Hey, babe?" he whispered. She opened her eyes. "Um, did you want me to stay the night with you?" he asked.

Brandi's eyes were wide opened and she sat up. "I'm not sure if that's a good idea, Kane."

Slightly embarrassed, Kane put his clothes on. Once he was fully dressed, he walked into the bathroom. A nude Brandi crept up behind him and wrapped her arms around his waist.

"Thank you so much for tonight, Kane," she said. "I really appreciate everything that you did for me tonight."

Kane softened up and smiled. "It was my pleasure, sweetheart," he said, turning around to face her. "I enjoyed myself too. I really did."

Brandi rubbed her nose on his chin. "I know that we just got busy like two porn stars but the only reason that I said it wasn't a good idea for you to spend the night is because . . . Well, that's not important. I just hope this isn't the last time that we're going to be seeing each other, though."

"Nah, babe," Kane replied, putting his arm around her. "It isn't the last time. I want to see you again."

Brandi kissed him on the lips. "That's what I wanted to hear."

After sharing yet another intimate kiss with Brandi, Kane said his good-byes and made his way to his car. On the drive home, he couldn't get the events of the night out of his head. Kane was amazed at how things went down so quickly; he hadn't expected to make a homerun with Brandi on their first date. But he wasn't going to judge Brandi because of it. He was just as guilty of being sexually attracted to her as she obviously was to him. And that was good to know.

"Damn, Sean," Kane said aloud. "You're gonna feel real fucked up when you find out that your bitch chose me!"

Chapter 9

Ever since Dollar came back from North Carolina that previous Friday morning, he hadn't wanted to do much of anything but sleep. By the time he finally got himself together, it was early Sunday.

Pissed about missing the entire weekend, Dollar decided to get out of the house and head to Brooklyn. With no real destination in mind, Dollar called up Peeto and few of their buddies from the old neighborhood. They all decided to go to Peeto's house, where they would sit in the basement, have a few beers, and catch some Sunday football on the seventy-inch LED television.

Little did Dollar know that his plans were about to change.

It was a little after two in the afternoon when Dollar got off the Belt Parkway/Pennsylvania Avenue in Brooklyn. As he made his way down the avenue, he got caught at a red light a few blocks away from the parkway. While waiting for the light to turn green, an attractive female in an Audi truck pulled up alongside Dollar's truck. Normally, Dollar didn't pay women much attention. But for some reason, this particular female caught his eye and it didn't take him long to figure out why. Just as luck would have it, she just happened to be the woman of his dreams.

Dollar quickly rolled down his driver's side window and began beeping his horn like crazy. "Ay yo, Brandi!" he yelled out of the window at the top of his lungs. "Brandi!"

When Dollar got her attention, Brandi leaned forward to get a closer look at him. She smiled when she recognized who he was. Brandi quickly rolled down her passenger side window. "Oh, my God!" she yelled. "Dollar? Is that you?"

Dollar felt elated. The woman that he had fallen in love with at first sight was right there before his eyes. He couldn't believe it. "Yeah, it's me, girl! Pull your vee over so I can get a good look at you!"

Dollar and Brandi pulled over the right side of the street and parked. As soon as Brandi got out of her truck, she ran up to Dollar and gave him a big hug. He hugged her back, lifting her off her feet.

"Oh, my God, Dollar!" she said, with her arms still wrapped around his neck. "How are you?"

Dollar released her from his tight embrace and stood back. Brandi was looking even more beautiful than what he remembered. The last time he saw her, she was a young woman, about twenty-one years old to be exact, and Shamari was a preschooler. Dollar gave her a nod of approval.

"Damn, Bee!" he exclaimed. "You look good as hell! Just when I thought that you couldn't get any prettier, I'm looking at this dime piece standing before me," Dollar said, with a look of admiration.

Brandi laughed and waved him off. "Oh, stop!" she replied. "Shoot, look at you! Last time I saw you, you had nothing but some peach fuzz on your face. Now you got a full beard and"—she stopped talking for a second to squeeze his right bicep—"and you got some big muscles, too! Wow!"

Suddenly, Dollar's face turned serious. "So what's up, Brandi? What's really been up with you? And how's your son?"

"Well, I'm doing very well for myself," Brandi said proudly. "I went to college, got myself a bachelor's degree, then I went back for my master's and got that, too. I've been a director for the Administration of Children's Services for the last twelve years. And my baby, Shamari? He works for the Sanitation Department now, has his own apartment, and a four-year-old son."

Dollar seemed impressed. "Really? That's what's up! By the way, did he ever tell you that I saw him on Rikers Island a few years back?"

Brandi rolled her eyes at Dollar. "Yes, he did! And what the hell were you doing in there anyway?" she asked, playfully punching him on the arm. "You're too much of a veteran to be going back and forth to jail, man!"

Dollar held his head down. "Yeah, you're right, Bee. But at that time, I got caught up in some hustling bullshit. I don't do that shit no more though."

"So what do you do now, man? How do you support yourself?"

Dollar sucked his teeth. "Come on now, girl! Now you of all people know that I always keep my money-making moves top secret! But on the real, I'm the owner of a successful trucking business. They don't call me Dollar for nothing."

"Same old Dollar," she said, giving him another hug. "You look great, though. And you didn't age one bit."

Dollar thanked Brandi for the compliment. "Where are you on your way to?"

Brandi sighed. "I was just about to head to the mall to return a few items and run some other errands."

"Why don't you follow me to the Lindenwood Diner? We can catch up over some brunch."

The Lindenwood Diner, a popular East New York eatery, was filled with Sunday morning churchgoers. Older women with their oversized hats and suited men holding

Bibles chatted it up in the front of the diner as they waited to be seated. Just as Dollar and Brandi walked through the front door, the small entourage of holy rollers entered the restaurant before them. They were escorted to their respective tables and not too long after, a smiling waitress guided the old friends to a booth in the back. Brandi slid into the seat and took off her wool coat.

Dollar found it impossible to take his eyes off her. Brandi put down her menu when she noticed him staring at her. "Yes, Dollar?" she asked, with a hint of sassiness in her voice.

He smiled. "I don't mean to stare at you but it's just that been such a long time since I've seen you."

"Yes, it has. So where are you living these days? Do you still live in that little-ass apartment on Ashford Street?"

Dollar frowned at her. "Hell no! I gave that apartment up years ago! I actually have a condo in Kew Gardens, Queens. Been living there for about five years now."

"So you live in Kew Gardens now? Wow! It's top dollar for property out there. You seem to be doing pretty good for yourself. What did you say that you did for a living again?"

Dollar waved her off. "Come on now, Bee! I told you that I'm about that trucking life! I'm not into anything illegal . . . anymore. I flipped all of that drug money I made and found myself a legit hustle. I was able to buy me that condo in New York and I have a winter crib in Miami, too. Not to mention, I made some good investments. Trust me, ya boy doing real good!"

Brandi rolled her eyes at him. "Okay, Dollar. Don't make me have to take my investigation to the streets. You know that it's not a problem for me to find out whatever I need to know about you."

The waitress walked over and they both put in their order. In the meantime, Dollar was thinking about what he was going to say to Brandi. He had so much to ask her but he had no idea where to start.

"So what's up with your love life, Bee? I know you got a man."

Brandi took a sip of water. "As a matter of fact, I don't. I'm just dating right now. What about you? Do you have someone special in your life?" she asked.

Dollar shook his head. "I have a few female friends but nothing serious."

Brandi smirked. "Dollar, you have always been this mysterious guy. I never really saw you with too many women back in the days and even though I knew you, I really didn't know you. What's up with your family? I never heard you talk about your family."

Dollar leaned back against the cushioned booth seat. "That's because I don't have no family, Bee. I was raised in foster homes all of my life and when I turned eighteen, the streets, Maleek, Gator, and Peeto became my family. I have a teenage son but him and I don't have much of a relationship with each other."

"That's so unfortunate, Dollar," Brandi said. "He's your only child, right?"

"Well, his mother and I never really got along and truthfully, I didn't really make much of an effort to be in his life. I can't blame his mother for that, though. I just couldn't stand that chick and it's a shame that my son didn't have a relationship with his father because of it." Dollar paused. "Isn't it funny but I used to always get on Maleek about that same shit."

"Maleek," Brandi said, repeating her son's father's name. "I hadn't really thought about him in years. Maybe I finally came to grips with his death."

Dollar frowned. "Speaking of Maleek, I heard some disturbing shit about his death," he said. He looked closely at Brandi's reaction to what he said. She didn't flinch.

Brandi shifted in her seat. "What about his death?"

"I heard that his murder was a hit. At least that was what the streets were saying back then. And the streets were also saying that you and that dude, Smokey, the cat from Virginia, were the ones who orchestrated the hit."

Brandi looked at Dollar with a straight face. He was amazed at how composed she was when he knew, just like him, that she was guilty as hell.

"Hell no!" she said. "Why would I put a hit out on the father of my child?"

"I didn't say that I believed the rumor, Bee. I just said that was what the streets were saying."

Brandi took a big gulp of water. "I was, you know, many things back then, Dollar. But honestly, I wasn't the type of chick to have the father of my child murdered! To do something like that is fucking nuts!" she said, looking away from his intense stare.

Dollar respected Brandi's tenacity but he was laughing on the inside. If only she knew that he overheard her talking to Smokey on the day that Maleek was murdered, she would probably run out of that diner, screaming at the top of her lungs. But the fact that she orchestrated a hit against her baby father had never been an issue for Dollar. He was more upset that she had sexual relations with Smokey.

Brandi screwed up her face. "Besides, I heard that the dude Smokey was the one who killed Maleek. Whatever happened with that Smokey situation anyway?" she said, continuing with her lie. "I was told that his body was found not too far from where Maleek was killed. That's a little strange, don't you think?"

"I don't know too much about the Smokey shit," Dollar replied, also lying through his teeth. "But hey, that was how the game went back in those days. That drug money was nothing but blood money and a lot of people lost their lives because of it."

"You're so right, you're so right." She paused for a moment. "So what's up with Peeto's fat ass? You know that he was the one who was responsible for my baby being locked up, right? He had Shamari out in the streets selling drugs or at least attempting to."

Dollar put his hand up. "Now, come on, Bee! Your baby wanted to do all that shit on his own! I admit, Peeto could have gone about the situation a little bit differently but you know how these kids are. They're fucking hard-headed! They never learn from our mistakes!"

"Shamari never knew about any of my mistakes, Dollar; at least, he didn't until you told him all my damn business!" Brandi said, rolling her eyes at him.

Dollar chuckled. "Oh, so it's my fault that you didn't keep it official with your own kid?"

"No, it isn't, but damn! You gave him a little too much information, don't you think?"

Dollar thought back to the Rikers Island stint.

The year was 2009 and he had to serve some time for a low-level drug charge that he caught that past summer. Naturally, Dollar was not happy about being locked up on Rikers. But he was even more pissed about being surrounded by the young, disrespectful inmates who were half his age.

The early afternoon sun was shining in Dollar's face, as he stood in the pen. He and the rest of the Bing inmates from his housing area were locked in the gated pens outside in the yard. They couldn't walk around but it beat being locked down for twenty-three hours a day. The one-hour recreation was just what the doctor ordered and Dollar took advantage of it.

As Dollar walked back and forth in the gated cage like some trapped animal, a young man in a neighboring pen caught his eye. There was something about the young man that looked vaguely familiar to him. He just couldn't put his finger on it.

"Yo, nigga, it's about time we got outside of that fucking rat hole. Shit!" he said. When the young man didn't respond, he said something else. "The weather out here is kind of nice," Dollar said loudly, trying to strike up some general conversation. "I was tired of being in that fucking sweat box! What about you, young blood?"

The younger man seemed surprised that someone was actually talking to him. "I didn't hear you, man. What did you say?"

"I said the weather out here is kind of nice," Dollar repeated. "I was tired of being in that fucking sweat box. What about you?"

"I'm just tired of being locked up, period, man!" he replied.

Dollar gave the younger man a visual inspection from where he was standing. "Yo, what's your government name, man?" he asked him, while staring at his familiar face. "Seems like I know you from somewhere, young blood."

Young blood seemed a little hesitant to give Dollar any information.

"The last name is Wallace," he replied, still reluctant to give Dollar his full name.

"Wallace. Wallace." Dollar paused for second. "Where does your family hail from, Wallace?"

"My family is from Bed-Stuy," he nervously replied.

"Oh, word? Bed-Stuy, huh?" Wallace nodded his head. "What's your pop's name? I think I know your pops."

Wallace really looked worried when Dollar asked that. "Ummm . . ."

Dollar understood Wallace's reluctance to tell him his personal business. "Listen, young blood, you don't have to be afraid to talk to me, man. I don't associate with none of these bitch-ass dudes in here! I'm about one of the realest dudes you're ever gonna meet on this rock. I been through it all and I done seen mad motherfuckers come and go. And I'm gonna keep it a hundred, maybe I'm just might be the person you needed to talk to."

Wallace took a deep breath. "Well, my pop's name was Maleek. He was killed when I was five years old. And my mother's name is Brandi. My mom's side of the family are the ones from the Stuy. My father's family is from East New York."

Dollar put his hand over his mouth. He was stunned by the news that Wallace had provided to him. "That's where I know you from!" Dollar exclaimed, covering his mouth and pointing his finger at Wallace. "You're looking exactly like your father, too. God bless the dead!" Now that everything came together, Dollar couldn't take his eyes off Wallace. "Damn, you look just like that nigga Maleek! Your name is Shamari, right?"

Wallace was taken aback. "Oh shit, yeah, how you know?"

Dollar chuckled. "Wow! Little Shamari!" He began reminiscing. "I was there when your mother and father first met. Brandi was about fifteen years old and she was going to Boys and Girls, the high school back then." Dollar shook his head. "Boy, your mama was off the chain! And she had one of the biggest crushes on your father, man. Shit, she was about to cut some broad over your daddy the first damn day she met him!"

Dollar laughed, as he continued with the memories. "Yeah, Shamari, we were some fly-ass young cats, man. And your pops? Shit, Maleek was my homie! That cat right there had a way with the ladies. He had swag for days!" Shamari smiled at that. "Him and your mother made a good couple but the way he did her . . ." Dollar drifted off. "Let's put it like this, I didn't agree with a lot of the shit that Maleek did when it came to your mother. But I kept my thoughts and opinions to myself."

Shamari seemed as if he knew what Dollar was talking about so he continued. "Now, Brandi was no angel. Like I said, you mother was off the hook! She used to get money out in the streets better than some of the dudes I knew. I'm not gonna lie, I think Maleek was kind of jealous of that. It was like he couldn't hang with his own girl when it came to hustling. She was smarter and prettier than him so naturally hustling dudes would gravitate toward her. Imagine your baby mother blowing you out the water when it comes to getting that money? How Brandi was getting down that was unheard of back in them days. If anything, your main chick is supposed to be the underdog, the bottom bitch. But Brandi was nobody's bottom bitch; she was on top. And she was nice with that hammer, too! She kept a biscuit on her at all times and would use it if she had to! Yeah, your mother Brandi was the truth."

"Sounds like she was," was all that the shocked Shamari could muster up to say.

Dollar was so caught up with the past that he had forgotten he was talking to Shamari. "How Maleek died was so fucked up, man. May his soul rest in peace!"

Shamari's eyes lit up. "How did my father die?"

Dollar sighed. "Well, me, Peeto, and your pops made the decision to move to Virginia. I thought that he would have taken you and Brandi with him. But he said that he was leaving everything in New York behind, which meant he was leaving your mother and you, too. When we got down there, the money was flowing and so was the bitches. Maleek was down there acting like he ain't never had pussy before! Shit, it was so bad that he refused to come back to New York, period. He didn't even want to come back to see you!"

Shamari frowned at that statement but that didn't stop Dollar. He just kept right on talking.

"Meanwhile, I was peeping Maleek's whole steeze. I was the one in his ear, telling him that not going to see his son wasn't right and honestly, Shamari, that dude wasn't trying to hear nothing that me or nobody else said."

"How did my father die, man? Do you know who killed him?" Shamari said, getting impatient with Dollar's beating around the bush.

"It was some country bumpkin named Smokey who killed Maleek. The streets tried to say that Brandi had your pops killed but I don't believe that shit for one minute! Then the streets tried to say that she was messing around with Smokey, even said they saw her in Virginia with Smokey, a few weeks before your pops got killed." Dollar waved off that idea. "Man, listen! Motherfuckers was lying and scheming so much back then, you didn't know who to believe! Then right after your father got killed, Smokey ended up dead too." He shook his head. "But, hey. That's how the game goes when you out in this world hustling, breaking the law and shit. We both know that it's only a few ways out of the game. I think you know about one of them ways, young blood, 'cause we living this shit right now! This jail shit is for the birds though."

Dollar banged on the gate to the pen that he was in. "Look, Shamari, I'm gonna tell you something, son: stay the fuck outta jail, man! I've been coming back and forth to this rock for most of my life and it's no joke. I can't even trust myself enough to stay the hell outta here. Do you have kids, man?"

"Yeah, I have a son. He's a month old," Shamari said.

"You see what I'm talking about?" Dollar said, getting all animated. "You need to be at home with your baby, man! Don't get caught up with this street shit. You don't want the karma to fall back on your son! See what I told

you about your father, right?" Shamari nodded. "Now look at what's happening to you! That's what I'm talking about!" He sucked his teeth. "You don't want history repeating itself. Get your life right, man! Anyway, how's your moms doing?"

Shamari attempted to smile. "She's good. She's got her master's degree and a good career. She's straight."

Dollar smiled at that news. "Good for her. I knew she was better than that hustling murder one bullshit. As smart as she was, I'm glad that she applied her brain to something other than the streets. Now you have to do the same thing, man. Follow in your mother's footsteps, not your father's, little homie."

Dollar paused for a moment and just stared at Shamari. Looking at him was like looking at a younger version of Maleek. He got a grip on his emotions and choked back tears. "Tell your moms that I said hello. And good luck to you, too, Shamari. Remember what I told you: follow in your mother's footsteps. But don't forget your pops. He still lives through you, man. Word."

A half hour later, the correction officers cuffed Dollar and took him out of the pen. As he was being escorted out, he gave Shamari a head nod. When Dollar got back to Four South, he discovered that he was already packed up and being transferred to another facility. He never got the chance to talk to Shamari again.

"Maybe I didn't need to tell him some of those things," Dollar said with a laugh.

"You think?" Brandi replied. She had to laugh too.

The waitress came to their table with their food. "But how was he acting after he told you about the talk I had with him?"

Brandi made her eyes flutter. "Okay, okay! I have to admit his attitude did seem a little better. He seemed a lot more mature minded after y'all's little talk," she said, while munching on her omelet.

"Exactly! He needed that man-to-man talk. Maleek was gone and your brothers were too busy getting locked up to reinforce some positive shit into their nephew."

At the mention of her brothers, Brandi put down her fork and rubbed her temples. "Please don't remind me of those Negroes! They're still putting my mother through the ringer and they're all in their mid-forties. I call them dumb, dumber, and dummy!"

Dollar laughed. "You ain't right!"

Brandi shook her head. "It's true!" She gave him a look. "You know, Dollar, it's crazy but I never realized how much I missed my people from back in the day until I ran into you today. How could I ever forget the times that you stood up for me when Maleek was beating my ass? If I never told you before, I truly appreciate everything you did for me, Dollar," she said, putting her hand over his.

Dollar squeezed her hand and continued to stuff some egg whites into his mouth. "It was no problem, baby girl. I already told you how I felt about you and what you deserved. You didn't deserve to be treated that way."

"No, I didn't. No woman deserves to be treated that way."

They continued to eat their breakfast and chat about the old days. After they finished their food, Dollar ordered some mimosas for them to make a toast.

"To old friends," he said. Brandi nodded her head and took a sip of the drink. "Yo, Brandi, listen, before we go our separate ways, I have something that I want to confess to you," he said.

Brandi's doe eyes opened wide. "What is it?"

"I was always feeling you," he said. Brandi blinked but didn't say a word. "Yo, ever since the day you got with Maleek, I thought that you were the cutest thing. And you had this way about you that I always respected. You was a no-nonsense chick who held down your man—"

Brandi cut him off. "Oh, God! Please don't remind me of none of the stupid shit that I did back then," she said, thinking about how she used to carry herself in her wild days. "I was so crazy!"

Dollar held out his arms. "No, no! I don't want to bring up anything from the past; I know the past is very painful for you and me too but I always thought that you were too good for Maleek. He didn't appreciate you like he should have. I used to always say to myself that if I ever had a chance with her, I would treat her like the queen she is."

Brandi began laughing and slowly clapping her hands. "Dollar, you never cease to amaze me! You still got your player game down pat!"

Dollar frowned at her. "Nah, sweetheart, I'm so serious right now," he said, feeling relieved that he'd finally got his feelings about her off his chest.

Brandi's facial expression changed. He could actually feel her staring at the frown lines forming in the center of his forehead.

"You are serious," she replied.

"I am dead ass!" he said. "It's no games to be played here."

"So what are you saying to me, Dollar?"

Dollar pulled out his phone. "I'm not saying nothing yet. Let's just exchange numbers and keep in touch with each other. Maybe I can show you better than I can tell you."

"Wow, I never saw this side of you before," Brandi said.

"And you're going to see plenty more sides of me. I'm a changed man."

Brandi smiled. "Yeah, right! You're probably the same old Dollar! You've always been such a slickster."

"I'm still a slickster but I'm a go-getter, too. When I want something, I go for it," he said to Brandi, giving her a sly look.

Brandi blushed and exchanged information with him. Soon after, they were back in their cars and driving away.

As Dollar headed for Peeto's house, he was elated. He couldn't wait to tell his right-hand man about Brandi. But then again, he decided to keep that news to himself. This time around, he didn't want anyone or anything ruining his chances of finally getting with the one woman he always loved.

Chapter 10

Across town in Canarsie, Kane was at his wit's end. He must've called Brandi's phone most of the morning but she still wasn't picking up. And that was something that Kane wasn't used to.

All of sudden, Kane's phone began vibrating. He anxiously answered the call, hoping that it was Brandi returning his call. But it wasn't who he thought it was.

"What's up, Kane?" India greeted him in that loud, raspy voice of hers. "What you doing?"

Kane shook his head, wishing that the call was from Brandi. *Damn, why did it have to be India?*

Kane had met India back in the summer of 2010, at one of Rasheed's yearly cookouts. Judging from her outer beauty, India was just what Kane liked. She was a younger woman, twenty-nine years old to be exact. Her body was tight and topped off with that beautiful face of hers, she was almost perfect.

But little did Kane know, she was a far cry from being anything like her twin sister, Asia. India was loud, abrasive, and worst of all, she was a lush. Rasheed tried to warn him about India's "ways" but unfortunately, Kane was driven by lust.

"I'm gonna introduce you to her, man," Rasheed said. "But whatever happens after this, I don't want to hear nothing about it. Consider yourself warned."

Kane took in all of India's physical attributes from where he was standing and licked his lips. "Whatever,

Rah. I ain't trying to fall in love with the broad. I just wanna get my dick wet. Damn, I wonder what the inside of her mouth feels like."

Rasheed stood there with a disgusted look on his face. "Come on, man! You can keep that to yourself." He waved at India and she walked over to them. "Yo, my man wanted to meet you. Kane, this is India. India, Kane."

Rasheed walked back over to the grill, leaving Kane and India by themselves.

"Mmm," she began, giving Kane the once-over. "You're kinda cute. I can take you down."

Kane was taken aback by her straightforwardness. "Oh, is that right?" he asked, with a raised eyebrow.

"Yeah, that's right, baby. You're my type of cat," she replied.

Within the course of a few weeks, the two hung out with each other a few times and did all of the sexual things that most adults do. But her brash behavior paired with alcohol only intensified India's ghetto antics. She began to display some clingy behavior, even started questioning him about other women. Pretty soon, Kane was ignoring India's phone calls and sending her straight to voice mail.

Now once again, India had started the calling. Hearing her voice made him regret even mentioning her name to Asia.

"Oh, hey, what's up, India?" he nonchalantly replied.

"Oh, hey, what's up, India?" she repeated, acting as if she was insulted by his indifference. "Thank you for sounding real excited to hear from me! Aren't you the one who told my sister to tell me to call you?"

Kane's jaw tightened. *Me and my big ass mouth!* He let out a long sigh. "Yeah, I did, girl," he said, angry at himself for the slip of the lip.

"Anyway, are you coming to Asia's baby shower this Saturday or nah? I would have sent your invitation in the mail but I felt like hand delivering it to you."

Kane laughed at her "kind" gesture. "Delivering it to me? Is that right? I got a mailman to do that, India," he said.

"Well, I'm your mailman today, Kane," India replied sarcastically. "And I'm not too far away from your house."

"Just bring the invite, damn!"

Within minutes, the persistent India was ringing the bell to his front door. Kane opened the door and immediately snatched the pink envelope right out of India's hand. But before Kane could say another word, she was on her knees with her coat still on and opening the zipper of his jeans. He was unable to resist her oral expertise; India commenced giving Kane a blow job right in the doorway of his house.

Kane closed his eyes, as India's juicy mouth went up and down on the shaft of his erect penis. The head of his rod was halfway down her throat, which tempted him to pull her inside of his house. Kane closed the door behind them and gave India exactly what she came for.

Two orgasms later, the fully dressed India was sitting on his couch and staring at him with an evil glare.

Kane buttoned up his jeans. "Yo, why are you staring at me like that? Aren't you supposed to be leaving?"

India folded her arms and rolled her neck. "I'm not leaving until you answer me this. I wanna know what's really good with you, Kane? With us?" she asked. "How long are we going to do this fuck thing?"

Kane plopped down in the single chair and looked up at the ceiling. He was in no mood for India's inquiries. He had given her the penis so she should have been on her way out the door.

"I don't have no fucking time for this bullshit," Kane mumbled while rubbing his temples. "You said that you were just coming over to drop off an invite to the baby shower. You're the one who started sucking my dick in the doorway! I didn't press you for the head or the ass!"

India hopped up from the couch and began walking back and forth. Kane prayed that he wouldn't have to physically remove the angry woman from the premises.

"Kane, me and you have been fucking with each other on and off for the past two years! When are you gonna make me your got damn girl?"

Kane almost choked on his own saliva. "Did you just ask when am I going to make you my girl? Yo, you're funny as hell!" he said, with a laugh.

"I don't see what's so fucking funny!"

Kane looked at India. Standing before him was a woman who was almost in her thirties who had the mindset and the lingo of a fifteen-year-old girl. If he was unsure of what he wanted in a wife or a girlfriend, he definitely knew what he didn't want and that was India.

"What the hell is this woman talking about?" the bewildered Kane asked. "You got damn women are nothing but one big headache, a headache that I don't need!"

The defiant India crossed her arms. "And you're one fake-ass, fronting dude, Kane, I swear you are! You don't know how good you can have it with me! I have a good job and I make my own motherfucking money. I don't need no man to take care of me! And I got some good-ass pussy! I can get any man I want!"

Kane chuckled to himself. He got up and began gathering the rest of India's things. He shoved the belongings in her arms and coat then gently pushed her toward the door.

"Look, India, we had a good time this evening. So please don't kill my vibe, okay? I have things to do so you have to leave now," he said, holding the door open for her.

India huffed and puffed but luckily for Kane, she didn't put up much of a fight. Instead, she smiled sweetly.

"You know what? It's all good, baby. I think you're trying to suppress how you feel about me. I get it, boo."

The relieved Kane watched as India walked down the front steps of his house. Before he could shut the door, she turned around and looked back at him.

"You are coming to Asia's shower next Saturday, right?" she asked.

"Of course, I'm coming! I wouldn't miss my boy's baby shower for the world!"

A disgusted look came over her face. "Hmmph," she said. "Oh, yeah, Rasheed is your boy. Damn, I wish my sister could have picked a better baby daddy." Her eyes rolled up in her head. "Anyway, I will see you Saturday and who knows? Maybe I can come home with you after it's over," she added, giving him a wink. "Night night, Kane."

Kane shook his head as he watched India get into her convertible. After she pulled off, he slammed his door and cussed Brandi under his breath. If only she would have answered her phone, he wouldn't have had to subject himself to India, the bugaboo. He reached for his phone and dialed Brandi's number again. This time, the phone went straight to voice mail.

"Damn!" Kane yelled, throwing his phone onto the sofa. Angry at himself for losing his cool over some broad he just met, he retrieved the phone to call up Rasheed to vent.

"What do you want, man?" Rasheed said.

Kane ignored Rasheed's rude greeting. "Your future sister-in-law just left my house."

"Ah!" Rasheed said, in disgust. "Please don't call her that! You know I can't stand that trifling-ass broad. You fucked her, didn't you?"

"Yeah, I did," Kane shamefully replied while listening to Rasheed's disapproving grunts. "Man, she called me up and said that she wanted to hand deliver your shower invitation to my house."

"Damn! She used that lame excuse on you, man? You should've known that it was a setup!"

"I know! I just told the woman to come on over and give me the damn invite."

"It has to be a good reason for you to want to still mess around with India, man. Anyway, what's going on with you?"

Kane fell back onto his couch. "It's Brandi, man. Me and her hung out last night, right, and we had a nice time, too. After the date, I ended up going back to her spot and you know what happened next."

"You smashed that?"

"Yeah, I smashed," Kane said, puffing out his chest. A visual recap of the night with Brandi had refueled his hurt ego.

"Damn! I can't believe that you smashed Sean's old chick! Does she even know that you and Sean are cool with each other, man?"

"Nah, she don't know about all that and she don't need to know until I feel that the time is right."

Rasheed cleared his throat. "You mean to tell me that Brandi is loving the crew and she don't know that she's loving the crew?"

Kane felt himself getting upset all over again. "I know you ain't talking about me, slime! You didn't tell your baby mama that you knew her ex-man until after you got the drawers!"

Rasheed got quiet at the mention of his son's mother. "Yeah, yeah, you right," Rasheed reluctantly admitted. "But you and Sean hang around each other sometimes so that's ten times worse. How do you think Brandi's gonna feel when she finds out that you know Sean?"

"Just because I know Sean doesn't mean that I had to know that they were dealing with each other! And man, listen, she shouldn't feel no way if she ain't fucking with the dude anymore, right?"

"Yeah, okay, Kane," Rasheed replied with a sigh.

"I don't give a hell about who Brandi used to talk to, Rah. All I know is that I'm trying to get at her and right now, I feel like she's shutting me out for some reason."

"What you mean, she's shutting you out?"

"I called her phone a few times and she hasn't called me back yet! What the fuck is up with that? She seemed like she enjoyed the cock last night."

Rasheed laughed. From what it sounded like, Kane didn't know how to handle a pro like Brandi. He decided that instead of butting in, he was going to sit back and watch how everything played out among Sean, Kane, and Brandi. To him, it seemed like the three were having a ménage à trois.

"She's probably just busy, man. Give her a chance, she'll call you back."

"You think so?" Kane asked, with a hint of desperation in his voice.

Rasheed tried to keep from exploding with laughter. "Yeah, man, she'll call you back."

Kane continued talking to Rasheed but his mind was still on Brandi. Twenty-four hours was way too long for him to wait for her to call him. And he had never been good with rejection. *What if her and Sean are secretly seeing each other?* He hoped this wasn't the case, for their sake. If there was anything that Kane hated more than rejection, it was being made to look like a fool.

Chapter 11

It was a typical Monday morning in the borough of Brooklyn. The sounds of schoolchildren's laughter could be heard throughout the blocks of Bedford-Stuyvesant. Working parents scrambled to get their toddlers and babies to the nearby day care centers. And at the corner of nearly every block, the security gates of bodegas went up in preparation for the influx of morning time customers.

From the looks of things, everything was pretty normal in the neighborhood. But for the newly married Sean, the weekend had proved to be an experience that he wouldn't soon forget.

Sean grudgingly rolled out of bed. The sweats from a sleepless night had his white tank completely drenched. He walked into the bathroom and threw the wet T-shirt into the wicker hamper. He washed his face, brushed his teeth, then looked at the clock. It was almost nine in the morning. In three more hours, Milan was going to be walking through the front door of their brownstone.

His wife's return was something that weighed heavily on his mind. After his act of infidelity, Sean was unsure of how he was going to act when she was around. Milan loved him and to think that he had been unfaithful to her. Her hand didn't call for that.

Sean couldn't stop replaying the images of him and Brandi having sex in his bed. She was such an insatiable lover. Their sexual chemistry was off the charts. Because of that, Sean found it exceptionally hard to resist her. His thirst for Brandi was increasingly hard to suppress, so much that Sean found himself picking up the telephone to call her that Monday morning. He had a strong urge to taste her one more time before he went back to being a loyal husband to Milan.

"Good morning, sunshine," Brandi said when she answered the phone.

Sean laughed, as he walked into his kitchen. "Hello, Miss Lady, how are you this morning?" he asked.

"I really don't have to be at work until twelve this afternoon. But I'm going in a little early."

A mischievous smile appeared on Sean's face. "Twelve o'clock, huh?"

"Yeah, twelve o'clock."

"Where are you now?" Sean asked.

"Actually, I'm still parked in front of my building. I didn't even pull off yet."

Sean's face brightened up. "Stay right there."

"Huh?"

"I said stay right there," Sean demanded. "I'm coming to see you."

"But, Sean, you can't come over here! Isn't your wife coming home today?" asked the confused Brandi.

"Yeah, she is but she won't be home for another three hours. I'll be there in twenty minutes."

Sean hung up the phone and ran upstairs to throw on some clothes. Soon after, he was in his vehicle and on his way to Brandi's house.

In Atlanta, Milan was in the passenger seat of a late model Porsche Panamera, sniffing a line of cocaine. The vehicle belonged to her best friend since college and one of Atlanta's most well-respected fashion bloggers, Antonio "Bam" Shelby. He was giving Milan a ride to the Hartsfield-Jackson Airport to catch her flight back to New York City.

Milan passed the small vial of cocaine to Bam. Feeling good, she put on her Chloe shades and let the cool fall breeze blow through the bundles of Brazilian body wave that was sewn on her head. She looked out the window at the city of Atlanta. She was definitely going to miss the place, especially the night life. The lounges and bars on Peachtree Street were where some of Milan's favorite haunts were located. And every time she was in town, she frequented Traxx, in the nearby Decatur. She was never one to shy away from anything adventurous and Atlanta was just the place for her to be that.

"Thanks for the ride to the airport, Bam," Milan said, high as a kite. "I truly appreciate everything you've done for me this weekend, boo, you just don't know!"

"It has been my pleasure, Miss Milan," Bam said, after sniffing some of the coke. He wiped his runny nose with a silk handkerchief. "I just don't know how you manage this lifestyle of yours, child! I mean, you're this fabulous career woman, a wife; you must have one hell of a husband, hunty! Mister man really has to be a cool guy to let the fineness that is Mrs. Milan Daniels travel alone!"

"Oh, please don't remind me about my husband," Milan said, while yawning at the same time. "I absolutely detest the fucking married life!"

Bam took his eyes off the road for a brief second to look at her. "Excuse me? I thought that you were completely and totally in love with your Seanie Poo! That delicious specimen of a man is for the gods, hunty! Yeeessss!"

Milan smiled. "Yes, my Seanie Poo is a handsome devil. And the dick is utterly divine but, sometimes, Miss Milan has a little taste for some fish, too! I always make sure that my licker license is on point," she added. "Seanie Poo don't know about that, though."

Bam gasped. "Oh, my stars! You mean to tell me that that man does not know that his beloved wife likes a little filet o' fish every now and again?" Milan shook her head. "Child boo! You are a complete and total HAM: a hot-ass mess! Don't you think that's something that should have been told to the poor bastard before you lovebirds took the plunge?"

Milan continued to look out the passenger window. "Please! You don't know how many times I wanted to keep it real with him, Bam, but, I didn't know how to do that. It's just that when I first laid eyes on Sean, he looked so . . . damn . . . good and at the time, my penchant for dark meat was working overtime!" Bam laughed. "But I didn't know that the man was gonna be talking about marrying me."

Bam rolled his eyes at Milan. "Girl, it sounds like you needs to pick you a side, honey! You're still straddling that fence! And to think that your clueless husband is at home, waiting ever so patiently for that box of yours."

Milan lifted her shades up and looked at Bam. "I have a confession, Bam," she said.

"Oh, my stars. Do tell!"

"Do you know Tuki Charles?"

Bam put his hand over his mouth, in amazement. "Yes, I do, child. Tuki Charles is that bitch in ATL, child! I swear, that woman makes a living off of showing up to various charity events and wherever the 'it' people are, honey! She is one bad mama jama, I tell you!"

"That's Tuki!" Milan turned around in her seat to face Bam. "Do you remember when I came down here last summer for that BET conference?" Bam nodded his head. "And that GLAAD event we attended that weekend?" He nodded his head again. "Well, Miss Thing walked right up to me and introduced herself. She told me that I had the most beautiful lips and eyes that she had ever seen!

After that, we kind of kicked it for a while and eventually exchanged phone numbers. We talked almost every day and honestly, that bourgeois, stuck-up attitude of hers is nothing but a front for the rich Atliens; she's a total sweetheart."

"Oh, my God! Why didn't you tell me that you and Miss Tuki were talking to each other? I don't think that she's stuck-up; she's divine! She is so, so hot, the epitome of a cool, classy, a dignified Southern belle, a certified Georgia Peach! But I would have never in a million years thought that she played for the same team! Hmmph. What a tangled web we weave, child!"

Milan laughed. "I wouldn't have thought that either but shit, I'm sure that her sexual orientation is no secret. Atlanta ain't that big, Bam. Anyway, we've been talking on the phone for some months now so when I came down here this time, she was ready for me! She had everything that she needed, too. I'm talking about the strap-ons, double-headed dildos . . . mmm mmm mmm! I'm telling you, I must have had over fifty orgasms in this one weekend alone, Bam." Milan leaned back in the seat and sighed. "Now I have to go back home and climb on top of this real-life beef sausage and I really don't want to. I so don't want to fuck my husband!"

Bam wiggled his French manicured hand at Milan. "Well, honey, I love me some sausage; that is my specialty, baby! No fish filet for this queen, honey!"

Milan wanted to laugh at Bam's joke but thinking about Sean and their marriage had suddenly put her in a sour mood. "I don't think that I want to be married anymore, Bam," she said, out of the blue.

"I will run this car off the road, child! What did you just say to me?"

"I don't want to be married anymore. I think that I made a huge mistake by marrying this man. I do love him, though. I realize that this whole hetero marriage bullshit is just not my thing! I don't want to be stuck with Sean for the rest of my life, raising babies and becoming some . . . some Brooklyn housewife. And Sean is a damn jail guard, for Christ's sakes! I mean, he's paid very well but I cannot fathom the idea of living my life as some CO's wife! Booooring!"

Bam yawned. "Stop! Please don't tell me anymore. I am going to fall asleep behind this wheel just thinking about your miserable future!"

"I think that I just married Sean to appease my parents." Milan sighed. "I need an out, Bam, a clean getaway. And I don't want to look like the bad guy, either."

"Sooo," Bam began. "Now you want to leave Sean? At that wedding, I saw two people who were truly in love with each other."

Milan gave Bam solemn look. "And I love Sean. I really do. But I can't live this lie anymore."

Bam exited off the highway and drove into the airport. "Oh, that is grand! Me and the children are so proud of you, honey, for finally wanting to come out of the closet. So when you make this break for it, are you going to stay in New York? Because if not, you can always come right on down to Buckhead, boo. You know you always have a room in my place."

Milan kissed Bam on the cheek. "That doesn't sound like a bad idea, sweetie. Shoot, Tuki's good box-eating ass would probably love it if I moved down here."

Bam giggled at the thought and gave Milan a high five. "I know she would, child. I know she would!"

***

In Brooklyn, Sean was bending Brandi over the kitchen counter and sexing her doggie style. He grabbed her hair from the back with left hand while using the right hand to massage her clitoris. Brandi screamed out his name, as Sean proceeded to go deeper inside of her vaginal walls. After a few minutes of this, he felt himself about to explode. But he stopped just as he was about to cum. He wouldn't dare pass the finish line without Brandi getting there first.

Brandi looked back at him. "Why you stop, baby?" she whispered. "You didn't have to stop."

"I felt like I was going to cum," Sean replied, kissing her on the back of her neck. "And I didn't want to cum without you."

Brandi turned around to face Sean. He lifted her on top of the counter and entered her again. He held her close while he ground inside of her. Brandi closed her eyes and threw her head back, taking in every inch of his girth. A few strokes later, she felt herself reaching her orgasmic peak.

"I'm cumming," she whispered. "It's right there, right there, baby."

"Cum," Sean mumbled. "Cum, babe. I'm right there with you!"

Brandi and Sean came within seconds of each other. Her heart felt like it was beating a mile a minute. She put her hand to her chest.

"It feels like my chest is about to explode," Brandi said, as she wiped the sweat from her brow.

Sean tried to respond to her but he couldn't speak. He just stood there, still holding his dripping wet penis in his hand. Once again, Brandi had rocked him.

"Damn," was all Sean could say. Brandi smiled at him and jumped off the counter. She pulled down her skirt and went to retrieve her panties from the floor. "You got some real potent pussy, baby. Damn!"

“You think so?” she said, with a seductive look on her face.

“I know so,” Sean replied, kissing her on the lips.

Brandi walked into the bathroom to prepare to take another shower. “So where are you off to now?” she called out to Sean. “Isn’t your wife on her way home?”

Sean woke up from the daze that he was in. “Damn! I gotta run and freshen up before she comes,” Sean said, pulling up his underwear and sweatpants, not bothering to wash up.

“Oh, really?” Brandi said, peeking out of the bathroom door. “So you come over here to fuck me and then run back home like a fucking lap dog to put up a front for the wife. Wow. What we won’t do for love!”

“Come on now, Brandi,” Sean pleaded. “I didn’t mean to make you feel a way. I was just telling you the truth.”

Brandi got into the shower. “Sometimes, women don’t need to hear the truth, Sean! When are y’all gonna get it?” she yelled, over the running water.

Sean walked to the bathroom and stuck his head inside of the door. “What did I say that was so bad, Brandi?” he asked, with a hint of confusion in his voice.

“Just leave, Sean. I’ll talk to you later,” she replied.

Sean stood there for a minute, trying to understand what he said that was so wrong. He hadn’t meant to upset Brandi; he didn’t want to anything to jeopardize what they had. But the truth of the matter was that he had Milan at home. And if Brandi was going to deal with him, she would have to respect his situation.

Sean waited around for Brandi to finish up her shower. When she came out of the bathroom, her body was glistening with water and she had a towel wrapped around her naked body.

“You still here?” she asked, with an attitude. “It’s ten-thirty, you know. Almost that time for your goddess to touch down again.”

Sean reached for her hands. “Look, Brandi, I didn’t mean to get you upset, babe. I apologize.”

“It’s cool. It’s just that I’m all into my feelings over you and this marriage of yours.”

Sean kissed her on the lips. “Don’t worry about my situation. We’re going to work this thing out.” He walked toward the door and unlocked it. “I have to be at work at three-thirty this afternoon. Call you around seven. Is that cool?”

Brandi managed to smile. “Seven is cool. I’ll be waiting.”

Sean slid out of the door and Brandi locked it behind him. As he made his way downstairs, Sean began contemplating everything that just happened between them. Things were moving a little too quickly and he could see that Brandi was not happy with the direction. He thought about how pissed Brandi was when he left. Her attitude toward his situation had him quite confused, especially when she was the one who appeared on his doorstep.

Now the married Sean felt extremely guilty about what had gone down between him and Brandi. He’d gotten hitched with the intentions of being a faithful husband. But Sean noticed how easy it had been for him to stray outside of his marriage.

Then suddenly, it hit him. He may have married Milan for all of the wrong reasons.

Chapter 12

Kane was awake since six a.m. that Monday morning. Around 7:30, he worked out for two hours at the gym. Working out always cleared his thoughts and more importantly, he didn't think about Brandi or any other woman for that matter. But as soon as Kane returned home, those feelings of loneliness started creeping up on him again.

Kane's ringing cell phone interrupted his thoughts. *Finally! The call I've been waiting for!*

"Hey, Brandi," Kane said, trying to sound as cheerful as possible. He really wanted to read her the riot act for not calling him. "How are you?"

"Hey, Kane," Brandi said. "What are you up to this on this fine morning?" she asked, sounding very cheerful and acting as if she had spoken to him the night before.

Kane began biting his bottom lip to keep from cussing her out. "Ah, nothing much. I was just thinking about you. Wondering why I haven't heard from you."

Kane paced the living room while he listened to Brandi give him a myriad of excuses as to why she hadn't called him after their late-night interlude. He could tell that Brandi was lying. Everything in that lie she told gave Kane every reason to treat women the way he did.

Kane waited for her to stop talking. "Wow. Sounds like you had a full day yesterday. The shopping, the grandson, the breakfast with an old friend . . . You're a very busy woman, aren't you?" he said, sarcastically.

"Yeah, I am. But I don't have a problem with making some time for you, Kane," Brandi said, as if she trying to soften him up. "It's just that after we hooked up, things got a little crazy for me, that's all."

"Right, right," Kane replied. "So when am I going to see you again? Or as a matter of fact, what are you doing this Saturday?"

"I'm not doing anything. What's up?"

"I wanted to know if you would like attend a baby shower with me. It's my boy's baby shower," Kane asked, with a smirk on his face. It was time for the big reveal. Kane knew that Sean would be there with his wife and the shower would be a perfect time to see if anything was going on between him and Brandi.

"A baby shower?" she repeated. "Ah, man, I haven't been to one of those in a while! That sounds cool. Should I bring a gift?"

"Don't worry about that. I got the gift thing covered. I just want your company."

"Aw, that's so sweet!" she said.

"I like you, Brandi," Kane blurted out. He was surprised at his own words. "I'm looking to see where this goes with me and you, know what I mean?"

"I think I know what you mean," Brandi hesitantly replied. "But, listen, Kane, I don't want to jump the gun with you or anything. I want us to take our time. Trust me, I've done that a few times and that just didn't work for me."

Kane sighed. "I hear that," he said, feeling like a jackass for sharing his feelings with Brandi. He quickly changed the subject. "In the meantime, put that date on your calendar, babe. I'll speak to you later."

"That's cool, Kane. You have a great day," she said, hanging up the phone.

After talking to Brandi, Kane walked over to his bar and poured himself a drink. "Damn!" he said to himself, as he guzzled down the glass of Hennessy. "How can I get this chick to fuck with me? She's not biting."

It was almost 11:00 a.m. Monday morning when Rasheed walked into Gordon's Tire, his rim and tire shop, located on Atlantic Avenue. Atlantic Avenue was a busy Brooklyn thruway and also the same street that occupied the newly built Barclay Center. Because of this, Rasheed's small business was definitely booming.

Rasheed turned on lights in the shop and immediately began checking the inventory for the store's supplies. As he was about to walk into his office, a knock on the locked glass door surprised him. Rasheed looked at his watch and frowned. He wasn't opening for another hour. When he opened the door, Sean was standing outside of the shop with a worried look on his face.

"What's up, slime? Where are you coming from?" he asked, giving Sean a pound, as he walked into the shop. "I thought that you didn't have to be at Rikers Island until three-thirty in the afternoon. Why you out so early?"

Sean shook his head and leaned on the glass counter. "I'm coming from Brandi's house, man."

Rasheed did a double take. "Did you just say that you were coming from Brandi's house?" he repeated.

"I ain't stutter, man! I just came from Brandi's house." Rasheed was silent. "Me and her got it on this past Saturday and we was back at it this morning before she went to work."

"So you and Brandi are fucking each other again?"

Sean plopped down in a chair and held his head in his hands. "I don't know what the hell we're doing, son. It's like I can't shake this woman!"

Now it was Rasheed's turn to shake his head. Two of his closest friends were involved with the same woman. Should he say something and possibly start a beef between the volatile Sean and quick-tempered Kane? Or should he keep what he knew to himself and risk losing the trust of both men?

Poor Brandi. The woman didn't even realize that she was being played. With Sean being a married man and Kane being a certified womanizer, she wasn't exactly in the best company.

"How did you end up sleeping with Brandi again, man?" Rasheed asked.

Sean looked at him strangely. "What do you mean, how did I end up sleeping with Brandi? Are you judging me, man? I know you ain't talking!"

Rasheed laughed at what Sean said. "I ain't judging you, homie, calm down! And you can't put me in the same category as you. I ain't the one who's fucking married!" Sean waved him off. "So now what's gonna happen with you and Brandi? And your marriage?"

"Hey, man," Sean said, putting up his hands. "Truthfully, I'm not really thinking about my marriage right now. Everything is pretty much good there. I've been too busy with trying to figure out how to keep things going with Brandi."

"Did you just say that everything is going pretty good in your marriage?" Rasheed laughed at that statement. "Not anymore, my man! Brandi ain't trying to be your side chick! And it might not be a good idea to put her in that position. You know she's probably still kind of bitter about you cutting her off."

Sean sighed. "Yo, Rah, you don't know what you talking about, man! I know Brandi very well and I'm telling you, that woman is in love with me! You saw how quick she was to hop back on the bandwagon again, right?" Rasheed stood there, looking at Sean in disbelief. "Now look at me. I'm in like Flynn and it looks like I'm going to be fucking that pussy anytime I want. And you know what she told me, bruh? She told me that she is always going to be with me, no matter what. What do you think that means?"

Rasheed continued doing his inventory. "That means that she is working on getting her some got damn revenge, man!"

"Damn, son! You don't give me no credit! I know these broads like the back of my hand!"

Rasheed sighed and greeted one of his workers as soon as he walked into the shop. He told the employee to start preparing for the day then walked Sean outside.

As the sounds of the Long Island Railroad rattled on the tracks above them, Rasheed tried to talk some common sense into his friend. Judging from the conversation they were having, Rasheed knew that he probably would have to handle Sean with kid gloves when it came to Brandi.

Rasheed put his hand on Sean's shoulder. "Look, man, I didn't mean what I said about Brandi being bitter and trying to get revenge on you and whatnot. It's just that you're my peoples and I want you to be real careful. I don't want you to lose focus, slime."

Sean gave Rasheed a brotherly hug. "You're my people, too, man. I appreciate you looking out for me." He looked at his watch and saw that it was almost 11:30. "Shit! Yo, Rah, I'm gonna hit you up later, man. Milan should be walking in the house in a few."

Rasheed gave Sean a head nod and watched as his friend disappeared from his sight.

When Rasheed walked back into his shop, he went in his office and closed the door. He sat at his desk, thinking about the situation with Brandi. As much as he didn't want Kane and Sean to be at each other's throats over the woman, he realized that he would have to take a step back; two male egos were at an all-time high. Keeping his mouth shut was something that he had to do. He just hoped the outcome wouldn't be a deadly one.

Chapter 13

Fresh off the flight from Atlanta, Milan walked through the door of her Brooklyn home, calling out Sean's name.

"Sean, I'm home!" she yelled. But there was no reply. She looked at the diamond Michelle watch on her wrist. It was 11:36 a.m. She wondered why her husband wasn't there to greet her. *Where could he be?*

Milan shrugged her shoulders and walked upstairs to the bedroom, leaving her bags downstairs near the front door. She was sort of glad that Sean wasn't at home; it gave her some time to regroup after her eventful weekend. Milan walked into her bedroom and fell back onto the bed with her clothes still on. As she was lying across the king-sized bed, Tuki Charles came to mind.

Tuki Charles was the young socialite daughter of a well-to-do African American financier by the name of Rodney Charles. Her father was featured in magazines such as *Black Enterprise* and *Ebony*. He even made several television appearances, with the likes of Tavis Smiley and Roland Martin to discuss African American consumers and finances.

Because of her father's connections, Tuki was well known in the most prominent circles of Atlanta's rich, prosperous, and even famous. But it didn't stop there. Tuki was a very beautiful woman with flawless honey-colored skin and exotic good looks, courtesy of her African American father and her mother's Hawaiian and Sioux Indian heritage. She had men clamoring for her attention but Tuki always politely shooed them away. With the exception of an occasional male escort for special events, she had an affinity for the same sex and she wouldn't have it any other way.

While Tuki made it perfectly clear that she was not interested in being with a man, she was definitely sure of what kind of women she was attracted to. They also talked about a few other things that made Milan quite uncomfortable.

"I want to ask you one question," Tuki said to her, as they sat by the fireplace in her luxury loft in downtown Atlanta. "Are you bisexual?"

Milan took a big gulp of her wine and frowned. She wasn't trying to give up an opportunity to be with someone like Tuki. The woman screamed money. "No," she lied. "I'm not bisexual. Why do you ask?"

Tuki breathed a sigh of relief. "Because I have no desire to be with a bisexual woman." She poured herself another glass of wine. "As a matter of fact, I am truly convinced that bisexual men and women are partly responsible for the spread of HIV. And I'm a strong advocate for AIDS awareness and finding a cure for the deadly disease. I can't take part in that."

To add to her disdain for bisexual women, Tuki went on to tell Milan about how her heart was broken while she was in college by her bisexual lover. The lover had suddenly broken off their relationship and got married to a man.

"Ever since then," Tuki began, eyes gazing in the distance, "I made myself a promise to walk away from any woman who was confused about her sexuality. I refused to be a part of some fad or be someone's personal experiment.

"I really like you, Milan," Tuki added, after helping herself to another glass of Pinot Grigio. "Ever since

we met at that GLAAD event last year, you've became like this important part of my life. I really enjoy our telephone conversations and I especially love being in your company. But honestly, sweetie, this long-distance thing is killing me! I find myself wanting to be with you all the time and I don't understand why we can't make this happen between us."

Milan started blinking real fast as she sipped on her wine. She didn't know what to say. Tuki just sat there, staring at her, patiently waiting for her reply.

"Well, um, Tuki, I feel the same way," she said, using her words very carefully. "I guess it would be really great if I could move to Atlanta but that means that I would have to uproot my entire life in New York. Relocation takes time and I don't want to move down here for a relationship alone."

Tuki stood up. At five feet nine inches and 130 pounds, she looked more like a runway model than some Southern socialite. She put her hands on her hips. "You won't be moving down here for just any old relationship, Milan," she said with an attitude. "And if you're worried about getting the career of your choice, that won't be much a problem, either. After all, my name is Tuki Charles; I'm Rodney Charles's daughter! My family has all of the necessary tools that you need to make it happen for you down here."

Milan poured some more wine into her glass. The truth was that Tuki didn't know that she was married. And after their heart-to-heart, Milan didn't have the heart to tell her that. Tuki had said it herself: she absolutely despised bisexuality and there she was, a self-admitted bisexual, perpetrating a fraud. Milan realized that she was just as bad as some womanizing man.

"I have to really think long and hard about that, Tuki," Milan replied. "Like I said, I absolutely love Atlanta but to live here permanently is a whole 'nother animal."

A look of disappointment came over Tuki's face. She plopped back down on the couch beside her. "So how about I come back to New York and stay with you for a week or two?" she said, giving Milan a soft kiss on the lips.

Milan kissed her back. "I wish you could, babe, but, um, I'm not going to be in New York for a few weeks myself. I have to go to Chicago in a few days to meet with a new recording artist for my label," she lied.

"Aw, they're working my poor baby to death," Tuki said, as she slid off the couch and stuck her face between Milan's golden brown thighs.

Without any hesitation, Tuki pulled Milan's thong underwear to the side and began giving her an oral treat right on the living room sofa. Milan began to moan softly, as she gently ran her fingers through Tuki's long hair. She was in heaven. Tuki's expert tongue explored the inner walls of her wet vagina. She wrapped her tongue around Milan's protruding clitoris, sending waves of pleasure throughout her body. Milan's eyes rolled in the back of her head and she began sliding down the couch onto the floor, as Tuki continued to lick, suck, and nibble on her. This went on until Milan exploded in the mouth of her female paramour.

Tuki stood up, face shining from Milan's juices. Not even bothering to wipe her mouth, she helped Milan up from the floor and led her into the bedroom. There she went into a drawer and pulled out some sex toys to help them proceed with their session. Tuki put on a hot pink strap-on and ordered Milan to lie across the bed. She did as she was told and opened her legs, ready to receive Tuki. Tuki entered her slowly and began fucking her with the hard rubber contraption. Milan could feel something tickling their clitorises simultaneously and it didn't take much time for her to have another orgasm.

They continued their freaky interludes until the very last night that Milan was in Atlanta. And every time she and Tuki made love to each other, it was always superb; the next time was even better than the last. Now that the fantasy was over, Milan's grim truth was setting in. She was a married woman.

Just as Milan sat up and was about to get herself together, she heard the downstairs door close and Sean call out her name.

"Milan? Are you up there, babe?" he called out from the bottom of the stairs. "Is my baby home?"

Milan rolled her eyes and took a deep breath. She knew that once Sean came upstairs, he would want to have sex with her and she definitely wasn't up for that. After the hot, steamy sex with Tuki, the thought of any man touching her was almost repulsive. Her lesbian side was in overdrive. But just like any wife or husband who was having an extramarital affair, she was going to have to pretend.

Sean walked into the bedroom and lifted Milan off her feet. He gave her a passionate kiss, only coming up for air to look at her. "I missed you so much, baby," he whispered. He put her down. "Those few days that you were gone seemed like weeks!"

Milan smiled. "Oh, boy, stop exaggerating!" she said. "Anyway, don't you have to get ready for work soon?" she asked.

Sean sighed. "Yeah, I do. But not before we have our fun," he replied.

Milan turned away from him and closed her eyes. She was in no mood to have Sean's stiff dick inside of her. She just wasn't feeling it. "Look, baby, I know that you want to roll around in the sack but I am seriously exhausted from that trip. I'm going to need like one day to recoup."

Sean looked hurt but he held it down. "Oh, okay, sweetheart. I guess I'll have to wait until you're recharged. Anyway, I'm gonna bring your bags and stuff upstairs. You relax, babe."

Milan kissed him on the lips. "You're the best, my love," she whispered.

She waited until Sean disappeared out of the bedroom to call Tuki.

"Hey, sweetie!" she said, when Tuki answered the phone. "I just wanted to tell you that I made it home safely and I'm going to get some rest now. After I relax, I will give you a call. Is that cool?"

"No problem, sexy," Tuki said on the other end of the phone. "I'll be looking forward to your call because we need to arrange the dates that I'm going to be coming to New York to see you."

Milan began to get nervous. "Coming to New York?"

"Yes, silly! I don't have a problem with traveling to New York, too! I have some friends and family up there I haven't seen in a while anyway."

Before Milan knew it, she was agreeing to the impossible. "Um, yeah, that sounds like a really good idea," she said.

"Then it's settled!" Tuki replied. "Anyway, you get you some rest and make sure you call me back when you get a moment."

"I will. I'll talk to you later, girl," Milan said, before disconnecting the call.

Just as she was hanging up the phone, Sean appeared in the doorway with all of her bags. He dropped them on the floor and looked at her. "Who was that?" he asked.

"Oh, that was Bam," Milan said, trying not to stumble over her words. "Remember my gay BMF from college? The one who came to our wedding?" Sean nodded his head. "Yeah, I hung out with him while I was in Atlanta. Just wanted to let him know that I had a safe trip home."

Sean laughed. "Oh. You said 'girl' so I thought you were talking to one of your girlfriends." He paused. "Well, technically, Bam is your girlfriend. Anyway, since there's not going to be any action in the sack today, let me start getting ready for this eight-hour jail bid that I'm about to do."

Milan watched as Sean gathered up his things to take a shower and exhaled once she heard the water running. She couldn't understand why she was so nervous. But then again, she knew why. The walls were closing in on her and it was too late to turn back now.

As Sean lathered up his body in the shower, he thought about the way that Milan was acting toward him. He wondered if she suspected anything and prayed that nothing came up. *Did she smell Brandi's fragrance on me? Is her woman's intuition kicking in and she's ready to accuse me of being unfaithful to her?*

Then Sean started to get some suspicions of his own. What if Milan was cheating on him? She went to Atlanta quite frequently for business and, because of his busy work schedule, he hadn't had the opportunity to go with her.

Sean didn't know what was going on but whatever it was, he couldn't allow his guilt to get the best of him.

By the time Sean got out of the shower Milan was in the bed and sound asleep. He tiptoed around the room, careful not to wake her from her restful slumber. He quietly grabbed his things for work and went into the next bedroom to get dressed.

It was almost two o'clock in the afternoon before Sean walked out the door and practically ran to his parked truck. If he didn't know any better, it seemed as if he was desperately trying to escape the lingering cloud of deception that had occurred in his home that weekend. Ironically enough, the gloomy corridors of his Rikers Island facility were looking like a ray of sunshine. He couldn't wait to get to work.

Chapter 14

Almost an entire week had passed. Brandi was more than happy to get out of the house even it was only to attend a baby shower with Kane.

Truthfully, Brandi was trying her best to avoid Sean. He had called her a few times during the week but she neglected to answer any of his phone calls. Brandi knew that she had better slow things down, for fear that she would fall in love with him all over again. She had to keep reminding herself how much he'd hurt her.

She was pissed that Sean had married someone else. A part of her wanted to destroy everything that Sean built with his wife. Then there was a part of her that actually felt sorry for the woman. Being a woman first, Brandi knew what it felt like to be in love with an unfaithful man.

Brandi pulled her vehicle up in front of Kane's house in Canarsie. She sat in her car for a few seconds, admiring the quaint brick home and its quiet surroundings. Before she could get out of her car, Kane was standing outside on his doorstep and waving for her to come inside. She quickly gathered up her bag, locked her car door, and met Kane at the door.

When Brandi stepped inside, it looked a layout from *Better Homes and Gardens* magazine. The dark hardwood floors were practically gleaming and the living room walls were covered with expensive wallpaper that screamed interior decorator. The cherry-colored leather sofa and love seat offset the beautiful linen draperies that framed the tall windows. Contemporary African American art hung from the walls and a pricey imported shag rug that was lying in the middle of the floor only added to the room's flair.

Brandi smiled. "This is nice," she gushed. "I would have never expected a bachelor's pad to look like this. Your place just screams . . . money!"

Kane ushered her to the couch and walked to the closet to get his coat. "Shit, my place ain't the only thing that screams money, ma. I love having the best that my money can buy."

Brandi continued to look around the house. "Well, it looks like your money can buy a whole lot," she replied.

Kane laughed at her comment and looked down at his watch. It was 6:00 p.m. on the dot. "So are we ready to go to this baby shower or what?"

Brandi stood up. "Yes, we are! I hope your friends don't mind me tagging along with you."

Kane frowned. "Tagging along?" he said, as he locked the front door behind them. "You ain't tagging along. I invited you! And trust me, they won't mind at all."

When they arrived at the baby shower, it was in full swing. Most of the guests had already arrived and the mother-to-be's presents were plentiful. Food was being served by caterers and the DJ was jamming.

Brandi looked around the hall. That was when she happened to notice a small group of females staring at her, as if she didn't belong there. She turned away from them, unfazed by their leering. She followed closely behind Kane, who was making his way through the small crowd and trying to get the expectant father's attention.

"Yo, Rah!" Kane called out.

As "Rah" made his way toward them, Brandi almost fainted when she discovered that Kane's friend "Rah" was Rasheed Gordon. He was one of Sean's closest friends. She couldn't believe how much of a coincidence it was.

Rasheed walked over to them and gave Kane a bear hug. Then he looked at Brandi and began rubbing his chin.

"Rah, I want to introduce you to a special lady, Brandi," he said, giving her a kiss on the cheek. "And, Brandi, this is my boy and the baby daddy of hour, Rasheed," Kane said.

Brandi put on a fake smile. "Hi, Rasheed, how you doing?" she said, while nervously shaking his hand.

Rasheed winked his eye at her. "Hello, Miss Brandi," he greeted her with a knowing smile. "Thank you for coming to my event, mama."

"You're very welcome," she mumbled.

Kane noticed Brandi's nervousness. "Are you okay?" he asked, with a look of concern on his face.

"Oh, I'm fine, I'm fine. I just need something to drink, that's all. A real stiff drink."

"You want me to get something for you?"

"No, no, sweetie, I'll be okay. You go ahead and talk to your friend. I'll just be over there by the bar," she said, pointing to the fully stocked bar across the room.

Brandi hurriedly left Kane's side and practically ran to the bar. She couldn't believe what was happening to her. She watched the front door like a hawk, knowing that it was only a matter of time before Sean stepped through the doors of that hall. After all, Rasheed was more like Sean's brother than his best friend.

She walked over to the bartender and ordered herself a double shot of Patrón. Before the cup could hit the bar, she had swallowed the contents in one big gulp. A few seconds later, another guest was standing on the left side of her, trying to order a drink too.

"What you drinking on, girl?" asked the female.

"I just took a double shot of Patrón," Brandi replied, looking a bit flustered.

"Hmm," the woman said. "Sounds good." She ordered herself a drink too. "Oh, my name is India and yours?"

"I'm Brandi. How you doing, India?"

"I'm doing okay. Just enjoying the scenery." Brandi nodded her head in agreement. "So who are you here for, Rasheed or Asia?"

"Well, actually I'm here for neither. I came with a friend of Rasheed's."

India took a sip of her drink and frowned a little. "Really? Who's the friend you came with?"

"I came with Kane. Do you know him?" Brandi asked.

India smirked. "Wow. You're here with Kane? Ain't that something."

Suddenly, Brandi remembered who India was. She was one of the women who were shooting her nasty looks when she and Kane first walked in.

"Yes, Kane. Is there a problem?" Brandi asked, instantly getting on the defensive. She ordered another drink from the bar.

India must have picked up on Brandi's tone and took it down a notch. "No, no, it's not a problem. It's just that I found it funny that me and Kane was just hanging out with each other a few nights ago and now he walks into my sister's baby shower with you! That's crazy," India said.

Brandi didn't respond to India's foolery. Instead, she gave the bartender a tip and took her drink. Ticked off, she started walking toward Kane, who was standing nearby with Rasheed. Just as she was about to grab Kane's arm to get his attention, she was surprised to see that Sean was standing there with them as well. Brandi instantly froze in her tracks, feeling like she was unable to move her feet. Kane noticed Brandi watching them and gestured for her to come over to him.

Brandi walked over to Kane, wishing that she could disappear into thin air. "Yo, Sean," Kane said. "I wanted to introduce you to my lady friend, Brandi. Brandi, this is Sean."

Sean stopped drinking from the cup that he had in his hands and stared at Brandi. He was unable to speak.

"Come on, man," Kane said, giving him a strange look. "Don't be rude! Say hello to my lady friend, man."

Brandi had a sick feeling in her stomach. "Hey, Sean. Nice meeting you."

"What's up, Brandi," he said, with a look of disgust on his face.

Kane wasn't paying any attention to Sean's facial expression. He gave Brandi a kiss on the cheek. "Yep, y'all dudes need to get used to seeing this face right here," he said, while rubbing Brandi's right cheek with the back of his hand. "You're going to be seeing quite of bit of her."

Suddenly, a woman appeared from the back of the hall and reached for Sean's hand. She was very pretty and slightly younger than Brandi, with a shapely figure.

"Hello," she said, extending her hand to Brandi. "I'm Milan, Sean's wife. What's your name?"

Brandi did everything in her power to keep from giving Milan the screw face. "Brandi. I'm Kane's friend."

"Oh, okay," Milan said. Brandi could tell that Milan was relieved when she said that she was there with Kane.

After Kane introduced the very pregnant Asia to Brandi, she pulled him to a quiet area to let him know what India had told her.

Kane was livid. "Who the fuck does that broad think she is?" he said through clenched teeth. "And why would she tell you that?"

"Um, I don't know, Kane," Brandi said sarcastically. "Maybe it's because you and her fucked a few nights ago!"

"So you believe that bitch?" Kane asked.

Brandi sucked her teeth. "You're missing the whole point, Kane. Who you have sex with isn't any of my business," she said. "I just don't want any of these bitches starting some shit with me, that's all!" She paused. "When I agreed to come to this shower with you, I didn't sign up for this bullshit! I don't want to have to kick nobody's ass in here tonight!"

Kane waved her off. "Go ahead with that, Brandi! I'm not letting anyone disrespect you. I'm gonna go talk to India and tell her about herself!"

Brandi grabbed Kane's arm to keep him from walking toward India, the troublemaker. "Don't do that. It's not worth addressing."

Kane stopped in his tracks. He kissed her on the forehead. "Yeah, you're right. Anyway, Asia is opening her gifts."

Brandi sighed. "Okay, I'll be there in a minute," she said. "I just have to use the restroom."

"Okay, I'll be waiting for you."

As Brandi was about to walk into a nearby bathroom, Sean appeared around the corner. They both stopped in their tracks and looked at each other for a few moments before they spoke.

"Look, Sean, I didn't know that you knew Kane," Brandi explained. "If I would have known—"

Sean cut her off. "Brandi, you don't have to explain nothing to me. You're a grown-ass woman," he said, with an attitude. "Fuck who you want to fuck."

Brandi was surprised and annoyed at his angry reaction. "You know what? You're right! I don't have to explain nothing to your married ass!" she replied, before attempting to walk away. But she didn't go far. Sean grabbed her arm and stopped her from going any farther.

"Don't get fucking fly on me, Brandi!" He shook her. "You're lucky I don't put my hands on you! And must I remind you that you and I have unfinished business. We ain't over! I don't give a fuck about no Kane!"

Brandi snatched her arm from Sean's tight grasp. "Kane is not my man, Sean. He's just a fucking friend!"

Sean's nostrils began flaring. "Are you fucking him?"

"What business is that of yours?" Brandi replied, with her nostrils flaring.

Sean pointed his finger in her face. "Yeah, you're fucking him," Sean said. "I could tell!"

Suddenly, Milan appeared around the corner. She walked over to Sean and wrapped her arms around him. "Hey, sweetie. What's going on over here?" she asked, with look of curiosity on her face.

"Nothing, babe," Sean replied, without taking his eyes off Brandi. "Brandi here was just asking me where the restroom was."

Milan put a hand on her hip. "But she's already standing in front of the women's restroom, honey," she said, with an attitude.

Brandi quickly stepped inside of the bathroom, leaving the couple to argue among themselves. As soon the door closed, she pulled out her cell phone and made a phone call.

"Hello? Hey, Dollar! I know that we haven't spoken to each other in a few days but can you do me a big favor and please come pick me up from this baby shower? I need to get out of this place before I fuck somebody up!"

Brandi gave Dollar the address before hanging up the phone.

A few minutes later, Brandi stuck her head out of the restroom to see if the coast was clear. Sean and Milan were gone. She walked out of the bathroom and was able to sneak past Kane, who was too busy making a toast to Rasheed and Asia to notice her. But she caught Sean staring at her, right before she slipped out of the front door.

Just as she thought she made a clean getaway, Kane walked up behind her near the front entrance of the hall. He grabbed Brandi's arm.

"Where are you going?" Kane asked, with a confused look on his face. "Didn't we come together?"

The stunned Brandi turned around to face him. "I'm leaving! Now go back and inside and enjoy your friend's shower. I'm outta here!"

Kane frowned and let go of Brandi's arm. "What is your problem? Is it about what India told you?"

"Fuck India!" Brandi exclaimed. "I'm not thinking about that cunt!"

"So what is it then? Why are you leaving?"

Brandi crossed her arms. How could she tell Kane that she couldn't bear to look in the faces of Sean and his wife? She threw her hands up. "Look, I just gotta go!"

Kane sighed and reached into his pocket for his car keys. "Okay. Let's go. I'll take you to your car."

Brandi stopped him. "No, that's okay. I have someone coming to pick me up."

"Who's coming to get you? One of your girlfriends?" he asked.

She rolled her eyes. "An old friend of mine is coming to get me, Kane."

Now it was Kane's turn to cross his arms. "Oh, yeah? Who's this old friend of yours?"

"You know, Kane, you're asking a hell of a lot of questions! Now who's coming to get me is none of your damn business. Just go back inside with your friends!"

But Kane refused to leave her side. They went back and forth for twenty minutes and were still going at it when Dollar pulled up in front of the hall.

Kane followed Brandi outside. "Yo, who the hell is that?" he asked.

"My friend! Go back inside, Kane!" she yelled, while walking toward Dollar's truck.

Kane yanked Brandi's arm again, prompting Dollar to step out of his vehicle. "What the fuck are you doing?" Dollar shouted. "Let go of her, man!"

Kane let go of Brandi's arm and stepped to Dollar. "Who are you to be telling me anything about my woman?"

"I'm not your got damn woman, Kane!" Brandi screamed at him.

Kane looked at her. "You are my woman! And I don't appreciate you leaving with this motherfucker!" he replied.

All of a sudden, Dollar punched Kane in the face and they began fighting each other right outside of the hall. One of the guests was a witness to the chaos and they immediately ran inside to alert Rasheed and Sean of what was happening. By the time the two friends got to the scene Dollar and Kane were really going at it. Brandi was screaming at the top of her lungs while trying to pull them apart.

Rasheed and Sean immediately stepped between the two men and broke it up. Brandi stood to the side, simmering with anger while Asia, India, and Milan looked at her like she was crazy. The other guests were whispering about the incident as well.

Rasheed held on to Dollar while Sean grabbed a hold of Kane.

"Yo, Dollar," Rasheed began, as he tried to catch his breath. "What are you doing on this side of town, man?" he asked. "I haven't seen you in years!"

"What's up, Rah?" the exhausted Dollar replied. "I came to pick up my homegirl and when I pulled up, I saw this punk motherfucker grabbing on her and wilding the fuck out!" he said, pointing at Kane.

"Fuck you, man! You came at me!" screamed Kane, while Sean pulled him away.

"Chill out before somebody call the cops!" Sean said, still holding on to the upset Kane. "We're gonna go back inside now!"

As Sean forced Kane back inside the hall, he gave Brandi a nasty look. Asia, India, and Milan followed them back into the hall, along with the rest of the guests. The only people left standing outside were Brandi, Rasheed, and Dollar. Rasheed finally let Dollar go and watched as he got himself together.

"You a'ight, man?" Rasheed asked with a hint of concern in his voice.

Dollar managed to smile at Rasheed and gave him a pound. "Yeah, man, I'm all right. It's just that when I pulled up, your boy was trying to manhandle my peoples and I wasn't having that!"

Rasheed looked at the somber-faced Brandi. She was standing off by herself, looking quite embarrassed and shaking her head.

"I apologize for ruining your baby shower, Rasheed. I really didn't expect for any of this to happen," Brandi said, her voice quivering with sadness.

Rasheed shrugged his shoulders. "Ah, don't worry about it. I'll go talk to Kane. Just get Dollar out of here."

Dollar apologized to Rasheed too and gave him a pound. Shortly after, he and Brandi hopped into his truck and pulled off.

Back inside of the hall, Sean and Kane were in the men's restroom together. While Kane stood in the mirror, tending to his busted lip, Sean was standing behind him, sulking.

"So how long have you and Brandi been seeing each other?" Sean asked.

Kane turned around and looked at him. "We just started talking to each other. Why?"

Sean leaned against the bathroom wall and shook his head. "You know that's my ex-chick, right?"

Kane pressed the wet paper towel against his swollen bottom lip. “Okay. And?”

“Yo, man, if you hurt her—” Sean warned.

Kane cut Sean off. “What you mean, if I hurt her? Like you hurt her, man?”

Sean frowned. “You don’t know nothing about me and Brandi’s relationship, homie! But what I do know is that you don’t particularly care for me and I feel the same way about your ass. And let me tell you something else,” he said, taking a step closer to Kane. “Don’t make Brandi a pawn in this dirty fucking game. If you got any issue with me, you deal with me. Leave her out of it!”

Kane threw the bloody paper towel in the trash and stared Sean down. “Fuck you, nigga,” he said, pointing his finger in his face. “Your married ass can’t tell me shit!”

Kane opened the door and walked out, leaving Sean standing there with a dumb look on his face.

Chapter 15

It was the midnight hour in Atlanta. Tuki walked into her spacious loft. She stepped out of her Louboutin heels and her Roberto Cavalli dress, leaving them on the floor, in the middle of the living room. She removed her La Perla bra and thong underwear and threw them to the side. Then Tuki slid into her heart-shaped king-sized bed with nothing on.

Tuki lay there, looking up at her vaulted ceiling. The effects of the Dom Pérignon Rosé she consumed earlier had her feeling real good. And the charity event that she hosted that night ended with a bang; she was so happy that everything came off without a hitch. But there was something missing that night or, rather, someone. That someone was Milan.

She tried closing her eyes but all she could see was Milan's pretty face. If Tuki thought long and hard, she could practically smell the natural scent of her sweet vagina. Tuki sighed loudly, as she wrapped the white goose down comforter around her nude frame.

Tuki turned over and looked at the clock on her nightstand. It was 12:06 in the morning. She couldn't stop wondering what Milan was doing. *Is she thinking about me? Who is she with?* Those were some of the questions that she had on her mind.

Not able to take the suspense anymore, she jumped out of bed to retrieve her cell phone from her clutch. She dialed Milan's number and anxiously waited for her to answer.

After the third unanswered phone call, Tuki became agitated. She dialed the number for the fourth, fifth, and sixth time and there was still no answer. She began pacing back and forth, making one last attempt at calling. This time, she left a voice mail on Milan's phone.

"Hey, Milan," Tuki said. "I'm, like, trying to call you and you're, like, not answering my fucking phone calls! I really don't know what to think about you, Milan, I mean, you always answer my calls. Are you with someone else? Do you still love me? Please tell me the truth, Milan! Don't fucking string me along!"

Tuki disconnected the call. Then she fell down to her knees and covered her face with her hands.

The spoiled Tuki always got whatever she wanted and it was no different when it came to her lovers. But there was something about Milan and her elusive behavior that was vaguely familiar to her.

All of Tuki's friends thought that Fabian Graham was so cute. She never denied that. He was the captain of their school's varsity basketball team and voted as the most popular boy of their senior class. Fabian was every high school girl's dream.

While Tuki thought that Fabian was subpar, he was telling her friends that he had a major crush on her. "Hook me up with Tuki," he would tell them and they would try to advocate for the handsome jock. But Tuki wouldn't bite. She was not interested in him at all, which only made her more attractive to him. It seemed as though Fabian, who was accustomed to the female attention, was intrigued by her aloofness. He thought she was playing hard to get. Little did he know, Tuki liked who he liked: girls. But of course, at that time, she wasn't ready to reveal that side of her.

One day, Fabian finally got the nerve to approach Tuki in the corridor of their Atlanta high school. He cornered her by her locker, refusing to let her past him until she gave up her telephone number. Not wanting to look like a prude, Tuki gave Fabian her information and much to her dismay, he started calling her at home every day after school. Fabian was such a well-mannered young man over the phone that her parents insisted on meeting the young man. Fabian was more than thrilled when Tuki told him the news and naturally, the moment her parents saw him, they were taken by his good looks and charm. And the fact that he was being scouted by several universities only added to the Charleses' delight.

Meanwhile, Tuki was not impressed with all of this. It had been some months since she and Fabian started seeing each other and now, he was asking for her most precious treasure. Tuki always dreamed of being with a girl the first time she had sex; she'd never imagined that she would be deflowered by some boy. Then she figured that giving up her virginity to a boy wasn't such a bad idea. She wanted to get that part out of the way and go on to live her life as a gay woman.

Tuki's moment of truth came the night of her high school prom. Fabian was smiling from ear to ear, as he accepted the crown for the homecoming king for the Class of 2000. Tuki stood by and watched as the homecoming queen placed a kiss on the lips of her date. Her friends were a bit ruffled by the gesture and ranted about how she should have been on that stage with Fabian. But the popular Tuki couldn't care less. She had too many other "grown-up" things on her mind to be bothered by something so trivial and juvenile as some pageant.

While some of her classmates would be heading to someone's house party after their senior prom, Tuki had used her credit card to reserve a room for her and Fabian at the exclusive Ritz-Carlton Hotel on Peachtree Street. Everything was going to be set up perfectly for the young couple. At her request, warm scented candles would be lit, the champagne was going to be on ice, and the rose petals were going to spread all over the king-sized bed. Tuki was probably more excited about the presentation than she was the actual process. But she had to make sure that things went off with a bang; after all, it was her first time having sex and she had a reputation to uphold.

So that night, after the prom was over, Tuki and Fabian hopped in their rented Bentley Phantom and headed to the Ritz. She made sure that she got Fabian all hot and bothered before they arrived at their destination. The moment they walked into the room, Fabian's love came down. He took her into his arms and kissed her. Then using his expert hands, he went under her prom dress and rubbed her clitoris until she had a mind-blowing orgasm before they even made it to the bed.

Tuki took off her $500 prom dress and threw it to the side. Fabian practically ripped off his rented tuxedo and climbed on top of Tuki. She felt his manhood growing and was shocked at the size of it. But she grabbed on to it anyway and rubbed it on her vagina, just like the women did in the porno movies she secretly watched from time to time. In the meantime, Fabian was in awe, amazed at the way Tuki was taking charge of their special moment. She slid his underwear off then opened her legs for him to enter.

"Put it in," she ordered.

And Fabian did just that. Tuki's eyes widened, unprepared for the pain of it all. He took his time with her, though, while making sure that she felt every inch of his manhood. Once he was inside of her, Fabian made love to Tuki. He must have cum at least three times and her orgasms were plentiful, as well. Fabian even licked her down there and to Tuki that licking was one of the best feelings in the world.

After the night was over, Tuki and Fabian went home, with wonderful memories of their prom night experience. They had sex a few more times after graduation and eventually, they went their separate ways. Fabian was accepted to Stanford University and Tuki was to attend Spelman University, right there in Atlanta. They remained good friends but never had any more sexual contact again.

It wasn't until Tuki's freshman year at Spelman that she had her first experience with a woman.

Tuki remembered seeing her exit the school library. She was an attractive woman, too; her beautiful golden-colored locks were piled on the top of her head like a crown. And she walked with her head up high, as if she was royalty. But she wasn't a student. Her name was Cassidy Sterling, a professor of sociology at Spelman. She was a well-known feminist and a strong advocate for women's rights. And she was off-limits.

"I am a queen," Professor Sterling would always say to her students. "And, ladies, we should all think of ourselves as such."

Professor Sterling was much older than the eighteen-year-old Tuki, thirty-two years old to be exact. It was rumored that she was a raging bisexual who had a strong appetite for men and women who were much younger than her. At first, this was just a rumor; Professor Sterling had managed to keep her personal life very low-key. That was, until she met Tuki.

Tuki, who was naïve to the bisexual rumors, was fascinated with the professor. She would secretly stalk the woman; she even changed her major from psychology to sociology just to see her. Her father wasn't too happy about that but Tuki didn't care. She was determined to be near the object of her desire.

One day, Tuki finally got the nerve to approach the professor after class. She waited until the other students filed out of the classroom to speak to the woman.

"Um, Professor Sterling?" Tuki said, as she watched the woman go through a stack of paperwork.

The professor looked up and smiled at her. "Oh, hello, sweetie," she said, in a singsong voice that sounded like music to Tuki's ears.

"Um," Tuki began, with some slight hesitation in her voice. "I'm so sorry to bother you but I was just wondering if you can go over something that we talked about in class today. I needed a little more information about the human relations stuff."

Professor Sterling pulled up a chair near her desk for Tuki. "Sure, sweetie. Have a seat. What do you want to know?"

"I wanted to know more about the homosexual community. Why is it there so much hatred against gay men and us gay women? I understand that everyone has their preferences but what about our, I mean, their rights?"

The professor cleared her throat and nervously shifted in her seat. "Tuki, I want to try to understand what you're asking here so that I can give you some clarification on this particular topic. But before we get started, I have to ask you something. Are you trying to tell me that you're gay?"

Tuki looked down. "Yes, I think I am. Um, I mean, at least, I feel that I am. But I have no attraction to men, just women."

Professor Sterling gazed into Tuki's eyes. "Okay. And you also know that we did not discuss that in class today. You do know that, right?"

Tuki smirked. "Yeah, I know. Can I be totally honest with you, Professor?"

"Shoot."

"I know this might be a little inappropriate but I have dreams about you. I mean, I think that you're so beautiful. Your skin, your eyes, your locks . . . I just can't get images of you out of my head. And I'm not sure that you are comfortable with what I'm saying right now but I just had to get it off my chest." Tuki stood up to leave. "Okay, that's all. You have a nice day."

As Tuki walked to the door, Professor Sterling called out her name. "Wait a minute, Tuki," she said. "Lock that door and come back here."

Tuki did as she was told. Professor Sterling got up from her seat and walked over to her. She placed a soft kiss on Tuki's lips. They began kissing each other, right in the middle of the large classroom. It didn't take long before the Professor had Tuki against the wall of the classroom with her face nestled between her legs. And that gratifying sexual experience was what solidified Tuki as a certified lesbian.

After that first round, the professor and Tuki kept their forbidden affair under wraps. They would meet up with each other after classes and off campus at the professor's one-bedroom apartment. It was there that the professor educated Tuki on how to explore the vagina and give her partner mind-blowing orgasms with her tongue. Not only was Tuki a quick learner, she was a dedicated student/perfectionist who had mastered her oral sex. She sucked and licked on the professor's delicious pussy until she got it right.

Then almost two years later, the façade that Professor Sterling had put on for the Spelman staff, students, and the lovelorn Tuki was beginning to unravel. She wasn't a full-fledged lesbian after all; she was a certified freak. She had a penchant for helping young women like Tuki come out of the closet. And she also had a thing for frat boys, preferably members of the Kappa Alpha Psi and Omega Psi Phi fraternities.

While Professor Sterling had Tuki believing that they were in an exclusive relationship, she was secretly having sexual trysts with a couple of Morehouse Kappas and Q Dogs.

When Tuki found out about these alleged trysts from a reliable source, she was devastated by this news. They had been seeing each other throughout her freshman and sophomore years without anyone suspecting a thing. Yet the news of Professor Sterling's activities was running rampant all over the Spelman campus. When Tuki confronted her about the rumors, not only did Professor Sterling admit that they were true, she tried to coerce Tuki into having a ménage à trois with one of her Morehouse male suitors.

Heartbroken, Tuki threatened to expose their forbidden affair to the upper echelon at Spelman. It wasn't too long after that threat that Professor Sterling resigned her position. But that wasn't the end of her. A few months later, some students talked about the beautiful wedding that Professor Sterling had and how handsome her husband was.

From that moment on, Tuki swore off bisexual women.

Throughout the years, Tuki had her share of lovers. But the scandalous relationship with Professor Sterling left her with a hole in her heart. Almost ten years later, she was still unable to trust or even get too close to anyone. And because of her trust issues, she was known in Atlanta's gay circles for being very promiscuous. She was what they called an "aggressive fem" with her preference being lipstick lesbians and soft studs. Then just as Tuki thought that she was going to be a playgirl forever, Milan came into her life. After meeting her, Tuki decided that it was time for her to settle down with one woman.

Tuki met Milan through mutual acquaintances, back in 2011, during a GLAAD event during Gay Pride Weekend in Atlanta. They started up a casual conversation with each other, immediately hitting it off. Milan told Tuki that she was a marketing assistant for Universal Records and that she was down there for a BET conference. Needless to say, Tuki was very impressed with Milan. Not only was she very beautiful, she also had that New York City swag that Tuki adored. It was definitely love at first sight for the socialite.

Tuki told her that she loved the way that New Yorkers talked. She used to imitate them by using her hands and speak with a phony Northern accent. Milan thought that she was hilarious and was complemented by her.

They talked about Tuki's life as a socialite and Milan let her know that she appreciated her beauty. They realized they were both in the life and Tuki suggested they exchange information.

That was over a year ago. Since then, Milan had made several trips to Atlanta. She was usually in town for business but she always found a way to fit Tuki into her busy schedule. As for Tuki, there was never enough time for them to spend with each other because she was just as busy with her own commitments.

For the last couple of months, she found herself questioning their long-distance affair. Tuki didn't complain with their arrangement at first but she felt that it was time to get to the bottom of things. She had to find out if Milan wanted to take things to the next level with her. In other words, Tuki was ready to commit.

Tired of stressing over Milan's unanswered phone calls, she grabbed her Apple laptop off her desk and logged in. From there, she went straight to the Delta

Airlines Web site to make reservations to fly first class into John F. Kennedy International Airport that Sunday afternoon. A few months back, Tuki had gotten hold of Milan's Brooklyn address from a check that the woman wrote for one of her charities. So with that bit of info, she knew that her impromptu visit to New York was not going to be in vain.

After putting in her credit card information, Tuki pressed one last button. A sinister smile came over her face once she received the confirmation number for her plane reservations.

"This bitch is gonna learn not to play with Tuki Charles," she whispered to herself. "I always get what the fuck I want. New York City, here I come!"

Tuki slammed the laptop closed and went to pack her things for her afternoon trip to the city. She couldn't wait to see the expression on Milan's face when she appeared on her doorstep.

Milan and Sean drunkenly stumbled into their Bedford-Stuyvesant home a little after two in the morning. Rasheed's baby shower had ended with a few of the guests taking the celebration to a local lounge bar for some more dancing and drinks. As the tipsy Milan fell up the stairs, Sean was right on her heels to help her up. When they finally made it to their bedroom, they practically tore off their clothing and engaged in some passionate sex.

An hour later, Sean was in a deep sleep and snoring loudly. Milan was unable to sleep so she quietly tiptoed out of the bedroom and downstairs to the family room. Once she was down there, she took out her cell phone to listen to her new voice messages. She had noticed that Tuki left an urgent voice mail for her and she wanted to hear it.

"Hey, Milan," Tuki said, in a solemn voice. "I'm, like, trying to call you and you're, like, not answering my phone calls."

The next few sentences weren't so subtle. "I don't know what to think, Milan, I mean, you always answer my calls. Are you fucking with someone else? Do you love me? Tell me the truth, Milan! If you don't love me, don't string me along!"

Milan began chewing on her bottom lip. She always did that when she was extremely nervous. And from the sound of Tuki's voice mails she had every right to be. Milan covered her face with her hands. She liked Tuki but she knew that she wasn't in love with her. Now the woman was sounding as if she was about to start acting real crazy. *What have I done?*

Not knowing what else to do, Milan immediately dialed her friend Bam's number.

"It is two in the damn morning!" Bam yelled, in a voice that was groggy from sleep. "Who is this and what do you want from my life?"

"Bam?" she whispered into the phone. "It's me!"

He yawned loudly in her ear. "Who in the hell? Girl, do you know what time it is?" he replied. "Folks in the South go to bed early, child!"

"Bam, Bam, please, I'm so sorry for calling this late but I really needed to talk to you!"

Milan could hear him groan. "Okay, girl, but make it quick! Samson is sleeping and I don't want to wake him up," he said, referring to his live-in boyfriend.

"This bitch, Tuki, done called me like a hundred and one times tonight! She left me a message or two on my voice mail, cussing me out and talking about do I really love her and if I don't not to string her along! What the fuck is wrong with that chick?"

"Oh, Lord have mercy! Sounds like somebody done got bit by the love bug, bayyybeeee!" Bam exclaimed. "And it sounds like you need to tell Missy Poo the truth, bestie."

"I can't do that!" she announced, looking back at the steps. She didn't want to talk too loudly so she took her voice down a few decibels. "I can't do that, Bam. I mean, I really, really like Tuki and everything. And shit, that long money of hers is enticing. She's young, gorgeous, and so my type. I don't want to lose that."

Bam sighed. "Well then, you need to tell your husband that you're bisexual."

Milan was appalled at the mere suggestion of revealing her down low lifestyle to Sean. "Hell no! That's out of the damn question. That man loves me and when he met me, he assumed that I was this . . . this virtuous woman."

Bam began laughing hysterically. "Lord knows, that poor man doesn't know his ass from his elbow if he thought that, hunty! You are serving up Janet Jacme realness!" Bam said, comparing Milan to the notorious porn star.

Milan was just too wrapped up in the Tuki issue to laugh at Bam's teasing. "Listen, Bam, I'm gonna need for you to try to talk to Tuki for me. Find out where the bitch's head is at. Make up some lie as to why I didn't answer her phone calls. You have to help me, Bam."

Bam sucked his teeth. "All right, all right!" he replied. "I will holler at her in the morning and give her a talking to. But if she comes for me, no tea, no shade, I will read her for filth, is that understood?"

Milan clapped her hands. "You're such a great friend! I love you so much, Bammy Poo!"

"And I love you, too, boo. Now get you some rest and don't you worry! Little Miss Shady Tuki will be just fine."

Milan hung up the phone and leaned back on the couch. After taking another peek at the staircase, she pulled some coke out of her robe pocket and took a sniff. Then she sat there in one spot, waiting for the drug to take effect. It didn't take long for Milan to feel the high. Pretty soon, she felt like she was sitting on a cloud, twenty-something thousand miles in the air. The coke helped Milan to stop worrying about the Tuki situation.

Milan grabbed Sean's iPod from the center table, put his Dr. Dre Beats headphones on, and began listening to music. She fell fast asleep on the family room's sofa with the headphones on her ears.

Chapter 16

That Sunday afternoon turned out to be a clear, sunny day. It was almost the end of October and the sixty degree weather was unusual for that time of the year. As people walked up and down Halsey Street, going to or leaving their resident churches, Sean and Milan were inside of their home, hanging out in their kitchen. They had just enjoyed a hearty breakfast but were sitting at the kitchen table in complete silence. The unusually glum Milan sipped on a cup of her favorite coffee and browsed the Internet on her iPad while Sean read Sunday's *Daily News*.

"So who was the bitch at the baby shower, Sean?" Milan asked, out of the blue.

Sean put down the paper and looked at his wife. "What bitch are you talking about?"

"What's her name? I think you said that her name was, um, Brandi! Yeah, that's the bitch's name. Brandi," she said. "Who was that, Sean?"

Sean frowned at her. "I don't know! I met her the same time you did!" he lied.

Milan walked over to the table, pulled out the chair and sat down in front of Sean. "You really think that I'm stupid, huh? I don't give a hell what you're telling me right now; you and that woman's body language didn't say that y'all just met. It said that y'all know each other, and know each other very well! Meanwhile, I know you, very well! You cannot tell me that you and that bitch ain't never mess around with one another before!"

Sean gave Milan the evil eye. “Look, you really don’t know me that well if you think that I have or had something with that Brandi chick. You saw who she was there with! And you saw her leaving with someone else, too! You saw that shit with your own two eyes!”

Milan took another sip of her coffee and stared at Sean. He continued to read the paper, ignoring her evil glare.

“I’m gonna have to watch your sneaky ass,” she announced, pointing at him. “You and your friends are some real sneaky motherfuckers.”

Sean threw the paper on the table and stood up. “I don’t have to listen to this bullshit!” He went to grab a leather jacket from the coat closet. “I’ll see you later, Milan.”

As soon as the front door slammed, Milan ran to the window. Once she saw Sean’s truck pull off, she reached into her robe pocket. She dialed Bam’s phone number.

“So what’s up, Bam?” she asked, as soon as he answered the call. “Did you speak to Tuki?”

“I was just about to holler at you, honey!” Bam replied anxiously. “You had better pack your bags and go into a witness protection program, child!”

Milan frowned. “What the hell do you mean by that?”

“Tuki is in New York, as we speak! I called her about an hour ago and she told that she just landed at JFK. She said that she was in a cab and on the way to your house in Brooklyn!”

Milan jumped up and down. “What?” she screamed.

“You heard me!”

Suddenly, her doorbell rang.

“Oh. My. God,” Milan whispered into the phone.

“What happened?” the curious Bam asked.

Milan looked out of the front window. There was Tuki, in all of her glory, standing on the stoop of her brownstone.

"Bam, she's here! What am I going to do?" Milan whispered.

"Is Sean home?" Bam asked. "Because if he is, chiiiild . . ."

"No! Sean isn't here! Me and him just had an argument and he walked out!"

"Oh, Lord! He's not there right now; that's a good thing. You don't have to answer the bell but what if the bitch comes back?"

"I don't know," Milan whined.

Bam sighed. "I don't know what to tell you, angel. No shade but Bam done did his part. Now you need to handle your business, Miss Thang, and call me back! I cannot do this with you and Miss Shady Pants right now!"

Milan disconnected the call. Then she slowly walked to the front door and opened it. As soon as she did, Tuki ran straight into her arms and began tongue kissing her on the mouth.

"Oh, baby, I missed you so much!" Tuki exclaimed, as she ran her hands all over Milan's body. "I missed my baby!"

Milan didn't respond; she was too afraid to say one word. She was just happy that Sean had left minutes before Tuki rang that doorbell. But he was going to eventually have to come back home and when he did . . .

Tuki walked right into the foyer area of the home. "Oh, my, this is so beautiful! I love brownstones! It's so New York!"

Milan tried to smile. "Yeah, thanks, Tuki," she replied. "What are you doing here? Why didn't you tell me that you were coming to New York?"

Tuki put down her oversized Louis Vuitton duffel bag on the floor. "I wanted it to be a surprise, baby! Don't I always tell you how much I miss you?" she said, wrapping her arms around Milan's small waist.

"But you never called to say that you were coming to New York, Tuki. You just popped up at my house and I live in another state, another city. You don't think that that's a little crazy?"

Tuki let go of Milan. "Are you saying that me being here is a problem?"

"Yes! It's a problem, Tuki!"

Tuki rolled her eyes at Milan and began walking around the house. She walked into the living room to inspect the pictures that were hanging on the wall and on the mantel of the fireplace. When she saw Sean and Milan's wedding picture, she almost gagged.

"What in the fuck, who in the fuck is that in that picture?" she screamed, pointing at the picture.

Milan took a deep breath. "That's my . . . that's my husband," she whispered.

Tuki walked up to Milan and pushed her to the floor. "Bitch, you're fucking married?"

Milan tried to get up from the floor. "Yes, I'm married, Tuki, but I wanted to tell you—"

Tuki screamed like a madwoman and began punching on Milan. She wrapped her hand in Milan's hair weave and tried dragging her across the hardwood floors.

"You bitch! I should kill your ass!" Tuki yelled, as Milan begged for her to let go of her hair. "Do you realize who you're messing with?" she asked, with the vice grip on Milan's weave.

Milan felt the braid from her sewn-in weave being lifted from her head and she tried hard to pry Tuki's hands off her hair without success. Instead, she got hit in the face with a few right hooks.

"I'm not up for a bitch playing me," Tuki said, through clenched teeth. "You and that Professor Sterling bitch."

Milan was in too much pain to make sense of what Tuki was saying or who she was talking about.

Tuki kicked her in the face with her Ugg boots. Milan's head slammed against the wall, causing her wince in pain. She spit blood from her mouth and onto the floor, as the love-crazed Tuki stood over her.

"Why did you lie to me, Milan?" she asked, with tears in her eyes.

Milan looked up at Tuki, who had a sinister look on her lovely face. She didn't have the energy to fight back. "I didn't want to tell you that I was married because I like you."

Tuki stomped her foot and huffed. "Oh, you like me, huh? That sounds like you're talking to one of your friends!" She walked back and forth for a few seconds. Tuki pointed to her heart. "You don't play with this right here! You don't do that, Milan! As a matter of fact, I'm going to need you to pack your shit and come back to my hotel room with me."

Milan was still holding her swollen face. "Come with you to your hotel room?"

"I want you to stay there with me until I leave for Atlanta on Wednesday."

Milan wiped some of the blood from her mouth. "What the hell am I supposed to tell my husband?"

Tuki bent down and grabbed Milan by the face. "I don't care what you tell that bastard! As a matter of fact, why don't you tell him the same got damn lies that you've been telling me?" She mushed Milan, making her fall back on the floor. "Get upstairs, pack your shit and let's go!"

Milan attempted to stand up and Tuki gave her a hand, by grabbing her by the collar of her robe. "And if you think about calling any cops or getting funny on me, not only will I tell your husband about us but I will have your entire life ruined. Your career, your marriage, and your fucking reputation will be shot to shit!"

The nervous Milan made her way up the stairs with Tuki following closely behind her. Tuki watched as Milan reluctantly packed a bag of clothing, cleaned herself up, and got dressed for the day. By the time they left the house together, Tuki had softened up a little.

"You know why I don't fuck with y'all bisexual bitches? It's because y'all bitches are all over the place, playing for both teams and leaving a whole lot of angry, bitter lovers behind. But for you, I will make an exception this time because I'm in love with you. And you're so lucky that you only caught that beat down, boo. 'Cause if I would've just wrapped my hands around your got damn neck and squeezed," Tuki said, grabbing Milan by the neck. "Your ass would have been dead!"

At this point, Milan was deathly afraid of what the seemingly unstable Tuki might do. She wiped the remnants of tears from her cheeks and walked out of the front door of her house, locking the door behind her. As she marched down the front steps, she realized that her lies were unraveling before her eyes.

Milan was a cocaine addict and had been since she was in college. She was bisexual but that wasn't the extent of it. She used to sell her body for money to well-to-do white businessmen. Milan fell in love with the material items that was gifted to her and she used the cash from her extracurricular activities to fund her lifestyle. Even her career wasn't off-limits. Thanks to one of her well-connected clients, she was able to screw her way into the Universal Music Group, as well.

Now Tuki was threatening to expose her for who she really was. Milan had to think of a way to get herself out of the mess.

They hopped into Milan's car and pulled off. As they sat at the corner of Halsey Street, waiting for the red light to turn green, Tuki grabbed her hand.

"Do you love me?" Tuki asked, with a serious look on her face.

Milan looked at the gorgeous woman sitting in the passenger seat of her Mercedes-Benz. What else was she going to say but yes?

"Yes, I do, Tuki. And I'm so sorry for lying to you," Milan replied, hating herself for getting caught up with the lovesick lesbian.

Tuki smiled. She leaned over and kissed Milan's bruised cheek. "That's what I wanted to hear, babe. I love you too."

Sean sat in front of Brandi's apartment building and contemplating ringing her doorbell. On the way to her house, he had tried calling her phone a few times but she just wouldn't answer him. Sean made another attempt at calling her. When he finally heard Brandi's voice on the other end, he did everything to keep from smiling. It felt good to know that she wasn't done with him, as of yet.

"What's up with you, Brandi?" Sean asked, getting straight to the point. "What the hell was that stunt you tried to pull last night? And who was that dude you left with?"

Brandi instantly got on the defensive. "I don't owe you any explanation, Sean. You're a married man so it's no need for you to worry about what stunts I'm pulling and who I left with!"

Sean chuckled at her sarcasm. He had expected her to say that to him. "Are you crazy? You do owe me an explanation! You're fucking with one of my homeboys!"

"And if I am, what are you gonna do about it? Don't you think that you need to be worrying about who your wife is screwing and not who's screwing me?"

"You know what?" Sean paused for a moment. He got out of his parked truck and locked the door. "Buzz the door. I'm coming upstairs to talk to you, face to face."

"Go home, Sean!" Then she hung up on him.

Sean shook his head. He was determined to get upstairs so that he could straighten things out with Brandi. He was also anticipating having some makeup sex with her after he smoothed everything over.

Instead of ringing her intercom, Sean waited downstairs for a few moments. When someone walked out of the door, he walked right into the building. In less than five minutes after getting hung up on, he was standing outside of Brandi's apartment and ringing her doorbell like crazy.

An annoyed Brandi swung the door open, with a visibly irritated look on her face. She stepped into the hallway and quickly closed the door behind her. "What do you want, Sean? Didn't I tell your ass to go home?"

"Let me come inside the house, Brandi. We ain't gonna do this in the hallway right now!" Sean tried pushing her to the side and put his hand on the doorknob but Brandi slapped his hand away.

"We're going to do this wherever I want us to do it!" she replied, pushing him back. "I'm tired of being nice to you, man. I'm so tired of men thinking that they can have their cake and eat it, too!"

Sean shook his head at her. "Wait a minute. Weren't you the one who mysteriously appeared on my doorstep? Oh, you don't remember that, do you? You didn't seem to care about me having my cake then, right? You wanted what you wanted and you got it! Now do you think that I'm gonna stand by and watch you fuck with one of my friends? Hell no! I want you to call that nigga, Kane, right now and tell him that it's over!"

The defiant Brandi crossed her arms. "You get a fucking divorce and then I'll tell Kane that it's over between me and him!"

Sean began backing away from her. "A'ight, cool! I see how you're getting down. Don't tell Kane nothing. *I'm* gonna tell him that it's over between y'all two! I'll talk to you later, Brandi."

Sean began walking toward the elevator but Brandi grabbed his jacket. "Wait, Sean."

He pulled away from her grasp. "What?"

She rolled her eyes in her head. "You don't have to tell Kane anything," she said.

Sean stood there, staring at Brandi. "Oh, I don't, huh?"

"Come here."

Sean walked back to Brandi and she gave him an intimate kiss. She got on her squatted down, undid his zipper and pulled his dick out of his pants. Then she started giving him head on the spot, right in the center of the hallway. He fell back against the wall, as she took every inch of him in her mouth. Sean felt the head of his hard dick rubbing against the back of her throat.

"Damn, girl," he whispered, as he held on to her head. He watched as she went up and down the shaft of his penis.

Sean did everything in his power to muffle the loud moans that he was dying to release. Brandi was a force to be reckoned with when it came to giving oral sex.

Brandi carried on with the act for approximately five minutes before Sean felt himself cumming. He ended up exploding in her mouth and she gulped all of his semen down like a professional. Brandi stood up and wiped the remaining jisms from her mouth. He stood there, staring at her in awe. She gave him a kiss on the cheek.

"There. Do you feel better now?" she asked, with a smug look on her face.

Sean sighed. "Hell, yeah! Who wouldn't feel better after that shit?" He fixed his clothing and kissed her on the lips. "Please don't forget about me, Brandi. You know that a brother need you in his life."

Brandi shook her finger at him. "You and bunch of other men. All y'all want is sex."

Sean sucked his teeth. "Look, I don't give a shit about other guys. You know what it is with us. Do what you want but I'm gonna always get some of that. That pussy belongs to me."

"Please, Negro," Brandi said, with a laugh. "You don't own shit over here."

"Keep thinking that. Like I said, I ain't going nowhere and neither are you. Later."

Brandi didn't respond or object to what Sean was saying. When he walked toward the elevator, she stepped back into her apartment and locked the door behind her.

Chapter 17

When Brandi stepped back inside of her apartment, she made a quick beeline for her bedroom. She opened the door and tiptoed around her bed, careful not to awaken the sleeping Kane.

Brandi wanted to burst out laughing at herself for being such a slut. There she was in the hallway, sucking Sean off, while Kane lay up in her bed. And Kane had made his way into her bed, even after getting into an altercation because of her. It was crazy what men would do for that three-ounce piece of flesh between a woman's legs.

And Dollar was such a sweetheart in all of this. He fought for her honor and continued to hang on as Brandi strung him along. She found herself liking him a lot but she just wasn't ready for him. She had a lot of loose ends to tie up before getting with a man like Dollar.

"I'm so sorry about what happened back there, Dollar," Brandi said after he picked her up from the shower. "I didn't know that things were going to get out of control."

Dollar smiled. "Apology accepted. But what's going on with you, Brandi?" Dollar asked. "You came too long a way to be involved with some messy dude like that. That shit back there only proves that you need to get with a dude like me, a grown-ass man who can take care of you."

Brandi smiled too. "I know, Dollar but I just got so much going on right now—"

Dollar cut her off. "Listen, Bee, I've been feeling you for mad years and I'm gonna be real; I always wanted to get at you. And I still feel that way. I ain't trying to rush you into nothing 'cause we just got back in contact with each other. But I hope you know that I will put a bullet in a motherfucker for you, trust me! So tread lightly with these lame-ass niggas you're fucking with."

I hope you know that I will put a bullet in a motherfucker for you, trust me! Brandi remembered taking a deep breath when Dollar said those words to her.

They pulled up in front of Kane's house. Before Brandi got out of the car, she wrapped her arms around Dollar's neck and hugged him tightly. He hugged her back when suddenly, they began kissing each other. Dollar's kisses were so calming, so sensual.

Brandi pulled back to take a good look at Dollar. She wiped her lip gloss from his face. "I have to go, Dollar," she said, with a hint of sadness in her voice. "I need to get home and get some rest. I will call you tomorrow though. Thanks for everything, baby."

Dollar unlocked the door for her and Brandi walked over to her vehicle, started it up, and pulled off. When they got to the corner of Kane's block, she went one way and Dollar went the other.

An hour later, Kane called Brandi's phone. She answered the call immediately and listened to him berate her like he was her man. But it was all good. She didn't care what he thought or said. He was the go-between, the guy who filled the empty space while she figured out what she was going to do with Sean and Dollar. It was too bad Kane didn't know that.

In the wee hours of the morning, Brandi got another call from Kane. This time, he was pleading with her to let him upstairs. He sounded a little drunk and very pathetic. Brandi found some compassion for the sap so she relented. Once he got inside of her apartment, Kane gave her some Hennessy dick that was out of this world.

Their late-night rendezvous ended with Kane lying in her bed, taking cat naps and waking up to her wet coochie all over his face. He sucked and licked on Brandi's vagina until her body started quivering. And of course, she pleasured him too. Kane fucked Brandi's mouth and eventually unloaded his semen down her throat. Just like she had done with Sean, she swallowed every bit of his babies.

Juggling the men in her life was becoming quite complicated for Brandi. But it felt damn good to be wanted, to be desired by three different men, with different personalities, from different walks of life. Kane was the wild card, who was spontaneous and a very passionate lover. Sean was the married man, an old love who Brandi wanted to keep close to her heart. And then there was Dollar, someone from her past, who definitely loved her more than she loved him.

Brandi's love life had gone from being super dull and unadventurous to a rollercoaster ride that she didn't want to get off of. Eventually the ride would have to end. And she could end up with one of the men or maybe none at all.

Not too long after Brandi walked into the kitchen to prepare Sunday dinner, she heard the bathroom door shut. A few seconds later, Kane emerged from the bathroom in his boxer briefs and walked up behind Brandi. He wrapped his arms around her, as she stood at the kitchen counter.

"Good morning, sunshine," he said. "Or should I say good afternoon?"

Brandi smiled. "You can say both. Good morning, good afternoon, sweetness."

Kane sat at the kitchen table and watched as Brandi sliced and diced some yellow onions. "What's on your agenda for the day?"

She shrugged her shoulders. "I don't know. What's on yours?"

"You."

Brandi laughed. "You're crazy."

"So what are we doing here, Brandi? I mean, look at what happened last night. You got me getting into fights with other dudes over you and all that."

"Yeah? And you had me come with you to a shower where my ex-flame and his wife are guests. What was up with that?" she asked, with a suspicious look on her face.

Kane shrugged his shoulders. "I didn't even know that you knew Sean, let alone slept with him before. I had no idea. But fuck him! What's up with me and you?"

Brandi walked over and kissed Kane. She gave him a nice kiss with tongue and everything.

"That was nice," Kane said. "Give me another one of those."

As Brandi kissed him again, she thought about how dirty she was. She hadn't bothered to rinse her mouth out after sucking Sean off and swallowing his cum. *If only he knew.*

The very pregnant Asia wobbled down the stairs of her home to open the door for her twin sister, India. The inquisitive India stepped inside and gave her sister a big kiss on the cheek while rubbing on her protruding belly.

"I can't wait for my niece to make her grand entrance into the world!" India said, as she walked into the living room. "I never thought that you were going to be the first one to get pregnant and ahem, keep it!"

Asia laughed and plopped down in her comfy armchair. "Yeah, everybody thought that you were gonna be the one with mad kids. You was always hot in yo' ass!"

India laughed then shook her head in disbelief. "Oh, my God, Asia! I cannot believe what happened at your shower last night! Kane's new bitch came there and started all that shit, got him into a fight with that dude and all that! He should have put his paws on that trick!"

Asia rolled her eyes at her sister. "After thinking about it, India, it really wasn't the woman's fault."

India frowned. "What you mean, it wasn't her fault? From the minute she walked through that door, I knew that she was nothing but trouble! Bitch think she cute, too."

Asia stopped India from going any further. "Will you listen, girl? I'm gonna tell you something and you better not say a word to nobody! I got the 411 on why homegirl was leaving the shower so early."

India jumped up and began doing the twerk dance. "Ooooh, girl, do tell!"

Asia laughed at her sister's silly antics but got real serious in a matter of seconds. "I'm gonna tell you this, India, and like I said, you better not say shit to Kane or nobody else. Rasheed would kill me!"

India waved her off and sat back down on the couch. "I ain't telling nobody nothing! Just spill the tea already!"

"Anyway," Asia began, flinging her hair over her shoulders. "According to Rasheed, Brandi and Sean used to mess around with each other a few years back. She apparently didn't know that Kane and Sean were cool with each other. So when she got to the shower, she was shocked to see Sean there. That's because they're still fooling around."

India put up her hand. "Hold up! Ain't Sean married to the little bougie chick? What's her name?"

Asia nodded her head. "Yes! He's married to Milan. And I can understand why she wanted to leave."

India smirked. "Hmmph," she said. "Well, I had to let the bitch know that me and Kane got our thing going, too," she said, simulating some sex moves.

Asia leaned back in the chair. "No, you didn't, India! Why are you always starting something?" she scolded. "You're too old for that messiness!"

India was taken aback by Asia's reaction. "'Cause got dammit, the bitch needed to know about me and Kane's relationship!"

"You and Kane don't have a relationship, India!"

India took off her shoes and put her feet on the wooden center table. "Oh, okay, we might not have a relationship, yet. But I promise you that we will have one real soon!"

Asia waved her sister off. "If I only could live long enough to see that shit." They both laughed. "But that dude Sean is a mess!"

"Yeah, I know all about Sean and his drama. My co-worker Yadira killed herself over him, too. I ain't never doing no crazy shit over a man."

Asia gave India a look. "Oh, really? What about the drama with Lamont and Sierra?" she asked, referring to Rasheed's son's mother and her husband. "I can remember the time when you were smiling all up in that woman's face and fucking her man, Captain Lamont Simmons, behind her back. You do remember that, don't you, India?"

India rubbed on her chin and smiled at the memory. Since then, Asia and Sierra were very cordial to each other. But she still hated India to that day.

After talking with her sister for the next hour and a half, India looked at the time and gathered up her things to leave. "Well, boo, I'm going to go home now and get some rest. Or maybe I'll give old Kane a call to see if we can hook up tonight."

Asia shook her head. "You and Kane would really make a nice couple, if you weren't such a chickenhead!"

India walked to the door with Asia following her. "Kane is the one that's passing up on a good thing, Asia. But it's all good. I'm going to get my man. Just you wait and see!"

Chapter 18

After leaving Brandi's place, Sean headed back home. When he arrived home, he didn't expect to walk into an empty house.

"Milan?" he yelled. "Milan? Are you here?"

He walked upstairs and looked in their bedroom. There were a few of Milan's things scattered on the bed and the hangers in her closet were in disarray. Sean checked the master bathroom and saw that her toothbrush was missing, too. He frowned as he walked back into the bedroom, trying to decipher what was going on.

"Where the hell did she go?" he said aloud. Sean grabbed the house phone and dialed Milan's number. The phone went straight to voice mail. "What the fuck?"

Sean walked downstairs to the family room and headed straight to the bar. He thought about the argument they had earlier that day and poured himself a glass of Jack Daniels.

While sipping on his drink, Sean began wondering if Milan was still upset about the Brandi situation. And he thought about how wrong he was for walking out of the house that morning. He should have at least tried to listen to Milan's gripes, tried to ease her fears and insecurities. But Sean didn't do that. He was only thinking about himself.

After having a few glasses of liquor, the worried Sean was at wits' end over his wife's mysterious absence. It was about eight o'clock p.m. when he called Milan's parents, even reached out to her brother and sister, who were as clueless of her whereabouts as he was. Sean didn't have any of her friends' phone numbers so he couldn't call them at all.

Sean walked back upstairs to their bedroom and started looking in Milan's closet. He hadn't done anything like that before but the search was imperative; he needed some answers.

Milan's large walk-in closet consisted of high-end clothing, designer bags, and a myriad of shoes in different colors and styles. Not knowing exactly what he was looking for, Sean snatched various clothing off the hangers and threw them onto the floor. After coming up with nothing, Sean stood there inspecting the huge mess that he made. Perturbed, he kicked her things to the side and walked out of the closet. Then he stood in the middle of his bedroom, looking as if he was in a daze. But he was contemplating his next move.

Sean's eyes went to the robe that Milan was wearing when he left that morning. He picked it up and put it to his nose. The terry cloth robe still had her scent on it. But while doing that, Sean felt something hard in the pocket.

"What is this?" he said. Sean reached into the pocket and pulled out an empty vial. The vial still had some white residue in it. "Is this what I think it is?"

Sean opened the vial and put some of the contents onto his tongue. The bitter-tasting white stuff was exactly what he thought it was.

The thought of his beautiful wife being addicted to any drug had Sean in a funk. He was failing as a husband and a protector. Sean shook his head as the vial rolled out of his hand and onto the floor.

Tuki marched through the sliding double doors of the Aloft hotel, located in downtown Brooklyn. Milan, who was following closely behind her, took a seat on the white leather sofa in the lobby. Once she was seated, she adjusted her oversized Chanel glasses to hide the bruising on her face.

Tuki stood at the front desk and waited to speak to an attendant. The moment that she turned her back would have been the perfect time for Milan to make her escape. But for some reason, she was too afraid to take that chance. She could just see Tuki going back to her house and telling Sean everything about their secret relationship. Milan figured that she would do her best to pacify Tuki until she left for Atlanta that Wednesday and explain her disappearance to Sean when she went back home.

The front desk attendant greeted Tuki with a smile. "Good afternoon, welcome to the Aloft Brooklyn! How may I help you today?" she asked.

Tuki kept a straight face. She was not in the mood for the woman's cheerful disposition.

"I'm going to need a room. I want a single bed, preferably king-sized," she quickly replied.

The attendant continued to smile at the serious Tuki. "That won't be a problem. Give me a minute to look that up for you." The attendant looked at the computer screen and typed in some information. "Okay, we definitely have a room available for you. How would you be paying today?"

Tuki rumbled through her Hermès Birkin bag to retrieve her wallet. She pulled out her American Express black card and handed it to the wide-eyed attendant.

"Put everything on that," she said.

After securing a room for them, Tuki gestured for Milan to follow her. As soon as they stepped into the elevator, Milan took off her shades and rubbed the side of her face.

Tuki shook her head. "I hope those marks are a reminder of how bad shit can get for you if you ever lie to me again," she said, pointing her fingers in Milan's face. "You're so lucky that I love you, girl."

Milan held back her tears as they got off the floor where their room was located. Tuki slid the card into the reader and the door opened. Milan walked in and sat on the bed, looking worn out from all of the drama.

Tuki put her Louis Vuitton duffel in the corner and the Birkin on the desk. She walked over to the bed and stood over Milan. Milan flinched, deathly afraid of getting hit in her face again.

"Why did you lie to me?" Tuki asked.

Milan sighed. "I . . . I didn't intentionally lie to you, Tuki. I mean, I do care for you and everything. I just kind of omitted my marriage," she stuttered.

Tuki began pacing the hotel room. "I can't believe that you're married. I can't believe that I fell for your type again."

Milan interrupted her. "I don't understand why there's a problem with me being attracted to men and women," she said, with a confused look on her face.

The frustrated Tuki stomped her feet. "Well, it's a fucking problem, Milan! Don't you see what you're doing? You're toying with people's emotions! Does your husband even know that you're attracted to women?" she asked.

Milan shrugged. "No," she whispered.

Tuki threw her hands in the air. "That's exactly what I'm talking about! You bi's inflict so much pain on people with your selfish asses! Choose a freaking side already!"

Milan tried to explain her plight. "But, but you don't understand, Tuki," she said. "I'm so on the fence with this! It's so confusing to live my life like this!" she cried, taking off her shades and throwing them to the side. She began weeping, covering her eyes with her hands.

Tuki sucked her teeth and collapsed in the chair across from Milan. "I ain't trying to hear your sob story, Milan," she said, with an angry look on her face. "What you need to do is tell your husband about us or else I'm gonna tell him. Simple as that."

Milan blew her nose and started yelling at Tuki. "Are you crazy? I can't tell Sean this shit! My got damn family don't know nothing about my lifestyle!"

Tuki let out a sarcastic chuckle. "So help me understand this. You're hiding behind your marriage, huh?"

Milan slapped her forehead with her hand. "No, marriage is not the some . . . some fake-ass marriage, okay? I really love that man, Tuki."

Tuki raised one eyebrow. "Is that right?" She laughed. "Well, how do you think he's gonna feel when he finds out that his beloved wife loves to eat pussy and get fucked with strap-ons?"

The fed up Milan sighed. "What do you want from me, Tuki?"

Tuki walked over to Milan and knelt down in front of her. She took her hands into hers and looked into her eyes. "I want you so bad," she whispered, while rubbing Milan's thighs. "You remind so much of my first love, the first woman I ever fell in love with. And I can't shake that feeling."

Milan clutched her chest. She brushed Tuki's hands from her thighs. Then she ran into the bathroom and locked the door behind her.

Milan sat on the toilet and went into her jeans pocket, once again pulling out her stress reliever. After one sniff, she could feel the cocaine going straight to her brain. She leaned her head back against the tiled bathroom wall, waiting for the coke to take its effect. Suddenly, loud knocks on the door interrupted her high.

"Milan, Milan!" Tuki yelled at her from the other side of the bathroom door. "What the hell are you doing in there?"

Milan ignored the knocking and snorted some more of the cocaine. A few seconds later, she opened the bathroom door with a smile on her face. She grabbed Tuki's face and shoved her tongue down her throat.

"Make love to me," Milan whispered in her ear.

Chapter 19

It was eight o'clock at night when Kane pulled into the driveway of his Canarsie home. He had a great time hanging out at Brandi's house for the better part of the day but it felt so good to finally be at his humble abode. He unlocked the door, disarmed the burglar alarm, and marched up the stairs to his bedroom. There, he stripped down to his boxers and climbed into his bed.

While Kane was lying in the bed and watching television, he began thinking about his life. His exaggerated sense of self-confidence was a front for what was really going on with him. He wanted to love someone and wanted someone to love him back. But it was so hard for him to reveal his true self to women. He had so much to hide.

Just like most people who had trust issues, Kane was in a relationship with a woman when he was a much younger, more volatile man. Gunplay and drugs were his forte, although his father had warned him about the dangers of the streets.

"Son," J.P. would say to him, "you don't want it with these streets. These streets are like a woman's pussy. Just when you think you done fucked it real good, there always one that can fuck it way better than you. And just like some women, these streets don't have no love or loyalty to nobody."

Of course, being the young whippersnapper he was at the time, Kane brushed his father off. He took to the streets anyway and along with Rasheed and the rest of their crew, created a reputation for himself. That reputation only fueled the fire, causing some major beef with rivals wherever he went.

One day, everything that J.P. said about the streets came to fruition. Kane was twenty-two years old when he killed an innocent man. He was involved in a shootout in South Jamaica, Queens, Forty projects, while going to see a girl he was seeing at the time. This resulted in Kane shooting the man, an older gentleman, coming out of one of the buildings.

The thought of his heinous crime brought tears to Kane's eyes. Fortunately for him, the police never found out who killed the man. But that was unfortunate for the victim's family. They had lost a patriarch while Kane lived his waking life, indulging in pleasures that the dead man would never experience. And the guilt wore on him every day.

The woman Kane was involved with at the time was the major player in the tragic story. He found out later on that she was the reason he was getting shot at in the first place. Because Kane had displayed a more mild-tempered, low-key side to the young lady, she assumed he was a "vick." So she set him up to be robbed by a group of her cousins and an ex-boyfriend, which led to the vicious shootout.

After the man was killed, the girl packed up her things and moved out of town. Kane never found out her whereabouts, promising himself that if he ever saw her again, she was going to meet her Maker. As luck would have it, Kane never saw the girl again. But he knew that one day he was going to meet his karma for the death of that innocent man.

And Kane was left with a distorted image of women. His father's cryptic message about the streets and the comparison to a woman was imbedded in his mind. Although he loved the female members of his family very much, being in a genuine relationship with one was somewhat of an enigma for Kane. He didn't think that it was possible for him to ever get close enough to a woman. But Kane knew that if he wanted love, he would have to try a different approach. And it all started with Brandi.

Kane had to admit that the short time he spent with Brandi was very enjoyable. He couldn't remember the last time he spent more than two hours with a woman, let alone spending the night with her. But Brandi was kind of different from the other women he dated. She was mature, goal-oriented, and considerably older than what Kane normally went for. There was something about her "been there, done that" attitude that got his attention. And there was an air of mystery about Brandi that Kane found himself connecting with. He just couldn't figure out what that was.

Kane turned over in his bed and began dozing off. Before he fell into a deep slumber, he went over the chain of events from the previous night. He hadn't blamed Brandi for the altercation with Dollar, even though he wanted to. But Dollar definitely had it coming to him and Kane couldn't wait to get his revenge.

It was around 12:00 a.m. Monday morning when Kane was awakened by a deafening boom. He immediately jumped up out of the bed and ran out of his room to investigate the noise. As soon as he opened the bedroom door, Kane was hit with a massive cloud of thick black smoke.

Kane began coughing nonstop, as the sounds of flames could be heard crackling beneath him. The smoldering heat sent him into a frightened frenzy, causing him to run back into his bedroom and slam the door.

Kane frantically looked around the room for his clothes. He grabbed his cell phone, his car keys, and wallet and put them into his pocket. Then he opened the second-story window and climbed out of it. As he hung on to the windowsill, he looked below him. Some of the flames were shooting out of the first-floor window. Kane closed his eyes and prayed for a safe landing.

"Please, God," he whispered. "Please help me."

Kane closed his eyes and let go of the windowsill. He fell to the ground, landing on the grass near the concrete driveway with a thud.

As Kane lay on the ground, the sound of shattering glass startled him. He tried to stand up but ended up falling back on the ground. While on the ground, Kane quickly crawled to the driver's side of his car and shielded himself from the flying shards of glass and debris.

A few of Kane's neighbors must have called 911 because pretty soon the quiet block was lit up with emergency vehicles.

Suddenly, Kane heard a familiar voice calling out his name. "Kane, Kane!"

It was Mr. Frank, the next door neighbor. He walked over and helped Kane onto their front lawn. His wife, Mrs. Frank, ran inside and came back out of the house with a comforter to wrap around Kane's shoulders.

Kane sat on the Franks' lawn and watched as the firefighters of Engine #257 pulled out the water hoses and began working frantically to put the raging fire out. A small crowd of neighbors had gathered outside the scene. They started asking Kane questions that even he didn't know the answer to. Thankfully, the Franks shooed the nosey neighbors away and insisted that Kane sit inside of their house while the firefighters put out the fire. But he couldn't move. The burning embers coming from his home had him in a zone. He couldn't believe what was happening.

An hour had passed and the fire was finally put out. Mr. Frank walked over to the fire captain and informed him that Kane was the homeowner.

The captain knelt down on the ground to talk to Kane, who was rubbing his injured left ankle. "So this is your house, sir?" he asked.

Kane nodded his head. "Yeah, it's my house, man," he replied, with a look on defeat on his face.

"Can you tell me what happened?"

Kane shook his head. "I was asleep in my bedroom when I heard this . . . this loud explosion. I got up to observe what was going on but when I got to the staircase, all I saw was this cloud of black smoke and flames! So I walked back into my room, threw my clothes on, and jumped out of the second-floor window. I think that I hurt myself from that fall, too," Kane said, cringing from the pain.

"Do you want an ambulance?" the captain asked.

Kane waved him off. "Nah, nah, I can drive myself to the ER."

The captain looked back at Kane's damaged home. The last of the firefighters were walking out of the house with their equipment. He sighed. "Listen, I hate to tell you this, Mr. . . ."

"Porter. The name's Kane Porter."

"Well, Mr. Porter, just to let you know, we found a bottle near the front window and it reeked of gasoline. It seems like this fire was started by someone throwing a Molotov cocktail through that window. Has anyone threatened you recently?"

At the sound of that news, Kane's mind began to wander. *A Molotov cocktail?* For some reason, an image of Dollar's face popped into his head.

"No, no, not that I know of," Kane said.

"Well, Mr. Porter, I think you might need to make a police report about this incident."

Kane watched as the fire marshal walked back to his crew. *Could it have been Dollar? Then again, Dollar doesn't know where I live. Or does he?* He thought about the night of the baby shower. After their scuffle, Kane was sure that Dollar dropped Brandi off to get her car out of his driveway. And based on what Rasheed told him about the hot-tempered Dollar, he wasn't above getting some kind of retribution after their fight.

The Franks helped Kane stand up on his feet. "Thank you, Mrs. Frank, Mr. Frank," Kane said. He gave the wife a hug and shook her husband's hand.

Mr. Frank patted Kane on the shoulder. "It wasn't a problem, son. Are you going to be okay? You know that you can stay with us while you get your house back in order."

Kane smiled at the kindhearted septuagenarian. "Oh, no, Mr. Frank! Thanks so much for the hospitality but I will be just fine."

The Franks waved at Kane and walked back into their house. The crowd of onlookers dispersed and went their way. After briefly talking to Kane about the suspected arson, the firefighters and police officers made their way off the block too. And just like that it was quiet again.

Kane stood outside of his house and stared at the external damage. The downstairs windows were broken or totally blown out and the brick front was untouched. But it didn't take long for Kane to walk away from the home. He didn't have the energy to deal with it at the moment. He hopped into his vehicle and pulled off.

But the normally composed Kane had barely driven off his block before he became overcome with emotion. He pulled over to the side and silently sobbed in the driver's seat of his vehicle. Shortly after getting his feelings in check, Kane made a phone call.

"Hey, Tabitha," Kane said to his sister when she answered the call. "I'm so, so sorry for calling you this late, but, can I stay there for a little while, sis?" He tried to explain what happened to his home when he began sobbing uncontrollably. Tabitha wouldn't let her brother finish the story.

"Kane, Kane!" she said, interrupting his tearful rant. "Don't you worry about a damn thing, baby bro! Everything is going to be okay! You can come right here and stay as long as you want."

"Thank you so much, Tab," Kane said, as he tried to calm himself down. "I love you, sis."

"And I love you too, baby bro. Come on through. I'll be waiting up for you."

Kane disconnected the call and took a deep breath. He turned his car around and began driving toward the Belt Parkway. Between his pounding ankle, his damaged home, and everything else that happened within the last twenty-four hours, Kane knew that being with family was the best antidote.

"Let me step on the gas and hurry to Tab's house," Kane said aloud. "Because I'm ready to kill some fucking body!"

Chapter 20

It was two o'clock Monday morning and the depressed India couldn't bring herself to get off her couch. She felt like she was losing what little sanity she had left. She had been feeling like that ever since Asia announced that she and Rasheed were having a baby. Wiping the lone tear from her face, India asked herself one question: *am I ever going to be happy?*

At one time, happiness for India was Chanel bags and Gucci shoes, but not anymore. She would have traded all of her material things just to have what her twin sister Asia had, which was a relationship with a man who truly loved her.

When am I gonna know what's it feels like to have a relationship? India wished that she knew the answer to that question.

And she had grown tired of being treated like a doormat. She was tired of men taking whatever they could get out of her and walking in and out of her life. She stood by and watched as the men she dealt with settled down or married other women, women who weren't her.

India knew that her looks weren't the problem; she was a strikingly beautiful woman. With her smooth olive-colored skin and thick jet-black hair, she bore an uncanny resemblance to Pocahontas. And her body was definitely well put together. She worked extra hard to keep her toned frame intact, by practically living in the gym.

India sighed, as she thought about her past behaviors. Growing up, she had been pegged the so-called "bad" twin. She was the sister who always found trouble, while the "good" twin, Asia, just followed her lead. India was fine with being a bad girl and adapted that image, in order to hide all of her insecurities. She had plenty of those.

India sat up and looked around the dark room, finally finding the strength to get up. She turned on the lamp and looked at herself in the large mirror. She didn't see pretty. She saw a broken woman, who was ugly on the inside and insanely jealous of her own sister. But aside from all of that, India saw a woman who wanted to have a man love her more than anything in this world.

It was 5:45 a.m the next morning when an exhausted India got out of bed and started getting ready for work. She yawned loudly and stared at the half-empty bottle of Hennessy sitting on her nightstand. The liquor and her excruciating headache were grim reminders of her emotionally taxing night.

A half hour later, India locked the door to her apartment. Just as she was about to walk down the stairs to the lobby, her cell phone rang.

"Who the hell is this?" she said to herself, as she dug in the bottom of her oversized handbag to retrieve the phone. She looked at the unrecognizable number on the caller ID.

"Hello? Who is this?" she asked, with a frown on her face.

The sound of female laughter could be heard on the other end of the phone. "Damn, I figured you probably recognize my got damn number. You don't never use it anyway."

India sucked her teeth. For the life of her, she couldn't recognize the voice, although it sounded very familiar.

"Come on now! Who the hell is this? I ain't got time to be playing with no bitch on the phone when I'm on my way to work!"

"Mmm hmm," the female said. "Same old India! You was always a mean motherfucker!"

When India got to the lobby, she stopped in her tracks. "Wait a got damn minute," she said. "Is this who I think it is?"

"Yes, it is! I don't know why you acting like you don't know your own cousin's voice, girl!"

India walked outside of her building and got into her parked car. Once she was in the driver's seat, she began screaming.

"Oh, shit! Tuki! Old country bumpkin-ass!"

It was her first cousin, Tuki. Born in Brooklyn, Tuki and her family moved down to Decatur, Georgia when she was only three years old. Her father, Rodney, was the twins' uncle and their mother's oldest brother. After hearing Tuki's voice, India felt bad. She really didn't visit her Southern family as often as she liked to.

Tuki laughed again. "Yes, it's Tuki, baby! How you doing, cuzzo?"

India sighed. "Girl, I ain't doing so good," she began. "Let's put it like this, these dudes be acting up and these hoes be letting them!"

"Yes, they do, girl!" Tuki replied with a laugh. "And that's exactly why I only deal with women! All men wanna do is fuck any and everything that got a wet, hairy hole! And they just aren't that attractive with all of their issues and nasty-ass habits. I can't take them!"

Now it was India's turn to laugh. "Tell 'em how you really feel, Tooks! So what have you been up to, girl?"

Tuki huffed. "Well, for one thing, you would never guess where I am right now."

"Where are you?"

"I'm in New York, child!" Tuki replied. India screamed into the phone. "I'm staying at the Aloft hotel, right in downtown Brooklyn."

India's eyes lit up. "For real? Oh, my God, Tuki! You're here? In Brooklyn? Oh, my God! I have to see you! When are you leaving?"

Tuki sighed. "Well, I'm going to be here until Wednesday, maybe a little longer, depending how things turn out here. But I have to get back to Atlanta by the weekend to take care of some business."

"What brought you to New York?"

"Hmmph," Tuki began. "Girl, I had to hop on me a quick flight to New York to come and serve this bitch with some act right. As a matter of fact, she lives right here in Brooklyn."

"Oh, damn!" India exclaimed. "How did y'all meet? How long you been dealing with her?"

"Well, I met this woman last year in Atlanta. She's a marketing executive for Universal Music Group and she's so beautiful. Like, I really love this girl, India. But why it took me to come all the way to New York to find out that this woman was married?"

India got on the entrance ramp to the Belt Parkway. "She's married! Get the hell out of here!" she said.

"Married, cuz!" Tuki continued her story. "I came to her house and when she opened the door, she looked real surprised to see me standing there. But I'm happy as all get-out to see her. So she lets me in and as soon as I walked in the house, there's a big-ass picture of her and got damn husband on their wedding day!"

"What the hell?"

"Exactly!" Tuki paused. "I cannot tell you how hurt I was, cuz! Like I said, I really love this girl. I mean, not only is she gorgeous, she's ambitious, she's everything I want and need in a lover! But this husband shit got me messed up, especially since I thought I had her to myself."

As India listened to Tuki's dilemma, she realized that her and her cousin had similar problems.

Tuki went on to tell her story. "India, I was so mad at this damn girl." India shook her head. "I beat her ass then made her pack herself an overnight bag and come back with me to my hotel for these next couple of days. What made this shit so crazy is that we ended up having ourselves a good old time after that. Sometimes, it takes a good ass whipping to set these hoes straight!"

India chuckled. "You gotta do what you got to do, boo! But what did you tell her? Did you give her some kind of ultimatum?"

"Yes, I did. I told her that if she doesn't tell her husband the truth about us, I'm gonna do it for her. I let her ass leave early this morning to go home and get ready for work. But I told her that she got until tomorrow evening to straighten this mess out."

"That's right, cuz!" India said, cheering her on. "You know how us Charleses do! Anyway, what's up with Uncle Rodney and Auntie?"

"They are fine, boo! And you need to bring your ass down there more often, help me spend some of Daddy's money. The family reunion only comes around every three years and that ain't enough!"

India switched lanes on the parkway. "I know, I know! I would have loved to come down there this past year but with Asia having this baby—"

"Asia's pregnant?" Tuki yelled into the phone. "Oh, hell no! I gots to see her! Did she have a shower yet?"

India felt bad. "Oh, damn, Tuki, the shower was this past Saturday! You missed it. But let's do this, you stay put at the hotel for the rest of the day. I'm gonna come through after work and pick you up and you can stay at my place for as long as you're here in Brooklyn. Before we head to my house, though, we can stop by Asia's crib. She will be so surprised to see you!"

"Oh, yes, I would love that! But I don't want to put you out of the way."

India cut Tuki off. "Girl, stop! You are my family, my first cousin, my blood! You're staying with me!"

"Awww! I love you, India! I swear, I miss you and Asia so much. Can't wait to see y'all!"

India exited off the Belt Parkway and onto the Van Wyck. She looked at the clock in her car. The time was 6:30 a.m. Roll call was at seven o'clock a.m. on the nose. She had less than thirty minutes to get to Rikers Island, take the route bus to her facility, and get into her uniform. She didn't want to be late.

"I'm going to lock your number in, Tuki, and when I get off work, I'm going to call you. By the way, what's your girlfriend's name?"

"Milan. Her name is Milan Daniels. She lives in Bedford-Stuyvesant, on Halsey Street. Do you know where that is?"

Milan? That's Sean's wife! A shocked India swerved her car into the other lane.

Chapter 21

It was six o'clock a.m. Monday morning when Milan crept into the house. After spending the night out, she knew that Sean would be upset with her. She had to come up with something and quick before he started jumping down her throat.

Milan tiptoed into the foyer and slid her overnight bag into the front coat closet. She took her shoes off at the door and then slowly walked up the steps, praying that Sean would not be in that bed when she got up there. But she wasn't that lucky. At the top of the stairs was Sean's shadowy figure. He was standing there, with his arms crossed.

"Where were you, Milan?" he asked, in a voice that was eerily calm. "I was worried about you."

Milan swallowed and looked up at him with her doe eyes. "Well, after our spat, I went . . . went to my girlfriend Ginger's house to clear my head," she lied. "I just needed to . . . to think about some things, about us and the direction that we're going in our marriage."

Sean let her walk past him and into their bedroom. She looked around, sort of half expecting to get a surprise from him, like roses or a gift, as an apology for walking out on her the previous morning. But there weren't any surprises and that was a surefire sign that Sean was pissed the hell off with her.

Sean stood in the doorway of the bedroom. "Ginger's house, huh?" he repeated. "Why didn't you call me?"

Milan went to take her shades off. Then she remembered that her face was bruised. She prayed that the M•A•C foundation she was wearing covered the bruising.

"Because we had an argument, Sean, and I was angry at you! Anyway, are you really going to do this with me right now? I would think that you would have been happy to fucking see me!"

Sean let out a sarcastic chuckle. "Happy to see you? I was about to file a missing persons report on your ass!"

Milan spun around. "A missing persons report? Are you serious?"

Sean walked up to Milan. "Yeah, I'm dead serious! And you got the nerve to walk up in my house, acting like I'm not supposed to be mad at you. Bitch, you musta lost your damn mind!"

Milan cut him off. "Bitch? Who are you calling a bitch?"

"You, bitch!"

Milan reached up and slapped Sean in the face. He threw her on the bed in an attempt to restrain her from hitting him again. The shades that Milan was wearing came off in the process.

"Let me go!" she screamed. "Get the hell off me!"

Sean looked at her face and immediately let her go. "What happened to you?" he asked, with a bewildered look on his face. "Who did that to you?"

Milan sat up. Her hand went to her bruised face. She tried to catch her breath. "What . . . what are you talking about?" she replied.

Sean snatched Milan by the arm and pulled her into the master bathroom. He flicked on the light, forcing her to look in the mirror at herself. "What the hell happened to you, Milan? Who did this to you? I want the truth because I'm ready to kill me somebody!"

Milan looked in the mirror. Although the swelling had gone down, her eye and face was still black and blue.

She thought that the heavy makeup would cover it but it didn't do a great job. Once she realized that she didn't have a story for the bruising, she began to cry.

Sean was unmoved by her tears. "I'm waiting," he said, shaking her by the arm.

Milan turned around to face him. "Sean, I . . . I . . ."

He let go of her. There was a look of disappointment and anger on his face. "I'm listening to you."

Milan walked back to the bed and sat down. "Me and Ginger hung out the other night and I got into a fist fight with someone at the lounge bar we went to and—"

"Come on, Milan! Do you really expect me to believe that? You're too bougie to be fighting in someone's lounge bar! And do you even know how to fight?" he asked with an amused look on his face. "I know that that ain't your style. Now come again."

"It's the truth, Sean! Damn! Why don't you believe me?"

"Okay, so call Ginger right now," he ordered. "Let me ask her!"

Milan hesitated. "Call Ginger? It's too early in the morning for that!"

"No, it's too early in the morning for your lies and your bullshit! Get that phone right the fuck now and call Ginger. I wanna talk to her."

Milan began crying again. "Sean, don't do this to Ginger! She had nothing to do with me leaving you and staying at her place. She was just being a good friend, really, that's all she was doing!"

All of a sudden, Milan's phone began ringing. She cussed under her breath for not remembering to put her phone her on silent before she walked into the house.

Sean stared at her in disbelief. "Aren't you gonna answer the phone?"

Milan took a deep breath. "For what? I'm talking to you!"

Sean grabbed Milan's pocket book and empties the contents out on the bed. Her cell phone fell onto the bed. When she tried to dive for it, Sean snatched it from her grasp. He looked at her caller ID and frowned. Then he answered the phone.

"Who is this?" he asked. The phone clicked off.

Milan began wringing her hands with worry. For her sake, she hoped that Tuki hadn't revealed her number and called. The image of their bodies writhing in the bed with each other for the night had Milan feeling guilty as hell. But what was done was done.

"They're calling you private, huh?" Sean asked, with a smirk on his face. "I guess you done told that nigga you're coming back home to your husband, huh?"

"Sean, it's no . . . no man, I promise you that," Milan pleaded with Sean not realizing that she was being very truthful about that.

Sean walked into her closet and came back with her robe. Milan was confused as to why he had her robe in his hands and what was about to happen. He began digging in the pockets, right in front of her. What he pulled out of the right pocket, Milan was not prepared for. He threw a half-empty vial of coke on the bed.

"What is that?" he asked, pointing at the evidence. "You got this all up in my fucking house. When did you start doing this?"

Milan held her head down. *I can't win for losing!* "I have no words, Sean."

Sean grabbed her face, making her look him in the eye. "Well, you better find some! Call your job 'cause you ain't going nowhere until I hear the truth!"

***

Back at the Aloft hotel, a bored Tuki paced back and forth. She looked out of the window at the dismal view of brick buildings and construction and began thinking about Milan. She smiled, as she thought about how intense their lovemaking was the night before. Tuki couldn't wait to taste her again.

"I'm so scared," Milan whispered to Tuki, while lying in her arms. "My family, my friends, and my husband don't know this side of me, Tuki. I don't even know how to tell them that I'm seeing a woman."

Tuki kissed Milan on her forehead. "Don't worry about none of that, babe. I got you. We will tell your people together, is that what you want?" she asked.

Milan kissed her on the lips. "No, no, baby, I want to do it on my own. I have to do this alone."

Tuki sighed. "Okay, baby. But just remember, if you need me, I'm there for you."

They ended that conversation with a kiss and some mind-blowing sex. Tuki gushed as she kept replaying their candid talks in her head.

Missing Milan, Tuki picked up the phone and dialed her number. She closed her eyes, waiting to hear the sweet sound of her girlfriend's voice on the other end. Unfortunately, when she called, the voice that answered the phone wasn't what she had expected to hear.

"Hello? Hello?" boomed the male baritone on the other line. "Who is this?"

Tuki looked at the phone and held on for a few seconds before the line went dead. She walked over to the desk and pushed the lamp to the floor, watching it break into a thousand pieces.

"Her husband is answering her phone now?" Tuki said, through clenched teeth. "I fucking hate him!"

Tuki took a seat and managed to calm herself down. She retrieved her phone and looked through her contacts, looking for anyone that she could talk to, in order to take her mind off her present situation. She smiled when she came across the number of India, her first cousin and her father's niece. Tuki figured it was right time to call India. They hadn't spoken to each other in months.

Naturally, India was happy to hear from Tuki and that made her feel a lot better. But their conversation took a turn for the worse when she learned that her cousin knew Milan very well.

"Tuki, I know Milan and her husband, Sean," India said.

Tuki stood up. "Are you freaking serious?"

"Yes. I'm serious! Me and her never hung out or anything but we crossed each other's paths a few times. She's been married to Sean for the last year and some change. They're basically newlyweds."

Tuki paced back and forth. "Newlyweds? What's up with her husband?"

"Sean is all right. That's Asia's fiancé's best friend. They're like brothers. But that Sean is off the hook, I tell you."

"What do you mean?" the curious Tuki asked.

"Some years ago, Sean was dating these two women, Brandi and Yadira. He had these bitches fighting over his ass and everything. To my understanding, Yadira was living with him and Brandi was allegedly his side piece. Needless to say, Yadira got wind of it. She was so upset that she killed herself right in front of him! She shot herself in the head!"

"Oh, Lord!" Tuki said, shaking her head. "What possessed that woman to kill herself?"

"I have no idea. But truthfully, you never know what Sean was putting her through. Men ain't shit."

Tuki sucked her teeth. "Um, yeah! That's why I don't fuck with 'em!"

"You might have a point there! But between me and you, Tuki, Sean is still messing around with Brandi."

Tuki's eyes widened. "Really? Do tell!"

India chuckled. "Let me just start by saying that Brandi is a home wrecking whore. Not only is she fucking with Sean, I heard that she's been lying up with my man, too!"

"Whaaaat? That bitch is wretched!"

"Ain't she? So scandalous! But it's all good. She is about to learn not to fuck with India Charles. As a matter of fact, don't fuck with a Charles, period!"

They both agreed on that. "I wonder does Milan know who she done went and married, India."

"Hmmph," India huffed. "That goes for the both of them!" Tuki burst out laughing. "Sounds like Milan needs to get put on blast, though."

Tuki shrugged her shoulders. "Well, not exactly. I was giving her the opportunity to tell her husband herself."

"Wait a minute, do you trust this chick? Fuck that. The Charleses always takes what they want!"

Tuki nodded her head in agreement. "Yeah, you're right. It's no need to wait around for her to bullshit me."

"Exactly! Or how about you and I give Miss Milan the little push that she needs to pack her shit up and leave that trifling-ass husband of hers."

"Are you suggesting that I tell her about Brandi?"

"Or how about I tell her about Brandi? Being that she is messing with my man, me telling Milan will make it sound a lot more believable."

Tuki clapped her hands. "That is genius, cuz! I love it!"

India smiled. "Yeeeess, boo! Anyway, I'm at the plantation right now. I'm going to give you call when I'm on my way to the hotel."

"Okay, see you then!"

Tuki disconnected the call and lay down on the bed. She felt so much better after speaking to India; she had shed so much light on Milan's situation. Now Tuki couldn't wait to pry Milan from the clutches of her husband.

Chapter 22

Dollar preferred to take care of all of his business during the morning time, right after rush hour, and Monday was the busiest day of the week for him. He would spend the first half of the day in different banks, where he deposited money into various personal and business accounts. Then Dollar would spend the other half of the day paying assorted bills and stocking up on supplies, such as paper and ink for his printers. With all of these things on Dollar's to-do list he still had one person on his mind. That person was Brandi Wallace.

But on this Monday morning, Dollar was slightly annoyed with Brandi. He thought about how he had gone to bat for Brandi when he picked up her up from the baby shower. She called him and he came running; he even had a physical confrontation with the guy she come to the shower with. Dollar never asked for any explanation as to why she wanted to leave and thankfully, no one got seriously hurt. But Dollar hadn't heard from Brandi since that night, which he found to be very odd.

Most men would have given up on pursuing this woman, Dollar thought. Not only was she extremely attractive but she was independent, outspoken, and definitely had a life of her own; she didn't need a man. But Dollar was so hell bent on getting close to her, he was unsure of what he had to do to get through to her. And it just didn't seem like he was going to ever get over that hump.

It was around twelve o'clock in the afternoon when Dollar finished taking care of his business. It was the first week of November and the streets of Manhattan were filled with tourists doing some early holiday shopping. Dollar headed toward the parking garage to get his truck when he got an idea. He would call Brandi at work to see if she wanted to meet up with him for lunch. It was worth a try.

Brandi picked up her desk phone right away, much to his delight. "Brandi Wallace speaking, how may I help you?"

Dollar smiled at the sound of Brandi's exaggerated professional voice. "Damn, your voice is like music to my ears," he complimented her. "What's up, boss lady? How are you?"

Brandi giggled. "Hey, Dollar! What's shaking?"

Dollar paid for the parking space then stood in front of the parking garage and waited for the attendant to bring his truck. "No, the question is what's up with you, Bee? I was your knight in shining armor Saturday and now I can't get a phone call? What's good?"

Brandi sighed. "No, no, Dollar, it's not like that! Don't think that I don't appreciate what you did for me the other night. It's just that I got caught up and didn't have opportunity to call you."

Dollar cut her off. "Keep it real. You just ain't feeling a brother."

"Please, Dollar," Brandi began. "Where did you get that from? I am feeling you! I do have my reservations and everything but I am feeling you."

"Reservations, huh?" he asked. "Look, Bee, it sounds like we need to talk. What about you taking some time off from your busy schedule and hang out with ya boy for the rest of the afternoon? And don't worry about the loss of income, baby. Dollar got you."

"Hmmph. I think that I'm going to take you up on that offer. I hate Mondays anyway."

Dollar smiled and tipped the attendant for bringing his truck to him. "That's what I'm talking about, girl! Hop in a cab and meet me at this parking garage on Thirty-fifth Street and Lexington. I'm gonna be sitting in my truck waiting for you."

"Will do," Brandi said.

It wasn't too long after they hung up the phone when Brandi appeared in a Yellow Cab in front of the parking garage. She walked right up to the driver side of his truck and knocked on the window. When Dollar saw Brandi, he rolled down the window and gave her a soft kiss on the lips.

"Come on to the other side and let me take a good look at you, gorgeous," Dollar said, as he watched her walk to the passenger side of his truck. She looked stunning in her color block cashmere coat, stylish short haircut, and high-heeled knee boots. Dollar got out and opened the door for her. He took the leather briefcase out of her hand and helped her into the truck.

"You really are a beautiful woman," Dollar said, giving Brandi another kiss on the lips before he closed the door.

"Oh, boy, stop," Brandi said, playfully hitting him on his arm. "You always know what to say."

"Of course I know what to say when it comes to you."

Brandi gave him a flirtatious look. "I bet you do."

Dollar got back into the vehicle and they were on their way. He took Brandi to one of his favorite restaurants located in the West Village for some delicious Italian food. He watched as Brandi enjoyed the chicken marsala dish she ordered. She gave him a wink when she caught him staring at her, along with a seductive smile. Dollar couldn't wait to finish the meal. By the time they were done it didn't take too much convincing for Brandi to come back to his condo with him.

When they walked into Dollar's condominium, Brandi did a twirl. She looked as if she was surprised to see that he had such exquisite taste. "I love your place. I didn't expect all of this!" she said, looking at the white leather furniture and colorful paintings on the pale white walls.

Dollar looked around at the same décor that he saw every day. "Yeah, I'm blessed, Brandi," he said, with a sigh. "But you look like you didn't expect for me to be living this good. It's obvious that you really don't know how I get down."

Brandi pulled off her boots before stepping onto the white area rug that was in the center of Dollar's massive living room. As he took her coat to hang up in the closet, Brandi didn't see his eyes roaming her shapely form.

"So what did you want to talk to me about, Dollar?" she asked, after he walked back into the living room.

But Dollar didn't want to talk. He walked over to Brandi, making her stand up and face him. He began kissing her, placing soft, juicy kisses on her lips. She reciprocated and wrapped her arms around his broad shoulders. She sucked on his lips and tongue, softly moaning as they ground against each other.

Dollar wasn't able to wait any longer. He lifted Brandi up and proceeded to carry her into his spacious bedroom. Once they were in there, he slowly began undressing her. He unbuttoned her shirt dress and instantly was turned on by the hot pink lingerie she wore underneath her clothing.

Brandi pulled Dollar's Hermès sweater over his head, unbuckled his belt, and jeans. He let them fall to the floor and kicked them to the side, as Brandi ran her fingers over his six pack and chiseled arms.

"Damn," she mumbled under her breath, while admiring his frame.

"I've always been in love with you," Dollar whispered.

Brandi eyes widened. That was the first time she had ever heard that from Dollar. "In love with me?"

He ran the back of his hand against her right cheek. "Because you were dealing with Maleek at the time, babe, and he was my friend, it wasn't the time."

Brandi got on her knees, pulled Dollar's underwear to his ankles, and started giving him head.

"Damn, Bee," Dollar moaned. He watched as she sucked and licked on his rod. "I didn't know you got down like this."

It was around seven o'clock in the evening when Brandi and Dollar finally got out of bed. They had spent most of the afternoon there, reminiscing about Brooklyn and laughing at some of the crazy things they used to do back then. Dollar even talked about growing up in different foster homes and how he used to ask God to find him a loving family to live with.

"I'm telling you, Bee," he said. "I can't count the number of foster mothers I had. I'm talking about from the time that I was a small child. My first foster mother had me from when I was a year old and she died from a heart attack. I was about six years old then. She had no real family so I had to go back into a foster care. After that, I was done off." Dollar went into a zone. "I was seriously fucked up, Bee. Because of my behavioral problems, I was unbearable to deal with and I had to be shuffled from home to home. The only place I ended up finding real brotherly love was from my friends and the old heads around the way. But I still regret not ever finding my biological mother and that shit still fucks with me to this day." Brandi kissed Dollar on the cheek. "So what's your story, Bee? What made Brandi the woman she is today?" he asked.

Brandi sighed. She started talked about her wayward brothers and how it felt to grow up without her father: a man her mother never seemed to want to talk about.

"For me, Maleek was my father figure. And for a long time, I did whatever it took to please that man. He practically raised me, which wasn't a good thing. But after he was killed, it was like I was released from those reins and I got my shit right. My son is to thank for that, though. I felt like, shit, my son done lost one parent to the streets. I damn sure didn't want him to lose another one, you know what I mean?"

Dollar nodded his head. "I know what you mean. It was too bad that I didn't form a tighter bond with my son. But that's what happens when you impregnate a fucking stripper. My son's mother was all about that money; that was her only love. It wasn't until she saw me getting my life right that she decided to shape up but by then me and my son's relationship was fucked up. She kept him from me so much that I just gave up. I didn't want to have to deal with her."

After their talk, Dollar realized that he and Brandi had so much in common. But he still had his worries. Dollar's biggest fear was losing her to someone else and the thought of that had him feeling a tad bit insecure.

Brandi looked him in the eyes. "Listen, I love you, Dollar. I always had the utmost respect for you. And trust me, I ain't going nowhere this time," she said, after he expressed his uncertainties.

Dollar breathed a sigh of relief. "But what about them other cats you fuck with, Bee? What you gonna do about them dudes?"

Brandi got up from the bed and slid into her panties and bra. "I have to admit that I'm scared of commitment, Dollar. I've been working through these damn issues but the truth is that it's hard for me to trust any man," she replied. "After Maleek, I just never been able to trust anyone."

Dollar had prompted her to come back to bed where he held her in his arms. "I'm not gonna tell you what to do, Bee," he said, kissing her on the forehead. "But sooner or later, you're gonna have to make a decision to settle down. We ain't getting no younger and I want you in my life. I ain't playing no games here."

Dollar kept replaying their candid talk as he watched Brandi put on her boots. He put his Timberland boots on too. "I want you to sleep on what we discussed today. I ain't gonna pressure you into doing nothing but I want you to remember something. Dollar has no patience and he hates waiting."

Brandi grinned at the comment. "Yeah, I know, man."

On the ride home, Dollar and Brandi continued to act like love-struck teenagers. When they pulled up in front of Brandi's building, they shared a sweet kiss. After the walls came down, it was like they couldn't get enough of one another.

"I really enjoyed our time together," Brandi said, as she was getting out of Dollar's truck.

Dollar smiled at her. "I did too, Bee," he replied. "But when am I going to see you again?"

Brandi paused. "How about this Friday? We can spend the weekend together."

"I can't wait, baby girl."

On his drive back home, Dollar couldn't stop thinking about Brandi. He couldn't believe that she was the young girl he fell in love with the very first time he saw her. Then Maleek turned her into a wildcat. He knocked her up at sixteen years old and then threw her to the wolves; the streets was nowhere for a girl like Brandi to learn her life lessons. Dollar couldn't stand Maleek for doing that.

Even though Brandi was all grown up now, Dollar could tell that she still had some of her old ways. She wasn't exactly an honest and upfront woman. She hid behind a smokescreen of lies but insisted that the men in her life come clean about their indiscretions.

Little did Brandi know, Dollar knew her truth.

He knew that she set up Maleek to be killed. He even knew that she had sex with his right-hand man, Peeto, back in the days. Then there was her involvement in the drug game. Brandi was no different from Dollar. They had committed some of the same crimes. She had robberies, kidnapping, and even murder under her belt.

But Dollar wasn't going to judge Brandi, for he had a few deadly secrets of his own. He was going to take those secrets to the grave with him and kill anyone who couldn't keep them.

Chapter 23

It was Monday afternoon when Kane was awakened by the smell of grits, eggs, and turkey ham being prepared in the kitchen of his sister's home. He arose from the bed and slowly limped up the stairs from the guest room in the basement. When he walked into the kitchen, he smiled. Najah, his twenty-one-year-old niece, was standing over the stove and preparing the food. "Hey, Najah," Kane said, greeting her with a big kiss on the cheek. "I didn't know that you were here."

Najah flipped the turkey ham over in the frying pan. The tantalizing scent of the food tickled Kane's nose.

"Good morning, Unc," she said, with a smile. "Yeah, I've been here for the weekend but now I'm ready to head back up to school in another two hours or so." She turned the eggs off and put them onto their plates. "Mommy told me about the fire, Uncle Kane. I'm sorry to hear about the house but I'm so glad that you got out of there in one piece."

Kane sat at the table and tightened the Ace bandage that was wrapped around his hurt ankle. "Thank you, baby girl. I sure appreciate that. And I'm glad that I'm okay too. It's a blessing that I was able to escape with just this busted ankle. I truly have to thank God for that, man."

Najah fixed Kane a plate and put it in front of him. Then she poured a glass of orange juice in a tall glass and handed that to him, too. Kane kissed his niece's hand.

"Thanks for the food, baby girl," he said. "Got your old Unc feeling really special this morning."

Najah made her a plate of food and sat down across the table from Kane. "It's not a problem, Unc. Me and Mommy are just glad that you made it out of that house alive!"

Kane looked at his sweet niece and smiled. Now that his living situation was in order, he was ready to get to the bottom of things. The mysterious fire wasn't just some kind of coincidence. He was convinced that someone was trying to take him out. And once he found out who that person was, he was going to deal with them accordingly.

After seeing Najah off to her car, Kane took a refreshing shower and got dressed for the day. He slid into the same clothes that he wore from the night of the fire, only they were freshly washed and pressed, thanks to Tabitha. Within minutes, Kane had his coat on and was heading out to Brooklyn to meet with an Allstate insurance adjustor. He didn't want to be late.

On the ride back to his house, Kane kept replaying the images of the fire in his head. There were a few suspects who came to mind when he thought about the fire. Dollar was one of those suspects for obvious reasons and Sean was the other. Sean might have been a correction officer but he had a violent history. He hadn't always been the most upstanding and law-abiding citizen he portrayed for the Department of Corrections. After their little run-in about Brandi, Kane didn't know what Sean was capable of doing.

When Kane arrived onto his block, his chest began to tighten up. He was experiencing the stress of everything that he was about to go through: the rebuilding of his home, a slight financial setback, and living with the fear that someone was really trying to kill him.

Kane parked his car in the driveway and breathed a sigh of relief. On the outside, the house didn't look as bad as he thought it would. But he was not prepared for how it looked on the inside. Kane walked into his two-story home and looked around in amazement. The sparkling hardwood floors squeaked as he walked throughout the bottom level of the house. Family portraits and other personal artifacts were strewn all over the place and his living room furniture was finished. Some of the items were burnt up and the rest had water damage.

After inspecting his things, Kane became overcome with emotion. He started throwing items around and kicked waterlogged debris all over the place. Finally, after a few minutes of letting off some steam, Kane continued his inspection. When he walked into the kitchen, he was happy to see that there was minimal damage. With the exception of the soot-covered cabinets and appliances, everything was intact.

Kane took a deep breath and slowly walked up the stairs to where the bedrooms were located. Thankfully, there wasn't much damage up there, either. That gave him some temporary relief. The insurance adjuster calling his phone interrupted his thoughts.

"Hello?" Kane said.

"Hello, Mr. Porter? This is Mr. Varick, the insurance adjuster. I'm standing outside of your house."

"Okay, great. I'll be right down to let you in."

It was the evening hours by the time Kane headed back to his sister's house on Long Island. The meeting with the insurance adjuster had gone even better than how he'd expected it to. And after being told that a check would be sent to him by the end of the week, Kane felt much better. His beloved home was well on its way to becoming habitable again.

Just as Kane was about to get on the parkway, he started missing Brandi. She didn't live too far from the parkway. He called her phone to see if she was home but the call went straight to voice mail. Naturally, he was aggravated because of this.

"I'm so tired of this broad!" Kane screamed, getting angrier at Brandi by the minute. Kane decided to pay Brandi another surprise visit. Instead of continuing onto the parkway, he got off the exit and headed to her house instead.

Kane arrived in front of Brandi's building and parked his car. Just as he about to get out, though, he noticed a truck idling a few feet away from his BMW. The slightly paranoid Kane quickly got back into the driver's seat. He was curious to see who was in that truck before he made another move toward the building.

It didn't take long for Kane to see exactly who was inside of the truck. It was Dollar.

"That's the motherfucker from the other night," Kane said to himself. "I never forget a face."

He felt his blood boiling as soon as he saw Brandi getting out of the passenger side. Kane rolled down his car window, desperately trying to overhear their conversation from where he was parked.

"Okay, Dollar baby," Kane overheard Brandi say. As luck would have it, she was talking a little louder than usual. "I really enjoyed myself with you today."

She walked to the driver's side of the truck, stepped onto the running board, and gave Dollar an intimate kiss through the open window. Not too long after that kiss, Brandi sashayed up the path leading to her building and Dollar pulled off as soon as she walked inside.

Now Kane didn't know what to do. He didn't know who he should be more upset with: Brandi, Dollar, or himself for caring too much. But he didn't ponder that thought too long. Kane hopped out of his vehicle and walked toward Brandi's building. When he walked into the foyer area, he saw Brandi standing by her open mailbox and looking down at her mail. Kane knocked on the glass to get her attention. Brandi looked up at Kane with a surprised expression on her face, slowly walking over to the door and opening it for him.

"Um, hey, Kane. What are you doing here?" she asked, giving him a bland kiss on the cheek.

"Trying to come see you," Kane replied sarcastically. He made an attempt to smile but the image of Brandi kissing his enemy, Dollar, kept running through his mind. "Let's go upstairs. We need to talk."

Brandi seemed a little hesitant but she gave in. "Oh, okay. Just let me close my mailbox."

When they walked into Brandi's apartment, she took off her coat and walked to her bedroom to put down her belongings. When she came back to the front, Kane was still standing by the door with a sour look on his face.

"Why don't you sit down, Kane?" she asked. Kane limped over to the couch but he didn't sit down. "Why are you limping? Did you hurt your ankle?"

Suddenly, Kane grabbed Brandi's arm and shook her. "You must think I'm fucking stupid, right?" he said, through clenched teeth.

Brandi's eyes almost popped out of her head. She tried to wrestle her arm from Kane's vice grip but to no avail. "Get the fuck off me!" she screamed at him. "Get off me, Kane!"

Kane held on to her arm and practically dragged Brandi into her bedroom. He slammed the door behind them and forcefully pushed her onto the bed.

"I just saw you get out of the truck with Dollar! And I saw you kissing him. Are you fucking this dude or something?" Kane asked.

Brandi paused for a moment. "I don't . . . No, we're just . . ." she said, trying to find the words to explain the situation with Dollar.

Kane threw his hands in the air and stopped her from going any further. "Do you wanna know what happened to me after I left your house last night?" he asked. Brandi had a blank look on her face. "Somebody threw . . . threw a fucking cocktail through my got damn living room window and my house caught on fire!" Her eyes widened with surprise. "Yes, my fucking house caught on fire! I could have easily been killed, Brandi. And this all came about after I had a fight with Dollar. Now answer me this. The night of the shower, did he drop you off at my house to get your car?"

Brandi didn't open her mouth to say a single word.

Kane chuckled. "Of course he did! He dropped you off and came back that very next day to kill my ass! That's what the fuck happened!" Kane yelled, while walking back and forth in Brandi's bedroom.

Brandi stood up. "You don't have any evidence of Dollar doing anything to your damn house, Kane!"

Kane walked up to Brandi and pushed her back down on the bed. "Oh, so you're taking up for this bitch-ass dude now?" He put his finger in her face. "It was because of yo' ass that this creep knows where I live. If you wouldn't have called him to come and pick you up from that shower, my house would probably still be intact today!"

"So you're going to blame me for this, Kane? It's not my fault that Sean . . ." Brandi stopped herself from talking by covering her mouth with her hand.

Kane frowned and got up in her face. "What the fuck did you just say to me? Did you just say Sean?"

Brandi sighed. "Nothing."

"Don't tell me nothing! What about Sean?" Kane asked, even though he already knew the truth.

Brandi covered her face. "The truth is that I used to be involved with Sean a few years back. When I saw him walk in there with his wife, I'm not going to lie; I kind of lost my cool. Then this India broad approached me about you; it was just so messy! I just decided that it was too much going on for me and I had to get out of there."

Kane nodded his head. "I see. So instead of you keeping it real with me about you and Sean, you had a third man come pick you up."

Brandi shrugged her shoulders. "I didn't know that things were going to escalate, Kane, I didn't know shit!"

Kane mushed Brandi in the face. She tried to jump up again but he pinned her down to the bed.

"You don't get it, Brandi," Kane whispered. "Dollar is trying to kill me."

Brandi struggled to get out of his grasp. "Dollar is not trying to kill you, Kane! You're bugging out right now!"

Kane began trying to kiss Brandi on the mouth but she resisted. He slapped her and grabbed her face, this time forcing his tongue down her throat. Kane began removing her clothing and pulled down his pants and turned her over. Brandi fought him tooth and nail but that didn't stop Kane forcefully entering her vagina. After a few strokes, she stopped protesting. She closed her eyes and began moaning loudly. Kane's aggressive behavior was obviously turning her more on than off.

"Kane, Kane, please stop," Brandi moaned between strokes.

"Shut the fuck up! This is my pussy," Kane said in her ear. "Don't you ever fucking forget it!"

"It's yours, baby, it's yours," Brandi willingly agreed.

After their hot and sticky makeup sex, all was forgiven and shortly after Kane was giving Brandi blow by blow details of the fire at his home. She kept trying to convince him that Dollar had no involvement in the incident but it fell on deaf ears. In addition to the accusations, Kane insisted Brandi stop seeing Dollar. That was when she put her foot down. She made it perfectly clear that she wasn't going to do that.

"Okay, Kane, enough is enough!" Brandi yelled at him. "You're not my man and I'm not your woman, okay? To be perfectly honest, I still love Sean and I can't guarantee that he and I will stop sleeping together! So there! There you have it!"

Kane sat there with a shocked expression on his face. "What?" he began. "Did you really just tell me that shit?"

Brandi threw Kane's clothes at him, hitting him in the face. "Yes, I did. Now I'm asking you to leave."

Kane reluctantly got dressed and kept giving Brandi nasty looks. Afterward, she walked him to the door. Before Kane stepped into the hallway, he turned around to look at her.

"You're missing out on a good thing," Kane said, through clenched teeth. "But if you wanna fuck Sean and Dollar, that's fine with me. Go right ahead. And by the way, tell your boy Dollar that if I ever see him again, I'm murdering his ass! Straight like that!"

Brandi frowned at him. "Fuck you, Kane," she said, slamming the door in his face.

Chapter 24

It was ten p.m. at the Gordon household. The loud chitchat among Asia, India, and their cousin, Tuki, had Rasheed at wits' end. The unexpected visit from his girl's long-distance relative interrupted what was supposed to be a quiet night for him and Asia. But when India walked in the house with the woman, Rasheed could tell from the smug expressions on their faces that trouble was brewing. He had no doubt about that.

Tuki was the twins' first cousin from Atlanta and she was a family member Rasheed never had the pleasure of meeting before. Even he had to admit Tuki was quite the looker, although she was a little too slim for his taste. Her exotic features, flawless olive complexion, and long, wavy hair gave him the impression that aside from her African American heritage, she was mixed with another race.

But there was also something that about Tuki that didn't sit too well with Rasheed; he just couldn't put his finger on it. When Asia told him that she came to New York to pay her and India a visit, he said some things that got her pretty upset.

"So you mean to tell me that after all this time, your cousin, Tuki, decides to come to New York to visit you all of a sudden? I've been with you for the last four years and have never even met this chick. You don't find her visit to be a little suspect?" Rasheed asked Asia, instantly pissing her off.

"Rasheed, why do you always have to be so freaking negative? You don't know all of my damn family and I don't know all of yours, okay? Damn!"

Asia's angry outburst didn't change Rasheed's mind. He had always been a good judge of character and usually his vibes were dead on. Because Tuki walked into his home with India in tow that gave him even more reason to be suspicious of her. Any time India was around, there was always some drama looming in the distance. Rasheed did not care for his future sister-in-law so poor Tuki didn't stand a chance.

Rasheed let out a long sigh. It was a crying shame that he and India would probably never be able to get along with each other. That was his fiancée's twin sister and they were extremely close, about as thick as thieves. At one point, they were almost inseparable but Asia stayed in hot water because of her fierce loyalty to India. When Rasheed put a stop to their shenanigans, India hated him for that.

Now just when he thought that India was finally cooling her heels, she appears on their doorstep with Tuki.

Rasheed could remember Asia talking about her uncle, Rodney Charles, who was a self-made millionaire in Atlanta. Uncle Rodney had a few children; he had two with his present wife and three other children from his first marriage. Rasheed had never met the man but this uncle was no saint in his book. "How does a rich brother allow his youngest sister to struggle with her two daughters?" Rasheed had asked Asia. He found out that the twins' mom was the black sheep of her family. She ran away from the South at seventeen years old to be with her older, dope-slinging boyfriend in New York City. And from what Rasheed knew of his future mother-in-law, her daughter India was a younger, watered-down version of herself. That explained why Uncle Rodney never bothered to extend his riches to his baby sister.

With Rodney Charles being a part of the upper echelon, that only meant one thing: his daughter Tuki was most likely a self-absorbed brat.

Rasheed had a close eye on Tuki. If he detected any similarities to India, she was going to be out the door. He didn't need or want any drama around him, Asia, or his unborn child, and that was a given.

Rasheed listened intently, as the women went on with their banter. "So, um, Tuki, why haven't you come to New York more often, you know, to visit your cousins?" Rasheed asked, rudely interrupting their chat. He took a sip of the Jack Daniels from the glass in his hand. "It's not like you don't have the money to hop on a quick flight to New York. Shit, from what I heard, you probably got your own damn jet."

Tuki looked at her twin cousins for an answer to Rasheed's question. They looked just as confused as she did.

Tuki rolled her eyes at him. "Um, not for nothing, Raheem—" she began.

Rasheed laughed. "No, no, sweetie. Let me help you out. The name's Rasheed. Rasheed Gordon," he said, sarcastically. "Now you may proceed with your reply."

Tuki rolled her eyes at him again. "Anyway, Raheem," she continued, messing up his name on purpose, "I don't think when or why my coming to visit my cousins, Asia and India, is any of your business. As long as they are good with me being here, there shouldn't be an issue. Thank you very much."

The cynical Rasheed let out a sarcastic chuckle. "No disrespect, ma, but when it comes to my girl and my unborn seed, everything that she's a part of is my business. I just don't want no drama around my family."

Tuki looked at Asia then pointed at Rasheed, who was leaning against the wall, staring at her. "Excuse me, Asia, where in the hell did you find this ghettofied Negro?" she asked, with a frown on her face.

"At the bottom of the barrel with the rest of the scavengers," India mumbled under her breath.

Asia hushed Tuki and India then stared at Rasheed with a pleading look in her eyes. "Listen, babe, could you please go somewhere? Me and India would like to talk to Tuki in private."

Rasheed sucked his teeth. "Okay, mama. I'll leave these broads alone, for your sake," he replied, pointing at her.

"Please do," Tuki shot back. "That's exactly why I can't fuck with no men, child! They're just too arrogant and cocky."

Rasheed heard what Tuki said and put his two cents in. "If you don't fuck with us men, who are you fucking with? Little boys or women?" he said, giving her a wicked look.

Tuki swung her long hair around her shoulders. "Just put it like this, Ramel. I like what you like," she replied, in a nasty tone. "I like pussy."

Rasheed walked out of the living room, dying with laughter. As soon as he was out of their earshot, he pulled out his phone to call Sean.

"I need you to come over to the house, man," Rasheed said, as soon as Sean answered his call. He closed the door to the family room.

"For what, man?" Sean asked, in annoyance. "I just got off work and I'm tired as hell. As a matter of fact, I'm turning onto my block as we speak."

Rasheed ignored Sean's complaints. "Listen, man, you have to come through here. India and Asia's cousin is here visiting them from Atlanta and I need some testosterone in this house, ASAP!" he pleaded.

Sean grunted. "Look, Rah . . ."

"Ah, come on, man! I'm over here, sipping on some of that Jack and shit. Come have a drink or two with your bro-ham, man. Come on."

"Okay, okay," Sean said. "I'm on my way. But I'm only staying for a little while. I'm kinda tired, man."

Rasheed ignored the statement. "How long before you get here, man?" he asked.

"Damn, man!" Sean exclaimed. "About five minutes!"

"Good! See you in a few, homie."

Ten minutes later, Sean was walking through the double doors of Rasheed's house. As soon as he stepped into the living room, he stopped in his tracks. The twins' cousin didn't look half bad. She was so gorgeous that Sean was almost at a loss for words.

"Excuse me, Cousin Tuki," Rasheed said, with a smile on his face. "This is my boy, Sean. Sean, this Asia's cousin, Tuki."

Tuki slowly stood up and reached for Sean's hand. "So you're the infamous Sean," she said, in a slightly flirtatious manner. "I heard so much about you."

Sean looked at Rasheed, wondering how the woman knew anything about him. Rasheed shrugged his shoulders, clueless as to what Tuki was talking about. India had a smirk on her face and Asia was none the wiser.

"You heard a lot about me?" Sean asked. "How can that be when this is your first time meeting me?" he added, looking at Asia and India to see if they told her anything about him. "Yo, let me find out y'all twins been talking about me to y'all cousin, man."

Tuki chuckled. "Oh, no, no! I heard about you from Milan. Milan Daniels is your wife, correct?"

Now Sean was really confused. "Yeah, Milan is my wife. But how do you know my wife?" he asked, giving Tuki a suspicious look.

"Well," Tuki began. "I met your wife Milan in Atlanta about a year ago and since then we've gotten really close."

India burst into laughter when Tuki made the last statement. Asia nudged her. Sean was totally oblivious so he just smiled.

"Well, anyone who's a good friend of my wife's is a good friend of mine's too. It's a pleasure to meet you. Tuki, right?"

Tuki nodded her head. "Likewise. So, where is Milan?"

"She should be at home."

"Really? I would love to see her. Would you mind taking me by your house to see her? I know she would be so surprised to see me."

Sean shrugged his shoulders. "I don't see that being a problem. Let me just call her," he said, pulling out his phone.

Tuki stopped him from calling Milan. "No! Don't do that. I really want to surprise her! She is going to get such a kick out of me walking in your house. She doesn't even know that I'm in New York right now."

"Oh, okay." Sean put his phone away and gave Rasheed a pound. "I'll be right back, man, I promise. Let me just run Tuki to the crib to see wifey."

Rasheed waved him off. "Ah, whatever, man," he replied, with a serious attitude.

Sean and Tuki got into his truck and drove a block away to his Halsey Street residence. He parked the vehicle a few doors from the house and helped Tuki out of the passenger side. Sean couldn't help but stare at her; she was such an attractive woman. He just knew that men of all different races and backgrounds clamored for Tuki's attention.

Sean unlocked the doors and they walked into the house together.

"Milan!" Sean called out to his wife from downstairs. "Are you dressed? Come down here. Someone is here to see you."

Less than a minute later, Milan quickly appeared at the top of steps, in her pajamas. She slowly walked the down the staircase, completely unaware of who was in the house. By this time, Sean and Tuki were sitting in the living room and all that could be heard were their muffled voices. When Milan stepped into her living room, she lost all of the coloring in her face. Sean was smiling and pointing to Tuki. He hadn't noticed the nervous expression on Milan's face.

"Do you know this young lady?" Sean asked. Milan nodded her head. "She's the twins' first cousin! I stopped by Rasheed's house on my way home and she was there. She said y'all knew each other. Isn't that crazy?"

Tuki walked over to Milan and gave her a kiss. But this wasn't a regular kiss on the cheek. It was a very intimate one, very similar to the ones that Sean shared with his wife on a regular basis.

Sean was in a state of shock at the unusual display of affection. "Yo, what the fuck is going on here?" he yelled, pulling the women apart from each other. He pushed Tuki against the wall and stared at the smirking woman like she had lost her mind. "What the fuck are you doing kissing my fucking wife like that? Who the fuck are you?"

Tuki didn't answer or give Sean any eye contact. Instead, she was glaring at Milan. "Tell him, baby. Tell your husband who I am to you."

Sean took a step back and grabbed Milan's hand. He looked at her. "What the fuck does she mean by that? Who is she to you?" he yelled.

The worried Milan snatched her hand away and backed up from her angry husband. "Um," she hesitated, as if she was trying to think of what to say.

"Let me help you with that, babe," said Tuki. "Sean, your wife and I are lovers. We've been talking to each other for the past year."

Sean plopped down onto the couch and stared at Milan. "You're gay?" he asked her.

Milan looked at Tuki then at her distraught husband. "I don't what I am," she replied, as she shrugged her shoulders.

Now it was Tuki's turn to frown. "What do you mean, you don't know what you are?" she asked. "We was just at that fucking hotel together and you had your got damn face between my legs!"

Sean stood up, grabbed the hat off his head, and threw it to the floor. "You're gay, Milan? You're motherfucking gay?" he screamed, in despair. Sean began pacing the living room. "So when you went missing, you was laying up with this chick in a hotel?" he asked. "You're gay and you have a fucking coke habit?"

Tuki was taken aback at the news of Milan's drug habit. "You're a cokehead?" she asked.

Milan didn't answer Tuki but Sean did. "Yep! Your lover is a cokehead! I just found some cocaine the other day and now I'm hearing about this gay shit!" he screamed at Tuki. Sean's attention went back to Milan. "It's like . . . it's like I married a fucking stranger!"

Suddenly, he walked to the front door and opened it. "You know what? I want you two bitches out of my got damn house, tonight! Milan, I will arrange for you to get all of your shit out of here by the end of this week. And I'm gonna have them divorce papers drawn up, too! I'm officially done with your lying ass!"

Milan watched in vain, as Sean walked away from the open door to run upstairs to their bedroom. He slammed the door so hard that it sounded as if it was going to come off the hinges.

Milan's blood was boiling. "What made you fucking do this to me, Tuki?" she asked. "I was the one who was supposed to tell my husband about us, not you!"

Tuki laughed at her. “Oh, don’t play with me, Milan! I know that you weren’t gonna tell him a damn thing. And I couldn’t allow that to happen; that’s why I came over here to do the dirty work for you. Now who should we tell next, your family, your friends? I can help you with that. And while I’m at it, should I tell them about your little cocaine problem, too?”

Milan sat down on the couch and covered her face. “I can’t deal with this shit right now, Tuki. Please get out of my house. I need a moment to myself!”

Tuki didn’t budge. “I’m not going nowhere without you! You heard what Sean said. He wanted both of us bitches out of here tonight! This means that you have to come with me, right the fuck now!”

Sean was upstairs in his bedroom, trying to calm himself down. He couldn’t believe that once again, he had managed to allow a crazy woman into his life. He felt so used. It seemed like Milan had just accepted his marriage proposal with the intention of hiding her alternative lifestyle from her loved ones. He would have felt better if she had cheated on him with another man!

Sean crept out of the bedroom and stood by the edge of the staircase. He listened intently at the heated conversation Tuki and Milan were having downstairs. The way they were talking to each other sounded as if they were in a serious relationship, much to Sean’s dismay.

Unable to take it anymore, Sean got up and walked into Milan’s closet. He began pulling all of her clothes and shoes out of there. He walked out of the bedroom and started throwing her belongings down the staircase.

“Sean!” Milan screamed at him from downstairs. “What the hell are you doing with my stuff?”

“Y’all bitches still here?” Sean yelled from the top of the staircase. He threw some boxes of shoes over the banister. Milan and Tuki jumped out of the way to avoid being hit. "I thought I told you and that bitch to get the hell out of my house!"

Milan was dazed, not knowing what move to make. And for once, the outspoken Tuki was at a loss for words. Fearing for Milan's safety, she insisted that they leave the house, just as Sean had told them to.

"Please, Milan," Tuki said, with a worried look on her face. "Let's just leave!"

Milan looked around at the articles of clothing, shoes, and accessories that were scattered all over the steps and foyer area. When she looked up, Sean was still throwing things over the banister. She took a deep breath, trying to build up the courage to confront him.

When Milan got to the top of the steps, Sean nudged her, causing her to almost tumble backward. She broke her fall by grabbing on to the banister. Tuki started to run up the stairs to help her but Milan stopped her.

"I got this, Tuki," she called out to her. "Just chill out. I got this!"

"You put hands on her again, motherfucker, and I'm gonna call the police on your ass!" Tuki yelled up at Sean.

"Fuck you, you box-eating lesbo bitch!" Sean screamed back at Tuki. "You're the one who came up in here and started all of this fucking drama! But since you wanna act like a man, come up here! I will beat the shit outta you, like a man!"

Sean's threats of violence and derogatory comments to Tuki were the final straw for Milan. She quickly slipped past him, and walked into the bedroom and directly into her closet to gather up some things. Sean followed her.

"Why are you messing with that woman, Milan?" he asked. "What was it? I wasn't man enough for you?"

"Please, Sean, don't make this about you, man," she replied to him. "It's not about you."

"So who is it about then?" he asked. "The bottom line is that you've been lying to me. If you were gay, don't you think that's something you should've shared with me when we first met?"

Milan slipped into a pair of Ugg boots and threw on a snorkel coat. She stuffed a duffel bag with bras, underwear, and sweat suits. After she finished packing up her essentials, she looked Sean square in the eye.

"First of all, I'm not gay! I'm attracted to women and men. And this is about me, Sean, not you," she said, with her voice cracking and tears running down her cheeks. "It's about me hiding who I was all of these years! I went to college, I got my degree, I got married. I did everything that everyone else wanted me to do! I even tried to be a good wife to you and then I met Tuki and I just couldn't continue this façade any longer." Milan looked up at the heartbroken Sean. "The bottom line is that I need to figure some shit out and get my life together because it's a fucking mess right now! Maybe this is the time for you to get your life together too, babe," She put the palm of her hand on his cheek. "I'm so sorry, baby."

Milan tried to kiss Sean but he pushed her away and watched as she walked out of their bedroom. A few minutes later, he heard the front door slam and then it was complete silence.

Sean picked up one of the lamps off the nightstand and threw it against the wall. He looked down at the scattered pieces of the busted lamp on the floor and thought about how eerily similar his life was to it. Then it hit him. *Milan is right. It is time for me to get my life together.*

Chapter 25

Milan practically ran out of her house to her parked truck, with Tuki trailing closely behind her.

"Milan! Milan!" Tuki yelled into the night. "Wait up for me!"

But Milan wasn't listening to Tuki. She quickly opened the driver's side door and started up her vehicle, ready to drive off and leave Tuki exactly where she stood. Just as she was about to pull off from the curb, Tuki appeared on the passenger side of the vehicle. Milan glanced at her lover and refused to open the door. *If it weren't for this bitch and her big mouth, I probably wouldn't be in this mess!* Milan knew that she was knee deep in a cesspool of feces, and from the looks of things there was no turning back now.

"Open the door!" Tuki said, as she stood outside of the truck and banged on the window. "Let me in, Milan! Please!"

A few seconds passed and Milan reluctantly opened the door but for one reason alone. As soon as Tuki slid into the seat, she blacked out and began pummeling the unwanted passenger with her fists.

"You dumb bitch!" Milan screamed at her, surprised at her own actions. "You ruined my fucking life!"

Tuki balled up her fists to hit Milan back but it was pointless. Milan was definitely getting the best of her.

"Stop! Stop!" Tuki cried out in pain, as Milan continued to give her body blows.

She even grabbed Tuki's long hair and began banging her head on the passenger side window, only stopping when she saw that Tuki was slowly losing consciousness. Milan grudgingly released her tight grip on Tuki's hair. Then she sat back in the driver's seat, trying to catch her breath. She was so physically and emotionally exhausted from everything that she'd been through that week. It was enough to make her want to leave New York for good and never look back. She glanced over at the dazed Tuki, who was leaning her head against the window, trying to regain her senses.

When Tuki did open her eyes, she starting rubbing her head. "Why did you do that to me?" Tuki asked, in a cautionary tone. She flipped down the visor to look in the lighted mirror. "Why were you hitting me?" she asked again, as she inspected her face for bruises.

Milan pointed her long, manicured nail in the center of Tuki's forehead. "You're lucky that I don't fucking kill you!" she replied. "You just had to go and ruin my marriage, didn't you? You just couldn't wait for me to tell my husband about us. You just had to fuck everything up!"

Tuki sat upright in the seat and pointed her finger back at Milan. "I didn't do nothing that you couldn't have done yourself! You're the one running around here acting like this . . . this devoted wife, and you ain't nothing but a DL lesbo, baby. Yes, I fucking said it! I know your type so well!" Tuki waited for Milan to respond but when that response didn't come, she continued talking. "Right now, your husband is back in that house, hurting just because you wanted to live a lie. But, oh well, I wasn't about to let you do that shit to me or to Sean! He deserved to know the truth!"

Milan thought about what Tuki what saying to her. Her life with Sean had become so humdrum and monotonous. She yearned for something different, something more exciting. That was where Tuki fit in. But truthfully, Milan didn't want to be in a full-blown relationship with the younger woman. Now that the cat was out of the bag, Milan could do whatever she wanted. She could finally live the life that she had denied herself for so long.

Before she pulled off, Milan reached into her bag and took out a vial of cocaine. She boldly sniffed the contents right in front of Tuki, who was sitting in the passenger seat and giving her a disapproving stare.

"I can't believe that you're going to do drugs right in front of me," Tuki said, while shaking her head in disgust.

As the cocaine began to take effect, Milan looked over at Tuki with her eyes half shut and a smirk on her face. The drug made everything very crystal clear to her. How could she really be in love with some spoiled, rich brat who would stop at nothing to get exactly what she wanted, even it meant ruining someone's life? And, after all that drama Tuki caused back at the house, it was painfully obvious that she was not only in love with Milan, she was obsessed with her.

Most people would desperately try to get away from Tuki but not Milan. She realized that Tuki was an asset, not a liability. The woman had major money, she had all of the connections and, most importantly, Milan could get anything that she wanted out of her. In the course of Milan losing her husband, she had gained a sponsor and a damn good one at that.

The smirk on Milan's face turned into a mischievous smile. She held the vial up to Tuki's nostril. "Why don't you have some, little girl?" she said, trying to persuade her to try the coke. "Trust me, it won't hurt you, little baby. You'll fucking love it. Go ahead and try it. It feels so good!"

Tuki took the vial from Milan, who showed her how to snort the cocaine from the back of her hand. Not too long after that lesson, Tuki tried it. Milan laughed, as she watched her grab her nose and squirm in the car seat.

"Wow!" Tuki exclaimed. "It burns a little but I have to admit that's some good shit!" she added, with a nervous laugh.

Milan grinned from ear to ear. "Isn't it great? I'm sure that there will be more where this comes from, right?" she said, suggesting that Tuki fund her habit.

Tuki snorted some more of the coke and gave Milan a seductive look. "Anything for my baby," she said. The two women started to kiss and grope each other's body parts. Things got so heated they were practically taking their clothes off in Milan's car.

Milan finally came up for air and wiped Tuki's lip gloss off her face. She started up the vehicle and drove off. "Let's hurry up and get back to the hotel," she whispered. "We got some things to do."

It was almost 11:30 at night when a worried India started calling Tuki's phone. She dialed the number several times but there was still no answer. She looked over at the pregnant Asia. All she could do was shake her head.

"This huzzy is not answering her phone!" the frustrated India said. "Where could she be?"

Asia frowned. "Rah!" she yelled. Rasheed quickly appeared in the doorway of the living room. "Could you please call Sean and ask him if Tuki is still at his house? She's not answering her cell and it's been almost two hours since she left this house."

Rasheed called Sean's cell phone twice but the call kept going to voice mail. Now it was time for him to be concerned about his friend.

"Sean ain't answering his phone, either," Rasheed said. He went to grab his coat from the closet. "I'm gonna go over there and find out what's going on. I'll be back."

Rasheed got into his car and drove to Sean's house. After parking his vehicle, he walked up the steps of the brownstone and rang the bell. When no one came to the door, Rasheed called Sean again. Shortly after the last call, he heard the locks on the front door click. As soon as Sean opened the door, Rasheed knew that something had gone terribly wrong.

Rasheed followed the visibly downtrodden Sean into his living room. He watched as his friend lay on the couch and covered his eyes with his forearm. Strangely enough, Sean was home alone, with no signs of Milan or Tuki in sight. Rasheed sat in the armchair across from Sean, waiting to get to the bottom of what went on there.

"What's up, bruh?" Rasheed asked. "Where's Tuki and Milan?"

Sean slowly sat up. He looked Rasheed in the eye and began telling him the story from beginning to end. The angry Rasheed stood up and began flailing his arms like a madman.

"I knew that that bitch was shady, I fucking knew it!" he exclaimed. "She came to New York for Milan, not to visit them twins!"

Sean nodded his head. "Yes, she did! And I'm gonna keep it real, man, this shit blindsided me. When Tuki said that she had heard so much about me, I didn't expect for her to say that her and Milan had been fucking each other! I just thought that they were acquaintances," he said, drifting off into deep thought.

Rasheed sighed. He felt bad for his friend. "Never in a million years would I have guessed that Milan was getting down like that but what do I know?" He walked over to Sean and put his hand on his shoulder. "Man, listen, man, you're gonna be a'ight! You can always find you a whole 'nother bitch if that's what you want and live your life, son. Some broads just ain't worth the tears or the time, know what I mean?"

Sean wiped the tears off his face. "This bitch got me crying like a little ho," he said, through clenched teeth. "Cokehead heifer!"

Rasheed paused for a moment. "Cokehead?" he repeated. "Who the hell is a cokehead?"

Sean shook his head. "Milan is a cokehead!"

Rasheed covered his mouth with his hand. "Wow! Damn, man! Yo, Sean, man, who was you married to?"

Sean got up and started walking around the living room. "I don't know, man!" He paused for a moment. "I just don't know who these bitches are anymore. They say they want a good man and when they get one, they fuck him over. I loved Milan, man, you know I did."

Rasheed cut him off. "Did you love Milan, homie? I mean, let's face it, you and her got married kind of fast. And you had just gotten over that Yadira shit, too."

Sean sighed. "Yeah, I loved her, man. I wouldn't have married her if I didn't love her. But, I don't know. I don't know what to do anymore."

Rasheed smiled. "So what's up with Brandi?" he asked. "Maybe a good piece of ass and some head will do a brother some justice tonight, you know, help you ease through the pain."

Sean rolled his eyes at Rasheed, trying not to laugh at what he said. "Man, fucking and getting my dick sucked is that last thing on my mind right now. I ain't no good, homie. I'll probably end up tearing Brandi's pussy to shreds!"

Rasheed started to laugh hysterically, causing Sean to do the same. "See, boy? That's what I like to see!" he said. "I want you to be happy, man. Just keep thinking about the bullet that you dodged with Milan. You don't have one kid with her and you ain't been married long enough for her to be entitled to any of your money! Let Milan keep her licker license; you divorce her ass and keep it pushing! Life goes on, man!"

Sean shook his head at Rasheed's advice. "What would I do without you, Rah?" he said, giving his longtime friend a bear hug. "It is time for me to really do me. Leave the past in the past and move forward!"

Rasheed nodded his head in approval. "Exactly!" He started walking to the door. "Well, let me get back to the house and tell these twins that their cousin is officially a home wrecking biatch!" Sean began cracking up. "I can't wait to do that!" he said, rubbing his hands together.

Sean kept smiling until he saw Rasheed get into his truck. But once his friend pulled off, those hurt feelings began creeping back in again, as he thought about how things had played out between him and Milan.

After making sure all of the downstairs lights were off, Sean made his way up the stairs to his bedroom. He plopped down on the bed and picked up the house phone's receiver.

"Hello? Health Medical Division, Gaines speaking," the woman said on the other end of Sean's phone call. He gave her his name and the Rikers Island facility that he worked in.

"I'm calling out sick for tomorrow afternoon," Sean replied.

"Nature of illness?" she asked.

Sean took a pause. *A broken heart!*

"Hello? Hello? Are you there?"

Sean couldn't come up with any illness. It was then that he decided to tell the truth about how he really felt. "I'm sick. Sick to my stomach," he said, in a remorseful tone.

"Oh, okay," the clueless woman began. "I got you down for sick tomorrow and nature of illness is a stomach virus. You have a good night, sir, and I hope you feel better."

Sean hung up the phone and got undressed, practically crawling into his bed. "Let me get a good night's sleep," he said to himself. "Gotta see this damn divorce lawyer in the morning," he groaned.

Chapter 26

After Rasheed came from Sean's house, he had a major attitude. He started telling Asia what happened with Milan and Tuki and, naturally, she was disappointed with her cousin's reckless behavior. Ironically, India was unmoved by the news.

"So you mean to tell me that Tuki was in town to be with Sean's wife?" Asia asked. "That's freaking bananas!"

Rasheed threw his car remote onto the wooden coffee table and sat on the couch. Then he started talking about India right in front of her. "And India was the one who brought that mess into the house!"

India crossed her arms in defiance. "What the hell are you talking about, Rah? You ain't gonna blame me for that shit!"

Rasheed waved India off. "Man, listen, like I said, you were the one who brought that shit over here! Ain't no telling what you and your cousin were plotting before y'all walked through that door!"

Asia, who was sitting next to India, gave her a nudge with her elbow. "India, did you know anything about Tuki and Milan's relationship?"

"What?" India replied, stunned by the question. "Hell no! I didn't know nothing about that! All Tuki said was that she wanted to see you, Asia, and I brought her here, to see you!"

Asia shook her head. "There's something that you're not telling me, India! I can always tell when you're lying because that bottom lip of yours begins to twitch!"

India tried to control the nervous twitch by biting on her bottom lip. "I swear to you, I don't know shit, Asia! And I don't know why your bitch-ass man," she added, pointing at Rasheed, "is always trying to accuse me of doing something!"

It was Rasheed's turn to chime in. "Because, you're always doing something!" When he stood up, his six foot four frame towered over the petite India. "The bottom line is that you're a miserable bitch and you can't stand to see nobody happy, not even your got damn sister!"

The two began to argue but they stopped when the pregnant Asia physically stepped in between them. "Stop!" she yelled. "India, you stay here! And, Rah, you go upstairs for a moment. Let me talk to my sister."

Rasheed grabbed his keys and stomped out of the living room. Asia listened for the upstairs bedroom door to slam before she started talking to her twin. She looked India square in the eye.

"I don't know what's going on with you, India," Asia began.

India cut her off. "Asia, I didn't do anything!"

Asia hushed her. "Like I said, I don't know what's going on, India, but I smell a rat. Whatever reasons Tuki had for being in New York is strictly her business; I'm not going to worry about that. But if I find out that you participated in this thing with Tuki and Milan, I'm going to ban you from my house, my baby, and my life. Do you understand me?"

India threw up her hands and fought back tears. "So you really would do that to me, Asia? After all of the shit that I did?" Asia held her hand up and India stopped talking.

"I don't want to hear nothing about what you done did for me! I always had your got damn back and you know it! You were the one who always was talking me into doing some negative shit. It's like you wanted me to be fucked up! And when I straightened up my act and got with Rasheed? You didn't like that, India. You weren't happy for me!" India wiped her tears and acted like she was unfazed by Asia's words. Asia gave her a look and let out a sarcastic chuckle. "You know what, India? I ain't gonna tell you what I'm going to do anymore; I'm going to show you. So please leave this house and don't bother coming to see your niece or nephew until you fix that fucked-up heart of yours, India."

India reached for her Louis Vuitton tote bag, her coat, and walked out of the front door without saying good-bye to her sister. As far as she was concerned, if Asia wanted to dismiss her from her life, she was going to learn how to deal with not having her sister around. And it was just that simple for the guilty India.

India turned off the car radio, preferring a quiet ride home. Considering the way everything went down, she had a lot to think about. When she arrived in the proximity of her apartment building, her cell phone rang. She looked at the caller ID and smiled when she saw that it was Tuki calling her. She felt relieved when she heard her cousin's voice.

"What's the deal, cuz?" Tuki screamed into the phone, sounding higher than a kite. "Where are you? What are you doing right now?"

India sighed. "The question is where the fuck are you, Tuki? We were worried about you, girl!"

Tuki giggled. "Child, I'm with my baby, Milan, right now!"

"Are you at the hotel with her?" India asked. "I thought I told you that I wanted you to stay with me tonight."

"She's with me!" Milan called out in the background.

Now India was annoyed. After the fallout with Asia, she needed to project her anger and Milan was the perfect target.

"Tuki, put Milan on the fucking phone! I need to talk to her."

Tuki gave Milan the phone. India had to move the phone away from her ears because she was talking loudly.

"Hey, cuz!" Milan slurred. "You know that we're cousins now!"

"Sorry but we ain't no relation, boo," India shot back at her. "So knock it off with the cousin shit, okay?" An evil smirk came on her face. "So, Milan, what's up with your husband?"

"Shiiiiit, fuck Sean!" Milan replied. "I'm finally free, girl!"

India wanted to get right to the point so she could hurry the drunken Milan off the phone. "Fuck Sean is right; you ain't got shit to feel guilty about! And don't feel like the bad guy, boo, because you're not the only one who's been cheating. Sean has been fucking around on you for some time now! And if you don't believe me, just ask Brandi Wallace. You do know who Brandi is, right?"

There was slight pause on the other line. India silently counted up to ten and like clockwork, Milan responded before she could get to the number eleven.

"Sean was cheating on me? With Brandi?" she said, in a barely audible voice.

"Yep!" India replied. "That's some foul shit, ain't it?"

Milan didn't reply to India. Instead, she passed the phone back to Tuki.

"Do you think that it was a good idea to tell Milan all of that crap about Sean? I mean, she seems real upset about it," Tuki said. "She just locked herself in the bathroom!"

India blew Tuki off. "Whatever. She'll be all right. Now you can have her, Brandi can have Sean, and I can have my man, Kane." India heard Milan call out Tuki's name in the background. "Anyway, go tend to your heartbroken little girlfriend."

Tuki sighed. "Okay. Kiss Asia for me and I'll give you a guys a call before I head back to Atlanta. And, India?"

"Yes?"

"Thanks for everything," she said, before hanging up the phone

Tuki's gratefulness actually brought a smile to India's face. Her cousin seemed pretty happy with her decision, even though she used unorthodox methods to get there. Meanwhile, India was tired of coming home to no one. Everyone around her was either married, living with each other, having babies, or in a committed relationship. All India wanted was a man to call her own. All she wanted was her happily ever after.

India had never told anyone but she contemplated suicide on several occasions. She just felt like she was undeserving of love. With her personal firearm, a Glock 16, stored in a lockbox on the top shelf of her bedroom closet, India could have easily taken the same route that Yadira did, ending a lifetime of misery and emotional conflict with one slug to the brain. As India thought about the way her life turned out, suicide didn't seem like such a bad idea at the moment. The things that Asia said to India made her wonder if her twin sister would live a better life without her.

India walked into her bedroom and reached for the unloaded gun. She took her hands and inspected it, like it was the first time she saw it. Then India began crying. She cried harder than she ever had in her entire life.

Chapter 27

Due to their hectic schedules, Dollar hadn't seen Brandi all week. But fortunately, they talked on the phone a few times a day so they were good in the communication department. And it was during those intimate telephone conversations that they learned a lot about each other.

Dollar had repeatedly expressed to Brandi that he regretted not being a better father to his only son. He couldn't understand how he allowed the tumultuous relationship with his child's mother and his lifestyle to affect his parental obligations to the boy. He wanted to change that.

"Why don't you call him up, Dollar?" Brandi told him. "I mean, it couldn't hurt."

So Dollar did just that and much to his surprise, Gregory Jr. was very receptive. Even his mother was cooperative. Reconnecting with his son made Dollar very happy and he had no one but Brandi to thank for the advice.

Now it was eight o'clock Friday night and the workweek was over. At least, it was for Brandi. Dollar had things to do on Saturday but he had no problem putting his business obligations aside for the new lady in his life.

It was mid-November and the wintry night air made it feel much colder than it was supposed to be for that time of the year. Dollar was sitting in front of Brandi's building, with the heat blasting in his truck, waiting for her to come downstairs. It was a date night for them and he couldn't wait to get his hands on her.

Dollar's octopus hands weren't the only things that were in store for Brandi. Now that it seemed as if they were one step closer to becoming exclusive, Dollar knew that he had to step his game up to impress a woman of Brandi's caliber. He opened the black jewelry box and smiled as he took another look at the two-carat tennis bracelet that he purchased for her, just the other day. All he could do was envision the expression on Brandi's pretty face when she saw the gift. It cost him a pretty penny but that didn't matter to Dollar; he could afford that and much more.

Dollar turned up the radio and began singing along with the music. As he basked in his glory, he didn't see the shadowy figure creeping on the driver's side of his truck. Suddenly, three gunshots rang out. The frightening sound of Dollar's screams and shattering glass pierced the silent fall night. Shortly after committing the heinous act, the mysterious ski-masked suspect quickly ran back into the shadows.

Unfortunately, the wounded Dollar wasn't that lucky. He was slumped over the steering wheel, with two shots to his neck and shoulder. Pieces of glass from the shattered driver's side window were all over him and there was blood everywhere. Dollar was slowly drifting in and out of consciousness. Thankfully, a male passerby walking his dog ran over to the truck and called 911 for help.

In the meantime, the excited Brandi didn't have any idea what had gone on. She wrapped the scarf that she was wearing around her neck before she exited her building and stepped outside into the breezy night air. Brandi had a huge smile on her face after spotting Dollar's truck near the driveway of the building. But that smile immediately turned to a look of terror when she saw the small crowd of people gathering around the truck. They were all staring inside of the driver's side window. Brandi's four-inch heels clicked loudly against the pavement as she ran toward the crowd. She had to practically push people out of the way to get to Dollar's vehicle.

"Dooooollaaaar!" Brandi wailed, once she laid eyes on the unconscious Dollar slumped down in the driver's seat. "Nooo! Oh, my God! Somebody call the cops, please! My boyfriend, my baby's been shot!" she cried.

Pretty soon, the block was filled with more than just onlookers. Plainclothes detectives and police officers from the 75th Precinct swarmed the crime scene. When the ambulance arrived, the cops handled the crowd control so that the paramedics could remove Dollar's limp body from the truck. They put him on a gurney and wheeled him to the waiting ambulance. In the meantime, Brandi was wrapped in the arms of one of her neighbors and crying hysterically. But before that ambulance pulled off, she was right by Dollar's side. She sat on the seat next to the gurney and held Dollar's bloody hand in hers.

"Please, don't die on me, baby," Brandi whispered to Dollar. "If you make it through this, I promise you that I will never leave your side again. Please don't die!"

As the ambulance raced across town to the Kings County Hospital trauma unit, the police started their preliminary investigation of the incident. Little did they know, the shooter was standing in the crowd of spectators, sans the ski mask, watching everything.

Somewhere in Brooklyn, Kane sat in his car at a red light. India called him earlier that day, practically begging him to spend some time with her. Naturally, Kane had his reservations about this. It wasn't a secret as to how much of a pain in the ass India was. She was not above calling him all times of the day and night, leaving texts and voice mails that he didn't bother acknowledging. But the bored

Kane decided to give India another shot. After being all wrapped up with Brandi, who had since moved on to Dollar, he needed a serious ego boost. And who better to do that than India?

Kane pulled up in front of India's building, checking out the address before he parked his car. She lived in a well-kept, pre-war building in the Crown Heights area of Brooklyn. The neighborhood itself was decent and gentrification had brought an onslaught of young yuppies from Manhattan to Brooklyn. Kane had never been to India's place but the neighborhood that she lived in said a lot about her character. With the way she carried herself sometimes, it wouldn't be hard to assume that she was from the projects. And that was what turned Kane off the most.

Kane rang the intercom and India buzzed him upstairs. When he got to her apartment, India surprised him when she opened the door. She was looking different from what he remembered. The India standing in front of him oozed sex. Her long hair was pulled up into a high bun. She was rocking the hell out of a cropped shirt, exposing her flat stomach and a pair of cutoff denim shorts that was showing off a little bit of cheek.

Kane paused. *Damn, she looks hot!* It was crazy but he had never taken a good look at India until that moment. She definitely was a physically attractive woman. If only she'd had the personality to match.

India stepped to the side so that Kane could come in. He walked inside and looked around her cozy apartment.

"Nice place, girl," Kane said, giving her a nod of approval. "Very nice."

India smiled and took Kane's coat, hanging it up in a nearby closet. Then she grabbed his hand and led him into the small dining area. There, she had the table fully set with plates, wine glasses, and candles. Kane smiled.

Initially, he thought this visit was going to be a typical booty call. But judging from the way that India was trying to impress him, her intentions had Kane thinking differently.

"Hey, I like this setup," he complimented her, as he slid into one of the chairs. "Candlelight, wine glasses . . . What gives, girl?"

India didn't reply. Instead, she walked into the kitchen and emerged with platters of food. She put the dishes on the table and poured some chilled Moscato into their glasses then sat across from Kane and told him to dig in. Kane took a bite of the grilled salmon and nodded his head.

"Damn, girl! Who knew you could hook up shit like this?" he said, giving her accolades on her cooking.

"It's a lot that you don't know about me, Kane," India calmly replied. "A hell of a lot."

Kane held his glass up and smiled. "I'm sure that I'm gonna find out a lot more about you tonight."

"I'm sure that you are," India said, with a flirtatious look on her face.

As they ate dinner, they chatted briefly about themselves. When Kane mentioned his house fire to India, she was visibly upset.

"Are you all right?" he asked, with a look of concern on his face. "Why did you get so quiet all of a sudden?"

India shrugged her shoulders and picked at the food on her plate. "I feel so bad about what happened to you, Kane! I'm glad that you made it out, though. I don't know what I would do if anything happened to you. Do you know who did it?"

Kane sighed. "Don't worry, babe. Daddy ain't going nowhere," he said. India laughed. "And yes, I have an idea who did it. But I ain't got no worries. That shit is gonna be taken care of."

India frowned at him. “Who do you think did it?” she asked, while taking a sip of her Moscato.

Kane waved her off. “It’s not important, babe.” He quickly changed the subject. “Anyway, what’s up with you, girl? To what do I owe this invite?”

India put down her fork and wiped her mouth with the cloth napkin. “I invited you over because I wanted to know what’s up with me and you. I mean, I really do like you, Kane, I do. But for the last couple of years, you’ve been treating me kinda fucked up; you would have sex with me and then don’t call me for weeks! I want to know, what is it about me that makes you treat me like some cheap whore?”

Kane took a moment to think about how to put his reply into layman’s terms so that India could understand. The truth was that she had been one of the fast ones. India was a woman who was willing to give up the panties to a man very quickly and then mistakenly assume that she could handle the outcome. But she couldn’t handle it. India was too insecure and needy to be sexually liberated. Kane knew what she really wanted was a relationship and maybe that was something that she should have specified when Kane first got with her. Perhaps, he would have shown her a little more respect.

“You have to remember when we first met, India, we jumped right in the bed with each other and honestly, that was all I wanted at the time. I wasn’t interested in being in no committed relationship with you or any other woman, for that matter.” A look of disappointment came over India’s face and Kane found himself trying to clean up his statement. “Look, India, you’re a gorgeous chick. You’re sexy and you seem cool but seriously, babe, your chill button is never on! And, in order for you to get what you want, it might be time for you to grow up.”

India agreed with Kane. "You're right. I do have a lot of growing up to do." She sighed. "Damn, I really like you, Kane. And I'm sorry that I portrayed myself like that to you. It's probably too late for us."

"Nah, it's not too late, babe. But I'm not gonna front, this is not something that gonna happen overnight."

"So, can I ask you another question? What's really good with you and that Brandi chick? Do you still fuck around with her?"

Kane hesitated to answer India, careful not to divulge any information about his and Brandi's relationship status. "Brandi and I are just friends," was all that Kane said. "And by the way, I didn't appreciate you telling her that you and I were seeing each other. That wasn't cool."

India rolled her eyes at Kane's statement. Once again, she fell right back into her messy routine. "So what? Fuck that bitch! I don't even know why you was fighting over her anyway!"

Kane shook his head and pointed his finger at her. "See? That's exactly what I'm talking about, India. You do too much. Press that chill button and relax, yo."

The slightly embarrassed India quickly apologized to Kane and insisted they finish up dinner. After dinner, they took another bottle of the chilled Moscato with them into the living room where India found a good movie on Netflix for them to watch. Just as the movie began, she cuddled up to Kane and surprisingly enough, he didn't object to that. He wrapped his arm around India, pulling her closer to him and even kissed her on the forehead. India relished the moment and didn't say one word. From the looks of things, she finally took Kane's advice: her chill button was definitely on.

Chapter 28

It was almost 1:00 a.m. Saturday morning and Brandi was still sitting in the waiting area of Kings County Hospital. She wanted to get word on Dollar's condition and wasn't leaving until someone told her something. Then, Brandi realized that she had no other choice but to stay.

Brandi began experiencing a myriad of emotions, blaming herself for Dollar's incident. She didn't know exactly who wanted to kill Dollar; it could have been someone from his past or someone from her present. Kane could have easily been a person of interest, especially after he accused Dollar of setting his house on fire. But Brandi was going to keep that to herself. Dollar would definitely have Kane's head if she revealed that information.

Brandi leaned her head against the wall. Just she was starting to doze off the surgeon appeared in front of her, still wearing his scrubs.

"Hello," he said, greeting the exhausted Brandi with a genuine smile. She quickly stood up and shook the doctor's hand. "I'm Dr. Hanover."

"Hello, Doctor," she replied. "How is Gregory doing?"

Dr. Hanover rubbed his chin. "Well, Gregory is a very lucky man. One bullet just grazed the left side of his neck, barely missing a major artery."

Brandi covered her mouth in shock.

"The other bullet was lodged in his shoulder. We were able to remove that bullet with no problem. But don't worry. Gregory is doing fine now. He's in stable condition."

Brandi breathed a sigh of relief and shook the doctor's hand again. "Thanks for everything, Doctor. Thank you so much!"

Dr. Hanover smiled at the relieved Brandi. "You're very welcome. Good luck to the both of you!"

Brandi watched as the doctor walked down the corridor toward the operating rooms. She sat back in her seat, ecstatic over the good news about Dollar's condition. After some minutes passed, she walked over to the nurses' station to ask what room Dollar was going to be in.

"He'll be ready in a minute, dear," the RN at the desk told her. "He's going into the room right now."

It was almost two hours before Dollar was wheeled out of recovery and into a private room. By this time, it was a little after three in the morning and way past visiting hours. But with the permission of the kindhearted nurses, Brandi was allowed to see him.

Brandi practically tiptoed over to his bed and gently rubbed his hand, as he slept. After feeling her tender touch, Dollar's eyes didn't stay closed for long. He gave Brandi direct eye contact and attempted to smile.

"Hi, baby," Brandi whispered, giving him a soft peck on the cheek. "I'm so happy to see you." Dollar tried to move but she stopped him. She made sure the bandages on his neck were in place and tucked him in. "You have to relax, Dollar."

Dollar sighed. "Who did this to me, Bee?" he asked, wincing in pain. "Please find out who did this shit to me!"

Brandi shook her head. "Look, Dollar, this is not back in the day, okay? We're older now. You have to let the police handle this matter."

Dollar cut her off. "Fuck that," he whispered. "Somebody tried to fucking kill me and I want that motherfucker's blood!"

Brandi was silent. Dollar was a firm believer in street justice. At that point, she knew there wasn't anything that she could say or do to change his mind about avenging the shooting. "Just focus on getting better and worry about that other shit later, Dollar," she replied with a sigh. "There's no need for you to get yourself all hyped up right now."

Dollar took Brandi's advice and instantly calmed down. She sat in the chair on the side of his bed and watched closely as he dozed back off to sleep.

As the sounds of Dollar's snores echoed throughout the room, Brandi silently prayed that the cops found the shooter before he did. If they didn't, there would be hell to pay.

It was the wee hours of Saturday morning when an intoxicated Sean called Brandi's phone. He dialed her number several times but didn't get an answer.

"Shit!" he said.

Sean's biggest fear was that Brandi had moved on. He'd been so busy worrying about Milan that he hadn't had the time to call her or anyone else. He put his iPhone down on the bar and gestured for the female bartender to come over to him.

"Give me another Henny on the rocks," he said, slamming his money down on the bar. "This is my last one, I promise."

The bartender shook her head and reluctantly poured Sean another glass of Hennessy. After serving him the drink, she grabbed his hand.

"Look, honey, I don't usually say this to my custies but it's no more alcohol for you," she advised, practically yelling at him over the loud music. "Do you have anyone who can come and pick you up?"

Sean picked up his cell phone and handed it to the woman. "Call Brandi," he slurred.

She took the phone from him and went into his recent calls. She found Brandi's number and pressed redial.

"Hello?" Brandi answered, in an annoyed tone.

"Um, hi, Brandi, this is Tasha, a bartender at the Hive Lounge. So sorry to bother you at this time of the morning but I have your friend here—"

"Who? Sean?" Brandi yelled into the phone.

"Yes! Sean! He's like pissy drunk and he asked me to call you, just to see if there's any way that you can take him home."

Brandi paused. "Thanks for calling me, Tasha, and this is nothing against you, sweetie, but please do me a fave? Tell Sean to call his fucking wife to come and pick his drunk ass up."

Tasha looked at the phone then glanced back at Sean. "Oh, okay, I'll do that. So sorry to bother you, Brandi."

"It's no problem, Tasha. Take care."

Tasha disconnected the call and gave the phone back to Sean. He raised his head, still in a drunken stupor. "What she say?" he asked.

Tasha gave Sean a nasty look. "She said for you to call your fucking wife," she replied, walking away from him with an attitude.

Sean looked down at the phone and shook his head. Then he dropped his head down on the bar and blacked out.

It was 7:00 a.m. Saturday morning when Sean opened his eyes again. This time, he was inside of his bedroom and lying in the bed with only his boxer briefs on. He looked around the room, trying to figure out how he got there. But for some reason, he couldn't remember a thing. Sean sat up. His head immediately started pounding, causing him to lie back down for a few minutes. It wasn't until he heard a sound in his house that he jumped up again.

Sean reached into the nightstand drawer for his gun. He slowly walked out of his bedroom and looked in every room upstairs to see where the sound was coming from. Then he heard a muffled voice coming from the living room. Sean frowned and walked down the stairs, careful not to make any noise.

When he got to the living room, he was more than surprised to see who was standing there.

"Milan?"

Milan hung up the phone and smiled at him. "Hey, Sean."

Sean put the gun on the living room coffee table and sat on the couch. "What are you doing here?" he asked, with an attitude.

"I just wanted to talk to you." Sean didn't respond so she continued. "I realized that the way things ended between us was very messed up. Everything was happening so fast that I didn't get the opportunity to tell you my side of the story."

Sean stopped her. "Tell your side of the story about what?" He waved her off. "What are you doing here, Milan?"

"Well, after I picked you up from the Hive Lounge—"

"Picked me up?" he said, with a confused look on his face.

"Yeah. Tasha, the bartender, called me from your phone and told me that you were in no condition to drive home. She asked if I could pick you up."

Sean breathed a sigh of relief. He remembered being really drunk last night and he was glad that Tasha looked out for him. "Oh, okay. Surprised that you came to get me after what happened the other night."

Milan sat next to him. "I'm not upset with you, Sean. I really do love you." She paused for a moment, as if she had something else on her mind. "But I want to ask you something. Why didn't you tell me that you and Brandi were seeing each other before we got together?"

It was Sean's turn to be stuck. "Who told you that?"

"That's not important. But what is important is you need to practice what you preach about being honest and faithful."

Sean didn't say a word. He was too busy trying to figure out who told Milan his business.

After a brief silence between them, Milan started talking again. "Look, Sean. I come to the realization that maybe I did misrepresent myself. But it wasn't like I was being dishonest; it's just that I wasn't too sure of which direction I was headed in. I was confused and ashamed of my attraction to the same sex."

Milan continued. "You deserve to be with someone who is going to give you a hundred percent of themselves, babe. I can't do that with anyone right now because I still got some shit to figure out about Milan. I'm an addict and I'm bisexual. There I said it. I gotta start keeping it real with myself before I can keep it real with anyone else."

Sean took Milan's hand into his. As he sat there and listened to Milan pleading her case, he realized that he was no better. He had cheated with Brandi before he even found about Milan's sexuality. But naturally, he wasn't going to admit to that.

"I apologize for not telling you that Brandi and I were involved with each other," Sean said, nonchalantly. "But that was a long time ago," he added, still refusing to be upfront about his connection with her.

Milan put her hands on her hips. "You really don't give a fuck if I'm hurt, do you?"

"Do you love her?" he asked, ignoring her question.

Milan paused, as if she was looking for the right answer. "She's okay. I mean, she's beautiful and rich but the way I feel about her could be more of an infatuation than anything."

"And this drug problem of yours. When the hell did that start?"

Milan got up from the couch and started walking back and forth. "Well, that started when I was involved with this female, a well-known heavy hitter in the music industry," she confessed. "Me and her used to party, get high together, and have sex for hours. Six months later, she left me with a broken heart and a cocaine habit. So it's been about six years now and I've really tried to stop doing it but it's so hard, especially when everyone I hang out with does the same thing."

Sean shook his head. "I can't believe what you're telling me, Milan. Here I thought that you were this . . . this innocent chick from Long Island and now I'm hearing about lesbian sex, cocaine, partying; this shit is crazy! But this lesbo shit . . ."

Milan started to get angry. "What the fuck are you, Sean, some homophobe? You don't like gay people or something?"

Sean stood up. "No, I ain't no fucking homophobe, man! What people do in their private lives, whether they be gay or straight, don't make me shit! But you? You're my fucking wife! You was supposed to have kept it real with me from the gate and you didn't. Got me out here looking like a fucking fool in front of everybody!"

Milan got frustrated with Sean's negative attitude. "I'm moving to Atlanta!" she blurted out.

Sean turned around and looked at her. "What you mean, you're moving to Atlanta?"

Milan ran her hands through her hair. "I want out of New York, Sean. I'm moving down to ATL, the second week in January. Right after the holidays."

Sadness and anger swept through Sean's body. "So you are in love with that gay bitch! You're moving down there to be with her!"

"I'm not moving to Atlanta for no chick!" she screamed at him. "I got a job offer with Universal." Milan plopped down in the armchair, calming herself down. "I've been meaning to tell you about it for a while; I just didn't know how to do it."

"So you had plans on leaving me anyway, huh?"

Milan shrugged. "I guess so, Sean. The truth is that I'm not really happy with this marriage. With marriage, in general."

"Damn," Sean said. "This shit is just fucked up all around the board! You're not happy with me, you're not happy living in New York . . . You're just not happy at all, huh?"

"That's what I'm trying to tell you."

Sean sat back down and stared at Milan. *Why do I always fall for the crazy bitches?* They both didn't say a word. After some minutes of silence passed, Sean spoke first.

"Look, Milan, I can sit up here and act like a bitter nigga about this whole situation. But the truth of the matter is that we got married for all of the wrong reasons."

"That we did," Milan agreed.

Sean sighed. "I think its best that we go through with that divorce, man. This ain't gonna work. And thanks for coming to get me from that bar. I appreciate that."

Milan smiled at him. "No problem." She grabbed her bag and car keys. "I'm glad that we were able to have this talk, Sean, you know, clear the air on some things. Anyway, I'm headed out to my parents' house now. I'm going to be staying there until I leave for Atlanta. I'll have my stuff outta here by the end of the week."

"You're going to your parents' house?"

Milan walked to the front door. “Yeah. I just said that.”

Sean stopped her from leaving. “Nah, Milan. You don’t have to do that. You can stay here until you move to Atlanta.”

“Thanks, Sean, but I wouldn’t—”

He cut her off. “It’s damn near three extra rooms in this house. Pick one,” he said.

Milan stood there, contemplating Sean’s offer. Then he wrapped his arms around her. As soon as he did that, Milan began to cry. Sean held her tightly, thinking about what life was going to be like without her. It was only a week ago that he and his wife were in the bed together, making love and reminiscing about the events that had occurred in their lives. It was definitely a sad situation.

Sean wiped her tears and kissed her on the lips. Naturally, she reciprocated. While they kissed, Sean began massaging Milan’s ample breasts then moved his large hands down to her butt, pulling her even closer to him. Then he lifted her up, carrying her up the stairs to the bedroom that they once shared.

Chapter 29

Tuki was extremely upset. She had been looking forward to her and Milan starting their new lives together that day. But unfortunately, it didn't look like that was going to happen and of course, that didn't sit too well with Tuki.

During their stay at the Aloft hotel, Milan told Tuki that there was a new job waiting for her in Universal Music Group's Atlanta offices. She was so ecstatic about the news that when she arrived back in Georgia that Thursday, she made airline reservations for Milan to fly down there Saturday morning.

"Well, baby," Tuki said, on the phone that Friday evening while Milan was still staying in their room at the Aloft. "Everything seems to be working in our favor. You're gonna be starting this new position in Atlanta and we can begin our new lives together. I can't wait!"

Milan smiled. "Yeah, it's gonna be some major changes," she replied.

"And that money I gave you," Tuki began, "is on me. You don't have to pay it back. Consider that your start up money."

"I appreciate the five thousand dollars, Tuki, but I'm going to pay you back. I promise."

"Please, honey! That's yours to keep. It's plenty more where that came from."

They talked for a little while longer until Milan called it a night. "Listen, sweetie," Milan said with a yawn, "I have to work in the a.m. I don't have all my clothes here so I need to get up extra early and get myself together. Staying in this hotel for the last couple of days has really thrown me off."

"Aw! Okay, baby, I understand. But make sure you call me tomorrow, okay? Sweet dreams."

Tuki hadn't heard from Milan since that Friday evening. She made several attempts to call Milan's phone, even leaving some nasty messages on her voice mail. But there still was no response. That was when the love-struck Tuki realized that Milan had definitely played her like a fiddle. She had taken the money that Tuki had given her to pay for that cocaine habit of hers, stayed at the Aloft for the extra days on Tuki's dime, and, most likely, went right back home to be with her husband. At least, that's what Tuki assumed she did.

Now Tuki was really stressed out.

"That bitch!" she screamed.

All of a sudden, Tuki flew into a rage and began trashing her luxury pad. She threw several wine glasses and plates onto the floor of the kitchen, flung her pricey Basquiat portraits and other expensive artifacts all over the living room. She even wrecked her walk-in closet that was filled with clothing, shoes, and bags.

Shortly after her tantrum, Tuki managed to calm herself down. But she still felt like a fool for being so naïve and gullible. Ever since Professor Sterling broke her heart in college, she always seemed to fall for the same type of women: the bisexual, experimental type of woman who's looking to "explore" new things. She was nothing but some science project to them and her bad choices in lovers were becoming a little too much for her to bear.

Minutes later, Tuki walked through her condo to inspect the damage she had done. She took a deep breath and slowly started cleaning up the mess. But as she was cleaning up the broken glass, Tuki began feeling down.

She needed something to minimize the pain of what she was feeling emotionally. Physical pain was her only savior.

Tuki walked over to the knife block on the counter and pulled out a small paring knife. She stared at it for a few seconds and began slowly cutting into her left forearm with it. Tuki closed her eyes and concentrated on the pain. The sight of her blood running down her arm and dripping onto the white tiled floor made her cry.

Then Tuki took the knife and cut deep into both of her wrists. Not too long after that, she sat on the floor of her kitchen and leaned against the cabinets. Tuki felt herself losing consciousness, as she bled out from her wrists. Tuki lay down on the cold floor and closed her eyes and just like that, she was out like a light.

Fortunately for Tuki, one of her neighbors had overheard her screaming and trashing the place earlier. Thinking it was a domestic dispute between two people, they had taken the liberty of calling 911. Two officers from the Atlanta Police Department were standing outside in the hallway and banging on her door.

"Miss Charles!" one of the officers yelled. "Miss Charles, open the door! It's the police!"

When the officers didn't get a response, the building maintenance was called. He came upstairs and produced the spare key for Tuki's place. When the worker opened the door, the police officers slowly walked inside with their guns drawn. While one of the officers checked both of the bedrooms, his partner walked into the living room and toward the kitchen, almost stumbling over Tuki's motionless body. There she was, lying on the floor in a pool of her own blood.

"Hey, Brody!" the officer called out to his partner. "In here!"

Brody ran into the kitchen and looked down. It had only been exactly three minutes after the suicide attempt and fresh blood was still seeping from Tuki's slit wrists. He shook his head and immediately pulled out his radio.

"Sector 19," he said. When the operator answered, he proceeded with the information. "We need an ambulance at 405 Peachtree Street, loft 10F! Hurry!"

In Brooklyn, the half-naked India walked into her living room with a big smile on her face. She was still on cloud nine, after spending a wonderful evening with Kane. She was happy that they were able to put some things into perspective and hopefully, their relationship was now going to go in a different direction. As India made herself a cup of coffee, she began daydreaming about her and Kane's future. She wanted the type of love that her sister, Asia, had with Rasheed: an unconditional, unequivocal love that no one could touch. India had spent most of her life looking for someone to sweep her off her feet, just as Rasheed had done with her twin.

She knew that Kane had numerous women at his beck and call day and night and, unfortunately, she had no control over that. But she wanted to give it a try. She wanted him so bad that she could taste it and she wasn't going to let anyone or anything stop her from getting with him. With Kane being twelve years her senior, that was a major turn on for her, as well. India was prepared to do whatever it took to show him that she was a grown woman, in every sense of the word.

India decided to start her path to righteousness by calling her sister. There were some things that were said and done and she wanted to apologize for them. She took her fresh cup of coffee into the living room and picked up her cordless house phone to call Asia. She was disappointed when the call went to the voice mail.

"Hey, Asia," India said. "Um, listen, I know that me and you kinda left things off on a bad note and I wanted to know if—"

Suddenly, her phone beeped. When she answered the other line, it was Asia. "What's up, India?" Asia said, in a dismissive tone. "You just called me?"

India swallowed, trying to find the right words to say to her twin. "Yeah, I called you." There was brief pause. "Look, Asia, I apologize for all of the drama that I caused over the years, man. I know that I haven't been the best sister in the world."

"Before you give me this speech, India, I was on the phone with Mommy right before you called."

India frowned. "Is everything okay?"

"It's real funny that you asked that, India, 'cause no, everything ain't okay."

"What do you mean everything ain't okay? What's wrong? Is Mommy sick?"

"No, Mommy ain't no sick!" the irritated Asia yelled into the phone. "But Tuki is! She tried to take her life this morning!"

India almost dropped the phone. "What do you mean? She tried to kill herself?"

"Yes, she tried to kill herself! She slit her fucking wrists, India! And you know why? It was over Sean's wife, Milan! Tuki told her father that she was in love with Milan and that she was upset because the chick didn't fly in to Atlanta that Saturday morning. When they checked Tuki's cell phone, she had called that woman over thirty something times!"

"Oh, my God! I didn't know."

Asia interrupted her. "Oh, my God is right! And this is all because you don't know how to mind your own damn business!" India was silent on the other end of the phone. "Messy shit like this is exactly why you and I can't fuck with each other, India. You're a miserable bitch and I don't want or need you, or your evil, fucked-up ways around my unborn child!"

"But, Asia, I didn't mean—"

"You didn't mean to do what? Tuki is lying in some hospital right now, losing her mind over some . . . some bitch. And Uncle Rodney and them are talking about committing her to a psychiatric facility because of it! Apparently, this isn't the first time she did this shit over a woman! And let's talk about you now. You don't get along with Rasheed. His son's mother can't stand your ass because you were screwing her husband. I mean, what's next, India, huh? Whose life are you going to fuck up now?"

India closed her eyes and took a deep breath. "Whoa, Asia, you're taking this too far! It's not my fault that Tuki lost her mind over Sean's wife!"

"It is your fault! You should have never, ever let her go home with Sean! You knew what her motives were!"

"You were there too, Asia! I didn't see you stopping her!"

"Because I didn't know what was going on, dummy! I really thought that Tuki and Milan were friends! You never bothered to tell me what was going on. Rasheed was the one who had to tell me what happened with Tuki and Sean's wife!" Asia paused. "You know what? You really ain't shit, India, you know that? Just live your miserable-ass life and stay the fuck away from me!"

All of sudden, the line went dead. India began to cry, as the onslaught of all the horrible things she'd done in her life hit her like a ton of bricks. The news of her cousin trying to commit suicide just let her know that she had truly crossed the line. Now her beloved twin sister wanted nothing to do with her because of it. It was definitely time for her to get her act straight.

A half-naked Kane walked out of the bedroom, yawning and stretching. He walked over to India, who was sitting on the couch, softly weeping. Out of concern, he wrapped his arms around her shoulders, pulling her closer to him.

"What's wrong, baby girl?" he asked. "I heard all of this yelling and whatnot. What's going on in here?"

India sniffed. "I just got news that my cousin, Tuki, who lives in Atlanta, tried to kill herself this morning."

"Damn!" Kane exclaimed. "I'm so sorry to hear that. Why did she try to kill herself?'

India shrugged her shoulders. "I don't know," she said, not wanting to explain what happened. "I just feel so bad for her."

Kane kissed India on the lips. "I know you do, mama. She's gonna be okay, right?"

India nodded her head. "I hope so."

"Aw, baby girl, it's gonna be all right," India continued to cry even harder. "Baby, baby!" he said, turning her face to his. "Look at me! What else is going on with you?"

India ran her hand across his cheek. "I'm in love with you, Kane."

Kane didn't reply to India's declaration of love. Instead, he held her tight, as she buried her face in his chest and continued to cry some more.

Chapter 30

An hour later, Kane walked out of India's apartment building and made a beeline for his parked vehicle. After comforting her, he had tried to find every excuse in the world to get out of there. Kane finally found one that worked.

As Kane got into the driver's seat of his vehicle, he was still thinking about what India said to him: she was in love with him. Kane laughed at that statement, as he pulled out of the parking spot. While he thought that India was physically beautiful, he wasn't interested in committing to one woman. He was upset with himself for mistakenly assuming that Brandi, a woman his age, was going to be the one for him. But Kane quickly discovered that older women played games too. He had never been one to chase a bitch, something that he would always tell his friends. Women were more apt to chase him and it was going to stay that way until he chose to do different.

When Kane got to the corner of India's block, the traffic light was yellow. It was only a matter of seconds before the light turned red. Without a second thought, Kane did the unthinkable. He stepped on the gas and blew through the steady red light. As soon as Kane drove his 2011 BMW into the intersection, there was a collision. The loud sound of twisted metal echoed throughout the neighborhood, causing passersby and residents of the surrounding area to run to the corner to see where the deafening boom came from.

In the middle of that intersection was Kane's car, which had come to a complete stop. The driver of the sixteen-wheel tractor trailer climbed down out of the cabin and literally broke down in tears right in front of everybody.

"He ran the red light! He ran the red light!" the driver yelled to a few nearby witnesses. "I tried to stop. Lord, have mercy on his soul!"

The onlookers gasped at the sight of the totaled BMW. The tractor had T-boned Kane's vehicle and it was almost split in half from the impact. And Kane hadn't been wearing a seat belt, causing him to be ejected from the car. His bloody, mangled body was lying in the middle of the street.

But Kane Porter was a fighter. When the paramedics arrived on the scene, he was still alive and his breathing was very shallow. He tried to say something to them but he was told not to speak. After putting the seriously injured Kane on the gurney and hoisting him into the ambulance, they quickly drove away from the scene. Police officers and firefighters were left to deal with the wrecked vehicle and a remorseful truck driver.

Rasheed, the father-to-be, was losing his mind. Asia was in labor and he was running in and out of the bedroom, desperately looking for her overnight bag to take with her to hospital. Her contractions were only ten minutes apart, which meant one thing: their baby girl was on her way!

As Rasheed looked for the overnight bag, he couldn't stop thinking about being in the delivery room with Asia. He was in no hurry to see his girl's vagina being stretched to the fullest capacity. Rasheed hadn't even done that when Messiah, his four-year-old son, was born. But Asia would never forgive him if he wasn't by her side, holding her hand and cajoling her during the childbirth process.

Rasheed had to laugh at his own nervousness. Throughout the years, he had done time in prison, was involved in shootouts, and saw more dead bodies than he could count. But the thought of seeing his newborn daughter being born had him shaken. "Rasheed!" Asia called out to him from downstairs. She was sprawled on the sofa with her legs open, feeling like she was going to give birth right in their living room if Rasheed didn't hurry. Rasheed finally found the bag, tucked in the corner of one of their bedroom closets. He shook his head at the oversight.

"What is the bag doing in here?" he asked himself. "I'm coming now, baby!" he yelled back at Asia.

In a matter of seconds, Rasheed was back down the stairs and in the living room, helping Asia off the sofa. It was a slight struggle, getting Asia down the steps of their brownstone and into his truck. He had offered to carry her but the frightened Asia would hear none of that. After making sure Asia was belted in the passenger seat, Rasheed climbed into the driver's seat and they were on their way.

As Rasheed sped down Malcolm X Boulevard, Asia chided him for driving like a maniac. "Don't speed, Rah!" she yelled, holding on to her rotund belly. "I don't want to fucking die!"

Rasheed slowed down. "Okay, okay, baby, I'm so sorry," he said, nervously. "It's just that I wanna get you to the hospital in time."

Asia waved him off. "I'm gonna get there." Suddenly, the pain of her contractions became very intense. "Oh, my God! Rasheeeeeed!" she screamed, writhing in the passenger seat of his Range Rover. "I can't . . . I can't make it to Methodist! It's too far! Take . . . take me to the nearest hospital! Please, baby!"

Rasheed was confused. “But, babe, I can’t—”

Asia’s wailing prevented him from finishing his statement. He reluctantly made a left onto Brooklyn Avenue from Atlantic Avenue. She wanted to go to the nearest hospital and Rasheed had to oblige her request. He shook his head and reluctantly headed to the nearest emergency room.

It was one o’clock on a Sunday afternoon when Brandi walked into Dollar’s hospital room. As she expected, he was fast asleep, doped up from the morphine that was running intravenously into his right arm. She crept over to his bed, giving him a soft kiss on the lips. When she did that, Dollar opened his eyes and looked around the room, as if he didn’t remember where he was. He smiled when he saw Brandi standing there.

“Hey, babe,” Dollar whispered to her. “Am I happy to see you.”

Brandi turned on the television for him. “I got your TV turned on and I brought you some fruit to snack on and some reading material,” she said, putting the items in the drawer next to his bed.

“Aww, thank you, Bee,” he said, grabbing her hand. She bent down and gave him another kiss on the lips. “That’s my girl.”

“Ugh!” she groaned. “I’m so glad that you’re okay, Dollar. If anything would have happened to you, boy . . .”

Dollar quieted her. “Shhh,” he said. “Let’s not talk about what could have happened. It didn’t happen and I’m grateful to be alive. That’s because God has a purpose for me and you too, girl. If I wanna make you my wife, a dude had no choice but to fight for his life.”

Brandi sat down in the chair. “Did you just say what I think that you said?”

He reached for her hand. "I didn't stutter! I said that I want you to be my wife someday, Brandi. I've been in love with your ass for years and now that I finally have you . . ."

Brandi frowned. "But we just got with each other. Don't you think that it's too soon for you to be talking like that?"

Dollar's hand went to his neck. "Check this out. I'm a man who knows what he wants. I done been through the fucking trenches and now I'm a self-made man. I have my businesses, my money, and, thanks to you, I have my son back in my life. And I ain't getting no younger, yo, and neither are you."

Brandi had to agree with Dollar. "Yeah, you're right. I'm a grandmother."

"Exactly! I know that you love me, Bee, but I'm in love with you. I always have been. I just want you to know that I don't have no problem taking care of you and fulfilling your every need. But we're going to do things right. As soon as I get better, I'm going ring shopping and you're going to plan us a wedding. You hear me?"

Brandi smiled. The idea of getting married always scared her, but for some reason she was ready for the plunge. Dollar seemed to be everything that she wanted in a man: he knew how to get money, he was handsome, the sex was phenomenal, and that was only half of his great qualities. Most importantly, Dollar seemed like he was a changed man. And Dollar loved the hell out of her. What more could a woman ask for?

"Yes, I hear you, babe. I hear you loud and clear!"

They both shared a laugh. "And another thing," Dollar began. "We're going to ask God for forgiveness, close those chapters from our past, and move on with our lives, okay?"

Brandi nodded her head in agreement. "I concur."

Dollar told her to come closer to him. "You have always been a beautiful sister, Brandi, inside and out. All you ever needed was the right man to see that and trust me, I see all of that. I love you, baby."

Brandi got up from the chair and gave Dollar a warm hug. "I love you too," she replied.

But the hug was a little too tight. "Ow!" Dollar exclaimed. "The neck, babe! The neck!"

"Oops, I'm sorry, baby!" Brandi said, while backing away from Dollar. They both shared another laugh.

Chapter 31

It was the middle of June and a clear Saturday afternoon. It was late spring and the streets of Bedford-Stuyvesant were filled with fully bloomed trees. From the looks of things, it wasn't hard to tell that the summer season was near.

Since the weather broke, Asia Gordon, first-time mother and the wife of Rasheed, spent a lot of her free time outside of her home. On this particular day, she was sitting on the steps, taking occasional peeks inside the stroller of her daughter, Miyah. She couldn't help but laugh at the baby, who was kicking her feet and gurgling at the excitement of seeing her mother's smiling face. As she stared into the beautiful eyes of the adorable six-month-old, Asia felt so complete.

"Hi, baby," Asia cooed. "Mommy loves you, do you know that? Mommy and Daddy love you so much!" Miyah made her baby noises. "Yes, we do, baby! Yes, we do!"

A look of contentment came over Asia's face. Her life had definitely turned out for the better. She was finally married to Rasheed, who was the love of her life. And the highlights of their family were their children: her baby daughter Miyah and her stepson, Messiah. She couldn't have asked for more.

Even with all of the positive things going on, there were still other issues that haunted Asia. She hadn't spoken to her twin, India, in a few months. The last time she saw her sister was back in late November, during Kane's wake. Asia felt badly for India. She knew that she was in a lot of emotional pain after Kane's death, considering she had always had a serious crush on the man. She regretted not being there for India in her time of need. Now looking at her baby daughter Miyah had Asia ready to make amends with her younger twin. Kane's untimely death was living proof that life was too short to not be speaking to her own sister.

While Asia bonded with her baby daughter, she hadn't noticed someone walking up on her.

"Hi, Asia."

Asia looked up and saw India standing there, staring at her. She was overcome with joy. She excitedly wrapped her arms around India and hugged her like there was no tomorrow.

"I was just thinking about you, India," Asia said, through happy tears. "Oh, my God, girl! I've missed you so much. I don't ever, ever want us to be apart again."

India consoled her sister while trying to hold back her own tears. But after a while, she couldn't help herself. She began crying too. "I missed you too, Asia. But I stayed away like you told me to."

Asia let her go and stepped back to look at her. "And when the hell have you ever listened to me, hussy?" she said, as she wiped the tears from her face. They both had to laugh at the truth. "Don't you ever stay away from me anymore! It's been six long-ass months, India and that's a long time to be away from your twin. We're supposed to be glued at the hip, remember?"

India chuckled. "Yes, it is. Seemed like I was missing one of my ribs all of those months." She looked inside of the stroller. India was instantly smitten, as she looked at her infant niece. "Oh, look at my niece," she exclaimed. "Asia, she is so beautiful."

Asia beamed with pride. "India meet Miyah Rashelle Gordon. Miyah, this is your auntie. Say hi, baby!"

Miyah began kicking her feet and making her happy baby noises. India put her hand to her heart.

"Hi, Miyah! Asia, she has your eyes and her daddy's nose and mouth. And I see a little of Mommy in her too," India said, while staring at her niece.

"Yes, she does." Asia looked at her sister again. "I'm so sorry for pushing you away, India. I will never do that again."

As India was about to reply to her, she caught a glimpse of her sister's left ring finger. "Asia? Those rings are off the hook! Are you what I think you are?"

Asia nodded her head. "Yes, yes, I'm married! We got married in Bermuda this past April, just me and Rasheed. But we're going to have a big reception, though, next month in July and I want you to be right there. Are you gonna come? You're invited, you know."

India didn't know what to say. "I don't know, Asia. How do you think Rasheed is gonna feel about me being there? I mean, shit, look at everything that's happened over the last couple of months. With Kane getting killed after the car accident, Tuki's suicide attempt, and with me and you not being on speaking terms for all of these months, he probably don't even want me around."

Asia hugged India again. "India, don't worry about no Rasheed. You're my sister. Trust me, the months that we weren't speaking, he felt effed up about it because he wants me to be happy. So you better be at my reception, India. I would have invited you sooner but you changed all of your numbers."

"Yeah, yeah, I know. I had to change my numbers. I heard that you were calling me at work but I just wasn't in the mood to talk to anybody, especially after Kane died. I was really going through it, Asia."

"I know you've been through it. But you're fine now, right?" Asia asked, while rubbing India's cheek.

India sighed and took a seat on the brownstone stoop. "So far, so good. I've been seeing a shrink for my issues."

Asia sat beside India and held her hand. "It's gonna be okay, India. You're going to be okay and I'm going to be right there with you. I promise."

India looked at her twin and broke down in tears again. "Thank you so much, Asia. I need all the support that I can get."

"Well, you got it, girl," Asia replied, kissing her sister's hand. "And don't you ever forget that."

Sean puffed on his cigar and sat on the steps of his Bedford-Stuyvesant home. He laughed to himself, as he enjoyed the beautiful spring day and thought about some of precarious situations that he put himself in over the years. Women were the root of his problems but they always flocked to him, mostly because of his good lucks, nice physique, and, of course, his charming demeanor.

Sean's biggest regret to date was what happened with Yadira. He felt like his actions were what sent her over the edge, causing the mentally unstable woman to take her own life. Her suicide was also a wakeup call for him. By marrying Milan, he thought that was proof that even a player like himself he could settle down with one woman. But that marriage had failed and now Sean was back to square one.

Before Milan came into the picture, there was Brandi. She was the perfect match for Sean. But like a fool, he let her slip right out of his grasp. After the traumatic incident with Yadira, Sean never once took it into consideration that Brandi had to deal with her own issues and guilt. He allowed his ego and selfishness to get in the way.

His attitude was definitely the demise of their budding relationship and unfortunately, Brandi was never able to trust him again.

When they reconnected with each other, Sean could tell that Brandi's feelings for him had changed. Sean found himself wanting her even more than the second time around but he was a married man and she was the forbidden fruit. Their whirlwind romance was very short-lived and he could tell there was a little animosity still lingering from their past dalliance. But Sean was convinced that Brandi truly loved him, which meant that she was going to come back to him someday. In his mind, she was going to always come back to him.

Chapter 32

Dollar exited the bedroom and walked into the living room of his two-bedroom condo. He smiled as he stood by and watched Brandi attempt to beat Greg, his fifteen-year-old son, at *NBA 2K13*.

"Ah, come on, Miss Brandi," Greg said to his future stepmother. "Can't you see that you're losing this game? I'm too official at this!"

Brandi wanted to laugh at Greg's bragging but she managed to keep a straight face and keep her eyes on the television screen. She wrestled with the controller, as she tried to get one of her players to shoot a three-pointer.

"Come on, you stupid game!" she yelled at the television. "These dudes are lucky I'm not their coach! They would be sitting on that damn bench!"

Dollar walked around the sofa and sat next to Brandi. He loved that she connected with his son, which only made him fall for her more. Brandi was the perfect partner who could do no wrong; she was what he always yearned for. And Dollar was ready to kill anyone who tried to harm her. She was his queen and no one was going to ever change that.

"Shamari is out of it," Dollar said to Brandi. Her grandson was sound asleep in the spare bedroom. "When I went to check on him, he was hanging off the bed. He sleeps like a grown-ass man working a full-time job!"

Brandi took her eyes off the game for a moment and kissed Dollar on the lips. "Yes, he does! And thanks, baby, for checking on him for me. Such a good man."

He rubbed her back. "What else am I?" he whispered in her ear.

"And you're my baby," Brandi whispered back then mouthed the words "I love you" to him.

"Come on, Miss Brandi," Greg chided. "You and my dad can smooch later! Let's do this!"

They all laughed. As Dollar watched them play the video game, he felt content. For the first time in his life, he knew what having a real family felt like. And it felt so good that he never wanted to let that go.

A few hours later, Brandi was in Brooklyn and dropping her grandson off to his father. When Shamari came downstairs to meet them, he was looking handsome as ever. Brandi smiled at her son. He was definitely a replica of his father, Maleek. They both had the same lean but muscular frame and flawless chocolate skin. And Brandi was so proud of Shamari. He had come a long way from being a rebellious teenager to becoming a hardworking, responsible dad.

"Hey, Ma!" Shamari said, kissing his mother on the cheek. "Thanks for holding down my baby boy for me today. I know it was last minute but I had some overtime that I wanted to do. Got these bills to pay, ya know?"

Brandi kissed Shamari on the cheek and wiped her nude lip gloss off his face with her thumb. "It was not a problem, baby," she replied. "You really don't have to take him today. He could stay with me tonight, you know. My sweet baby truly enjoyed himself with his Nana today," she added, giving the younger Shamari a kiss on the cheek, too.

Shamari smiled. "Nah, that's okay, Ma. His other grandmother wanted me to bring him to her anyway so that he could go to church with her in the morning. Where did y'all go today?"

Brandi took a deep breath. "Well, we went to Chuck E. Cheese's earlier in the day, caught a movie with Dollar and his son, Greg, and then got something to eat. After all of that, I spent some of the evening trying to beat Dollar's son at *NBA 2K13!*" Shamari laughed. "You know I can't play those video games for nothing!"

"Ma, you never could play those games! But one thing I could say, you always tried to play with me anyway. And I understand why you tried to play with me."

Brandi felt herself getting choked up. She always went out of her way to make her son feel loved and make him believe that he didn't need a father in his life. But after Shamari went to jail, Brandi started thinking otherwise. Maybe the female substitution of a father figure was no good for him. Shamari was acting out and it was apparent that he needed male guidance. As a woman, she couldn't give him that. But fortunately, life lessons and his son's mother's untimely death helped him to grow up. Even though her grandson didn't have his biological mother, he had his father in his life. After all, who else can raise a man better than a real man?

Brandi hugged her son. "I love you, baby."

"I love you too, Ma," Shamari replied, as he hugged his mother back. Little Shamari let go of his father's hand. He went off to the other side of the lobby to play by with toy cars that Dollar purchased for him. Shamari looked at his mother.

"So what's up with you and Dollar? Do I see marriage in your future?"

Brandi beamed with pride. "I think he's the one," she said. "Me and Dollar have history together and that history is what kind of connects us, you know?"

Shamari put his hand on his mother's shoulder. "That's what's up, Ma. I'm happy for you. Dollar seems like he's a cool cat and I like the fact that he got some legal money.

That means he could hold my Mama Dukes down the right way!" Brandi laughed at that statement. "I don't want you to be with no broke-ass Negro!"

Brandi happily agreed. "Yeah, you're right, son. I don't need that."

"But, Ma, I do have one small issue with Dollar. I'm not too cool with some of things that he's done in the past. I did my homework on him. A few of my dudes was up North with Dollar and they said that he was no joke with the hands, the banger, and the gun. And I don't want you to get caught up in his bullshit, excuse my French, and you end up getting hurt. And the person who shot him last year was never found," Shamari said, giving his mother a shrewd look. "If he find out who did that, you know that Dollar is not about to let that ride."

Brandi nodded her head. "No, no, no, baby! It ain't even like that. Aside from that incident, Dollar is on chill mode. He's a businessman; he ain't trying to lose no money by trying to kill somebody! That doesn't make any sense."

Shamari still had his reservations. "Okay, Ma, I'm just saying. I don't want no problems and I don't want to end up back in jail for killing this dude Dollar! And I want you to be careful too. He's really into you, I could tell. I see the way he looks at you, caters to you. So all I'm saying is to be careful with your movements, Ma." Brandi sighed. "And you have to leave Sean alone."

Brandi frowned at him. "Ain't nobody thinking about no Sean!" she said with a slight attitude.

Shamari grabbed his son's hand and gave his mother the side eye. "Come on, Ma. You still have strong feelings for Sean. I may be your son but I ain't no fool."

After Brandi left Shamari and her grandson, she thought about what he had said to her. *Leave Sean alone!* It was great advice, coming from someone who was so close to her. And Shamari knew exactly how she felt about Sean.

Shamari's comment had the adverse effect on Brandi. When she got upstairs to her apartment, she picked up the phone to call Sean a few seconds after she walked through the door.

"Hello?" Sean said. Hearing his voice had Brandi hesitant to respond.

"Hi, Sean, this is Brandi. How are you?" she said.

She listened as Sean laughed in the background. "Wow! What's up, sweetness? You good?" he asked, sounding happy to hear from her.

Brandi couldn't contain her giddiness. "Yes, yes, Sean, I'm fine. Just, um, checking on you to see how you were. You've been on my mind lately."

"Is that right? I'm surprised that you even thought about me. I would've called you but I figured that you have a man by now."

Brandi sucked her teeth at his wisecrack. "Anyway, how's your wife doing, Sean?"

"I don't have a wife anymore, sweetness. I'm happily divorced."

Brandi got quiet. She had to get her thoughts together before she started talking again. "Are you serious? I can't believe that you're divorced, Sean! You seemed so happy with your wife. What happened?"

"Man, I don't even want to talk about it. She lives in Atlanta now so I don't ever have to see her again! But the question is what's up with you and that Dollar cat? Heard you were kinda happy with homeboy," Sean said.

"Um, yeah, I'm happy with homeboy," Brandi said, mocking him. "Are you happy being single?"

"I would be happier if I can have you."

Brandi cut him off. "Sean, please."

"Why don't you just come see me, Brandi?"

"Sean, I—"

It was Sean's turn to cut her off. "Please, baby, I miss you."

Brandi started to sound worried. "Sean, we can't do this. I . . . I'm in a relationship now."

"And? What the fuck does that mean?" Sean asked, in a sarcastic tone. "I ain't thinking about Dollar. I asked you to come see me. Please, Brandi?"

It didn't take much convincing to get Brandi out of the house and on her way to Sean. She knew that what she was doing was wrong but she craved the excitement.

Chapter 33

It was 9:00 p.m. at night when Brandi rang Sean's bell. He came to the door with nothing but a robe on, not making things any easier for her. He had the robe slightly open to reveal his baby-oiled chest and abs. Brandi held her breath, as she slowly stepped into the foyer of his home. Before she could say one word to him, Sean began taking off her clothing. Brandi didn't object to it one bit. She was ready for everything that he had in store for her.

"You had better brought this pussy to me," Sean whispered in her ear. He removed her panties, got on his knees, and stuck his face in her crotch. Brandi almost fell backward while Sean used his expert mouth and tongue to suck, nibble, and lick on her pussy.

Brandi grabbed Sean's head, as if she was trying to pull him deeper into her vagina. "Sean, I have a man," she moaned. "I can't. I can't do this."

Sean heard what Brandi said but didn't reply to her. He just continued to make a full-course meal out of her clean-shaven vagina and she was loving every minute of it. Brandi peeled Sean's robe off him. His body looked exquisite. This time, she got on her knees and blessed him with her fellatio skills. Now it was Sean's turn to scream and moan. He was in heaven.

Unable to hold back any longer, they took off all of their clothing and had sex all over Sean's house, from the kitchen counter to the bathroom sink. Brandi couldn't get enough of Sean. She wrapped her legs around his waist, practically begging him to fuck her harder. He bent Brandi over the couch, long dicking her in the doggie-style position. She screamed and yelled his name, urging him to stop because the pain was so intense but she really didn't mean that. Brandi loved rough sex and having her pussy pounded; even Dollar knew that about her. Sex with him was super but there was something else about Sean that she just couldn't resist.

The two freaks ended their sexual romp in Sean's bedroom. They lay in the bed, with Sean hold Brandi in his arms.

"I love you to death," Sean said to her. He kissed her on the forehead. "It just doesn't seem like we're going to ever be together but you know what? That could be a good thing. Maybe it's just best that we remain secret lovers."

Brandi sighed. "I can't agree with you more, Sean," she replied. "It's much better the way it is between us."

Their adoration for each other was too intense, too passionate for real life. Instead, they chose their sanity over their love.

After spending almost three hours exploring every inch of each other's bodies, they hopped in the shower together. Feeling refreshed, Brandi refused Sean's offer to spend the night with him. Instead, she put her clothes back on and prepared to leave. Sean wrapped his robe around his naked frame and walked Brandi to the door. They shared an intimate kiss, vowing to keep their rendezvous on the hush.

"Good-bye, Sean," Brandi said, as she walked down the stairs.

Sean hadn't expected for Brandi to say good-bye to him. "Why does that sound so final?" he asked her. But Brandi didn't reply to him. Sean watched as she got into her vehicle and he closed the door.

Sean walked upstairs to his bedroom and walked into the closet that once belonged to his wife. He pulled out a metal box that contained his off-duty firearm. But that wasn't the only weapon in that box. Along with his personal firearms was the throwaway weapon that he used the night he tried to kill Dollar. Sean's jealousy had gotten so out of control that he resorted to attempted murder. And after he shot Dollar, he discreetly stood amid the group of spectators and watched as Brandi broke down in tears. It was then he knew that Brandi really loved Dollar, which hurt him to the core.

Sean groaned, as he thought about how close he had come to murdering Dollar that day and getting rid of him for good. But when he discovered that Dollar had pulled through, Sean came to his senses. He was going to spare Dollar's life, at least for the time being.

Poor Kane. Sean smiled. He thought the Molotov cocktail he threw into the man's house that night had done the trick. Sean had imagined the raging fire burning Kane to a crisp and, when that didn't happen, him being pissed off was an understatement. If that sixteen-wheeler hadn't taken Kane out, Sean was definitely going to finish him off.

Sean laughed when Kane acted as if he didn't know Brandi when he met her at the Hive Lounge that night. What Brandi didn't know was that Kane was a known habitual liar who would stop at nothing to make Sean look stupid. The fiercely loyal Rasheed had sworn Sean to secrecy and told him everything that Kane said.

"Yo, slime, I have to tell you something, man," Rasheed said one day, while they were at his house drinking and watching ESPN. "That dude, Kane, is fucking with Brandi. I had to tell you about it 'cause you know that I don't like that snake shit. You know if he would do it to

you and you're my man, he would do it to me. What you gonna do about that shit?"

Sean smiled. "I'm gonna kill that motherfucker," he replied with no sign of remorse. "Guess I gotta bring my murder-for-hire skills back, huh?"

Rasheed took a sip of his liquor and smiled. "Dudes don't know that you were one of the best who did it. They keep letting that fucking badge of yours fool them."

At Kane's wake, Sean looked down at the dead man lying in his all-white casket. No one noticed the sinister smile on his face.

Sean leaned over the casket, pretending to kiss Kane on his cold, clammy cheek. Instead, he whispered in his ear. "If you didn't die in this accident, I was going to murder you myself," he told the cadaver.

Sean took his robe off and climbed into his comfortable bed. As he was dozing off to sleep, he kept thinking about Brandi. He thought about her full lips, her sweet nectar, her beautiful face and how obsessed he really was with her. He didn't want to envision her being with Dollar and not him.

Sean began tossing and turning in his bed and wasn't able to fall asleep. The voices in his head were getting louder than they had been over the years. They kept asking him question after question and he felt compelled to answer them. But it was that one voice that kept nagging Sean to do things that he had never done before.

"What did you say, Yadira?" Sean replied, talking to an imaginary person in his dark room. Sean never told anyone but he could feel Yadira's spirit following him throughout his house. He knew that people would not believe him; they would call him crazy. But Sean didn't think that he was in need of psychiatric help. It's just that when Yadira talked, he was the only person who listened to her, who could hear her. It was only right because she did the same for him.

Sean began laughing hysterically, as if someone had told him a very funny joke. “Okay, okay, you were right, Yadi,” he said with a sigh. “Being in love does make you wanna kill somebody.” Suddenly, Sean paused, as if he was contemplating what to say. “Look, Yadi, I wanna ask your opinion about something.” Sean paused again. “I wanna kill Brandi. What do you think?”